A Proposal Worth
Waiting For

RAYE MORGAN
TERESA CARPENTER
MELISSA McCLONE

MIX
Paper from
responsible sources

FSC C007454

is produced from independently certified FSC™ paper to ensure
a forest management

information visit www.harpercollins.co.uk/green

and bound in Spain
Encional

MILLS &
BOON

First Published in Great Britain 2018
By Mills & Boon, an imprint of HarperCollins*Publishers*
1 London Bridge Street, London, SE1 9GF

A PROPOSAL WORTH WAITING FOR © 2018 Harlequin Books S. A.

The Heir's Proposal, A Pregnancy, A Party & A Proposal and *His Proposal, Their Forever* were first published in Great Britain by Harlequin (UK) Limited.

The Heir's Proposal © 2013 Helen Conrad
A Pregnancy, A Party & A Proposal © 2015 Teresa Carpenter
His Proposal, Their Forever © 2015 Melissa Martinez McClone

ISBN: 978-0-263-26459-3

05-0118

FSC
www.fsc.org

This book ... certified FSC™ paper to ensure
responsible ... management.

For more i... formation visit www.harpercollins.co.uk/green

Printed and ... d in Spain
by CPI, Ba...

THE HEIR'S
PROPOSAL

BY
RAYE MORGAN

Raye Morgan has been a nursery school teacher, a travel agent, a clerk and a business editor, but her best job ever has been writing romances—and fostering romance in her own family at the same time. Current score: two boys married, two more to go. Raye has published more than seventy romance novels, and claims to have many more waiting in the wings. She lives in Southern California, with her husband and whichever son happens to be staying at home at the moment.

This story is dedicated to Bets in Santa Fe.

CHAPTER ONE

TORIE Sands was shivering so hard her teeth clattered together. Not only was she cold, she was—well, sort of scared.

What in the world was she going to do? She'd come out onto this spit of land when the sun was still shining, California-beach style, and she'd gone on a sentimental journey around the rock, looking for her childhood in the caves. She'd forgotten how quickly the weather could change out here—not to mention the water level.

Now she was stuck. The spit turned into an island at high tide. And the fog had come in—not on little cat feet, but like a wild herd of ghostly mustangs, silent and deadly, sweeping in with a vengeance.

She remembered now. This sort of thing was called a killer fog when she was a kid and living up on the cliff above, the only child of the Huntington family butler. She knew she should be able to swim or wade to the shore, but she couldn't see land and the current was running hard toward the open sea. If she got caught up in that...

A crack of thunder made her jump. Great. Now it was probably going to rain.

How was she going to get out of here? She hadn't

told anyone where she was going. Her cell phone was telling her No Service. She hadn't brought along any flares. Could she possibly spend the night out here? No!

And then she was eaten by the slimy sea monster...

The phrase came sailing into her head from some long-forgotten campfire story from her childhood. Ah, memories. She shivered that much harder.

Okay, time to call for help. She hadn't seen another soul as she'd come sashaying down through the dunes and across the wet sand bridge, but just in case... After all, what other option did she have?

"Help!" she yelled as loudly as she could. "Help! I'm caught out here on the island. Help!"

Nothing. Just the sound of water slapping against the shore in rhythmic waves. In the distance—the far, far distance—she could hear the lonely call of a foghorn. She pulled her arms in close and winced as the wind slapped her hair into her eyes. This was no fun and she was bordering on hysteria.

"Mrs. Marino?" A deep male voice came arcing through the gloom. "Are you out there?"

She gasped with relief. Human contact! Maybe she wasn't going to die out here in the cold after all.

It took her a moment to register the name, though.

Mrs. Marino? What? Oh. That was the name she was going under so as not to alert the Huntingtons as to who she really was. She shouldn't give out any hints that it was a phony.

"Yes," she called back, surprised to hear how her voice quavered. "I'm here. What should I do? How do I get back to the other side?"

"Just hold on. I'm coming to get you."

She took a deep breath and closed her eyes for a

moment. She was already in love with that voice. He sounded hard and male and sure of himself. *Confidence.* That was the key word here. Hopefully, the man would fit the voice and she would be safe. Hopefully.

Marc Huntington was growling softly as he began to pull off his jacket and then his long-sleeved knit shirt. This was not exactly the way he'd planned to spend his afternoon—rescuing one of the vultures who had come to Shangri-La, his family estate, to pick the bones clean.

He knew the situation. There was no money left. He'd come back home just in time to watch his heritage be destroyed. Unfortunately, his ten years in the military hadn't equipped him with the kind of funds needed to pay the back taxes his mother had ignored for too long. Selling the entire estate seemed to her to be the only way to deal with the problem and she was the official owner. It was her call.

So Shangri-La was up for sale. His mother's elaborate advertisements had produced a set of eight visitors here for the weekend, here to look the place over and come up with their offers. Every one of them was a grifter as far as he could tell. He could have cheerfully watched them all drown.

Well, not actually. His years as a Navy SEAL had ingrained the protective, rescuing ethic in his mind so thoroughly, it would take more than pure loathing to cleanse it from his soul. It was a part of him. How did you unlearn something like that?

"Talk to me," he ordered the stranded lady he couldn't see. "As I go through the current, it'll help keep me on course."

"Okay," she called back, sounding less scared now. "What shall I talk about?"

He was growling again. What did it matter what she talked about? He wasn't going to listen to anything but the sound of her voice. Her actual words weren't important. Maybe he should tell her to recite the details of the terms she was planning to offer in buying out his family estate. Hah.

"Sing a song," he suggested, looking down at his board shorts and deciding not to strip quite that far. He'd taken off the shirt and jacket because he might have to swim if the water was deep enough. But going down to his boxers wouldn't help much. "Recite a poem. Whatever."

He stepped into the icy water, feeling it wash against his legs even though the fog was so thick, he could barely see anything. Across the way, he could hear the woman beginning to sing something. She had a nice voice. He stopped and listened. Whatever that was she was singing, it had a familiar sound to it, like a Celtic folk song. Where had he heard that before?

He shook his head. It didn't matter. If she could keep it up, he would find her soon enough. One last growl and he plunged into the current, heading for the high, clear voice he heard through the fog.

Torie heard him coming through the water. He was getting closer. Sweet gratitude surged through her system. She raised her face to where the sun should be and sang harder and higher, trying to give him a clear signal as to her location.

And then she heard splashing very close and in a

minute or two she began to make out the dark shape of a man coming toward her.

"Oh, thank God," she cried as he approached. "I was afraid I was going to have to spend the night out here in the cold."

He didn't speak and as he came closer, she could make out his features and she began to realize he had a familiar look to him. She frowned. Oh no! It couldn't be.

He stopped a couple of feet away. "Mrs. Marino, I'm Marc Huntington. Marge is my mother. Just so you know I' m not some random beach bum."

Her heart began to thud in her chest. Marc Huntington. What was he doing here? It had been years since she'd seen him—at least fifteen of them. She'd heard he was overseas, in the service, fighting bad guys and raising hell.

But here he was, staring at her and looking none too friendly, despite his polite words. "How did you get out here, anyway?" he growled. "And why?"

He didn't recognize her. That was a relief. But why should he? She barely recognized him—and wouldn't have if she'd met up with him anywhere else. The last time she'd seen him, he'd been about half this size, a lanky, smart-mouthed teenager who probably didn't even know she existed.

Now he was all corded chest muscles and wide shoulders, with dark hair that tended to fall over his forehead and crystal-blue eyes that seemed remarkably hostile. Bottom line—he was pretty much the most gorgeous man she'd ever seen. She drew her breath in sharply and couldn't say a word.

His brow furrowed. "Are you okay?"

She nodded. It took two tries before she could speak.

"Uh…I'm…my name is Torie… But I guess you know that. I was just exploring the caves and the fog came in and…and…"

"Okay," he said impatiently. "No problem. Your husband was getting excited when you didn't show up for tea. Everyone is out looking for you."

Husband? Husband? She didn't have a husband. Oh. But she did have Carl Marino, and he was pretending to be her husband. She had to keep that straight in her mind.

"I'm sorry to be a bother," she said, finally getting control of herself. The shock of coming face to face with the man version of the boy she'd had a crush on for years had thrown her for a loop, but she was getting her balance back. She had to remember he was the enemy, just like everyone else in the Huntington family—the enemy she'd come to slay like a proverbial dragon.

And now here was one of them, saving her from the cold. A bit awkward, to say the least.

"I lost track of time."

He nodded, his blue-eyed gaze skimming over her bare arms and legs in the skimpy sundress she'd worn. "Next time, bring a jacket," he suggested gruffly. "It can turn cold fast."

And she'd known that. After all, she'd spent every summer of her childhood right here on this very beach. But it had been a good fifteen years since her last visit and she'd been so excited to see her old secret places, she'd forgotten about the vagaries of the weather.

"I'm okay," she insisted, despite her chattering teeth. "Are you going to lead me back?"

He looked her up and down and, for the first time, there was a hint of humor in his eyes.

"No," he said. "I'm going to carry you."

"What?" She began to back away from him on the sand. "No. You can't carry me all the way back."

"Why not? I'm trained to carry awkward loads, and you definitely look like a lightweight anyway."

She stopped and glared at him. Was he making fun of her? Why the hostility when he thought he'd only just met her?

"Awkward and bird-brained at the same time?" she asked crisply. "I didn't realize you knew me that well."

His mouth twisted. "That isn't what I meant."

"No, but it's what you said."

His look was long-suffering. "Mrs. Marino, your husband is having a fit back at the house. He seems to think you're likely to walk off a cliff or something, unless you're carefully watched. So I intend to make sure you get back safely." He made a gesture with his head. "Come on. Let's get this over with."

She looked at him, at the smooth, hard flesh she was going to have to touch in order to do what he'd suggested, and her heart began to pound like a hammer. There was a time when she'd dreamed about touching him—but that was when she was half in love with him from afar. Now, the thought was horrifying. He was the enemy. She couldn't do it.

"No," she said. "I'll follow you. I'll...I'll hold on to..." She was going to say, *your shirt,* but he wasn't wearing one, and the only alternative was the back of his low-slung board shorts. The thought of sticking her fingers down there made her gasp.

He watched her, waiting as her face registered a growing realization of the problem.

"Exactly," he said, his voice mocking. "I'll carry you," he said again.

She was shaking her head. "I don't think so."

His patience was running thin and it showed. "Listen carefully. There is a hard current running through the deepest part of the channel, right where we have to cross. If it knocks you down, the strength of it could carry you right out to sea. Then I would have to swim out after you, and I don't know how successful I'd be. It's safer for all concerned if you just let me pick you up and ..."

"Isn't there some other way?"

His frown was getting fiercer. "What is your problem?"

She drew in a deep breath and told him with a glare. "You're almost naked, you know."

He gave her a look that said he thought she was nuts. "You're not exactly well-covered yourself. If we'd been swimming, you wouldn't think twice."

"But..."

"Look, every minute we delay, it's only getting worse. Come on." His quick smile was sarcastic. "I'll be gentle, I swear it."

By now she was seriously annoyed with him. He wasn't even trying to see this from her point of view—and he had no interest in exploring alternatives. She looked around, trying to think of some way to avoid this, and he took a step forward and grabbed her, swinging her up into his arms. It was pretty obvious he wouldn't mind just chucking her over his shoulder, good to go, but when she shrieked he relented and straightened her so that one arm was under her knees and the other behind her back. She threw her arms around his neck to avoid being dropped, and they started off.

He was impossibly hard and exciting to touch, but even worse, his incredible warmth worked on her like a drug. She was clinging to him, trying to get closer. She closed her eyes and took it all in, trying to pretend he wasn't the boy she used to watch with stars in her eyes.

Those stars had dimmed when the Huntingtons had fired her father, accused him of crimes and kicked her whole family out of what had long been their beloved home. Let's face it, the Huntingtons had pretty much destroyed her family and torn apart their lives—and all over a lie. Nothing had ever been the same again and the pain and resentment still smoldered deep inside her.

But she'd never been in stronger arms. It felt good—as long as she didn't think about who he really was.

The water was surging against him and she could feel the effort it took him to keep his footing. He almost went over at one point, splashing a spray of seawater against her legs, and she cried out, holding on more tightly, pressing her face against his neck.

"I've got you," he told her gruffly. "Just a little bit more. We're almost there."

She peeked out. She couldn't see a thing but the cold, clammy gray of the fog. How did he know they were almost there? She couldn't tell. But she knew one thing—his skin against hers felt like heaven. To think she'd been resisting.

But the fog was lifting and she began to see the shore herself.

"Here we are," he said, and she could feel the difference in the way he was walking. They'd hit dry sand. He began to lower her and she felt a pang of regret.

"Put on my jacket," he told her as he picked it up off the sand and handed it to her. She did as he suggested. It was big and heavy, made of denim with a few studs at the pockets—and it still felt warm, as though his body heat had lasted.

She turned to look at him. His arms were raised and he was pulling a long-sleeved thermal shirt down over his head. She watched, marveling at the interplay of muscles, and then gasped as she noticed the deep, ugly scar that disfigured an area of his rib cage.

Her shocked gaze met his ice-blue eyes as the shirt came down into place and covered everything—the muscles and the scar. She blinked at him, feeling breathless.

She wanted to ask about the scar, but the look in his eyes told her not to do it. Still, she had to say something. It was only right.

"Did you do something horribly brave that saved the day?" she asked a bit too quickly.

His look was dismissive. "No. I did something horribly stupid and ended up injured, which is something you never want to let happen."

"Oh. Of course."

But she didn't want him to think she was just a snotty brat. She needed to let him know she did appreciate what he'd done for her.

"Thank you," she said at last, feeling almost shy now that they were on firm ground and about to end their rescue encounter. "I really appreciate it. I mean…"

"What I'd appreciate," he said, his voice calm but icy, "is some answers."

She'd been stopped in the middle of her sentence,

and she was still staring at him. "Uh…answers? About what?"

"About what you're doing here. Why you came."

She blinked at him, a flicker of panic near her heart. Had he really caught on to her so quickly? "I…we came to see the estate, of course. It's for sale, isn't it?"

He nodded, waiting.

"Well, we came to see if Carl wants…I mean if we want to buy it. Isn't that what this is all about?"

His gaze never left her eyes. "You'd think. That's what all eight of you people came for, to spend the weekend looking over the property, evaluating it." His eyes narrowed. "I would have thought the house itself would be the main attraction. Either that, or the patio, the waterfall area, the huge front yard. And yet you'd hardly dropped your bags in the bedroom before you were off to see the caves. And your husband was off to nose around in the old vineyard area." He cocked an eyebrow. "What gives?"

She frowned at him. She hadn't realized Carl had gone off on his own sightseeing mission. She had to admit, it might look odd that the two of them had been so driven by alternate goals so immediately. She ought to do her best to quell all suspicions—if she could.

"What do you mean, 'what gives?' Nothing. We're just interested in everything, the house, the land, the beaches. I'd heard about the caves and…and I wanted to see them for myself."

He didn't look convinced. "The caves are cool, but they're hardly the best feature on the estate." He eyed her speculatively. "They do have a lot of historical significance," he said. "Smugglers seem to like them, and have since the old Spanish days." His gaze narrowed and he added acidly, "Is that what you were doing out there? Hiding something?"

She wanted to laugh out loud at such a silly suggestion, but she could see that this was no joke in his mind. "If I were, I wouldn't tell you about it, would I?" She bit her lip, regretting her words before she'd finished uttering them.

Keep it friendly, Torie, she told herself silently. *Save the anger for when you've got the ammunition.*

She quickly added out loud, "I'm going to enjoy seeing everything. It seems to be a wonderful property."

"Oh, it is that." A stormy look filled his blue eyes. "And it's worth a whole lot more than my mother is asking for it." He gave her a faint, sarcastic smile. "But you know that, don't you?"

A crash of thunder seemed to give an eerie emphasis to his words and large raindrops began spattering around them. Torie was shivering again.

CHAPTER TWO

THUNDER rolled and the rain began in earnest. Looking up, Marc swore under his breath.

"The fog no sooner thins out than the rain comes," he grumbled. "Come on. We'll never make it back across the dunes. Head for the tool shed just beyond the ice plant over there."

He pointed toward a wooden structure only a few hundred feet away and they ran for it, reaching it in moments, the threat of a downpour chasing them. Luckily the door wasn't locked and they tumbled in, breathing hard and laughing. Marc slammed the door shut, holding back the cold, wet wind, then turned to look at her.

They were both still laughing from the run across the sand, but Torie saw the humor fade in his eyes, and she looked away quickly.

"This shouldn't last too long," he said. "We might as well have a seat and wait it out."

The interior of the shed seemed clean enough, with tools piled along one side and bags of gravel and peat moss stacked along the other. They sat down on the plastic bags and listened to the rain pound on the roof. A couple of leaks appeared along the walls, but they weren't bad. Neither of them spoke, and the rain was too loud to try to talk over anyway.

Marc's head was turned away, looking out a small window at the rain, and Torie had time to study him, the back of his head and the angle of his neck and the width of his shoulders.

She shivered again, but not with cold. She was beginning to realize this wasn't going to be easy. How could she ever have imagined it might be? For fifteen years, she'd hated the Huntingtons. They'd seemed like monsters in her mind. She'd ached to find a way to clear her father's name and turn the world right again.

But now that she'd come face to face with them, things looked a bit different. If she'd succeed, she needed to be smart about it. She was going to have to stay strong. Reality had a way of cancelling out fantasy every time.

They were just people. That didn't mean they weren't guilty of some ugly things. But they were still proving to be only human—for now.

First there had been Marge, Marc's mother. When she and Carl had come up the front walk and climbed the steps to the wide porch and the huge front door, her heart had been pounding so hard, she'd thought she might faint. And then the door had swung open and there was this short, redheaded woman in a simple pants suit, welcoming them to Shangri-La with a warm smile. She didn't look much like the Cruella de Vil monster Torie had been remembering her as all these years. In fact, she looked more like a Brownie den mother. Sort of a letdown.

Marc's older sister Shayla had shown them to their rooms. She was a little closer to the mark. She'd always been snooty and full of herself, and things hadn't changed. But Torie had to admit, even she didn't seem like a fiend close up.

There had been two boys in the family, Marc and his older brother Ricky. Torie had assumed, as she and Carl had first arrived, that both young men were off living their own lives somewhere by now. The surprise had been to find Marc here.

Of course, the one most to blame for what happened, Marc's father, Tim Huntington, usually called Hunt, wasn't here at all. He'd drowned when his sailboat capsized in the bay years before. She would never be able to confront him. There would always be a hole in her soul for that.

In her dreams, she came charging up to Shangri-La and found the evidence to clear her father, presented it to Marge and Shayla with a flourish, and had them dissolving into tears of regret and apology. She would demand they write up a complete retraction and send it to the *Alegre Beacon*, the local paper. The little town of Alegre would be thrown into an uproar. The mayor would name a special celebration and present Torie with a plaque commemorating the day.

And Torie would take the plaque back down to Los Angeles and present it to her mother. That was her dream.

At least, it had been for years. She'd recently discovered evidence that cast a shadow on those hopes. Was there more to all this than she'd ever known? Possibly. And that was the main reason she was here today.

The downpour was almost over. The noise on the roof had faded to a dull drumbeat. Marc turned and looked at her, his blue eyes full of skepticism.

"So tell me about Carl," he said without preamble.

Her eyes widened. She hadn't really expected that. "What about him?"

"How long have you and Carl been married?" he asked her.

She frowned. She hated questions like this. She really didn't want to lie. But what could she do? Try to avoid it, she supposed. Just dance around the facts any way she could.

"Not long," she said brightly.

"Newlyweds, huh?"

She gave him a vague smile. She couldn't imagine Carl as a newlywed—not to anyone. He was a fairly cold, unemotional person. Business deals were all he cared about. Her accompanying him here was all part of a bargain to him. He needed to pretend to have a wife—she needed a way to get onto Shangri-La without letting the Huntingtons know who she was. They'd struck a deal.

"Any kids?"

"No. Oh no."

"I guess not if you always ask for separate bedrooms."

She flushed and her eyes flashed, but she held her temper. "Carl snores," she said, reciting the excuse they'd given when they made their reservations. That had been her one demand when Carl had asked her to come along. It had to be separate bedrooms, no matter how strange that looked.

Marc's eyes narrowed. "Carl's a bit older than you are, isn't he?"

She wasn't going to dignify that with an answer. Suddenly the bag of gravel felt hard and uncomfortable, and she got up to stretch her legs a bit. There wasn't much room for pacing, but she did her best.

"Where did you two meet?"

She glanced at him. The question flustered her. Her fingers were trembling. He was going to figure this whole charade out, wasn't he? He wanted to catch hold of a string and begin to pull it all apart. She could see it coming. But she had to make an attempt—keep her finger in the dike, so to speak.

"I…uh…he hired me to plan some cocktail parties for his business clients."

"You're a party planner?"

"And a caterer." She nodded, brightening to a theme she knew well and something she didn't have to skate around. "Yes. Any event, large or small. I can make it magical."

"I'll bet you can." His smile was ironic. "So you partied and you fell in love?"

She frowned, not trusting him at all. "You might say that."

Okay, it was time she got a little tougher. She couldn't let him think he had the upper hand. Turning, she glared at him.

"Listen, Marc. What's with the third degree? What is this intense interest in my private life?"

His wide mouth twisted. Maybe he was coming on a bit too strong.

There was no doubt he was suspicious—suspicious of every one of the visitors they were stuck with for the weekend. The last time they'd had an influx of strangers like this had been shortly after his father had died, drowned just outside the bay when his small sailboat had capsized. Once the word had spread that he'd taken the Don Carlos Treasure down with him, fortune hunters had come crawling all over the place. None of them believed that the old Spanish fortune that had been in the Huntington family for over a hundred years had really gone down into the sea. Everyone thought if he just looked hard enough, he would find the hiding place.

And the place searched most often were the caves. Of course. The caves had been where the treasure was first found. And the caves had been where the treasure had been hidden the first time it had disappeared.

But not this last time. Experts had gone over the place with a fine-tooth comb. There was no treasure, not anymore. It was pretty obvious his father's suicide note had said it all. The Don Carlos Treasure had gone back to the sea, from whence it had come.

Ashes to ashes, dust to dust and Spanish doubloons back to Neptune.

So was that what this pretty young woman had been looking for in the caves? Of course it was. Why else would she hurry right out there? She even had the look of a treasure hunter—always hopeful.

His gaze held hers for a long moment. There was a spark of humor in his eyes, but that didn't make her feel any better about this air of tension between them. Finally, he actually smiled.

"No big deal," he said. "Just making conversation. Passing the time." He slid off his bag as well and faced her in the small space. "I think the rain has stopped. Let's go."

She took a deep breath and watched as he left the shed, then hurried to catch up with him. He started across the dunes, striding quickly in the wet sand, and she had to run to keep up. His legs were much longer than hers.

About halfway to the cliff, he stopped, turning to watch her arrive at his position.

"Rest a minute," he said.

"I wouldn't need to if you wouldn't go so fast," she said testily.

"Sorry." But his gaze was restless. He looked toward the large white house up on the cliff. "I can't help but wonder what they're doing up there," he said, mostly to himself. He shook his head. "What is she thinking?"

"Who?" Torie asked, though she was pretty sure he meant Marge. "What's wrong?"

"'Turning and turning,'" he muttered, along with some other words she couldn't make out. He was staring into the distance. "'The center cannot hold.'"

"What?"

He looked directly into her eyes. "I think I'm in need of some 'passionate intensity'," he said.

Funny, but those words seemed to strike a chord with her. "Me too," she said. "Where do I go to get some?"

His grin was quick and then gone just as quickly. "Try a little Yeats," he suggested. "That just might be your answer."

And he was off again across the sands.

She came behind him, muttering about Lawrence of Arabia, but he didn't go as quickly this time and she arrived at the end of their mad scramble across the dunes only seconds after he did.

"My dear Mrs. Marino." He said with a touch of sarcasm. "We have reached the end of the line. I think we'd better part company here."

"You're not going up to the house?"

"Not yet. I have things to do in another part of the estate."

"Oh. Well, I guess I'll see you later."

"Unfortunately, I think you're right."

He sounded bitter, but before she had a chance to analyze that, he stepped closer and grabbed the two sides of the jacket, acting as though he was straightening the collar, but she was pretty sure he was really just trying to make a point—and maybe trying to establish his sense of control. The way he pulled on the jacket, she had to look up into his face.

"I still want to know what the hell you were doing in the caves," he said, his voice low and harsh. "You want to come clean now, or wait until I've got more information to go on?"

She stared up at him, shaken. His face was only inches from hers. "Uh…nothing. I was just exploring. I…I love the beach and I…"

But an expression flashed across his face and suddenly he was frowning, studying her features, his gaze sliding over every angle.

"Do I know you?" he asked softly.

Her heart was thumping so hard surely he could hear it. "I don't think so," she said quickly. "Now if you don't mind…."

"But I do mind." He pulled harder, bringing her up to where she could feel his warm breath on her face as he spoke. "And I'll give you fair warning. I won't let Shangri-La be trashed. Any excuse I can find to disqualify any of you, I'll use it."

She stared up, mesmerized by his voice and his eyes.

A shout from the cliff area turned them both in that direction. Carl was coming down the wooden steps.

"Torie!" he called. "Thank God you're okay."

She looked at Marc. He stared back, not letting go of the jacket. For a long moment, their gazes held. There was a look deep in his eyes, a mood, something that told her he was a bit of a loner, that he couldn't trust anyone enough to let go. Her heart seemed to melt, something in her yearned toward him. Someone ought to teach him how to trust. Too bad she was exactly the wrong person to expect that from.

She was the one who'd been lying to him all along. When he found out, he would discard her like yesterday's news.

But Carl was coming and it was obviously time to draw apart.

"Just keep that in mind, Mrs. Marino," Marc said coolly. "I'll be watching you."

He gave her one last impenetrably hard look, then turned and walked away.

Torie groaned as she watched him go. Marc Huntington would be watching her. Great. Maybe this was turnabout for the way she used to watch him when she was fifteen. She had to bite her lip to keep from laughing a bit hysterically, and she turned just as Carl reached her.

Tall and slim with thick auburn hair, Carl was handsome in an older way, and came across as very sure of himself. But right now, the man looked nervous.

Maybe Marc had threatened to watch him, too.

"What are you doing?" Carl whispered loudly, glancing toward where Marc was disappearing through the brush. "You're going to ruin the whole thing if you start messing around with young guys."

Messing around?

She drew back, offended. "He just saved me," she told him tartly. "I was in danger. Sort of."

"Where were you?" Carl asked, looking perplexed.

"Where were *you?*" she countered, pulling the jacket close around herself. "I heard you were out looking at the vineyard. I thought it was the house you were interested in."

His gaze shifted in a way that startled her. Was that a guilty look? He grabbed her arm and started leading her toward the stairs, muttering as he went.

He was annoyed but not really angry. She knew he didn't really care anything about her personally, he just didn't want anyone to get suspicious. And when you came right down to it, she felt the same way about him. The two of them were more like partners in this enterprise than anything else. They were definitely not a couple.

Carl looked back over his shoulder as they started up the wooden stairway. "Stay away from that guy," he said. "I can tell he's nothing but trouble."

"His name is Marc Huntington," she told him, in case he didn't know. "He's Marge Huntington's son."

"He didn't recognize you, did he?" he asked in alarm. He knew all about her childhood here in Shangri-La.

"No. I don't think so."

"Good."

She eyed him curiously. "I would think you might want to get friendly with him, not avoid him," she said. "He would probably be a good source of information about the property. And maybe have a little different perspective than his mother has." And then she remembered what he'd said just before Carl arrived. Maybe there was really no point in getting closer to Marc.

Maybe it would be safer all around if Carl kept his distance.

Carl shrugged. "I think I can gain more by exploring the place on my own," he said, giving her a pointed look. "And that is something you are going to help me with."

"I am?"

He nodded. "Sure. What do you think I brought you for? You grew up on the place. You know all the secrets." He gave her a crafty smile. "Don't you, darling?"

They'd reached the wide front porch and Marge Huntington was holding the door open for them, clucking over how everyone had been worried about Torie, freeing her from having to answer Carl's surprising statement. But she couldn't stop thinking about it. As she went up the stairs to dress for dinner, his words echoed in her mind.

You know all the secrets.

Something in his words chilled her. Maybe it was time she faced a few facts. She'd ignored her own doubts about Carl because he was giving her a chance to come back to Shangri-La, a chance she'd never have had without him. He'd told her he wanted her along to give the impression he was a stable married man, to help his chances of buying the place.

But now that they were here, she was beginning to realize there was more to it. When he'd quizzed her about her life her as a kid, she'd been happy to spill out just about everything she could think of. The trip down memory lane had been worth it. But now his interest seemed more pointed, less general. What was he after, anyway? That started her shivering again, despite the warmth of Marc's jacket.

The room she'd been given was a little heavy on the pink accents for her taste, but it was certainly charming. There was an old-fashioned canopy over the bed and plush, heart-shaped cushions everywhere. There were two doors besides the entryway—one to the private balcony and the other to the bathroom.

She shrugged out of Marc's jacket and threw it over the back of a chair, then walked out onto the little balcony and leaned out over the white wooden railing with its Victorian ornamentation. She could just barely make out the red tile roof of the butler's cottage where she'd lived as a child. Just seeing it brought a lump to her throat.

"I'm back, Huntingtons," she whispered to herself. "I'm back and I'm going to find out what really happened fifteen years ago when you fired my father and destroyed my family." She flipped her thick blond hair back with a toss of her head. "Get ready for it. I want some answers, too."

Shangri-La.

The name conjured up images of the mysterious East, and yet, the Huntington estate was plunked right in the middle of the California central coast and looked it. The house was a huge old rambling Victorian, perched on a cliff over the ocean, and there was nothing mysterious about it.

Torie did a little exploring, disappointed to find the grounds had been changed here and there. The beautiful rose garden that Mr. Huntington had been so proud of was a barren mess, and the trellis along the ocean cliff was gone. A new set of buildings lined the driveway and a new pool complex filled what had once been the tennis court area. The changes gave her a sick, empty feeling and she went back into the house, slipping quietly down the hallways to get a feel for the place.

She found the kitchen, and just as she turned to go again, Marc appeared in the doorway.

"Looking for something?" he asked, gazing at her skeptically.

She blinked, feeling guilty for no reason at all. "Just a drink of water."

He went to the cabinet and got down a glass, then poured her a drink from the pitcher next to the sink. Turning, he watched her levelly as she drank it down.

"Shouldn't you be attending to your husband?" he said, his voice soft but filled with a sense of irony.

"My...?"

Funny. Whenever Marc came near, she completely forgot that she was pretending to be married to someone.

"Uh, no," she said quickly, using a phony smile as a cover-up. "Carl is actually pretty self-sufficient."

"Lucky you," he noted, his gaze cool.

She smiled at him but he didn't smile back and she retreated quickly, pulse beating a bit too fast. This might be Shangri-La, but it wasn't paradise. Too many conflicting emotions for that.

Another name came to mind as Torie sat at the dinner table, looking at the eclectic gallery of other perspective buyers. Actually, she was reminded of the cantina scene in the original *Star Wars*. A den of villainy, no doubt about it. Not to mention strangeness.

There was Tom, the jovial Texan whose booming laugh filled the room and bounced from the walls.

Sitting next to him was the stylishly dressed Lyla, a pretty young widow from Los Angeles, who looked upon them all with a sense of disdain flaring her elegant nostrils. Andros, a Greek restaurateur, and his wife Nina, seemed pleasant and friendly, but Phoebe, the voluptuous blonde in the low-cut dress, and Frank, the vaguely sinister-looking real estate broker who dressed as though he was trying out for a role in a local production of *Saturday Night Fever*, were a couple she wouldn't have wanted to meet in an alley on a dark night.

Marge Huntington presided at the head of the table, attempting to tame them all with pleasantries and offers to pass the au jus. She hardly looked any older than she had fifteen years ago, her flaming red hair flying like a flag. Torie remembered seeing her out sunbathing on the beach and hosting luncheons for the local women's groups.

She'd been jumpy at first, wondering if the woman would remember her, but Marge hadn't given her a second glance. She didn't recognize her—and why should she? Her name had been Vikki then, short for Victoria, and she'd been short and chubby, with mousy brown hair and no personality that she could remember having. A typical plain Jane sort of girl, short on friends and scared of her own shadow.

That was then. This was now. She'd learned a thing or two about making herself ready for her place on the stage of life. She was taller, thinner, blonder—and definitely more confident.

Even so, sitting at the table with the woman made Torie a little nervous. Every time her eyes met Marge's, she felt a little surge in her heart rate. She couldn't help but think her hostess was going to begin to recognize her at some point.

But maybe that wouldn't happen. After all, Marge was pretty self-absorbed. As long as she was the center of attention, she didn't seem to need anything else.

She'd been prepared to face Marge, but it had never occurred to her that Marc might be here. She wondered if that was going to be the fatal flaw. Marc could very possibly ruin all her plans.

The food was good—cold trout and roasted Cornish game hens with a warm caramel apple pie for dessert. She noticed that the butler, a semi-handsome young man whom they called Jimmy in an annoyingly casual manner, was exchanging the sort of looks with Marge that usually meant bedroom visits late at night—but she didn't care. She was just glad her father wasn't here to see the Shangri-La butler being so unprofessional. He would have been appalled.

Marge welcomed them all and laid out the plans for the weekend.

"I want you to love Shangri-La like we do," she said, smiling at each in turn around the table. "I want you to feel what it's like to have the ocean in your front yard. I want you to explore the gardens, the vineyards, the cliffs. I want you to ride into town and visit our quaint little stores. Once you get a true feeling for the place, for the possibilities, I know you'll see how it could change and enrich your life."

The Texan gave a grunt of amusement. "And then you're hoping one of us will be ready to 'change and enrich' yours with a nice ownership bid, aren't you?"

Marge didn't flinch. "Of course. That's the whole point, isn't it?"

Everyone laughed, but a bit tentatively, glancing sideways at each other. After all, if they did all love the estate, they would all soon be fighting each other for the chance to own it.

Lyla began going on and on about the invigorating effects of fresh sea air while Phoebe was throwing flirtatious glances at the Texan. Torie looked at Carl sitting next to her and found that he was staring at his food as though his mind was off in some other place.

And then an odd thing happened. The hair on the back of her neck was rising. She glanced up quickly and found Marc leaning against the doorjamb, arms folded across his chest, watching her coolly. He was wearing a long-sleeved jersey shirt that said Airborne just above where his forearms sat. He had the look of a man who was deciding who was naughty and who was nice. She was afraid she could already tell which category he had her in.

Funny. A look like that from Marc Huntington would have sent her running for a hiding place in the old days. But times had changed. She was all grown up and had a temper of her own. So she raised her wineglass as though toasting him and smiled.

His face didn't change but something glittered in his eyes. Was that a hint of humor? Couldn't be—not in a tough guy like Marc. She shrugged, raised her chin and put the glass down. He was obviously in fight mode, just searching for ways to stop his mother's plans. She actually had no interest in either side of that struggle. She had her own agenda.

Marc stayed where he was and studied each one of the characters around his family dining table in turn. Every one of them seemed have hidden motives. Every one of them needed to be watched.

Or was he just being paranoid? Too many months on the front lines of war tended to do that to a man. He had to watch out. He'd known others from his line of work who ended up raving against reality, seeing assassins behind every tree. He didn't want to be like that.

His biggest problem right now was that his gaze kept getting tugged back to Torie. Wasn't there a phrase for that? He couldn't keep his eyes off her. That was it.

There was no getting around it—something about her appealed to him in a core, involuntary way. It was visceral. It came from inside him and he couldn't get it to stop.

He didn't trust her and he certainly didn't trust Carl. He'd already put in a call to an old friend in local law enforcement who sometimes worked with the FBI to see if he could find out something about Carl. The man just had a gangland look about him. What in hell a woman like Torie was doing with scum like that, he couldn't imagine. He didn't want to believe what that pointed to—that she was just as bad as he was. Or at least, willing to tolerate his badness.

But never mind. It wasn't as if he was falling for her or anything. It had been a long time since a woman had really yanked his chain and he thought he'd been pretty much inoculated against it.

He was a Navy SEAL for God's sake. He'd been out and seen the world and the world had done it's damndest to him. He'd been shot at, he'd been attacked by a man with a knife and a deadly grudge, he'd been in bar fights. He'd been loved by some beautiful women and hated by others. He'd lived, and he planned to live some more.

But what he hadn't planned for were the feelings, the emotions, that coming home had delivered like a blow to the gut. Coming back to Shangri-La, seeing its majestic beauty again, remembering his life, his father, his brother, and all that they had meant to each other—those emotions had surged through him and pierced his heart, cutting to the soul of who he was and where he came from.

His gaze kept shifting back toward Torie. He liked the look of her. There was love and laughter in that face, and a lively intelligence. Most women he'd known had one or another of those qualities. But she seemed to have them all in spades.

But there was something else that teased his imagination. Every now and then when he looked at her, he caught an expression in her eyes that he couldn't quite analyze. Was it sadness? Regret? Or fear? She was always quick to erase it with a smile and he hadn't had time to get a fix on it yet.

But he knew one thing about her for sure—she wasn't in love with Carl. That was clear. She might be in love with someone, but this guy wasn't it. A little part of him felt a twinge of jealousy.

He grimaced. Ridiculous. He could admit she attracted him, but even that was off limits. She was married, and even if she didn't love Carl, that was a situation he would stay a million miles away from.

At the same time, he didn't trust her. How could he? She lied every time she spoke to him. Why didn't he hate her for it?

No. He couldn't hate her. Even her lying was cute, like a kitten who couldn't help but bite you.

Whoa. He seemed to be about to hand her carte blanche for anything. This was ridiculously dangerous. He had to get out of this mood and fast.

He shifted his gaze to his mother. Except, she wasn't really his mother. It had been drummed into his head that he had to call her that, but it had never penetrated his heart. She wasn't his real mother. She was his stepmother. She and her daughter Shayla had come into his father's life after his biological mother had died. Now she ruled the roost here at Shangri-La, and that was just wrong.

He and Shayla had always been at daggers drawn. But Shayla was older and his brother Ricky had been forced to deal with her. Marc had flown under the radar, staying out of Shayla's way and pretending she didn't exist.

Poor Ricky had been battered daily by the attacks Shayla dealt out. Now that he looked back, he wondered how his brother had put up with it. If only he'd been there for Ricky more often. If only he'd taken some of the blows himself, maybe Ricky would still be alive.

Maybe. Sure. It was no use thinking 'maybe'.

So he'd come back to his ancestral home to find his stepmother and his stepsister about to throw away the Huntington legacy that was over a century old. No one could pay enough to make the sale worth it. At least, that was the way it seemed to him. They wanted to sell the place and go live it up in the Bahamas. As if money could make up for losing their heritage.

This was a no-go as far as he was concerned. It was not going to happen. This property belonged to generations of Huntingtons and these interlopers were not going to be allowed to ruin that. He was the only real Huntington here, and he was going to have to put a stop to it.

CHAPTER THREE

A FEW minutes later, dinner over, Torie had to brush past Marc in order to leave the room.

"Waiting to high-grade the leftovers?" she asked mockingly in a soft voice for only him to hear.

"That would lead to starvation with this greedy crew," he murmured back to her.

She'd meant to get past him and move on, but something in his smoky blue eyes caught at her and she paused, held in his gaze for a beat too long.

"I get first pick at all times," he added arrogantly. "Or I don't play at all."

She flushed. He was so obviously trying to rattle her, and, darn it all—it was working. She should have known it was very foolish to taunt the tiger. A sharp retort came to mind, but she bit her lip and held it back, flipping her hair over her shoulder with a toss of her head and looking away as she walked on.

She could feel his gaze follow her like a brand on her back, but she just kept going. She'd come here to Shangri-La with a purpose—she wanted to find facts and clear her father, and that meant snooping into things. It might be best not to tempt Marc with reasons for him to want to follow her around.

She needed to stay as far away from this man as she could manage.

She joined the others on the wide terrace. The rain had cleared out the fog and now it had gone away as well. Twilight wasn't far off, and in the light that remained, Marge suggested they all join her in an excursion to the pier. She wanted to show them the boathouse and the dock. They all gathered into a group and began the long tramp down to the shore, but Torie noticed that Carl had slipped away and she hung back.

"I want to run up and get a jacket," she told Marge. "I'll catch up with you."

Just before she started up the stairs, she heard a muffled thumping down the hallway, and she followed the sound into the library. There was Carl, knocking on wooden panels as though he expected one to slide open at his touch.

"Searching for a secret compartment?" she asked a bit caustically. "Not cool, Carl."

He whirled to face her, his thin face intense. "Just checking the quality of construction," he said unconvincingly.

"I'll tell you what the construction is like," she responded, a bit impatient with him. "It's old. This place was built about a hundred years ago. And it's held up all this time. I wouldn't worry about how sound it is. If you buy it, obviously, you'll have to get some expert advice. Structural engineers and architects."

"Yes, of course," he said, frowning at her as though she were being a nuisance. He hesitated, then sighed and moved closer so that he could whisper. His dark eyes were darting about the room, strangely impatient. "But these old houses have false fronts and hidden passageways. I'm just checking it out." He frowned at her. "Did you know about any? Did you ever find one?"

She shook her head. He was really turning out to be a little strange, wasn't he?

"Carl, I never even came into this house when I lived on the property. My father worked here, but I didn't. We lived down by the gate, at the butler's house. I never even came onto the porch."

"You're sure?"

"I'm sure."

He gestured toward a glass cabinet in the corner of the room.

"So you never saw the bag of Spanish gold they used to keep in that display case?"

She turned and stared at it. An empty showcase was a sad thing and she realized it must have looked that way for the last fifteen years. Why had they left it like this? Did they think the Don Carlos Treasure would turn up again someday? From what she understood, it was at the bottom of the sea.

"No," she said softly. "I never saw it." At least not there.

There was a noise in the hallway and suddenly Jimmy, the current butler, appeared in the doorway, looking surprised to see them in the library. Torie gave him a friendly smile and told Carl, "I'm just running up to get a jacket. You ought to go on out and meet the others. They're taking a look at the old boathouse. You might just be interested."

Carl nodded, but he was eyeing Jimmy speculatively, and Torie took the opportunity to escape before he began questioning the man about construction facts. She raced up the stairs to the bedroom and was about to reach for her velour hoodie when she noticed that Marc's denim jacket was still lying where she'd tossed it on the chair. She hesitated. Something about it appealed to her on a primitive level. She ought to get it back to him.

Instead, she found herself pulling it on and posing in front of the full-length mirror. It was big and heavy and rough and it looked completely wrong for her slender frame—and she knew she had better get it off before Carl came up and saw her in it. But she hugged it to herself, thinking it had a male smell that could be seductive if she let it be. For just a moment, she remembered how it had felt to be in Marc's arms, coming through the fog. That made her smile at herself in the mirror.

"Go ahead and wear it if you want to," Marc's deep voice said.

She whirled, gasping in shock. There he was, standing in the doorway to her bathroom, a pipe wrench in his hand. Her face went instantly to crimson and she shed the jacket as though it had just caught on fire.

"What are you doing here?" she cried out. Surprised, embarrassed, humiliated—she was all three at once.

She could tell he was trying not to smile, but he just couldn't help himself, and when his grin broke out, it was wide and sardonic.

"Just a little sink repair," he said, waving the wrench at her. "I thought you'd gone down to the beach with the others."

She dropped the jacket on the floor and glared at him. "I hate you," she said unconvincingly.

He laughed, which only made her more angry. "Totally understandable," he acknowledged.

"I was just…just…" There was no way to explain what she'd been doing, prancing around in his jacket in front of her mirror, so she gave it up. "You ought to let people know when you're in their bathroom."

He shrugged. "Exactly why I came out when I did. I wanted to make sure you didn't do anything you'd regret." He couldn't help but grin again. "I've got to admit, you look a hell of a lot cuter than I do in that jacket. Maybe you should keep it."

She glared at him. "I don't want it," she said emphatically as she threw it toward him. Her face was beginning to cool down. For a moment there she'd been afraid she would explode with the agony of it all. Things were better now—heart rate slowing, skin cooling, breathing getting back to normal. Maybe she was going to be okay.

"What were you really doing in here?" she asked him, frowning suspiciously. "Checking around for some answers to those questions you were talking about?"

"Why?" He cocked a curious eyebrow her way. "Are there some answers lurking where I could find them?"

Her green eyes narrowed. "You tell me."

He shook his head as though she thoroughly amused him. "I didn't go through your things," he told her patiently. "And I really don't plan to. Not yet anyway."

She glared at him. "Not ever!"

He considered her words for a moment. "How about this?" he said. "You go ahead and give me some answers now. Then I won't be tempted to go digging at all."

She hesitated, searching his smoky eyes for reasons to believe he was being straight with her. What would he be digging for, anyway? Did he really think she was some kind of scam artist? Or that Carl was?

That gave her pause. After all, she wasn't too sure about Carl herself anymore.

"We could try that," she said, attempting to sound reasonable and watching his reaction. "We could both ask each other. Take turns."

He made a face as though he thought that was going a little far, but still he said, "If you want."

"Ask me something," she challenged. "I'll see if you deserve an answer or not."

He nodded, considering. "And I'll see if I can trust anything you tell me."

Her chin rose and her eyes blazed. "Trust is a slippery thing."

"You got that right." He carefully put the wrench down on the desk. "Okay, let's just try it." He shrugged. "You start."

She thought for a second, then said, "Here's one. Why are you so mean?"

He threw his head back and groaned. "That's such a girlie question. There's no way I can answer that."

She shrugged, nose in the air. "I rest my case. You can't be trusted."

He glared at her. "You've got to ask things that get to substance, not feelings."

She glared back. "Okay, let's hear your great question."

"Okay." He looked at her for a long moment, then shoved his hands down into the pockets of his jeans and frowned. "Here's what I want to know. Why would you lie about being married?"

Her heart flipped over and began to pound. Her hands curled into fists. "So now you're calling me a liar?" she said breathlessly.

"Oh yeah. Beyond a doubt."

She flushed. What could she say? He was right.

"You're just grasping for things to make me angry," she charged, knowing it was a weak one. "You don't have any proof."

"I don't need proof. I've got common sense and my own two eyes." He gave her a half smile. "In fact, I've got a whole list of reasons that tell me you two aren't married."

"A list?"

"Yeah."

She turned away, panic fluttering in her throat. "You know, I don't need this…" she began, but a shout from the direction of the beach stopped the words in her throat and they both went out onto the balcony, looking toward where the sound had come from.

"They've started back," Marc said. "Looks like you missed your tour of the boat house."

They both leaned on the railing, looking west and watching a gorgeous sunset. All traces of the fog were gone now, and the sky was streaked with red and purple. The ocean was silver blue.

Marc rubbed his eyes as though they were tired and he looked again, shaking his head. "It's so damn beautiful," he said softly, almost to himself. "I'd forgotten how much I loved the evening sky out here."

She looked at him sideways. "You haven't been back here much lately?"

"No. Not at all, in fact. I've mostly been overseas."

She thought about that for a minute. If she'd come earlier, he wouldn't have been here. And that would have been a good thing. Wouldn't it?

"When did you get discharged from the military?"

"A while back. But I only came home two days ago." His mouth twisted. "I've been gone over ten years and it all still looks so much the same. You'd think the land would show the scars of..." He winced, then shrugged, letting the thought go. "Anyway, I can't believe how much this place means to me. I can see my history everywhere I look."

He pointed. "See that broken gate to the rose garden? See how it lists? That happened when I told my high-school sweetheart I wasn't the marrying kind. She slapped me and then slammed that poor gate so hard, it almost fell off the hinges."

Torie tried to remember who that would have been but the memory didn't surface. "At least you recovered," she murmured.

"Yeah. Sort of."

This time his grin was open and sweet and her heartbeat quickened just seeing it.

But he wasn't finished. "See that pile of rocks by the oak tree? That's where my brother and I buried our old dog Neville."

"Oh." Torie gasped. She'd forgotten about Ricky. Two years older than Marc, he'd been a shyer, more remote figure, sort of awkward and a bit of a computer geek. What had ever happened to Ricky?

"We had a funeral service and put that dear old dog in the ground," Marc said. He shook his head, a half smile lingering on his lips.

"Where is your brother?" she asked, hoping he would tell more.

He didn't answer for a long moment, and when he spoke again, his voice was gravelly. "Gone. I can't believe how long it's been. He died just over ten years ago."

"Oh no!"

The news went through her like an electric shock. It was horrible to think of Ricky gone. And all this time, she'd never known about it. She felt a trembling deep down that shook her. Ricky had never been anything much to her. Not the way Marc had been. She'd demonized him in her mind because he was part of her enemy—the Huntingtons. But was that fair? He was part of her past, too.

There was too much tragedy in the world. Ricky, Marc's father, her own father—all gone. Tears shimmered in her eyes and she covered her mouth with her hands, as though holding back the dark side of life for all she was worth.

He watched her for a moment, wondering why his brother's death would seem to touch her like this. That was a part of the fascination he had with her—she was always surprising him. Just when he thought he had her all figured out, she would do or say something that showed him how useless it was to make assumptions.

Turning, he looked out at the grounds again, searching for something he could use to change the subject.

"The red tile roof you see in the distance used to be the butler's house," he pointed out, hoping to distract her.

It seemed to be working. She'd turned her attention to where he'd indicated.

"He had a little girl who used to hide in the apple tree while I was washing my car over there by the shed. She'd wait up there, eating apples, until the car was sparkling clean and I was gone and then she would throw the apple cores down on my just-washed car."

"No she did not!" Torie said before she thought. But

it wasn't true! She would never have done such a thing. Would she?

He looked at her in surprise. "How would you know?"

She was flushing again and still wiping tears from her eyes. This was not a road she wanted him to go down. She had to change the subject and nip this in the bud.

Turning away, she went back into the room and sank down to sit on the bed. "Listen, you were going to tell me why you got this nutty idea that Carl and I weren't married," she reminded him. Better that than memories of the chubby little girl in the apple tree. "You said you had a list."

"That's right." He followed her back in, standing in front of her and looking down at her. "You want to hear it?"

She took a deep breath and made herself smile. "Sure. And I'll shoot down every one of your items. Go."

"Okay." He cleared his throat. "To begin with, I'd say Carl has a passion, but it's not for you."

He said the oddest things!

"Gee thanks," she retorted.

He gave her a curious look. "I hope that doesn't break your heart."

"Hardly. Go on. I thought you had a whole list."

"I do. Here goes." His head tilted back and he began to go through the reasons, counting them off on his fingers.

"No ring on your finger. No ring on his. Separate bedrooms. You two sit at a dinner table like strangers. Newlyweds usually can't keep their hands off each other."

Her lower lip stuck out and she took a deep breath. "Circumstantial evidence. What else?"

He turned and held her gaze with his own for a long, long moment before he spoke. And then he said, in a soft, husky voice, "The way you look at me."

She gasped sharply and her cheeks colored again. "You don't play fair, do you?" she said breathlessly, looking at him wide-eyed, knowing she probably looked hurt rather than angry. Because that was pretty much the way she felt.

He hesitated. She could see the indecision in his eyes. Then he reached out and touched her cheek softly with his fingertips. One casual caress and his hand was gone again.

"Torie, I don't mean anything personal by that. I just mean that like any healthy young woman, you're attracted to men. Not just me. It could be anybody. You're not committed to one guy yet and it's written all over you."

He was so right about everything—probably why he was annoying. The more he talked, the less she found she could argue back about.

Still, this was not fair. She turned back to glare at him. "It's all none of your business, you know."

"Wrong." He shrugged, his eyes cool and mysterious. "You came here under false pretenses. You claimed something that isn't true. I should send you packing."

She drew in a quick breath. "No. Your mother can do that if she wants. But you have no standing to do it. You didn't invite us."

"I didn't invite you," he repeated, shaking his head.

The bitter twist was back in his mouth. "You're right. It's up to my mother. If she doesn't care that you lied to get in here, why should I?"

Her courage took on new life. "You got that right. Good for you."

"Tell me this, Torie." He moved closer, looking down into her eyes. "Just exactly why are *you* here?"

"Me?"

"Yes. You." He shook his head. "You're not married to Carl. You don't care if he buys the place or not. What do you want out of all this?"

"I..." She closed her eyes and swayed a bit. She wanted to tell him the truth. She wanted to tell him that she'd lived here in the past, that if he thought hard, he would remember her, that his family had ruined her family and they ought to face that fact—and help her get to the truth. That was what she wanted. But she didn't have the proof to back up those claims. Not yet. Soon, she hoped to lay it all before him. Very soon.

"I'm helping Carl," she said. "Believe it or not, he thinks he needs me. He thinks portraying himself as a married man gives him more gravitas to make his case and submit his purchase plans."

"No." He shook his head slowly, his gaze travelling over her face as though sure the truth was in there somewhere. "That's not it. I don't think Carl wants to buy Shangri-La at all. He doesn't have that land-grab look in his eyes."

She threw out her hands, palms up. "Okay Mr. Know-It-All, then what *did* we come here for?" She waited, breathing fast. What was he going to guess? Did he have any idea?

"You got me." His blue eyes searched her dark ones.

"I don't know. I don't know why you came. I don't know what you were doing out at the caves. I don't know who you really are. But I intend to find out." He flashed her a lopsided grin, his eyes filled with mischief. "So be careful, baby. Just remember. Like the song says, every move you make."

"You'll be watching me," she said, trying to keep the resentment out of her voice but not entirely succeeding. "Got it."

CHAPTER FOUR

"WHAT was that?" Lyla's coal-black eyes were wide and startled. Her stylishly short hair was swept back in two wings at the sides of her face, making her look all the more surprised. "Was that a wolf?"

It was well after dark and Jimmy had started a fire in the fire pit on the patio overlooking the ocean. The others were gathering there, and Torie had joined them. The strange, high-pitched cry, wild and unnerving, had come during a lull in conversation.

"It sounds like a coyote," she told the pretty woman reassuringly. "They usually shy away from humans. I wouldn't worry about it."

"Hey, no problem," the man named Frank told her with a leering smile. "No one's going to let a lovely lady like you get eaten by wolves."

"Define *wolves*," his wife Phoebe interjected caustically, looking daggers at Lyla.

Torie turned away. She was definitely staying out of this one. The drinks had been flowing freely for over an hour now, so the voices were getting higher and laughter was ringing throughout the patio area. That was good as far as she was concerned. At some point, she was hoping to feel safe in slipping away and following her own plan. It was just a matter of time.

She sank down into a deep wicker chair, staring into the golden flames that were leaping higher and higher, ignoring the others and letting memories creep up out of her subconscious.

She remembered parties around this very fire pit—but not parties that she ever attended. She remembered slinking about in the shadows, watching as Ricky or Marc gathered here with their high-school friends, envying them their abandoned joy, wishing…she wasn't sure what. But wishing with all her heart anyway for something…someone.

She glanced out into the trees, wondering if there was anyone watching the way she'd watched. Sure enough, there was Marc. He wasn't exactly hiding the way she had, but he was watching. Right now, he had his attention trained on someone else, though, and that made her smile. He was so busy keeping tabs on everyone. What made a man so paranoid?

But she knew very well what did that. It affected her, too.

He glanced her way and her gaze met his and she made a face, hoping to annoy him. Then she winked, for no reason at all. She caught the ghost of a smile on his face before he turned away and started watching the big Texan who was enthralling one and all with tales of his cowboy days herding cattle out on the range, heading for the Chicago stockyards.

"Has this guy ever heard that trains took over that job about a hundred years ago?" Frank muttered as he walked past her.

She glanced around the circle. Once again, Carl had

disappeared and she frowned. What was his problem, anyway?

Someone put a stick in her hand and she noticed, vaguely, there was something white attached to the end of it.

"Oh my gosh," Lyla cried out as someone handed her one too. "Toasted marshmallows on a stick. Are you serious?"

Torie blinked, realizing she was right. Dutifully, she began waving it toward the flames but she wasn't particularly interested in the results.

"You're letting it burn," a low voice said from behind. Marc had come in from the cold and he reached out and took the stick from her, turning it expertly so that it browned evenly. He handed it back.

She gave him a questioning look, then stared at the gooey mess on the end of her stick. "I'm supposed to eat this?"

"You'll love it."

"I doubt it."

He took it off the stick and popped it into her mouth before she could stop him. That made her laugh. It was good, sugary and crisp on the outside, creamy on the inside, and delicious in a simple, childish way.

"Okay, now you have to eat one," she said.

The look on his face told her it would be a cold day before that happened.

"Where's Carl?" he asked, looking around at the others.

That reminded her. He thought she was a crook, and if he knew who her father was, that would probably clinch the deal in his mind. She had to be careful.

"You got me," she responded to his question about

Carl. "There's no telling where he's gone or what he's up to."

He gave her a quizzical look, then shook his head, looking at her so intensely, she felt suddenly chilled.

"Let's get out of here," he said, his voice low.

Something surged in her chest. "What? You and me?"

"Yeah." His eyes shone in the shadows. "I want to talk to you. Alone."

She felt the pull he had over her, but she could resist that. She bit her lower lip, thinking fast. She didn't have time to talk. She had to get going on her plan, and she didn't want him following her.

The first thing she wanted to do was to get to the house she'd lived in as a child, the one with the red tile roof, and do a little exploring. Luckily, Jimmy wasn't living in it and it seemed to be empty. In fact, it seemed no one had lived in it for years. All the better for finding something left behind that might ignite a memory or her imagination in ways that could help her.

"I don't think that will work," she said, looking away. "People will notice."

"And you care? Why?"

She frowned at him. "Because I'm a decent person, Marc. I want people to notice *that*. Maybe you don't. But I do."

Funny what amazing thoughts came tumbling out of her head because she felt she had to fight back against him. She'd never thought this position over, but now it seemed to be hers.

"And there's something else," she told him. "Look into my eyes. Do you see someone who's attracted to you?" She glared at him. "Do you see someone who looks susceptible to your load of bull? Because I don't. And I want you to acknowledge it."

He stared at her and shook his head as though he thought she was nuts. "Okay," he said. "Point taken. I was wrong. You don't have a thing for me. I can accept that."

"Can you, Marc?" She glared harder. "Good. Because I don't have a crush on you. So don't expect it."

His mouth twisted in half a grin. "All right. Sorry I ever brought it up."

"Okay." She took a deep breath.

His mouth twisted and his gaze was sardonic. "But you're still not married to Carl. Isn't that right?"

She sighed and tossed her head, letting her hair fly behind her, then looked toward the fire. When she looked back, he was gone.

But he wasn't far away. Every nerve ending he possessed, every element of caution, was on edge. There was something going on here. He could feel it in the air. He wasn't sure what it was—but he was going to find out.

Was Torie involved? Undoubtedly. His gaze kept getting pulled back to her, leaving him halfway between bemused and annoyed. Something about her nagged at him—as though there was something he'd forgotten, something he'd filed away and put into the wrong drawer. Something just didn't compute. Why did she look so familiar?

And where the hell was Carl? A part of him wanted to go looking for him, but then Torie would disappear. Better to stay. Someone had to keep an eye on her.

She spoke to the Texan and laughed at something he

said back, but her gaze quickly returned to search him out. What expression did he see on her face? Defiance? Anger? He wasn't sure what it was, but it only aroused his interest. He couldn't stop looking at her. She was getting ready to make a move and he wanted to be sure he knew about it when it happened.

But the night was young and Marge had plans for them all.

"Come on, everybody," she announced, calling them all to gather around the fire pit. "I've got Jimmy bringing in more wood. We'll sit around the fire and tell stories."

"Ghost stories?" Lyla asked, looking worried.

"No," Marge said, laughing. "Let's get back to the reason you're all here. I think each of you should talk about Shangri-La and what you would do to change it into your own special dream. How about that?"

Torie couldn't hide her smile. Marge was turning out to be quite a saleswoman. She glanced over at where Marc was standing, a beer in his hand, looking watchful.

Of course, she thought. *I'm surely not the only one he's got his eye on tonight, and that's obvious.*

Marge was trying to perk the party up, to generate some enthusiasm among the people crowding close to the fire, trying to get warm.

"Come on people. Dig deep. Think back. Recall patio parties and fireplace sing-alongs from your early days. Think of the potential here." She looked at the faces turned her way. "Come on, Lyla," she said. "What would you do if you owned this place?"

Lyla smiled, looking dreamy, and stepped out into the light. "I see this property as a setting for an entertainment center. I'd set up a stage and put on theatrical performances, drawing audiences down from the Bay Area and up from Los Angeles."

"Lots of luck on that one," the Texan chortled. "Both of those are long drives. You'll get an audience of ten or so per show."

Lyla shrugged elaborately. "I'll start with that. But we would grow. Word of mouth..."

"Here's my plan," Phoebe chimed in happily. "I would love to have a spiritual retreat for our friends. Some are show-business people, some are politicians. They could come here and be refreshed by nature. I would put in a natural swimming pool right here, with a waterfall and vines hanging over it. I would have Greek statues all around the water."

"That sounds like Hearst Castle."

"Yes. I love Hearst Castle."

"That's okay if you're as rich as Hearst was," the Texan said. "Otherwise, better aim a little lower, I'd say. Stop dreaming."

"A human must dream," Andros protested grandly. "We have a dream too, me and Nina. We would make this place into a first-class destination resort for Mediterranean clients, people who want something different. Our restaurant would be the core project, of course. We would make the best Greek restaurant in the world, right here, an old-fashioned supper club. And we would turn the house into a hotel...."

Nina chimed in, telling them about her ancient recipes handed down through the family grandmothers. "Old-country charm supported by modern technology," she declared. "We have such plans."

"No way," the Texan said dismissively. "You're all aiming to go broke in the first year."

"Oh yeah?" Frank retorted. "Then what's your idea, cowboy? A dude ranch?"

"Hell no. I have no interest in drawing other people here. The first thing I'll do is hire a geologist and a mining engineer and start drilling holes."

"Holes?"

That got everyone's attention and they all stared at him raptly.

"Sure. We would tear this place apart. I'm bettin' on gold, lady. There was a pretty good vein that tapped out in the nineteenth century not far from here. I'm bettin' we can track it down and…"

"Are you serious?" Marc said, frowning fiercely.

"California gold. That's what the state is known for. There's gotta be some somewhere. I'm bettin' on these here hills."

"You're crazy," Frank said, and four or five other voices joined in, each with a different view of the possibilities of finding gold.

"How about you, Torie?" Marge asked as the argument died down. "What do you and Carl have in mind?"

Torie tried to deflect the question. She didn't want to get caught up in this. "You'll have to ask Carl himself for that."

All eyes were turned her way.

"We're asking you," Frank pointed out.

"Me?"

"Sure. Aren't you involved?"

"Oh. Sure." She cleared her throat. What the heck could she say? She had no idea what Carl would want. Everyone was waiting. She felt cornered.

But then it came to her—not Carl's dream, but her own. It was a picture of what Shangri-La had been twenty years before when she'd been a child. She realized now how much she'd loved it, how central it had been to her universe—the core of her being—the place that had molded her identity.

"If I had this place all to myself," she began, staring off at the moon drifting off over the ocean and leaving a trail of silver behind, "I would build a trellis along the walkway at the top of the cliff and grow wild roses all through it."

She went on, caught up in the memories, and conjured up every detail of what the place had looked like in its glory days, when she was a child. Just bringing back those pictures made her heart sing. She smiled as she talked and wondered if this was what love felt like.

Marc grimaced as Torie began, tempted to go look for Carl while he knew she was occupied. He had to stop falling for the spell she seemed to weave so easily in his head and in his body. But he hesitated, and once she'd started talking, he was really listening to her words. Frowning, he concentrated. What she was saying sliced through him like a knife. The picture she was painting was one he recognized. It fit his childhood.

She knew this place. She'd been here before.

He looked over to see if his stepmother had noticed, but her attention was wrapped up in smiling at Jimmy. That made his stomach turn and he swore softly, shaking his head. Then he looked back at Torie.

Who the hell was she anyway?

Torie came out of her reverie and looked around. Everyone was staring at her and she felt her cheeks heating up. What had she said that seemed to have enthralled them all?

Her gaze met Marc's. He looked as though he couldn't believe what he'd been hearing, and then he jerked his head in a way that told her he wanted to talk to her privately. Something in the look on his face made her think she might want to comply this time.

She waited until the conversation began to buzz around the fire again. And when no one seemed to be paying any attention to her, she rose and slipped out of the firelight, meeting Marc on the walkway through the palms.

"What is it?" she said as she came up to him.

He was standing with his arms crossed over his chest, staring at her. "Who are you?" he demanded.

She drew in her breath and her pulse began to sputter. "I'm…I'm just Torie…"

"Torie who? What's your real last name?"

She started to speak and he stopped her.

"Don't give me that Marino nonsense. Your *real* last name."

She shook her head, looking away. The masquerade hadn't lasted very long, had it? "Listen Marc…."

"No, you listen. That little tale you spun out there by the fire was a perfect description of what this place used to look like twenty years ago. How did you know that?"

She tried to smile but his eyes weren't friendly at all. She had a sinking feeling inside. She wasn't very good at this deception stuff. She couldn't possibly tell him everything, but maybe she could let a few things go.

"I used to live here," she told him frankly.

He stared at her, shaking his head.

"It's true. I'm Torie Sands."

"Sands? As in…?"

She drew in a deep breath and came clean. "Jarvis Sands was my father."

He stared at her. "The butler."

"Yes."

"The one who stole the Don Carlos Treasure."

"No!" she said fiercely. "He never did. He was falsely accused."

Marc's head went back. "As I remember it, he went to jail…."

"He was never formally indicted and the treasure was found. He was released." She shook her head, wishing her eyes weren't stinging with tears. How could her emotions about that time be so close to the surface when it was so long ago? "It was all a horrible mistake."

He was frowning, his gaze ranging over her face, studying every feature as though he could randomly rearrange them and get to the truth. "You used to live in the gatehouse."

She nodded, holding herself together with effort.

"Your name wasn't Torie though, was it?"

"No. It was Vicki." She shrugged. "Actually, Victoria."

He was looking at her in wonder. "You were the chubby little girl who used to throw things at me from the apple tree."

"I never threw anything at you," she replied, wishing she didn't sound as though she were pouting. "But I was that little girl."

"Vicki Sands." He nodded slowly. "Sure, I see it now. That *was* you." He shrugged as though hardly knowing what to think. "I can't believe it." His gaze sharpened. "So what are you doing here, Torie? Why did you come back?"

She searched his handsome face and considered telling him the truth. She wanted to. But was that smart? After all, what she was here for was to prove his family wrong. He wasn't going to help her do that, was he? The best thing that could come out of this was if she could convince him to leave her alone and let her get on with it. She wasn't going to get anywhere with him hanging around.

She shrugged and looked away. "Nostalgia, I guess. I thought it would be fun to see the old place again."

"Really." His skeptical take on her statement was obvious. "I see." His head tilted to the side as he considered her words. "So that's why you went straight for the caves. It had something to do with the Don Carlos Treasure. Of course."

"No." She turned, wanting to defend her actions, but she saw the disbelief in his eyes and she was glad she'd kept the truth to herself. "Actually, I went out there because I used to play in those caves and I wanted to see them again. For old time's sake."

"Right."

He didn't believe her but she tried to get past that. After all, what did she care if he didn't believe her? All she really wanted from him was to be left alone. Still, there was something she had to say.

"I…I heard about what happened to your father," she told him. "And despite everything, I was sorry he had to go that way."

He frowned. "What do you mean, despite everything?"

She blinked at him. Didn't he remember how it was?

His father had been the one who'd had hers arrested. There was certainly cause for her to resent the man. Her father had loved working for Hunt, as they called him, and had felt personally close to him. The way his old friend had turned on him had seemed a complete betrayal. It was a major factor in his taking his own life.

She frowned and turned away, fighting back emotion, but he didn't seem to notice that she hadn't answered.

"Wait. I'm trying to remember. Didn't your father die shortly after you moved back down to Los Angeles that year?" he asked her. "I thought my father had told me that."

She nodded, holding tears back with all the strength she had. There was no way she was going to cry in front of him.

"Yes," she said gruffly. "My mother always says he died of a broken heart." She coughed, covering up how her voice was shaking. "But actually...actually..." She turned and looked right into his face. "Actually, he shot himself."

"Oh God." His face registered pure compassion for a moment, and he reached out and touched her arm. "I'm sorry, Torie. I don't think I knew that."

She shrugged, forcing back the lump in her throat and pulling away from his hand.

"Funny," he said softly. "So both our fathers committed suicide. How strange."

"Oh!" She stared at him. His eyes looked troubled in the dark. "I didn't know. The papers didn't say... I thought..."

"It was an accidental drowning? Yeah, we got that

announced and it stuck, luckily. But he left a note. We knew he died on purpose."

She felt as though she'd been slugged in the stomach. She'd had no idea. She'd spent a lot of time resenting the man, but to hear he'd been tortured enough to want to end it all changed a lot in her heart.

Impulsively, she reached out and took his hand. "Oh Marc, I'm so sorry. I didn't know."

He gazed down into her face. Tears still shimmered in her eyes. He looked at her pretty mouth and everything in him hungered to kiss her. Why? Just because she was pretty? Just because she was so close? No matter how much she appealed to him, she wasn't available. She might not be married to Carl, but that didn't mean she was free.

Deliberately, he pulled away from her touch.

"Carl," he said, reminding himself as well as her. "What's the deal with him? What's he looking for?"

She shook her head. "I really don't know. He hasn't told me." She hesitated, thinking fast. She needed to keep her cards close to her vest. She shouldn't tell him too much. "I thought he was interested in buying the place and wanted to check out all the details. And that's probably all it is."

"But you don't know."

She bit her lip. What could she say? "When you come right down to it, I don't really know him all that well," she admitted. There was no use trying to maintain the fiction that they had ever been married. It was too late for that.

"I've worked for him a few times. He found out I grew up here, so when he decided to come check it out, he asked if I wanted to come and pretend to be his wife."

She looked up into his eyes, hoping she was coming across as undeniably innocent—because that was what she was. Wasn't she? Sure she was. She was using Carl, but he was using her. They both knew the score. It was basically an arrangement of convenience for both of them.

"I thought it would be fun, so I agreed to come with him." She shrugged. "Other than that…"

A call came from the fire-pit area. It sounded as though the others were preparing to go to their rooms for the night. Torie's heart fell. She wouldn't have time to go to the old house and do the investigating she'd planned to do. Even if she could lose Marc, it was just too late. The others would be looking for her.

She gazed up at his face, surprised at how he seemed to get better-looking by the hour. Was it really him? Or was it her?

"I'd better get back," she said.

He nodded, but as she began to turn away, he caught hold of her arm and pulled her around to face him.

"Promise me one thing," he said huskily, his gaze hooded. "Keep your door locked tonight."

Her eyes widened. "You mean…?"

His grip on her arm tightened. "I mean keep your door locked. I don't trust Carl."

"Oh no. He would never…"

Something flickered in his eyes. "He's a man, isn't he? And you're a very attractive woman. I don't trust him. Lock that door."

She took a deep breath. For some reason, her heart was beating wildly. She didn't think of herself that way, and she didn't really believe he meant what he said about her. But still…

"Okay."

"I'm going to check it. I'll give you a knock like this…" He demonstrated against a handy tree trunk. "So you'll know it's me. Just checking."

She searched his eyes and shook her head. "Why are you doing this?"

He thought for a minute, his brow furrowed, and then he shook his head too. "You got me," he said. "I guess it's for old time's sake. After all, you're sort of like a baby sister to me. Aren't you?"

She laughed shortly. "No," she said emphatically.

He shrugged and his hand loosened on her arm. "Okay. I guess I just want to make sure you're okay."

She nodded. "Fine. I can accept that."

"Good."

He looked down and for one, heart-stopping moment, she was sure he was about to kiss her. Marc Huntington was going to kiss her. How many times had she dreamed of this moment? She waited, ready, lips slightly parted, heart beating like a jungle drum. He stared down at her for a long moment, and then something changed in his eyes and he turned away.

"Good night, Victoria Sands," he said gruffly. "Sleep well. I'll see you in the morning."

And he melted into the shadows of the trees.

Her breath was coming fast, as though she'd just been running hard, and her face was burning. She felt like a fool. When would she ever learn? Marc Huntington was not for her. Never would be.

Back at the house, she managed to evade Carl as she passed the fire pit and made it all the way to her bedroom before he caught up with her.

"Hold it," he said, thrusting his shoulder in the way of her closing the door. "We've gotta talk."

"Carl, it's been a long day. I need to get some sleep."

"You can sleep all you want, but I need some help first. I need you to update the map."

She sighed. The map she'd drawn of the Shangri-La estate was rough at best. She'd done it from memory and given it to him back when they were first planning this little adventure. In some ways it had been a labor of love and she'd enjoyed dredging up all her old stories as she worked on it.

"What's missing?" she asked.

"The caves." He pulled a folded paper out of his jacket and looked at her quizzically, his gaze cold. "I'm just wondering. Why did you leave out the caves?"

That was a good question and she wasn't really sure what the answer was.

"Listen Carl, just leave the map with me and I'll get them sketched in by lunch tomorrow."

"No," he said, a hint of anger beginning to surface in his voice. "I need it tonight. I need…"

"Is there a problem?"

They both jumped and turned to find Marc coming down the hall toward them.

"Something I can do to help?" he asked silkily, staring at Carl.

Carl grabbed his map back and shoved it into his jacket, shaking his head and looking resentful. "No. It's nothing." He began to retreat toward his own room. "Okay, Torie. We'll deal with it in the morning. See you then."

She looked at Marc and he raised an eyebrow. "I

know," she told him. He didn't have to say it. "Lock my door. Don't worry. I will."

And he was right, she mused as she prepared for bed. Carl had seemed so harmless when she'd agreed to come on this trip, but he'd changed. There was an intensity in Carl she'd never noticed before. She wasn't sure if she could say that she trusted him any longer.

She knew Marc didn't. But then, he didn't trust her either, did he?

Later, as she drifted into sleep, she thought she heard shouting. She sat up and tried to analyze what it was, but the sounds had faded by the time she was awake enough. Maybe she'd dreamed it. She lay back down but what little sleep she got after that was fitful. It was hard to let go when she knew that she was planning to get up and go exploring in a couple of hours anyway.

Plans that looked easy to execute from a distance always looked so impossible once you got face to face with the time to act. It was 1:00 a.m. and Torie's eyes were wide open, waiting for her little buzzer alarm on her cell phone to sound.

She felt as if she hadn't slept a wink. A part of her tried to justify just rolling over and going back to sleep, but she'd come all this way and she knew she couldn't miss this chance.

Her heart was beating in her throat. Was she really going to do this? Was she really going to start sneaking around, looking for information? Maybe it would be better to wait until morning when the light would be better and she could just be casual and find people to ask questions of.

"Coward!"

She said the word aloud, goading herself into action as the buzzer sounded and she reached out to stop it. She couldn't let this opportunity pass without taking advantage of it.

"Carpe diem," she added firmly, just for fun. Yes, she would seize the day. What else had she come for, anyway?

CHAPTER FIVE

TORIE slipped out of bed and reached for her clothes, pulling on leggings and a heavy sweatshirt that came down almost to her knees. She tied her hair back quickly and went to the doorway, opening it as quietly as she could. This was an old house. Just how badly were the stairs going to creak? She stayed as close to the banister as she could get and hardly made a sound.

The rooms downstairs were silent. She hesitated at the door, waiting for something to stop her, but nothing moved. Once out the door, she was free.

Now she was on a path she knew well. She didn't even have to think about it. Her feet knew where to step. She'd taken this route so many times in her childhood.

The night was clear and even though there was no moon visible, there was enough light to see where she was headed. The sounds of the frogs and crickets, the scent of the ocean, the breeze on her face—it all was so familiar, she found herself smiling as she hurried toward her old house as though she was truly going home. She rounded a corner and ducked back off the path as the flash of headlights from a passing car hit close to her. Who in the world was driving around at this time of night? From the snatch of laughter she heard, she could make a guess. Marge and Jimmy had been out and about.

She turned back and looked at her goal. Almost there. She stopped behind a small stand of palms to get the lay of the land, and she stood very still, shivering. Was it the cool air or a nervous reaction? For a moment, she thought about Marc and wondered what he was doing right now. Was he asleep? She certainly hoped so.

Finally she was on the front porch, the one she'd run onto as a girl, calling out, "Hey, Mom, what's for lunch?" as she threw down the latest shells she'd collected at the beach, or the prettiest rocks she'd found in the hills. The flame of nostalgia made her ache inside, but it was a good ache. Those were good days.

She tried the front door. It was locked. That was hardly surprising. Never mind. She knew other ways to get in. She made her way to the back of the house and found the window to her old room. It looked firmly closed and solid as a rock, but she knew that a little push here and a jiggle there and a shove in the right direction would loosen the sash and the window would slide up easily. She hadn't forgotten how to climb through, and in another minute, she was in her old room.

Pulling out her little flashlight, she played it against the empty walls. It was amazing, but no one had painted the rooms since her family had left. There was her growth chart by the door, milestones marked off in pencil. And there was the splotch of purple color where she'd thrown a paintbrush at the wall in a fit of anger. She stood and stared, breathless. Here it was, evidence that she really had lived here. For some reason, that choked her throat and filled her eyes with tears.

She went out into the hall and then the family room. The scrapings where chairs had brushed the walls, the mark on the door where her old dog Nanny had scratched to go out a few too many times, the old bulletin board where her mother had put up bits and pieces of her schoolwork or articles that interested her—all were still there. Had she stepped back in time?

The kitchen tore apart that theory. There was ample evidence that people had lived here since her day. The refrigerator was not the one she knew. The cabinets had been painted white and a relatively new-looking microwave sat on the counter.

That set her head back on straight. This wasn't her house. But she did have things she needed to do here.

The attic. That had been her goal from the beginning and she made her way through the living room to the hallway where the little structure that held the attic ladder hung from the ceiling. And how, without a stepladder or a piece of furniture, was she supposed to reach it to pull it down?

Her heart sank and she looked down the hallway and around the room. The heating register stood out against the wall, and there, leaning against it, was a long handled iron key for working the temperature controls. Could it possibly be long enough?

It was. She bit her lip as she worked hard to release the little rickety ladder, and her work paid off. It unfolded before her eyes, giving her access to the attic door. She climbed up quickly and tried to shove the door open. It didn't budge. She pushed and pulled and tried to pry it open, but nothing seemed to work.

And then she heard footsteps…a man's footsteps. She doused her little flashlight and pulled her legs up into the enclosure, heart racing. Anyone who came into the hallway would notice the ladder was down. But would they look up and see her perched there?

The footsteps came into the hallway. She tried to hold her breath, but she was already short of oxygen and rapidly falling into panic mode. Luckily, he just didn't stop walking, moving back and forth, just out of sight, making too much noise to hear her and her problems. The beam from his flashlight skittered around the walls, but didn't aim her way. She caught a glimpse of a shoulder in a black pea coat at one point, but she couldn't see enough to identify the man. All he had to do was glance up and she would be caught.

Suddenly, he stopped moving. Her heart nearly jumped out of her chest. Had he seen her?

No. He switched off his flashlight. He'd heard something, or had a sudden idea, because he turned and began to stride quickly toward the door. Now she was afraid he would get away before she could see who he was, and she slid down the ladder and sneaked silently toward the front room.

He was headed down the driveway toward the highway. She slipped out into the night and tried to stay hidden in the trees, following him the best she could. Was it Marc? Or Carl? She still couldn't tell.

So when the strong arms grabbed her from behind, she was completely unprepared and let out a shriek before the hand slapped down hard over her mouth.

"Hush," Marc growled in her ear. "It's me."

Her heart stopped and then started up again. She sighed, relaxing in his arms. It was just Marc. Everything was okay.

She tried to rouse her own sense of jeopardy. After

all, what made her think Marc was a good guy? Still, his arms felt right around her and she turned her head to feel the heat of his face against her cool cheek as though she'd been waiting for just that.

"Torie, I'm not going to hurt you," he told her huskily, and she nodded.

"I know," she whispered back, even though she really had no reason to know that at all. She couldn't stop shivering and he held her more tightly against his body as though to calm her.

For just a moment, he indulged himself and turned his face into her hair. She smelled good and she felt even better. He didn't want to let go. He wanted to hold her and run his hands up under her sweatshirt and…

But he wasn't going to. Too tempting. Too stupid. Too dangerous. And most of all, a big distraction from what he had to do.

Instead, he slowly released her and she turned to face him.

"Hi," she said, peering at him in the dark. The features of his face looked as though they'd been cut from stone. "What are you doing here?"

"Looking for you, I guess," he said, his voice laced with sarcasm.

She frowned. "Who was that man?" she asked him. "I couldn't get a good look at him."

His mouth twisted. "Don't you know?"

"No! Was it Carl?"

"Weren't you meeting him out here?"

"Marc!" She threw up her hands in exasperation. "No, I wasn't meeting him. I wasn't meeting anyone. I'm actually surprised to find so many people out wandering around in the middle of the night." She glanced suspiciously into the trees. "I wonder who else is out there."

Marc glanced in the same direction. "There's no telling, but I wouldn't be too surprised to find a Texan, doing placer samplings here and there."

She smirked at him with impetuous impertinence. "Are you watching him, too?"

He surprised her with a sudden grin. "No. The man's an open book. I don't have to."

"Unlike me and Carl," she said, eyes flashing a sense of barely concealed resentment.

He didn't bother confirming her accusation, but it was more than true. He'd been following Carl when he'd come across Torie doing the same and he had to make the call—the lady or the tiger? He could only choose one. He'd gone with the one he would rather be with, and that had probably been a mistake.

See? Too tempting. Too dangerous.

Still, he might be able to get information out of her he would never get out of Carl. From what he could tell, there was little rhyme or reason for the way Carl was zigzagging all over the estate, looking for who-knew-what. What he couldn't figure out was—why was Torie tailing the guy as well?

"Just what is Carl looking for?" he asked her again.

She shrugged. "You got me."

He frowned. "You're the one who brought him here."

"No. I used him to get here, but that's as far as it goes."

He studied her as well as he could in the darkness. Basic instinct told him she was telling the truth. What the hell—he was going to take a chance on that instinct.

It usually worked out best when he did, despite his natural inclination to want to see proof for everything.

"I wish I could figure the guy out," he told her. "I saw him leave the house and then I checked your room and you weren't there, so I took off after him."

"Where did he go?"

"Nowhere that made any sense."

She frowned. "So you thought you'd follow me for a while to see where I was going?"

"Why not?"

She groaned. "This is crazy. We're all running around in the middle of the night following each other. It's like a Keystone Kops episode. Going in circles, getting nowhere."

"I'm not getting nowhere." He gave her a twisted smile and reached for her hand. "Come on."

"Where are we going?"

"Somewhere." His hand curled around hers as though he didn't trust that she would come along if he didn't force the issue. "Back into the house. I want to see what you were doing in there."

"No." She pulled back, obliging him to turn. "You know what? It's none of your business what I was doing in there. You can't stop me."

She knew she sounded childish. She felt childish. Maybe that all went along with her being in her childhood home. At any rate, it annoyed Marc enough that he yanked on her hand, pulling her in close and glaring down into her eyes.

"While you are here, you *are* my business. I thought we'd already established that. But in case you're still not convinced, let me say it again. I can kick you off the estate and send you home any time I want to. And I don't have to ask Marge first." He gave her that twisted smile again. "So be nice to me."

"I'm always nice," she protested, but her breath was coming faster.

"Prove it." His voice lowered huskily. "Tell me why you're out here in the dark, dark night. Tell me what you hope to achieve."

She drew in a sharp breath. He was obviously stronger than she was and he could force her to go along with him if he wanted to. But he didn't need to force her. She could probably use his help. So she traded in complete rebellion for the chance to be a smart aleck instead.

"Wisdom," she said crisply. "Revenge. Closure. Truth."

He looked at her for a long moment and then he grimaced and his shoulders seemed to relax.

"That's a tall order," he said, his voice lighter. "Life doesn't usually give out free passes. I'm afraid you're probably going to have to work very hard for all those things, and never actually be satisfied with the results."

She closed her eyes, but a complete and detailed picture of him stayed in her mind. He had it all—looks, strength, a natural honesty that might be a façade, but was still impressive as hell. She wanted to trust him. Could she take that leap? She stared down at the hand that held hers and pondered that question.

Her first impulse was to keep it all to herself, not to let him in. But she didn't have time to wait this out. The only way she was going to get into the attic was if someone helped her. The only someone she could even halfway trust right now was Marc. Could she take the risk? What choice did she have? Besides, he was going to see the ladder and make his own assessment.

Should she go ahead and tell him? Why not? What did she have to gain by avoiding it? She made the decision and suddenly, she felt calm inside.

"Okay. Here goes." She raised her face to him again. "I'll tell you what I was doing. I was looking for something, anything, that might give me a new lead on finding out what really happened when my father was fired."

He stared down at her and shook his head. "Torie, that was a long time ago."

Her chin rose. "About time we got to the truth then."

He drew in a long, deep breath. "You really loved your father, didn't you?"

"Oh yes. Above all else."

He winced and she frowned, wondering why. Didn't he ever love anyone? Didn't he know how brave it could make you?

Or was it the other way around? Did he think no one had ever loved him that way?

She couldn't help all that. She had to move forward. If she could bring him along, so much the better.

The front door was standing open, just as she'd left it when she crept out. Moving quickly, they walked right in. Marc turned on his flashlight and did a quick survey of the empty room.

"There's nothing here. What's it been, fifteen years? What did you think you would find?" He looked at her. "Or were the walls going to talk to you? Spill all the secrets."

"I want to get into the attic," she told him. "The door seems to be sealed."

He moved closer, searching the depths of her green eyes. "What's in the attic?" he asked softly.

She had to steel herself not to start shivering again. "I'm not sure."

He shook his head. "You're going to have to do better than that. You must have something in mind."

She shrugged and it felt like surrender. She would tell him what she had to, but she couldn't tell him everything.

"My mother told me there were things left in the attic," she said slowly. "I...we left in such a hurry, we couldn't take everything."

He nodded. "That was a long time ago," he noted again. "Other people have lived here since."

She took a deep breath and tried to smile. "I know. But I have to look and see." She met his gaze and tried to maintain her dignity, but she knew he could see the pleading in her eyes. "Please, Marc. I really need to see what's in the attic."

He gazed at her for a long moment. The sweet, quiet way she'd asked him made him want to help her more than anything else! If she would put away the threat of antagonism that always seemed just a comment away, they might get on quite well with each other.

He shrugged. "Let's go take a look."

To her chagrin, he shoved the attic door open with no problem at all and then followed her up into the dusty area. The light from his flashlight made eerie shadows as it flickered through the beams. The ceiling was low and they both had to bend over to make their way toward where boxes and old suitcases were stacked.

Torie sorted through the boxes quickly, then turned to the luggage. Most items belonged to other people, but there was a suitcase that looked familiar. Marc gave the locks a jab with his pocketknife and they sprang open.

Torie stared at what was inside, more moved than she'd expected. These were the remnants of another life, far, far away, but she recognized them immediately. Her mother's wool coat. Her own band uniform. Her father's sweaters.

And beneath all that, a photo album and a stack of papers. She went through the papers anxiously, heart beating. Marc watched her, wondering what she was looking for. He didn't ask again.

She'd set the photo album aside carelessly and he wondered why. He picked it up and leafed through it while she searched, holding the flashlight high. There was that chubby young girl Torie had once been. Seeing the pictures made him smile.

"How did you manage to make such a big change from the annoying little squirt you used to be?" he asked her dryly.

"Magic," she shot back, not looking up from her search. "I traded a cow for a handful of beans."

"Right."

The pictures showed a loving family living at Shangri-La—his home—and none of them were any relation to him. Sort of weird. Jarvis the butler was just as he remembered him—full dignity with a touch of reserve. He remembered Torie's mother, too, a pretty woman with a slightly worried, fragile look.

"Darn," Torie muttered at last, sitting back. "It's not here."

He waited for a moment, but she didn't say any more, and he moved impatiently.

"What? What are you looking for?"

She ignored him and began to put things back in the suitcase.

Assuming she would want the photo album, he held onto it.

"Take a look at these pictures," he said, opening the album to a shot of Torie in her younger, more rounded past.

She took a deep breath and shook her head, avoiding even looking his way. "I can't," she said, her voice strangely choked. "Not now. I just can't."

He watched her curiously, touched by the emotion he heard in her voice. Life hurt pretty much everybody, one way or another, but it seemed life had really done a number on Torie. Still, he couldn't believe she wouldn't want the pictures eventually. He tucked the album under his arm and led the way back down into the house.

"What now?" he asked her.

She looked tired and a bit defeated. Not finding whatever it was that she'd been looking for seemed to have crushed her for the time being. He had a fleeting thought that this might be the time to press her, to poke around in her psyche and get to the truth of what she was doing here, what she really hoped to accomplish. But when he looked at her sad, pretty face, he didn't have the heart for it. Maybe later.

"I guess I might as well go back to bed," she said, holding her chin high with seeming effort. "I can't really look any place else until it's light."

He raised an eyebrow. "Are you going to give me a hint?"

She glanced at him, then away. "What do you mean?"

"What are you looking for? What did you think you would find in that suitcase?"

She stared at him and he knew she was mulling over her options.

"You never know," he said softly. "I might have already found it. I might have hidden it myself."

"Hidden what?" she challenged, blinking rapidly.

He shrugged. "What you're searching for. Why don't you tell me what it is?"

She took a deep breath, looking at him sideways. He was sounding so reasonable and looking so gorgeous. It wasn't fair. Marc wasn't fair. He thought he could manipulate her. And maybe he wasn't far off the track. He had to know she'd always had a thing for him.

She had to convince him that all embers of that fire had gone cold long ago. And they had! After all, he was one of the people, one of the family, who had been so cruel to her father. She had to remember that.

But she was at a dead end. She'd searched the caves. She'd searched the attic. She had no other leads.

"My mother thinks my father had a journal," she said softly, avoiding his gaze. "She thinks he put things down that might help me—might show the way to the truth." She shook her head. "I don't know. I never saw it. I was just hoping..."

She stopped. Tears were choking her voice. He stared at her, wanting to take her in his arms. She looked so sad, so lonely. But he wasn't ready to give her the benefit of the doubt. Not yet.

What was it about this woman that seemed to crash right through all his normal defenses and touch him at his core? They were fighting over something here and he couldn't concede. Not without getting something for his side.

"I've never found a journal," he told her. At least he could be honest with her. "Are you sure it exists?"

She shook her head, avoiding meeting his gaze. "I'm

not sure of anything." She looked up at him, tears shimmering in her haunted eyes. "I'm not even sure my father was innocent. What do you think of that?"

He raked his hard fingers through his hair, leaving spikes in every direction. He could see she was tortured and he wanted to grab her and hold her and tell her it was going to be okay—but he couldn't.

"I don't think," he told her, mostly because he didn't know what to think of that statement. "I just react."

She nodded. She shouldn't have said that. It was true, but no one else needed to know. She couldn't un-say it, but she could throw some other things out there into the mix to lessen its impact. Hopefully.

"Okay. React to this." She took a deep breath and her green eyes looked like bits of shattered emeralds. "I've hated your family for fifteen years. I think you caused my father's suicide. If it hadn't been for the way you all handled it and how disgraced you made him feel, he would be alive today." Her voice was firm, but the edges were trembling, just a little bit. "What's your side say?"

Her words stung. He turned away. His natural reaction was to lash out at her, but he held it back. She was talking crazy. Her words, her emotions, her reasoning, everything was jumping all over the place. She wasn't really making sense. And maybe that was because she really didn't have any solid proof of anything. It was all conjecture, all an attempt to fill in a past she just couldn't understand.

Understandable. Still, he had to balk when he heard her using his family as an excuse to cover up her family's heartbreak. But that didn't mean she wasn't in pain. He could see it. He could feel it. Her soul was writhing in agony.

And he had a sudden insight. If it was true what she'd told him, if she really didn't know for sure if her father was guilty, if this was more a search for truth than a search for proof—then she had a kind of inner integrity that was rare to find.

Still, it didn't mean she couldn't be capable of some pretty underhanded methods to get to where she wanted to go. He'd seen enough of the raw and untamed side of humanity to know it was always lurking. Never trust anyone. That was his motto.

"My father was an honorable man," he said softly, leashing his anger. "If he did something that hurt your father, I'm sure he had a reason. He didn't have a mean bone in his body."

Tears were sliding silently down her face. Her mouth twisted. "I know," she whispered. "I...I loved your father, too." Her voice broke. "He was so kind to me. I can't believe... Don't you see?" She hugged herself, arms wrapped tightly. "That's part of the problem. It just doesn't make sense that he would treat my father like an evil person. He ...he..."

She couldn't go on. He started to reach for her, but she turned away. "Torie," he said, but she shook her head and moved further away.

"Let's go back." She started off down the trail. He followed close behind.

He wasn't sure what he wanted to do. Everything in him rebelled at her calling his father a villain. He didn't believe it. He'd known the man too well.

But at the same time, he suspected her father had probably been treated badly. Why? How? Had he really been guilty of the original theft? Or what? He wanted to get to the bottom of this as much as she did.

"By the way," he said as they walked along the path. "The Greeks have gone."

She stopped and whirled, staring up at him, remembering the shouts she'd thought she heard in the night.

"What? What happened?"

He shrugged. "Turns out they weren't very Greek. And they definitely weren't on the up and up."

Her shoulders sagged and her face was truly sad. "Oh no. I liked the Greeks."

"Sure you did," he said as they started off again. "That's part of their game. They spend a lot of time at events like this, or resort gatherings, endearing themselves to people with money and trying to get some of it."

She sighed sadly, looking up at the house as they approached. All the windows were dark. Hopefully everyone was asleep—even Marge and Jimmy. "So there's no idyllic little Greek supper club?"

"No."

"No little Greek grandmother with secret recipes from the old country?"

He gave her a half smile. "Sorry."

She shook her head. "It's a real shame. I liked that story."

"Yes."

They'd reached the porch and slowly took the steps, one at a time, until they were in front of the door.

"How did you find out?" she asked, turning to face him again.

His face took on a hooded look and he shoved his hands down into the pockets of his jacket. "I've got some friends in law enforcement. I made a few calls."

She looked at him, tilting her head. Was that a subtle hint that she and Carl had better watch their steps?

"What did your sources have to say about me?" she asked tartly.

He started to grin, then cut it short. "I'll let you know when I get the full report."

She reacted badly. That wasn't something she had wanted to hear. "You see this face?" she asked him, pointing at it. "Once again, this isn't adoring reverence for you. This is what we call anger. Anger and resentment and…"

His kiss stopped her words. He couldn't help it. It had to be done. Right now, she needed to be kissed, and he was the man to do it.

It was just a kiss. A kiss wasn't a surrender. It didn't mean he believed her. It didn't have anything to do with guilt or innocence. It was just an expression of desire, or maybe need, or maybe something even deeper. But that hardly mattered at all. It just was.

She gasped, her hands rising up to push him away, but they didn't try very hard. His mouth was hot and his arms were strong and she began to melt. And just as she began to enjoy it, he pulled away.

"Good night, Torie Sands," he said roughly, hunching deeper into his jacket. "Go to bed."

She felt slightly dizzy. "Where…where are you going?"

"I think I'll just take one more turn around the area. See what's shakin'." He gave her a quick grin as he turned to go. "See you tomorrow. Breakfast is at nine."

CHAPTER SIX

BREAKFAST was served on a wicker table on the terrace overlooking a clear blue ocean beneath a clear blue sky. It was a beautiful morning. Just what any real estate agent would have ordered if such a thing were possible.

Torie slipped into a chair beside Carl. He looked dreadful, like a man with a serious hangover.

"What's the verdict?" she murmured to him as she reached for a small glass of orange juice that was perched tantalizingly on a silver tray.

"The verdict?" he responded sharply, jumping as though the word startled him.

She looked at him impatiently. "What do you think of Shangri-La? Are you going to buy the place?"

"Buy the…? Oh, uh…" He moved restlessly in his chair. "I haven't seen enough yet," he muttered. Then he seemed to remember who she was and he frowned at her fiercely. "And you haven't been much help. You keep disappearing."

"You were the one disappearing last night," she said. "What were you looking for out there in the dark?"

He glared at her, then leaned closer to talk without being heard by others. "Look, way back when we first started talking about this, you told me you used to go with old man Huntington on his rock-hunting trips around the estate. Didn't you?"

She nodded carefully, wondering where he was going with this.

"And I asked you to draw up a map of all those places you used to go with him. His favorites. Didn't I?"

"Sure."

He glared. "You didn't put the caves on that map."

The caves. She should have known it would come back to the caves.

"Yes I did. I sketched in where they are along the coast."

"Vaguely. No detail. And when I went out there, I realized there was no way I was going to be able to search them." His nostrils flared. "They're like a maze. It must take forever to know where all the hiding places are in those caves. You didn't give me a clue."

She stared at him, wondering at the intensity she was seeing in his face. "You know Carl, maybe if you told me what you're looking for, I could help you better."

She stared at him. He stared back.

Come on, Carl, she thought silently. *Tell me you think you're going to find the Don Carlos Treasure. Admit it. Let's get it out in the open.*

He took a deep breath, his eyes smoldering with anger. She almost thought he'd heard what her mind was thinking.

"Just make a map of the caves," he said. "That's all I ask."

She smiled and waved as Lyla called out a good-morning greeting, walking out toward the edge of the terrace. Her smile faded as she realized where Lyla was headed. Marc was sitting on the broad stone wall, dangling his legs over the side. Lyla laughed as she kicked off her stiletto heels and prepared to join him.

Torie turned back to the man beside her, feeling a bit more grumpy than she had seconds before.

"Carl, I was a kid when I knew the caves that well. That was fifteen years ago. Do you really expect me to remember…?"

He leaned so close his hot, thick breath was on her cheek. "What were you doing down there yesterday?" he demanded. "What's in those caves?"

"Nothing," she said back, recoiling and frowning at him. "That isn't the only place I went. I walked up and down the beach, remembering things from my childhood and just enjoying seeing it all again. I walked past the boathouse and went into the canyon to the little redwood forest."

"Redwood forest? What redwood forest?" He pulled out the map and curled it open at one end. "You didn't put any redwood forest on here."

"I guess I forgot it," she said coolly. She'd had about enough of Carl and she welcomed the chance to throw him off the scent of the caves. "Here, let me fix that." She snatched up the map and opened it to the coast area, grabbing a pen and quickly drawing in a tree where the canyon should be. "There it is." She handed the map back to him. "Have yourself a ball," she told him caustically.

She started to gather her things with every intention of leaving Carl and going over to the stone wall to see what Marc and Lyla were doing, but it occurred to her that she ought to warn him.

She turned and looked at him, wondering how she could have let herself pretend this man was sane and safe. Anyone could have seen he was nothing but trouble—ugly trouble. And now she was stuck with him. She sighed, but resigned herself to a duty warning.

"You heard about the Greeks?"

"No." He glanced around and didn't see them. "What?"

"It appears they were not what they seemed." She gave a little cough of a laugh. "Just like us. Funny, no?"

He looked uneasy. "What are you talking about?"

She leaned close and spoke softly. "Marc has connections with local authorities. They have connections with the feds. He asked for a background check and got one. The Greeks are not even Greek, and they are out on their ears."

He stared. "Are you kidding me?"

She shrugged. "Would I kid about a thing like that?"

He rose, shoving his plate aside. "I've got to get out of here." He glanced at his watch. "Okay, I'll be back." He looked up and jabbed a finger in her direction. "And I want you to be available at noon." He glared at her fiercely. "You're going to lead me through the caves."

She swallowed hard. Something about his obvious burning anger was beginning to put her on edge. "I told Marge I would join the group in a hike along the cliff after breakfast. I don't know if we'll be back in time to…"

"Be back," he said coldly, almost snarling at her, his eyes suddenly looking very bloodshot. Reaching out, he gripped her upper arm painfully. "I'm going to need you. Understand?"

"Okay," she said a bit breathlessly. "Okay. Take it easy. I'll be here."

He nodded, obviously trying to get a grip on his emotions. "Good. I'll hold you to that." And then he turned away, walking quickly in the direction of the stairs and toward the rocky shoreline.

She rubbed her arm, watching him go. The man was beginning to scare her. She turned, planning to go to where Marc was, but he was gone. Lyla sat alone, swinging her legs over the side, and that was not an inviting scenario. Torie turned back toward the house. It was probably time to get ready for the hike.

An hour later, the hike was in full swing. Their little group was straggling toward the cliffs about half a mile from the house. Torie was walking behind Frank and Phoebe and wishing she knew where Marc had gone. She was on edge and conflicted and not sure what to do next.

She regretted allying herself with Carl. He was obviously some sort of underhanded crook, and she didn't want to be associated with him any longer. She knew it looked bad, that it made her look less than honest herself. What did Marc think? She was afraid she might just know.

Marc had been her crush from the time she was about ten years old. He'd never looked twice at her, except for various, vague incidents in their past. But on the whole, he didn't know she existed most of the time. But she certainly knew about him.

She'd watched him grow from a gawky but adorable teenager to a slender willow of a young man, strong and sharp, smart and quick, brave but restless. He'd gone off to join the military because he needed something in his life, needed to do something, be somebody. She'd only been fifteen the last time she'd seen him, but she'd known what he wanted to do and she'd understood his hunger for life. She'd felt a bit of an echo of it in her own heart at the time.

And now he'd come home, thicker, stronger, more wary of life and its challenges. He'd been through some things out there in the world, things he wasn't going to talk about. You could see it in his eyes. He didn't seem to trust anyone or anything anymore. It made you wonder what he'd seen, what had been done to him, what he'd had to do to others that he might regret. He was a man.

And when he'd kissed her, he'd been her dream come true. She'd gone up to her room and slipped into her bed and stared at the ceiling, and gone over it—feeling his mouth on hers again, catching her breath in a gasp of sensual excitement like she'd never felt before.

No. Sorry, world. Those embers were not dead after all. The smoldering excitement of Marc was very much alive in her heart and soul, and she knew it would be hard to smother it at this point. Hard—or maybe darn near impossible.

She shook herself to get rid of the dream and forced her focus back on the hike. Marge was calling out instructions.

"If you keep a sharp eye out, you may just catch sight of sea otters hanging around that black rock you see there in the bay," she was calling back to everyone. "And up the beach a bit, you'll see sea lions basking in the morning sun."

Their group consisted of Phoebe and Frank, Lyla and the Texan and Torie herself. And, of course, Marge, their fearless leader.

It was a beautiful morning but Torie couldn't conjure up much interest in the scenery. She was wondering what Carl was getting into and if Marc was there to stop him. She should be there, too. What was she doing going on a nature hike when time was racing, running away from her? She needed to get back to the project at hand.

Last night hadn't done her much good, but it had clarified a few issues. She knew now that Carl wasn't interested in buying Shangri-La, never had been. What she didn't know was what he *was* after. Something, that was for sure. And he seemed pretty crazed about getting to his goal.

One of the first things she planned to do was to see if she could find some of the old employees, someone who might remember her father. She knew it wouldn't be easy. But surely someone knew someone. In order to get to a position to make any headway, she would have to get friendly with an employee.

The Greeks were crooks and they were gone. The Texan wanted to find evidence of gold-mine potential on the property. Marge wanted to get enough money to head for the Bahamas—maybe with Jimmy in tow. So what about Phoebe and Frank? Maybe they actually wanted to buy the property. Who knew?

Marc didn't want his ancestral home sold out from under him. Torie could understand that. And he didn't trust her, but he didn't hate her either. Would that change? Would he start to hate her once he knew.... knew about the little bag of Spanish gold doubloons she had hidden in the lining of her suitcase? She shuddered and closed her eyes, stricken and breathless just thinking about it. She had to find the truth—find it before anyone found those doubloons.

The sea lions came into view. Barking nastily, they flopped their huge bodies on the warm sand and threatened each other with dire warnings of terrible sea-lion battles to come. The little tour gathered around the edge of the cliff and stared down at them, fascinated. There was nothing cuddly about these beasts.

"Take pictures," Marge advised. "But don't try to go down and get close to them. They're not friendly and just might hurt you if they get mad enough."

Lyla came to stand next to Torie as they watched the noisy animals complain about their lot in life.

"They remind me of some ladies I lunch with," Lyla said with a laugh. "Never happy." She turned to look at Torie. "So, are you and Carl ready to make a bid on this place?"

Torie laughed. That seemed so far from her reality now. "Not yet, I'm afraid. How about you?"

Lyla sighed. "I do love it." She arched one carefully painted eyebrow. "Now if the son came as part of the estate, I might do some serious thinking about it."

"You mean Marc?" Torie said, stunned at the thought. "I doubt he's for sale."

"Oh no, honey." Lyla was the one laughing now. "Everybody's for sale. You just have to find the right price."

She was still laughing as she started toward the other side of the area, as though she found Torie immensely naive and it really amused her. Torie bit her lower lip to keep from saying something mean, but the encounter didn't improve her mood.

The incessant barking of the seals was setting her nerves on edge. She turned away from the cliff, shading her eyes and looking back toward the house. As though summoned by her impatience, a large horse appeared, coming toward them.

She stood where she was, transfixed, staring at the approaching animal. And then it got close enough to make out the identity of the rider. Marc, of course.

Marc. She felt as though there was something glowing inside her. She knew he was coming for her. She stood where she was and waited.

"Oh look," Lyla cried, noticing him too and beginning to wave. "Marc's got a horse. Oh, I love riding! Marc! Over here!"

As he rode closer, his mother started yelling at him, but he didn't pay any attention to her. The horse was big and black, a beautiful mare, and he reined her in as he came near, making her walk softly up to where Torie was waiting.

She resisted the temptation to give Lyla a smile, but she had one for Marc.

"Come on," he said, leaning down and reaching for her hand. "I want to take you to the village. There's someone there you're going to want to talk to."

She reached up to meet him and he pulled her up in front of him, effortlessly. She slipped into place with hardly a wasted move. Marge was still yelling. She looked back and smiled at them all. And then they were off.

They rode along the edge of the cliff, the blue ocean on one side, the stand of tall, green eucalyptus trees on the other. Torie felt glorious. The wind was in her hair, Marc's hard, strong arm was around her, holding her in place, and the large, wonderful horse was beneath them. The whole scene was magical and she knew she would never forget it. If nothing else, she would always have this.

When she saw the village ahead, she knew the magic would be fading, and she regretted it. If only they could always ride like this...on and on and into the night. This felt like something she'd been born for.

She leaned back and his face was there, near her ear.

"You want to go down by the beach before we go to the village?" he asked her.

She sighed and nodded. "Yes," she told him. "Let's do it."

There was a dirt road down the hill and then a paved road that came in and led to a boat-launching area. The beach was deserted. Sea gulls dove at them, then retreated to a nearby buoy to call at them from a safe distance.

She slid down off the horse and he swung down after her. They stood side by side, staring out to where the waves crashed outside the breakwater.

"Why is the movement of water so mesmerizing?" she asked him.

"I don't know." He turned to look at her, eyes hooded. "Maybe something in us wants to return to the sea."

There was a sense of danger in his gaze that disturbed her and she looked back toward the water.

"When I was a little girl," she told him after a moment of silence, "I loved *The Little Mermaid* movie. I would wander around, leaning against the furniture and looking lovesick, singing the Ariel song until everyone around me went mad with it." She laughed softly, remembering. "They were threatening to tape my mouth shut if I didn't cease and desist."

He grinned, looking at her sideways. He remembered

hearing her singing in the old days. That must have been why she'd sounded so familiar when she'd sung in the fog. "Don't tell me you actually caved in."

She gave him a look of pure cheek. "What? You think I'm a complete narcissist?"

"No. I think you're stubborn as hell though."

She laughed and turned toward him, but he was frowning as he studied her face. "You know, I'm starting to remember more about you," he said. "You were around more than I remembered at first."

"Or more than you noticed at the time."

"Was that it?" He shrugged as though he wasn't convinced. "I know one thing. When I reached down for you at the cliff, and you took my hand and vaulted up in front of me on the horse, I suddenly realized we'd done that before."

Her eyes widened. Now he was bringing up things she'd forgotten herself. "Oh. Yes! That time I was walking home from the village…"

"And you found a lost dog—a little white one."

"With the sweetest little black nose." She grinned. "I was trying to carry him back with me but I had a bag of groceries I'd picked up for my mother and I kept dropping things."

He nodded, his blue eyes filled with humor. "I must have been about sixteen."

"And I was about eleven."

"I was riding Brown Sugar, my favorite Indian pony. I passed you and I think I said 'hi.'"

"Hah!" She gave him a mock glare. "You didn't say a word."

He frowned. "I must have said 'hey.'"

"No you didn't. You were much too cool to deign to speak to a little girl like I was."

He looked at her for a long moment, then sighed. "I think you're wrong," he said, slightly grumpy. "Anyway, I looked back and you dropped your brown paper sack and macaroni noodles went into the air like a bomb had been set off, and the little dog jumped out of your arms and began to bark its head off."

She winced. Some memories were just too painful. The sense of humiliation she'd felt that day came back to her in a wave.

"So I turned around. By the time I got back to you, you had it all back in your arms, but you looked like you were going to drop everything again any minute. I told you to give me the dog and the groceries."

"And I thought you were going to ride off with them and leave me there."

"But I didn't. I stashed the groceries in my pack and the little dog in my shirt, and then I reached down for your hand."

She laughed softly, staring off at the blue horizon. "And I felt like Cinderella," she said.

She remembered that feeling. As though the prince had asked her to dance. She'd been on cloud nine all the way home, even though she knew he wasn't exactly enjoying it as much as she was. Still, the most handsome boy she'd ever seen was being nice to her—for the moment. It made her whole summer brighter.

"I named him Snowcone," she mused. "I loved that little dog."

"Whatever happened to him?"

Her face clouded. "My father insisted on sending a notice to the paper and the real owners showed up three days later." She shook her head. "I begged him not to do it, but you know what my father was like. Strictly by the rules."

Marc looked at her speculatively and she raised her chin. She knew it sounded as though she was feeding him her vision of her father's character, but she didn't care. It was the truth. He might not know it, so she might as well let him in on it.

"Yeah," he said, then looked around to where they'd tied the horse. "I guess we ought to get going."

She nodded and followed him, still amazed and gratified that he'd remembered so much. There hadn't been many incidents between the two of them but what there were still shone like gold in her memory. She pulled her way up to ride in front of him again, wishing they could just head on down the beach. She closed her eyes and felt Marc's arm tighten around her.

But the ride slowed and finally came to a stop.

"We're here," he said, close to her ear, and she sat up straight and looked around.

The village had an old-fashioned, quaint look. Red-tile-roofed cottages were scattered all up and down the hills, most with flower gardens overflowing with blooms. Boats filled the small marina, many apparently working fishing trawlers. The business district boasted a coffee shop, a small market with bait shop, a real estate office and a rustic tavern with a wooden statue of an ancient mariner out front. The place looked about as it must have looked in the 1920s when it began as a tiny beach resort.

"You ready?" he asked her.

"Ready for what?" she asked, still floating in the

mellow nature of the sunny day and only half interested in anything else.

"Ready to talk to Griswold."

She turned to look back at him. "Who?"

"Griswold. Don't you remember him? The chauffeur. He was there when it all went bad."

"Oh." She shivered and steadied herself. "Oh!" Griswold. Of course. He might have some answers. He was just exactly who she needed to talk to. She turned and smiled at Marc.

"Perfect," she said, starting to get excited. Then she looked at him in wonder. He really was going to help her. "Thanks. This is…really cool."

He laughed softly and shook his head, still holding her against himself as though he really didn't want to let her go. "Let's go see him before you get too appreciative," he warned. "You never know."

"Of course." She set her shoulders and tried to get tough. This was important. She couldn't be getting all silly over Marc and expect to maintain the sharp edge she was going to need if she was going to get anywhere.

They pulled in closer to the front of the tavern and dismounted. Marc tied the horse to a post at the entryway.

"Where did you get this nice horse?" she asked, stroking its velvet nose and getting a snuffle in return. She knew that Shangri-La didn't have any horses these days, though they'd had a well-stocked stable when she'd lived there before.

"I went down to visit with an old rancher down the road," he said, stopping to give the animal a pat as well. "Both his sons were friends of mine in high school and now they're both in the military. He's having trouble keeping his livestock exercised, so I volunteered to take this little lady out for a spin."

"She's a beauty," Torie agreed.

Two girls in tiny bikinis with beach towels thrown over their shoulders strolled by on their way to the sandy shore. They gave Marc the eye with youthful enthusiasm, making Torie laugh.

"Girls always did like you, didn't they?" she noted as they gave him a backwards look and disappeared around a corner.

He glared at her. "You think that's funny?" he challenged. "You try living with it. They're everywhere and they're a pain in the neck."

She laughed harder. "Poor baby. Such a burden."

He turned and glared at her, then paused as though really seeing her for the first time. A slow smile crept into his eyes. "I'm sure you get your share," he said.

Her laughter faded and she was suddenly uncomfortable. "Not me," she said, trying for a light tone that didn't quite work. "I'm not the type."

"Baloney."

A new warmth had come into his gaze and it was heating up her cheeks.

"You're not very self-aware, are you?" he said as he finished up securing the horse.

Now she was embarrassed and blushing crimson— but not in a bad way. She'd never considered herself a beauty and she knew in her heart of hearts that she wasn't. At least she never had been before. She was pretty enough on a good day. But she didn't have a face that turned heads. And yet something in Marc's eyes was telling her that she did, and suddenly, she was walking on air.

He smiled and gestured toward the tavern. "Shall we go in?"

She turned looked at the door, just a bit hesitant. "How do you know Griswold is in here?"

"From what they tell me, he's always in here."

He took her hand in his and she took a deep breath. This could be it. This could be where she finally learned the truth of what had happened all that time ago. She looked up at Marc. He gave her a wink and she smiled. Time to face her father's past as if it were her own. She lifted her chin and walked in.

CHAPTER SEVEN

MARC let Torie go ahead and followed a few steps behind. This was her show, her quest. He wasn't even sure why he was supporting her this way. She said she was here to find out what really happened fifteen years ago, whether her father was unfairly accused, whether he shouldn't have been fired. If that was true, if that was really her goal, she was basically trying to prove his family's actions wrong—maybe even illegitimate.

And where would that take them all? Did she think she could find the truth—or maybe even the treasure—somewhere and show them all her father had been slandered?

Not likely. Insurance investigators and the police had both taken their turns at searching for the gold. And then, through the years, treasure hunters had come sneaking onto the property to try their own methods. No one had found anything yet. As far as he was concerned, that treasure was at the bottom of the sea. His father's goodbye note had said that was what he was going to do with it. Why did everyone keep trying to find something that just wasn't there?

Torie was only the latest, and she said her search had a new twist. Was she lying? Was the treasure really all she wanted, just like everybody else? He was pretty sure that was what Carl was after. And she'd come with the man, so it all fit together.

And yet, he didn't want to believe she was lying to him.

He groaned softly, hearing himself and hating his own weakness. He knew all about lying and being lied to. He'd been through it often enough to consider it a normal part of human relationships. Why would Torie be any different?

As they walked into the dimly lit tavern, he glanced about the room. People were scattered around at tables and along the bar, mostly men. There was one stocky, blond young man who waved, but he didn't recognize him. There didn't seem to be anyone there that he knew.

Torie was still flushed from his compliments a few minutes earlier and looking prettier than ever. He had to grin as he noticed one man after another stealing a glance her way. And true to form, she didn't see it at all.

And then he saw the man they were after, sitting at a corner table, looking as if he'd staked a claim to it long ago and wasn't going to give it up for love or money. He pointed him out to Torie and they made their way there.

Griswold was drunk. There was no getting around it. He was a pale, boney shadow of the dapper man he'd once been. He gazed up at Torie with bleary eyes and didn't have a clue who she was, even after she told him. Jarvis Sands was a name that seemed to spark some recognition.

"Jarvis? Jarvis? You mean, the butler at Shangri-La? Sure. What about him?"

"Do you remember him? Do you remember what happened?"

He frowned at her. "I should have had his job, you know. They only made me chauffeur because the lady wanted to swan around in front of her friends. They didn't need me. All I did was wash cars all day." He shook his head. "No. I don't remember nothin'."

"How about the Don Carlos Treasure disappearing? You must remember that."

He was frowning and it wasn't apparent whether he had actually heard her question. "He told me not to go, but I went anyway," he said sadly. "I went and he was right. I shouldn't have gone."

"Who? My father?"

He looked around as though he felt trapped and Marc reached out to pull her away.

"It's not much use," he said quietly. "He's in no shape to talk. From what I hear, he never is. If he ever knew anything at all, it's probably lost to history by now."

She nodded reluctantly. She was bitterly frustrated. Somehow she'd been counting on finding employees from those days and now that she'd found one, he was useless.

"You know, its sort of crazy," she said to Marc as they were leaving. "Almost everyone from that generation is either dead or ruined in some way. It doesn't seem right."

"Anecdotal," he muttered as he led her out. "Don't let life depress you. There are plenty of good things to think about."

She looked up into his face and shook her head, still disappointed, but vaguely amused. "*You're* giving happy-talk advice? Now I've seen everything."

"I have my happy moments," he protested. "I even get optimistic sometimes."

"But not for long, I'll bet," she said dryly.

They were outside by now and they both noticed the blond man from inside the tavern had come out and was leaning against a huge black Harley. He waved as they approached, then straightened and came toward them.

"You don't remember me?" he said, smiling in a friendly fashion.

Torie gasped. "Is it Billy Darnell?" she cried.

He nodded. "You got it."

Torie reached out and grasped his hand in hers. "You remember Billy," she said over her shoulder to Marc. "Alice was his mother. The cook at the estate back in our younger days."

"That's me," Billy said, looking pleased.

"It's so good to see you! How's your mother?"

"She's fine. She lives down in LA now. She likes being close to my sister and her family."

"Of course." Torie thought quickly, going over the past. Billy was a year younger than she was. Being children of the Shangri-La staff, they'd spent some time together, though they'd never been particularly close. But when you were eleven and twelve and there was no one else around to hang with, you made do.

"Billy and I used to go on day-long mineral-collecting trips with your father," she told Marc. "We would trek out along the cliff at dawn, backpacks full of drinks, snacks and lunches, and your father would lead us to the most interesting places, nooks and crannies that you would never think existed if you just drove by them. And he'd find some quartz or some rocks with hornblende or muscovite and he'd use his rock hammer to break specimen-sized pieces out of the rock. Then Billy and I would wrap them in paper and pack them away in canvas bags and then tote the bags home for him." She grinned at Billy. "We had a glorious time."

"That we did," Billy said, grinning right back.

Marc nodded at the reminder and listened to them reminisce, but the whole thing created a bit of an empty feeling in his soul. He'd known his father was interested in rock collecting, but he'd never really paid much attention. He'd only listened with impatience whenever his father tried to talk to him about it. Which might have been why he never got invited along on any of these expeditions. Probably because he was too old when the hobby began to appeal to his dad. He'd been seventeen when Torie was twelve.

Still, he wished he'd known, wished he'd participated. It seemed more and more that there was a whole side to his father that he had known nothing about. He would have been a good man to get to know.

Too late now. He grimaced. He wasn't used to feeling this sort of regret. It made him uncomfortable. He looked at Torie, and for some reason, he felt a little better. She was like a light into the past that he'd been ignoring for years. She was helping him clear up some things. For the first time, he realized he was actually glad she'd come back to Shangri-La.

Torie brought up the treasure and Marc began to listen more carefully. Billy remembered it, but he claimed he didn't know anything about what had happened to it, other than the newspaper accounts about Hunt having dumped it in the sea, and didn't think anyone else knew anything new about it either.

"There's really no one else still left around who was working at the place in those days," Billy said earnestly.

"Except Griswold, of course. But he's not much use these days."

They chatted for a few more minutes, and then Torie gave Billy a hug and they said good-bye. He rode off on his motorcycle; they got back on the horse.

"I'll drop you at the house," Marc told her. "I've got to get this little lady back home before she starts to worry about lunchtime."

She smiled, liking that he had a sense of understanding for a horse. Okay, it was time to admit it. Down deep, she knew him well enough to know he was a pretty good guy. Unless something had changed him while he was overseas, he was one of the best men she'd ever known. Maybe his family had been cruel to her father—he hadn't been involved. Not directly anyway.

Closing her eyes and letting the sway of the ride take her, she mused on life and the U-turns she seemed to find all along the way. So far, it had been a disappointing day as far as her aims and goals were concerned. What if she never found out the truth about her father? What if the truth was hidden somewhere and no one alive knew where it was? Could she live with that? Could she go back home and find a way to be happy? Could her mother snap out of the depressive state she'd been in for years?

Not likely.

Even more scary, what if she found out the truth and it was worse than she'd ever believed? What if her father was really and truly guilty? What if there was even more to it, more things he had done? Her mind cringed away from those stray thoughts. Some ideas were just too painful to explore.

Too soon, Shangri-La loomed on the hill ahead. She

remembered she'd told Carl she would be back in time to go over the map with him again. That hadn't happened. The time had long passed. He was going to be angry.

Oh well.

She turned back to look at Marc.

"Can I come with you to your neighbor's?" she asked him. "I don't want to go back to the house just yet."

He nodded, his face unreadable. "Sure," was all he said.

But he didn't complain when she leaned back against him. He was strong and warm and she had a sudden fantasy of letting him be her champion in the world. She could use one. The only problem was, she had a feeling he wasn't in the market for a girl like her. After all, she tried to get his attention before, when she was a chubby young adolescent. That hadn't worked out so well.

Now she was back and he only cared because she was threatening his family's reputation with her crazy theories and searches. But at least he was paying attention now. She smiled at the irony of it all.

"How can big things happen—big, important things that change the shape of our lives—and a few years later no one remembers anything about them?" she asked him over her shoulder.

He didn't answer for a long moment. Finally he leaned forward and spoke softly in her ear. "The people who are directly affected remember. Sometimes it takes a surprise to get them to open up to the past once they've tried to put it behind them. But they remember when they have to."

She wasn't sure she bought that. It seemed as though her father had passed through this life without anyone much noticing him. He'd tried so hard to be a good man and good at his chosen profession—and he'd done well at both. But when his heart got broken, so did his spirit—which started the chain of tragedy that pretty much ruined her whole family. And no one seemed to care.

If only the treasure had never disappeared. If only they had stayed and she'd finished her childhood here where she belonged. He would still be alive today, and her mother wouldn't be the faded shell of a woman that she was. Everything would have been so different.

She glanced back at Marc. His father might still be alive, too. And Ricky? She didn't really know what had happened there and Marc definitely bristled whenever she asked questions.

If only she could pretend she was any closer to finding out about her father. She'd always had a feeling deep in her heart that clearing his name would change everything. It wouldn't bring any of those people back to life, of course, but it would surely brighten her mother's life—and her own.

Funny, but in some ways she had begun to realize that she felt close to Marc. He was a part of her past. She might even venture to call him a part of her present. There was a reserve in him that appealed to her.

And then she frowned, wondering if it was really just a certain dignity that set him apart—or was it actually a wariness, and a basic distrust of her and who she was.

They delivered the horse to the neighbor and got into Marc's long, low sports car. She expected him to turn for home, but instead, he took a side road that took them on a curvy two lanes into the hills. He pulled into an overlook and turned off the engine.

"Wildflowers," he said by way of explanation.

She looked out and sighed. "Wow. How beautiful."

The hills were covered with masses of golden California poppies fighting for space with sky-blue lupine and bright yellow mustard, all dancing in the breezes. In the distance, looking back at the way they'd come, she could see the blue ocean. Oaks and flowering purple bushes filled the valleys. It was one of the most beautiful places she'd ever seen.

They got out and walked to the edge of the overlook, leaning against the guardrail that had been put up for just that purpose. She breathed in the beauty, but all the while, she couldn't ignore the sense of presence in the man beside her.

She finally turned and smiled at him. He didn't smile back, but his eyes were warm and she was beginning to think they might have a tender moment, if she played her cards right. Her heart began to thump a bit harder.

And then he pulled her right back into the maelstrom.

"Have you decided what it is that Carl's looking for yet?" he asked her.

Carl. Her shoulders sagged and she felt a pang of guilt. He must be wondering where she was. But she knew he would want more than simple work on the map. He was going to insist she come with him to the caves and show him what she knew. She wanted to avoid this at all costs.

"Uh...no," she responded evasively. "Why? What's your theory?"

He shrugged and looked out at the hills. "I think he's after the same thing most people who come nosing around here are after: the Don Carlos Treasure."

"But..." She hesitated, biting her lip. This was what

really bothered her. "I thought your father sent it to the bottom of the sea when he sailed out that awful day. Wasn't that the story? And then his boat capsized and he...he..."

"He went down with the treasure. At least, that was what his suicide note said he was planning to do."

"Is there really any proof that he took the treasure out there with him? Does anyone know for sure if it's really down there?"

He didn't answer. She watched as his handsome face turned to granite. Reaching out, she touched his arm.

"I'm sorry, Marc. I know it brings up unhappy memories to talk about it."

He turned and stared down at her. "If we don't talk about it, we'll never get to the truth. And this may surprise you, but I want the truth as much as you do."

She searched his eyes. Was that really true? What do you know? Just as he had decided that, she was becoming more ambivalent. What if the truth only made things worse?

But Marc seemed to be transitioning into a philosophical mood. He leaned out over the railing and looked toward the ocean in the distance and went on, almost as though to himself.

"You know, I hadn't thought about it all, the whole situation, for a long time. Years. I was sort of blocking it out." He glanced sideways at her. "There were a lot of people at the time who asked the same questions you just asked. How did we know the treasure was truly gone? We had people coming here in droves, sneaking onto the property, digging up the rose garden, moving logs around, trying their best to find out where he'd actually hidden the treasure. It was like the California gold rush all over again."

"How awful." She glanced away, wondering if he looked at her as one of those scavengers. Why not? In a way, she was like them. Only she already had a part of the treasure. He just didn't know about that, and she hoped she was going to leave without him finding out. What she was after was the explanation. That was all.

"It didn't let up for a long time. Marge was always calling the police, and then there would be a confrontation. I didn't have to deal with it, since I was overseas. But I sure heard a lot about it."

"From Marge?"

"Yeah. She wanted to sell from the beginning. I kept trying to talk her out of it."

"But she kept things going around here."

He nodded. "I've got to give her that one. She did okay for a good long while. She kept writing me about these great offers she was getting, and then they always fell through. After awhile, she gave up. I hadn't heard from her about selling for about five years now." He ran his fingers through his thick, dark hair. "But this time she's determined. This time, she's going to sell."

"And this time, you want to stop her."

He was silent and she stood beside him, so close and yet so far. She could feel that he hated this, that he didn't want his family estate going to strangers. She wasn't sure how finding out the truth about the treasure would help him deal with that. A part of her wished she knew a way to help him. There was nothing she could do.

"So you're not in the military anymore," she said, more to fill the silence than to find out anything new.

"Not really. But when you've been in as long as I

have, a part of you will always be in there. It gets in your blood."

She nodded. That made sense to her. The military could be a pretty intense experience, one that changed many people forever. She looked at him candidly. "What are you going to do with the rest of your life?"

He laughed, leaning back with both elbows on the railing. "That's what I like about you, Torie," he said, his gaze ranging over her in a way that made her tingle. "You don't play games and beat around the bush. If you want to know something, you just ask."

She gave him a quick smile. "You, on the other hand, try to change the subject and don't give straight answers."

"You want an answer? Here goes." He took a deep breath and gazed off at the horizon. "I got experience in a lot of things in the service. Security, business management, electronics, diplomacy, espionage." He looked at her. "I even filled in as a wedding and bar mitzvah singer from time to time."

"You're kidding." The picture that conjured up made her laugh out loud.

"No," he protested, half laughing himself. "I was pretty popular at it."

"I'll bet." She could see the young girls swooning now.

He rolled his eyes at her amusement, but he went on.

"So when I got out, I started looking around at opportunities. But my mind kept going back to Shangri-La."

"Of course," she murmured. Her mind did too. All the time.

"I started wanting to come home. The more I thought

about it, the more it seemed to pull at me." He turned to look at her more closely.

"You know, this is a wonderful place. There are a lot of options right here on the land. My grandfather made his fortune as a breeder of racehorses. My father spent a few years developing a world-class vineyard, selling his grapes to the best wineries along the coast."

"I remember that."

He looked at her, one eyebrow raised. "What do you think of me putting in a winery right here?"

"It would take a lot of start-up money, wouldn't it?"

He nodded. "Yes, it would." He shrugged and the faraway expression was back in his eyes. "Aw, what the heck. No point living in dreamland. Marge is going to sell, come hell or high water. She's got that look of determination in her eyes. She wants out of here. And I don't have the resources to stop her."

There it was again, that note of pain the tore at her when she heard it. "Will she give you a part of the proceeds if she does sell?"

"Why would she do that?"

She shrugged. "Maybe because you're like a son to her. Stranger things…"

His laugh was short and cold. "Not Marge. She wants to take the money and run. And she really doesn't owe me anything. She's the lonely widow. I'm the ne'er-do-well stepson. Never those minds shall meet."

"It just seems…"

"Community property," he said shortly, pulling himself upright and starting back toward the car. "I'm not a part of that."

She followed behind, kicking her feet into the dirt. "It doesn't seem fair."

"My only claims are emotional and courts don't much care." He turned to look at her. "Besides. I'm a grown-up. I should be making my own way in the world."

She stared at him, suddenly realizing that he was as much stymied by Shangri-La as she was. She couldn't move on with her life because these unanswered questions haunted her.

And he was no better. He couldn't stop loving Shangri-La, even though he had no hope of ever running the place as his father had done, and his grandfather and all the Huntingtons before that right into the days when Spaniards roamed these hills and tall ships cruised the coast.

They were a pair, lost and lonely, wandering in the wilderness, looking for a home.

"Making your own way is one thing," she said softly. "Losing your home is another."

They'd reached the car. He pulled her door open and held it. She appraised his tousled hair, his clear blue eyes, his incredible handsomeness, and she felt a surge of emotion. Was it affection? Or the sense that they were kindred souls who ought to join forces to fight the darkness? Whatever it was, the impulse took hold and she went on her toes, threw her arms around his neck, and kissed him on the mouth.

"Thanks, Marc Huntington," she told him, smiling at his startled look as she stepped away again. "Thanks for helping me get home that day with Snowconc in my arms. Thanks for being here to help me now."

"Anytime," he murmured.

But he didn't reach out and pull her into his arms as she had secretly hoped he would do, and his eyes were hooded, giving no hint at what he thought about what she'd done.

They rode in silence all the way back to Shangri-La, but she didn't regret that kiss.

The group was lounging sleepily on the patio furniture arranged casually on the terrace, enjoying the scenery. The sound of the surf in the distance, the cries of seagulls, the platoons of dignified pelicans swooping past—all very seductive selling points for Marge.

Torie hurried past, giving them all a wave after she noted that her fake "husband" wasn't with them.

Marge glanced up and scowled. "Where've you been?" she demanded.

Torie stared right back. "Out," she said with an artificial smile. "Looking for facts. Looking for truth."

"Truth," Marge said in mock disgust, but she was looking more sharply at Torie, as if she was beginning to see something familiar about her. "Good luck finding any of that in this world," she muttered.

Torie turned her back and headed for the stairs, wondering what it would be like to get that woman in a small room with third-degree lights shining in her lying eyes. It wouldn't hurt to have a few grizzled old investigators to help her crack the woman's defenses. She smiled to herself.

"Oh, Carl said to tell you he was exploring the caves again," Lyla called after her.

"Thanks," she called back, taking the stairs quickly. And then she paused, looking at Carl's closed door. If he was out at the caves, this was a perfect opportunity to take a look at what he might have in his bedroom.

Should she? Why not.

After all, she was looking for facts, wasn't she? And Carl was looking for something else. She had a feeling she knew what that something was, but it would be good to confirm it. And anyway, she wanted to know what he was up to.

She looked up and down the hallway. There was no one coming. Quietly, she slipped into the room.

Carl seemed to be a very neat man. No discarded clothing littered the floor. Nothing was hung on the chair. His suitcase was closed and propped against the desk. Papers were stacked neatly on the nightstand and she looked through them quickly. They seemed to be old insurance claims and she didn't see anything interesting on them. The corner of his briefcase was barely visible under the bed and she pulled it out and opened it. Inside was a sheath of newspaper clippings. The first one to catch her eye bore the headline: Gold Doubloons Show Up Along the Central Coast.

Gold doubloons. That was what the Don Carlos Treasure had been mainly made up of. She snatched the clipping, stuffed it under her shirt, and prepared to leave. The last thing she wanted was to be found sneaking around in Carl's room. Just the thought gave her the shivers.

And that was the moment she heard footsteps coming down the hall toward where she was.

CHAPTER EIGHT

TORIE's heart began to hammer and her breath seemed to be stuck in her throat. She glanced around the room, zeroing in on the closet, the only place where she might hide in. But if she got caught in there, it would be ten times worse than just hanging out as though she was waiting for him.

Quickly, she sat down on the bed and stared at the door. If he came in, she would have a story ready. "Where's that map?" she would say. "I thought it might be here so I could work on it."

He wouldn't believe her, but at least she'd have a cover story.

The footsteps paused, as though someone was about to knock. She bit her lip and held her breath. A shriek of laughter came from downstairs and someone called. She couldn't tell who it was or what they were saying, but it seemed to get to her visitor. He—or she—seemed to turn, and the steps went back toward the stairs. She let her breath out slowly, listening intently.

She then slipped out again and into her own room, where she threw herself down on the bed and tried to regulate her breathing and calm her pulse. That had not been a fun few minutes she'd just gone through. She didn't want that to happen again. That probably wasn't Carl who'd stopped at the door and then left. Whoever it was would likely be back though.

She pulled the article she'd stolen out from under her shirt and looked at it. She had to show this to Marc.

But she needed to get cleaned up first. Rising from the bed, she pulled off her rumpled clothes and put on a fresh pair of designer jeans and a soft blue sweater. Then she stopped to take a closer look at the article.

It was dated nine years before and seemed to have been printed in a county newspaper. Gold Doubloons Show Up along the Central Coast. The article claimed that a stash of the ancient coins must have been found lately, since coin dealers were reporting that people from the area were selling them in numbers that hadn't been seen for years.

"Nine years ago?" she muttered, frowning. How could that have any impact on today? She should have taken more of the articles. Too late now. She wasn't going back there.

Folding the article, she stuck it into a pocket of her jeans, then turned to look at where she'd stowed her suitcase under the bed. Reaching down, she pulled it out, found her key and unlocked it. With her hand, she felt along the lining. It was still there—the little bag of Spanish gold.

Her heart started pounding again. Could it really be a part of the treasure? What else could it be? And why had she found it among her mother's possessions just a few weeks before?

She shook her head. "Daddy, Daddy, what did you do?" she whispered to herself. Then she closed the suitcase and put it back under the bed, pushing it far enough back so that no one would notice where it was unless they were down on their hands and knees, looking for it. She couldn't really think of more she could do.

With a heartfelt sigh, she started downstairs. Detouring into the kitchen, she snagged a sandwich on her way out. Suddenly, she was ravenous.

At the doorway, she looked down on the little party on the terrace. Marge and the Texan were having a loud argument. Phoebe and Frank seemed to be taking sides—against each other. Lyla was pouting and playing up to Jimmy. Somehow she had to get past this nightmare bunch and find Marc again.

"Hey, you," came a half whisper from across the hall.

She whirled, and there he was, just coming out of the library.

"This way," he said with a jerk of his head. She followed him to a small French door at the end of the sitting room. A moment later they were slinking down a garden path and into the eucalyptus trees.

"You read my mind," she told him. "I was not looking forward to joining that group."

"You're wise beyond your years," he said, glancing back toward the house. Then he looked back at her, his blue eyes sparkling. "Have you ever been to the car barn?"

She had not, though she remembered hearing about it years before. The car barn had been Ricky's domain and Ricky's hobby was race-car driving.

"Never," she said.

"Until now," he told her. "Let's go."

It was a long walk and they weren't in any hurry. Stone benches had been set out here and there many years ago. They spent the next fifteen minutes remembering other times they'd been this way.

"The trees weren't quite so thick then," she recalled, looking up at the tall redwoods around their path. "You could see the ocean from here."

He nodded. "I remember when you could see the whole coastline from here, all the way down to the caves and up to the village."

"I wonder if Carl is back from the caves," Torie mused. Then memories of the newspaper article popped into her head. "Oh! I've got something to show you."

She pulled out the clipping. "What do you think of this?"

They stopped and sat on a nearby bench. He read the whole thing before he said a word.

"So where did this come from?"

She couldn't avoid the guilty look her face took on. "I took it from Carl's room. He had a stack of them, and some old insurance papers in a folder."

"And this is all you got?"

She nodded. "I just snatched it up and ran like a rat."

He gazed at her for a long moment, then shrugged.

"I remember this," he said. "I wasn't here, but a friend sent me this article when it first came out." He shook his head as though dismissing the importance of the clipping. "I thought at the time that either someone had a fertile imagination or a new stash of doubloons had been found."

He looked into her eyes and she frowned. Somehow his show of earnest common sense was ringing false with her. Was he trying to con her for some reason?

"Shangri-La isn't the only large estate along the coast you know," he said somewhat defensively. "There are plenty of cave networks too, along with hidden canyons. Back in the eighteenth and nineteenth centuries, the Spanish were all up and down this coast. I'm sure there were many places that were used for hiding various treasures, and I'm sure most people who find them keep it pretty quiet."

"But they have to let others know when they go to coin brokers to try to cash in," she noted.

He nodded. "Sure. And that doesn't happen very often. Mostly, people would rather keep the treasure for themselves. To people like my father, the historical value is more important than the cash you could get for it."

Was that understandable? Maybe. "Where did the Don Carlos Treasure originally come from?"

"My grandfather, William Canford Huntington. He found it in the thirties. He was trying to map the caves and ended up breaking down a ledge to be able to reach further in. Behind that ledge he found a pile of gold doubloons and other coins, along with some jewels. The bag they had been in had been eaten away, but the coins were bright and shiny as they'd ever been." He smiled, remembering the stories he'd heard. "But you must have seen it. My father had it in the display case in the library for years."

She shook her head. "I don't think I ever saw it."

"It was right in the house all the time I was growing up."

"That must have been quite an exotic display. But I never went into your house. I wasn't a guest, you know." She blinked with mock innocence. "Just a humble servant's child."

He rolled his eyes and groaned.

"It was stupid, of course, to have it just sitting there. It should have been in a security deposit box at the bank. But you can't show it off if it's not there."

"Ah, vanity."

"Vanity and greed."

He rose and held out his hand to pull her up. She took it, looking into his face to see if he'd had any new thoughts about her.

Just checking, she told herself. But she was disappointed once again. The man just didn't feel the things for her she felt for him. *Pity.*

And then they reached the car barn. She never would have found it on her own. It was a large, echoing warehouse-sized garage built into the side of a hill. The entry consisted of a set of huge double doors, but they were impossible to make out in the gloomy forest area. Weeds and vines covered it and years and years of branches and leaves and sifted dirt had been built up against it by the wind and rain. Luckily, Marc remembered where it was supposed to be and once he found it, the two of them worked for a good twenty minutes at removing debris before they were able to pull the doors open.

"God only knows what we're going to find in here," Marc said as he cleared a path for her. Before going in, he found the fuse box and threw a breaker, making sure they would have lights inside.

What they found when they went in was amazing. The door seemed to have kept the place hermetically sealed and it was like stepping back into past times. The inside was probably as clean as it had been when Ricky had last been working there. There were six bays, four of them filled with cars. Two of the cars were elegant models from the twenties or thirties, one restored and the other in the process of being so, both beautiful reminders of a bygone age.

"This one's an Auburn Boattail," Marc told her proudly. "I helped Rick with it a lot. It's beautiful, isn't it?"

"Gorgeous. Like something from an old movie."

He nodded. "The other's an old Mercedes. Both these cars were my grandfather's. When he realized how good Ricky was with cars, he gave them to him, along with this place. Ricky spent all his time here. In fact, most of the time over those last few years I think he lived here."

Opening a side door, he revealed a small room with a cot and some bedding.

"Ricky's apartment," he said with a smile. "He even had a small cook stove and a lot of supplies over there in the cabinets."

"And an ancient microwave," she noted, pointing it out.

"Right. I can just imagine the gourmet feasts he was able to serve up in this place." Marc's eyes had a faraway look. "Ricky and I were never real close. But he was my brother. And I miss him."

His voice cracked just a little bit in the last sentence and he made an impatient move, as though he could erase it. She had a lump in her throat. She was finding herself in tune with him more and more, feeling what he was feeling. Or at least, trying to. Maybe she ought to cut it out. Before she knew it, she was going to get herself in too deep.

She tried to remember Ricky. He was taller and thinner than Marc, and a few years older. He always seemed preoccupied and she had the feeling he never really saw her at all. She was invisible as far as he was concerned.

He was always thinking about cars and he obviously had zero interest in younger kids of any type. She never took it personally.

Not the way she took Marc's lack of interest. His hurt.

"I think my father came out here to see what Ricky was working on," she said slowly, thinking back. "I remember him talking about it. I think he liked Ricky a lot."

He nodded.

"Marc, what happened to Ricky? How did he…?"

A spasm of pain crossed his face, but only briefly. "What would you guess?" he said shortly. He waved toward the other two cars, a souped-up Mustang and something else she didn't recognize that was also kitted out. "Amateur race car driver dies in crash. Some make it to the pro level, others die trying."

His voice was bitter. She glanced at him quickly, but he turned away.

"At least he was doing what he loved," she tried tentatively.

He swung back and glared at her. "That's supposed to make me feel better? People say it every time and it doesn't help anything at all. It's so lame."

She winced. He was absolutely right. "I'm sorry. I was just trying…"

Now *her* voice was breaking and he groaned and reached for her, pulling her in close and burying his face in her hair. "I'm the one who's sorry," he said gruffly. "You're a sweetheart and I don't need to be yelling at you."

She raised her face. It felt so good in his arms and she wanted to stay there forever. Was he going to kiss her this time? There had been so many chances and he'd passed them all by. She wanted to taste him so badly. Couldn't he read that in her eyes?

He looked down. There was something smoky in his gaze, something sensual, an awareness and a sudden flash of something that might be desire. She caught her breath and yearned toward him. He leaned closer, his lips almost there.

And then his face clouded and he seemed to pull himself back with a jerk, even pulling his hands from her shoulders. Turning, he walked toward the cars.

She closed her eyes and drew in a deep, deep breath. When would she ever learn?

They spent some time looking at the cars and he told her a bit about them. Fifteen years had passed since Ricky'd left them here, and they were hardly even dusty.

"It almost feels as though he might walk in that door any minute," Marc said. "Everything looks so much the same."

She nodded. "I'm glad you brought me here," she told him. "I'm glad to know more about your brother. The picture is more complete that way."

Marc was rummaging around in a cabinet. "Hey, look at this," he said, pulling out a wine bottle. "From the Alegre Winery. Bottled in 1994. Made with our grapes."

She laughed. "If only we had some wineglasses."

He produced them with a flourish out of the same cabinet. There was even a corkscrew. He started to open the bottle, then looked around.

"We can't just drink it here on the floor of a working garage," he said. "We need a little elegance."

The Mercedes from the 1930s had that in spades. He

opened the door, pulled forward the back of the passenger seat, and escorted her into the beautifully upholstered back seat, then went around to the driver's side and slipped in beside her, bottle and glasses in hand.

The crimson wine poured into the crystal glasses and sparks of light and color flew around the room. Torie raised her glass and he met hers with his. They clinked, looking into each other's eyes. Suddenly there was an air of excitement trembling in the atmosphere.

"To Shangri-La," she said. "And all it's glory."

"To truth," he countered. "And to us finding it soon."

She bit her lip. She didn't want to think about that right now. She was here in a beautiful, luxurious car, the sort of car rich people drove to mansions in the old days, the kind of car movie stars stepped out of to begin their walk on the red carpet in front of movie premiers. She could smell the leather, see the gleaming paneled wood, feel the soft seating, and here in her hand was a gorgeous glass of wine.

But best of all, she was in touching distance of the man she had always been almost in love with. It was a magic moment and she didn't want to waste it on painful subjects.

Sipping the wine, she let the bite of it warm her throat and she smiled at him. She wasn't a drinker. This was going to go to her head right away. She ought to be careful.

"More?" he asked, holding up the bottle.

"Lovely," she answered, surprised to see that her glass was empty. She'd never had wine so delicious before. And she seemed to be thirsty.

They talked softly for a few minutes, going over their day, their ride to the village, their stop to view the wildflowers. She told him about a friend who ran marathons and he told her about a friend who raised Siamese cats. Their bottle was empty, but he produced another.

And then he told her, looking deep into her eyes, "You know what your biggest problem is?"

The fact that you won't kiss me? But she couldn't say that aloud, even though the wine was making her feel giggly.

"No," she said, melting in the thrill of his gaze. "Why don't you tell me?"

He suddenly seemed very wise. "You trust too much."

She reared back, not sure she liked that. "In what way?" she asked carefully.

He looked at her as though trying to decide something. Finally, he reached out, cupping her chin in his large hand, as though he meant to study her face, and she let him, though her heart was fluttering in her chest like a lost bird. When he finally finished his thorough observation, she sighed as he drew away again.

"You trust Carl to bring you here, even though he's probably a crook," he said quietly. "You trust things people tell you as long as they're nice about it." His mouth curled in a wistful smile. "Worst of all, you trust me."

"I do not," she said stoutly.

He grinned. "Yes you do."

She blinked rapidly. "Well, at least I give people a chance. You don't give anyone the benefit of the doubt. You don't trust anyone, do you?"

His eyes narrowed. "Trust is for suckers."

She drew back, frowning. "That's a horrible attitude."

He shook his head as though she just didn't understand, and he took her hand in his.

"Let me tell you a little story. Something short and sweet. Something that will give you the picture of the world I live in, and why I think trust is overrated."

She smiled, her fingers curling around his. For some reason what he'd just said seemed so very amusing. "Lay it on me, baby," she said, leaning toward him.

A look of alarm came over his handsome face. "Hey. How much have you had of that stuff?"

She giggled. "Sorry. I was just trying to get in the mood."

Moving with calm deliberation, he took the glass from her hand and put it out of reach.

"See, this is what I mean. If you were smart, you would be very wary of what I might do if you get a little tipsy."

"Don't worry," she said bravely. "I've got all my wits about me. Such as they are." She laughed out loud.

He gave her a baleful look, but he settled back and continued his cautionary tale. "Okay. This happened years ago, when I was young and still a nice guy."

"Unlike today." She nodded wisely.

He frowned his disapproval of her chattiness. "Unlike today," he allowed. "I was in South East Asia. The country doesn't matter. But I was on a mission. A pretty dangerous situation. And I fell in love."

Now he had her complete attention.

"Oh," she said softly.

"The area was beautiful. White-sand beaches. Sweet, friendly people. My mission was to extract something important from the desk of a local plantation owner. My job was to get in and get out. Under no circumstances was I to interfere with local customs or get involved in local affairs. No roiling the waters."

She nodded to show she understood completely. "And I'm sure you did a very good job of it, didn't you?"

He stared at her for a moment, then laughed softly. He touched her cheek, looking at her as though he enjoyed the view. "Yes, darling. I always did a good job. But right now I'm talking about the girl I fell in love with."

"Oh." She felt so sad all of a sudden and she wasn't sure why.

His face took on a faraway look.

"She was so beautiful, so tiny, so fragile, like a flower. I was pretty young and I fell like a ton of bricks. She enchanted me. She told me how her family had sold her to the plantation owner because they were desperately poor. They had eight other children to feed. She was one too many."

"How terrible."

"Yes. The plantation owner had promised to take good care of her, but he'd lied. She was so unhappy. She told me whispered tales of how cruel he was."

He shook his head, remembering his naive reaction. "I was outraged. I burned to protect her. I couldn't get her out of my mind. So I did something very stupid."

"Uh-oh."

"Yes. Uh-oh. You see, when my mission was complete, I took her with me."

She'd known he would end up being the hero. "Good for you."

"No. Not really." He grimaced. "We travelled for two days and finally reached the city and I got us a hotel room. I had so many plans in my head. I thought..." He stopped, looked at her and his mouth curved in a bitter smile. "Hell, what does it matter what I thought? I woke up at dawn the next day and she was gone. And so was all my money."

She gasped. "Oops."

He looked at her and started to laugh. "It's like you've got an alter ego just waiting inside you," he noted. "She can only come out to play when you drink. Is that how it is?"

"I don't know what you're talking about," she said very primly, sitting up straight like a good girl.

He laughed again, then shook his head. She looked like an angel, her blond hair flying like gold threads around her face, her green eyes sparkling, her eyelids heavy with the effects of the wine. The need to kiss her came over him like an urgent wave, choking him for a moment. He had to look away and breathe hard a few times to get himself back on track.

"Okay, I'll wrap this story up. The beautiful girl I thought I was in love with not only stole all my money, she fingered me to the local crime gang. I got away from them, but I took a little memento with me."

Pulling up his shirt, he showed her the scar.

"See?" he said as she gasped, wide-eyed, at the ugly wound that contorted his beautiful skin just below his rib cage. "That's what you get when you trust someone."

Reaching out, she put her warm hand over the damage. And then, without thinking, she leaned down and pressed her lips to it.

As he felt the heat radiating from her mouth, he sucked in his breath, then reached to pull her up.

"Torie, you'd better not..."

She ended up in his arms and all his determination

not to touch her melted away like April snow. What had he been saying? It was gone. All he could think about was her warm, wonderful body against his and her hot, tempting mouth so close.

He kissed her. He felt a twinge of guilt. After all, she might not be doing this if it weren't for the wine. But it was too late to use that as a reason to pull away. He was kissing her and she was the most delicious thing he'd ever had.

She sighed and bent back as though offering him something more than a gesture. Something in that move hit him directly in his natural male response center.

Desire bloomed in him like a small explosion. He wanted her. He wanted his mouth on hers and his tongue exploring her heat, and he was getting that. But he needed more, and the need was beginning to grow in a way he wasn't going to be able to control. He had to hold her hard against him and he had to touch her breasts and make her cry out so that it would make him even more crazy and… and…

He had to stop. It was becoming obvious that she wasn't going to stop him and he'd counted on that. He'd have to do it himself.

"Torie." He tried to pull back.

She whimpered when his mouth left hers and she reached with her warm, provoking hands to slide against his skin and lure him back.

"Torie."

"No," she whispered, flattening against him. "No, don't leave me."

"Torie, we have to stop."

"No." She shook her head, her eyes tightly closed,

as though that would make his common-sense thoughts go away.

"Yes, Torie. We have to stop."

She still pressed against him, her face to his chest. Her sigh was deep and heartfelt and he began to stroke her hair. In moments, she was asleep.

He held her there, taking in her fresh scent and her soft feel. An emotion swept through him and he wasn't sure he knew exactly what it was—but it touched his heart. He knew that. A part of it contained a tug on his sensual responses, but there was more. He felt the warmth of affection, the strength of protectiveness, and he couldn't stop looking at her and how pretty she was.

Still, it was all crazy. He'd been in love and it never came to anything good. It usually meant a certain type of heartbreak. It had been a good five years since he'd even chanced it, and he'd vowed never to let it happen again. So he was okay. He was protected, inoculated against the disease. He wasn't going to worry about it.

But he was going to enjoy this. This, he could handle.

So he sat there and held her and waited for her to wake up. And he thought about his situation.

Why was he here? What exactly did he want out of all this? He wanted to save Shangri-La. That was it. He wanted his home to stay in the family. And since he was the only real Huntington left, that meant he wanted to keep it himself.

He'd tried to talk to Marge about him becoming caretaker while she went off and did what she felt she had to do, but she didn't want to hear about it. Marge wanted money. She wanted enough cash in hand to leave the country and live on for the rest of her life. If she could get that from any of these people she had gathered here, she would be gone like a flash. And he just didn't have that kind of a bankroll.

So what were his options? Few and far between—not to mention, weak. If the fortune-hunter crowd was right and the Don Carlos Treasure was hiding on the estate somewhere, things would be different. But he didn't believe that for a minute. His father's suicide note had been stark and emphatic. He thought the treasure was cursed and he wanted it at the bottom of the sea. Marc had no doubt his father had done what he said he would do.

So why was he helping Torie? Why was he letting her dream? Maybe because her dreams connected with his own in an odd way. She wanted to prove her father didn't steal the treasure. He wanted to know what had actually happened. She wanted to clear her father, he wanted to exonerate his own. And maybe help to fix something that had haunted his family—if it could be fixed.

And that was why he wanted to help her find the journal. Who knew? There might be something written in there that could clear up a lot of questions—and put some ghosts to rest.

But that was a pretty slim thread to put his hopes on and he didn't really expect anything even if the journal was found.

He looked down at Torie's pretty face, her lashes making long shadows on her cheeks as she slept. He had to smile. To think that chubby little girl throwing apple cores on his car had grown up to be something like this—and possibly his only hope at getting to the truth. That made his grin wider.

Still, he wasn't sure about her. There was a huge element of distrust in his gnarled soul. He'd been lied to one too many times. He didn't trust anyone and, if he was honest with himself, he had to admit she hadn't proved herself at all. She'd just become so appealing to him that he was willing to give her a pass—for now.

Wasn't that it?

CHAPTER NINE

TORIE was somewhat surprised to wake up alone in the back seat of an ancient luxury car, but she stretched and yawned and smiled. She was still a little fuzzy in the head, but she knew that something good had happened. And then she remembered what it was and she sat up straighter and sighed happily. Now the only problem would be if Marc regretted it.

She wondered where he was, but then she heard someone rummaging around in the storage room at the end of the hall and she assumed it was him. She sighed. There wasn't much point in sitting here waiting for him to come back as though she was hoping for a rerun. Something told her that wasn't going to happen.

She ran her fingers over the leather seat and turned to look at the beautiful dashboard with its hand-rubbed mahogany trim. They just didn't make them like this anymore. There was even a long shelf just under the dashboard, running the width of the car. Ladies probably stored their long kid gloves there after the party was over. She smiled at the thought, and then her gaze sharpened. There was something pushed far back into the shelf. You could hardly see it but when she bent low, she could just make it out. It looked like a small notebook of some kind. Maybe the sort of thing people wrote their mileage down in. Or…

Her heart began to beat like crazy and her breath choked in her throat. A journal? Her father's journal? She pushed forward to the front seat and leaned to reach for it. And at just that moment, Marc came back into the room.

"Hey sleepyhead," he said, carrying a couple of cans of car wax in and stowing them away on a shelf.

She jerked back, pulling her hand in and turning scarlet. "Oh, uh…hi."

He grinned at her, probably thinking her pink cheeks were the result of her thinking about the snuggle they'd shared. But that was just as well, because she suddenly realized she wasn't going to tell him what she'd just seen. If it turned out to be the journal, she wanted a little time to see what it had in it. Who knew what sorts of things her father might reveal in something like that?

"Find something?" he asked curiously.

"No. No." She shook her head and tried to smile.

"I've been out looking through the shelves." He gestured toward the storage room. "I didn't find anything either."

She gazed at him out the car window. "Thanks for letting me take a little nap," she said cheerfully. "I hate to be a girl who can't hold her liquor, but better to sleep than to do something crazy."

He grinned again. "Oh, I don't know. Crazy can be good too."

She gave him a look and laughed, and he turned back to the storage room, disappearing in through the door.

She reached out quickly and grabbed the little notebook, and then her hands began to tremble.

Her father's little leather journal. His name was embossed on the front cover in gold—Jarvis Sands. And inside was the handwriting she knew so well. She flipped through it quickly. There was someone else's handwriting on the last few pages. She only had to read a couple of lines to realize it had to be Marc's father who had added his thoughts.

But Marc was coming back. She could hear him approaching the doorway. Quickly, she closed the journal and jammed it down deep into the back pocket of her jeans.

She had the grace to flush again as he came out and smiled at her. The guilt made her look and feel nervous. But he would just think she was still shaky over what they had shared. She wasn't going to show the journal to him until she knew for sure what it revealed. She just couldn't see any way around it.

A few minutes later, they left the car barn and walked out to the cliff that overlooked the ocean. The sun was low in the sky. The people back at the house would be preparing for dinner about now. They were going to have to decide what they were going to do.

But not yet. For now, they found a fallen tree and sat on it while they watched the sun move toward a sunset. He made no move to get closer, and she knew instinctively that he wasn't planning to kiss her again. Did he regret doing that earlier? Who knew? It made her a little sad to think that he might. Still, there was nothing she could do about it now.

"What a beautiful view," she said softly.

He nodded. "Think of being a local Native American in the nineteenth century and watching Spanish galleons come sliding into the harbor," he said. "We had an archeologist doing a paper on this area one year. He found evidence that lots of ships stopped along this part of the coast. Can't you just picture how that would have been?"

Yes, she could picture it. She'd lived her Spanish-era fantasies on her own on the beaches and in the caves from early on. Such a great place for a child to grow in.

Tears filled her eyes and she blinked hard, angry with herself for letting it get to her again. She stared out at the ocean, throwing her head back to feel the wind in her hair. She was filled with sadness and a wave of nostalgia. She'd been so happy here as a child—despite any latent insecurities. The mood in the fresh ocean air was filled with peace and a sense of well-being. Life had been like that here—right up until the day her father had been accused of stealing.

That was the dividing line. Everything had begun to fall apart on that day and it had only gotten worse since.

She'd had good times with friends and success in her job. She couldn't claim it had been all angst and torture since her fifteenth year. But her father's agony had been a dark cloud over her family.

His eventual suicide and her mother's breakdown had only made things worse. She felt as though her heart and soul were restless, looking for answers, aching for closure. Could she ever find happiness without knowing? It felt to her as though that would be impossible.

Rising, she rose and walked out to the edge of the cliff, looking down at the rocks below. Then she turned to watch Marc in the gathering gloom.

"So tell me this," she said. "What was the official story? What did you hear at the time? What do most people around here believe happened?"

He looked back at her coolly. "About what?"

Her eyes narrowed. "About when my father was fired."

He sighed. It was pretty plain he didn't really want to go over it. But he did.

"Okay. Here's how I remember it. I was in premed at UCC, living with a couple of friends in an apartment off campus. It was a Sunday, late at night. My father called to tell me the Don Carlos Treasure had gone missing."

"Wait. What were the circumstances?" Walking back, she sat beside him again. She wanted to be sure she got this right. She might never have another chance.

"Circumstances?" He shrugged and thought back. "I'm not sure."

"Here's what I remember," she said. "And believe me, I've gone over this in my mind a thousand times. My family and I had been gone that weekend. We were up in Monterey to see the aquarium. Your father was at some geology lecture in Los Angeles and your mother was off on a trip with friends. Palm Springs or somewhere like that. Ricky was at a comic-book convention in Oregon."

He shook his head, his gaze hooded. "I don't remember all that, but you were there. I wasn't."

"That's just it. None of us were there. When we got home, no one else was back yet. Even the rest of the staff was gone. No one else was due back until Monday morning. But about an hour later, my father went up to the house to get back to work. Even though he didn't have to." She almost rolled her eyes. "He always had that darn sense of responsibility toward the place—and toward your father. He wanted everything perfect for when Mr. Huntington got home."

Marc nodded and almost smiled. "That is how I remember him. I know my father had a lot of affection for him at the time."

She nodded too. "Your father got back unexpectedly about eight. My father went out and met him on the drive. He told him the treasure was missing. He'd gone into the library and saw that the display case was empty. He'd been searching for the last hour, in a panic, hoping someone had just moved it. Your father rushed in and they both spent rest of the evening searching."

Marc frowned. "Didn't they call the police?"

She shook her head. "My father came home about midnight and told us what had happened. He said Mr. Huntington didn't want to call them until he'd talked to everyone, just to make sure someone hadn't borrowed it and was bringing it back. He didn't want to start a scandal."

He stared at her. "Any idea who he had in mind?"

She held his gaze for a long moment before she answered. "No." She sighed. "The next day, after everyone was back, the police were called. They questioned everyone. And someone accused my father."

Marc looked at her sharply. "Just because he was the one who was alone in the house at the pertinent time?"

She hesitated. She'd run out of proven facts. Now she was going to venture into speculation. "I think someone gave them more to go on than that. Someone made some things up about my father. Someone who had a reason to need the money and might have stolen the treasure themselves."

"Need the money," he repeated softly. "So now you've got a motive."

"Maybe."

They were both silent for a few minutes, and then Marc spoke, his tone emotionless. "My family was having lots of money problems fifteen years ago. Did you know that?"

"I...no, not really." To tell the truth, that shocked her.

"Mostly tax issues as I remember it. I had to work full time in college. Marge had to give up some renovation plans she had because we didn't have the money for it. My father had some property in Hawaii and he sold that. We were scraping the bottom of the barrel for a while there."

"I didn't realize that."

He considered, then turned to look into her eyes. "You don't suspect me."

She waved that away. "Of course not."

"Or my father."

"No."

"Or the cook, or Griswold, or any of the staff."

She shrugged. "There doesn't seem to be any backing to suspect any of them."

He raised an eyebrow. "Ricky?"

"Ricky?" She was shocked at the thought. "No, of course not."

He knew the name of the person she suspected, but he set that aside. "What about a random theft? A burglar? Someone from the village?"

She shrugged. "Always a possibility."

He nodded. "And then there's the obvious one." He took a deep breath before he said it. "How about your father?"

She winced. "That was what they decided. A few days later, they arrested him. They took him up to the county detention center." Her voice trembled as she remembered. "It was horrible."

"Yes."

She took a deep breath, wishing she could blot out the memories of that time. "He claimed innocence. My mother fell apart. I had to withdraw from my school and stay home to take care of her." She shook her head, holding it together. "I don't think she ever recovered. Not really."

"I'm sorry, Torie." He looked at her, then away, raking fingers through his thick hair. "I feel a bit cut off from all this. I wasn't there, didn't know all the details. I wish I'd been more involved."

She threw out her hands, palms up. "You were away at school. You couldn't help it."

"The next thing I heard," he said, "was that the treasure had been found buried in the caves. Right where the Spaniards had put it in the beginning." He shook his head. "Seems odd, doesn't it?"

"Yes." She tried to steady her voice. "There still was no hard proof my father was involved. The police found the treasure, and he was released right after that. But..." She shrugged helplessly. "He was fired anyway. And still under a cloud."

Marc grimaced and looked out toward the ocean.

"You'd think once the treasure was found, they could have at least given him a chance," she murmured.

"Be realistic, Torie," he said a bit firmly. Then he seemed to regret his tone. He turned toward her. "Actually, my father considered your father a good friend as well as the best butler he ever had. I'm sure he tried to find a way to keep him on. I think there were others who counseled that he had to go."

Her voice hardened. "You mean Marge."

He hesitated, then coughed and looked away. "When it came to Marge, I'm afraid my father didn't seem to have much of a defense on anything."

She took a deep breath, knowing she was going to sound bitter, but determined to let it out anyway. "So because he couldn't stand up to Marge, we were thrown like refugees into the street."

His head went back and he frowned at her, but he tried to keep his tone light. "Hardly. I'm sure you drove off in a car."

She shook her head. "You know what I mean."

"I know what you mean, and I know it was painful. Unfair, too. But things in life are often unfair. Most people find a way to get over them."

She glared at him. She knew what he was saying was true, and his manner wasn't cold or lacking compassion, but these hard truths weren't what she wanted to hear right now.

"What else?" she asked shortly. "What did your father ever tell you about it all? What did he say about my father?"

Marc thought that one over for a few minutes, then raised his head and looked at her.

"My father didn't say anything about it when I came home that year. It was sort of the big unmentionable. Everyone tiptoed around it."

"Oh."

That obviously wasn't going to satisfy her. He sighed, threw her a rueful smile and dug a bit deeper.

"It wasn't until about a year later, when Ricky died that he talked to me about it. It was the night after the funeral. He'd had too much to drink and he couldn't stop crying. Neither could I. It was…pretty awful that night. But at one point, he started talking about the treasure. He said that maybe we should have left it in the caves in the first place. Maybe fate—or the ghost of Don Carlos—had tried to put it back where it belonged."

She shook her head. "I wish I could buy that."

"Yeah." He looked at her sideways. "At that point he had the treasure in a safety deposit box at the bank. No more display in the library case."

She nodded. "Did he say anything else?"

"Yes." He sighed and stretched out his arms. The sun was almost gone and it was starting to get cold. "Actually, he blamed all our troubles on that bag of gold. He thought it seemed like a curse on the family. Like nothing good had happened since the treasure was found and brought into the house." He glanced her way. "He went through the list. My mother dying. His marriage to Marge. The financial ruin he was facing. Having to fire your father. And then, Ricky."

She almost smiled. Despite everything, she felt a warm spot for Marc's dad. His heart had been in the right place most of the time. And she'd always known his marriage to Marge was a rough element in his life.

It was tempting to find a way to blame everything on Marge—but she knew that was the easy way out. She wanted to know the truth, not just something that might be true to make herself feel better.

Rising again, she walked to the cliff and watched the sky turn red as the sun disappeared over the edge of the earth. It was always startling how quickly it began to disappear once it got that close.

"Why isn't there anyone who knows anything else?" she asked into the wind. "Why doesn't someone come forward? I just have this feeling…" Throwing out her arms, she turned back to face him.

"You know, I corresponded with local authorities quite a few times over the last year, trying to see what I could dredge up. But nobody tells me anything. All the people who work in law enforcement around here are young. They're all different from the ones who worked here then. No institutional memory at all."

He nodded. "The trail has grown cold."

"But how are we going to find out just what were the facts?" she cried, her frustration quivering in her voice. "Why did this happen?"

Marc moved impatiently. "Face it, Torie. You're never going to know it all. Some things just aren't knowable."

She stared at him. "You really are cynical, aren't you?"

He held her gaze with his own hard blue one. "I try to be."

She frowned at him fiercely. "So tell me, Marc. What do you think happened? Be honest. Was my father guilty? Tell me what you think."

Marc stared back at Torie's impassioned face. What did he think? Did he have to make a statement right now? Did she really need to know everything going on in his brain?

No. What good would it do her to know?

"Forget it, Torie," he said, rising to walk toward her. "I'm not going to play that game."

It wasn't until he got a few steps away that he realized tears were running down her face.

"Torie," he began, reaching for her, but she whirled and started off in the opposite direction as though she couldn't bear for him to see her crying.

"Torie, wait."

He went after her. She knew he was coming and she started to run. The next thing she knew, she'd tripped on a rock. She'd been moving fast and the momentum sent her sprawling at the rim of the cliff, suddenly half over the edge and sliding toward the rocks below.

"Torie!"

He had her in seconds, pulling her back up to safety. She clung to him, tears forgotten as she gasped for air and looked down at the disaster she could have fallen to.

"Oh my gosh! Oh, thank God you caught me."

I'll always catch you.

He held her tightly and swallowed hard. Had he really thought that? Good thing he hadn't said it aloud.

"Are you okay?" he said instead, letting her go enough to be able to get a good look at her.

"I don't think so," she admitted, flattening her hand on his chest. "My ankle feels like it's being stabbed."

He swore softly as he pulled her up in his arms and carried her back to the fallen log. Placing her carefully, he pulled off her tennis shoe and took a look at the ankle. It was swelling fast.

He looked up at her doubtfully. "I don't think you're going to be able to walk on it."

"Oh, sure I am. I've got to." She slid down and tried. "Ouch!"

He shook his head but a smile was creeping through. "You're cute," he told her, "but silly. You can't walk on that. I'm going to have to carry you back."

"Never!" she insisted.

Not again. That first time had almost done her in. But really, it wasn't her own peace of mind she was worried about. It was a long way back to the house and she was no lightweight, no matter what he said. Gallantry was all very well, but common sense was better.

"You did that once when we didn't have that far to go. You're talking about almost a mile here, and through some rougher terrain."

"No problem."

She held him off. "Listen to me. I happen to know you have a golf cart back at the house for running around on the estate."

He looked surprised. "You're right. I forgot about that." He hesitated, then shrugged. "But I'm not going to leave you out here waiting in the dark. Besides, I want to get you to a doctor as quickly as possible."

Her ankle was throbbing and she wanted to get back to the house and put an ice pack on it. She began to relent. Once she got back to her own room, she would have time to look through the journal and…

She reached back to feel for the journal, which was supposed to be in her back pocket. It wasn't there. Panic began to race through her blood. She looked at the area around the log, trying not to be too obvious. Nothing. Then toward the edge of the cliff where she'd fallen. There it was, lying out in plain sight. She looked at Marc quickly, hoping he wouldn't see it. But how was she going to get to it without him noticing? And how was she going to get to it at all with her ankle this way?

"I'm going to carry you back," he said decisively.

"But…" She tried hard to think of a way to stop him but nothing came to her. She was beginning to think she would have to leave it behind and come back later— only hoping that a squirrel didn't take it home for some light reading.

"Ready?"

"No, I…" Nothing popped into her mind. Nothing at all.

"Oh, wait," he said. "I wanted to take some of that car wax back with me. Think you can carry it for me?" he asked her.

She nodded, suddenly hopeful.

"Okay. I'll be right back." He went back into the car barn.

She rose quickly, gritting her teeth to hold back her cry of pain. She grabbed the journal and pushed it back into her back pocket, then made her way back to the log, sinking down just as Marc reappeared at the clearing.

"Okay, let's go," he said, handing her the car-wax cans.

She breathed a sigh of relief. He hadn't noticed a thing.

He swung her up into his arms and she clung to his neck with a sigh. If nothing else, this would be a great chance to hold on to him. She was beginning to think that very action could get to be a habit with her.

He started off through the forest. It was pretty dark now, and he had to watch his step. She clung closely and breathed in the scent of him, just this side of swooning.

"You all right?" he asked.

"Absolutely." She sighed.

"How's the ankle?"

"It hurts." She tested it and flinched. "Yes, it's not too good. You know, I hope this isn't going to inhibit my activities." She frowned. "I was thinking, maybe I ought to try to talk to Billy again. He seems to be the only one who has any links to anyone who might be useful."

He hesitated. "Well, that's fine," he said slowly, "but you do understand that Billy was lying, don't you?"

"Lying?" She looked into his face. "About what?"

"My father."

"What are you talking about? I was there, remember? I know he went rock hunting with us...."

"No, not that. About not knowing anything about the treasure and what happened to it himself."

She stared at him. "How do you know?"

He shrugged. "I've got some training in intelligence work, you know. And I could see his eyes flicker a certain telltale way when the subject came up."

She thought that over for a few seconds, then looked up again. "So you think he really knows something?"

"I know he does."

She moved restlessly. "Let's go back there tomorrow. Let's talk to him."

"No." He gently squeezed her against his chest. "Let's leave it alone. Let it simmer. See what comes out in the wash."

She frowned and felt pouty. "You're mixing your metaphors."

He grinned. "But you get the general idea I was trying to communicate, don't you?"

"Yes." She looked up at him, eyes flashing. "You don't trust many people, do you?"

His face went hard as stone. "I don't trust anybody."

"Even me?"

He looked down and paused, then with a half smile, he said, "Especially you."

"Why?" She felt a sense of outrage, and yet...

"You have all the reason in the world to lie to me. Your motivations are as clear as your pretty green eyes."

And that was exactly why she wasn't going to show

him the journal until she'd read it herself. If he didn't trust her, she surely wasn't going to trust him. And that was that.

CHAPTER TEN

THE others were back sitting around the fire pit in the dark. The flames leaped high into the air, giving their faces an eerie quality.

"Do you see Carl?" Torie asked as she craned her neck to see them all.

"Yes," Marc answered. "He's there."

"Darn. I was hoping he would have given up and gone home by now."

"Listen," he said softly to her, pausing before they went in to greet the others. "I'm going to put you down by Carl. You keep him occupied. I've got to call the doctor, but as soon as I get that done, I want to go raid his room."

"What?" she cried, alarmed. "Oh no, I don't think you should do that."

"Sure I should. I want to see those insurance papers. I think they might be very interesting."

She frowned. "But I think he might be suspicious."

"Of course he is. That's why you'll sit down here by him and keep him from going up to his room while I'm in there."

"But..."

"It'll work, don't worry."

He carried her into the middle of the group. "Wounded soldier here," he announced. "I'm going in to call the doctor."

They all gathered around, everyone exclaiming over her and talking at once.

"It's just my ankle," Torie said. "It's really painful but I don't think it's life-threatening."

"Let me take a look," Lyla said, pushing through the others. "I used to work as a physician's assistant before I got married to my beloved departed husband. I might be able to call upon my lazy brain cells for some helpful memories of what to look for with these things."

"Oh," Torie said, surprised. "Thanks, Lyla. I'd appreciate it."

Marc gave her a wink and disappeared up the stairs.

"It certainly looks like a sprained ankle," Lyla said after manipulating it to moans of pain from Torie. "That means mostly ice and lots of rest are needed. If you've got some bandaging, I can wrap it up and make it almost usable for walking. Which you should keep to a minimum."

"That would be great," Torie said, truly grateful for the help from the woman.

Marge went bustling after bandages, Jimmy brought out some ice, and Lyla went in to wash her hands. Phoebe and Frank clucked over her injury, asking for details, then went inside as well. It was getting chilly. Torie was finally alone with Carl. He leaned close, his eyes bloodshot and angry.

"Do you want to explain to me what the hell is going on?"

"Carl, I …"

"I brought you here for a reason. You keep disappearing on me."

She got a chill from the fury in his eyes. She could see it throbbing at his temple. He was really upset.

"I know, Carl, but..."

"I didn't expect you to go chasing after hot young guys. I didn't realize you were that sort of girl."

She stiffened and glared at him. "I'm not 'that sort of girl' and you know it. I came to pretend to be your wife so you would have the sort of presence you might need to put in a bid on the property. Now I can see that you never planned to do any such thing. You lied to me."

"What do you care?"

"I care about being lied to. And I'm not going to help you."

"Oh yes you are," he said harshly. "Tomorrow will be the last chance. You're going to have to go with me."

"To do what?"

"Help me navigate the caves."

She gaped at him. "You may not have noticed, but I've sustained an injury. It's going to be kind of tough to make a hike to the caves with a sprained ankle."

He stared at her ankle. It was swelling up like a balloon, despite the bag of ice she'd encased it in. He started to swear, one ugly word after another, and then he surged out of his chair, turning toward the house— the house where Marc was probably going through his room right now.

"No, wait Carl," she cried, grabbing at his shirt to keep him there. "Wait. Come here. We need to talk."

"I'm done talking with you."

"No you're not. We need to work this out. Maybe we can..."

He ripped his shirt out of her hands and backed away. "Draw me a good map of the caves," he snarled. "Do that and we can talk all you want to."

She knew he was headed upstairs and she had to stop him. If he caught Marc in his room, she didn't know what would happen.

She tested her foot. Stabbing pain shot through her ankle and up her calf. She gasped with it. Too much. She couldn't do it.

"Carl," she called after him. "Come back here."

He was almost to the stairs. "Why should I?" he called back. "What have you done for me?"

"I have to tell you something. Something private. Please. Come back."

He stared at her as though weighing the possibilities, then reluctantly walked back across the patio. She almost collapsed in relief, but she couldn't let up. She had to find a way to keep him here.

"Come here," she coaxed. "Closer. I can't shout this."

Finally he came close enough and her hand shot out again, fingers tangling quickly into the fabric of his shirt, holding tight. "Closer," she said again.

He looked down as though he was afraid she was going a little crazy. "I'm as close as I'm gettin'," he said firmly.

She leaned and pulled him even closer, whether he wanted it or not, then hissed in his ear, "You're after the treasure, aren't you?"

He looked startled and tried to pull away, but she had him. He tried to peel away her fingers, but she clung on tightly, desperate to keep him from going upstairs to his room.

And then, Marc was back, and she sighed with re-

lief. Her hand loosened on the shirt and she half collapsed into her seat.

"Hello, Carl," Marc said coolly as he approached
them. "How are you doing?"

Carl grimaced and looked away. "I've been better,"
he grumbled.

"I'm sure you have." Marc's smile was humorless.
He was carrying a folder of papers and he didn't try to
hide it. Carl glanced at it and away, then did a double
take and blanched. Marc's smile widened.

"Say, Carl." He gazed at him levelly. "You know,
I don't think you ever said exactly what you do for a
living."

"Who? Me?" Carl blinked at him nervously. "Uh,
well, various things. I'm a businessman really. Mostly
import-export stuff lately."

"Ever spent any time in the insurance game?" Marc
asked him casually.

Carl stared. "Insurance game? What do you mean?"

"Ever work for an insurance company, Carl? Ever
done any claims adjustment? Fraud investigation?
Things like that?"

Carl seemed to pale. "Listen, my past work experience has nothing to do with anything. I'm not officially
applying for anything here. It's none of your business."

Marc's smile was pleased. "Thanks, Carl. That's all
I needed to know."

He handed Torie the folder and reached under her
knees to swing her up into his arms. "Come on up to
my room," he told her. "We're fixing it up as a sick bay
for you. Lyla is going to tape your ankle up and then
we'll see where we are."

Torie looked back at Carl as she was carried up the

stairs. He was staring after them, mostly trying to see what Marc had in that folder Torie was holding. And he looked very worried.

She sighed and leaned against Marc's shoulder as they left the area where they would be seen by others. "Why are we going to your room? Wouldn't mine do just fine?"

"It would not." He paused and looked down at her face. "I've had some information from my friend. He left me a message. He said, and I quote, 'Carl's one of the bad guys. Nothing outstanding on him at this time, but I wouldn't leave him alone with the silverware.'"

That was an uncomfortable thing to find out about the man she'd been pretending to be married to. She shuddered, but kept up the good fight anyway. "And how does this effect me exactly?"

"He seems to have a reputation for treating women badly. I'm not going to risk it. I'm keeping you close."

"Oh." Her gaze flickered up to his face. "So you're telling me that you're a danger-free zone yourself?" she asked him archly.

He grinned. "Hell no. But I promise to keep the rough stuff curbed for now. Until you're well and can fight for yourself."

She smiled back. "Deal," she said.

He started down the hallway. She looked at his beautiful smooth skin and the way his hair barely curled around it. She had a sudden impulse to drop a long, slow kiss on the side of his neck, but she managed to hold it back.

"So are you going to tell me what you found in Carl's room?" she asked instead.

He flashed her a smile and kicked open the door to

his room. "All in good time," he told her. "Right now, Lyla is here to bind up your ankle."

"Ah."

She looked around as he plopped her onto his king-sized bed and sure enough, there was Lyla with a Cheshire-cat grin, playing with her beads and looking truly entertained.

"So Marc tells me he's fixing this room up to be your recuperation center. How handy for him." She batted her long eyelashes his way. "And will you be staying here, too?"

"Of course." He openly laughed at her. "I have to keep an eye on her condition at all times." He shook his head. "Though it's really none of your business."

"Of course not. And yet, I have a feeling this innocent young woman might need an older, wiser friend to help guide her through the tangled thicket of the male attention I'm beginning to sense here. If you know what I mean."

Marc smiled, but dismissed her at the same time. "I know just what you mean. But I think we can do without it."

Lyla shrugged and looked at Torie. "Just keep it in mind. I'm here if you need me."

Torie smiled at her but she didn't know quite what she could say to that.

"Didn't you have a husband when you first got here?" Lyla noted, putting a double knot in her long string of glass beads and tossing the end of it over her shoulder, out of the way.

"You mean Carl?" Torie gave her a shaky smile. "That was just...well, that's inoperative now."

"Inoperative." Lyla laughed out loud. "I see. That

explains the strange situation with the separate bedrooms. I did wonder about that."

Marc chuckled. He couldn't resist. "You see, Carl is
a shy fellow—socially inept. He felt intimidated by all
you real-estate sharks and he thought he might need
Torie along for moral support."

"Ah. Perfectly understandable." By now Lyla had
manipulated the foot and analyzed what she could of
the injury to the ankle. She gave the skin a light massage, then prepared the elastic wrap. "It seems to be a
nasty one, dear," she told Torie. "But I think we can
wrap it tightly enough so that you can use it at about
fifty percent tomorrow."

"Oh, I hope so."

Lyla looked up with a smile. "Big plans?" she asked
with a smirk.

"No!" She gave the woman a look of pure annoyance. "It's just that I'd rather be able to walk than not."

"A universal desire, my dear."

Marc was laughing. "You are a sly one, Lyla."

She smiled at him, her black eyes glittering in the
lamplight. "I try to be." She patted Torie's knee as she
finished up. "Now take two pain pills and call me in
the morning." She looked up at Marc. "Have you got
something for her?"

He nodded. "Thanks, Lyla. I appreciate it."

"No problem. And don't forget to take her down to
the clinic for X-rays." She looked from Marc to Torie
and then back again, gave a small resigned shrug, and
smiled wistfully. "Have fun, you two," she said, and
she was gone.

Marc found a couple of pills and a glass of water and
then he handed her her pajamas and her toothbrush.

"Oh," she said, looking at him with wide eyes. "You went into my room too."

He frowned at her tone. "Does that bother you?"

"No, of course not." But it did. He could see it on her face. He frowned. There was that sense again that she had something to hide. He hated distrusting her, but she kept giving him cause.

Better to find out now than later, he reminded himself silently as he waited with his back turned for her to change out of her clothes. But when he turned back and looked at her, her cheeks pink, her smile irresistible, he pushed that aside.

He was going to trust her as far as it went. They were partners in this quest, at least for the moment.

"The only things I saw in your room were the pajamas I was looking for and your toothbrush," he told her. "Carl's room was a different story."

"You found the stack of papers I told you about?"

He nodded. "There were more clippings, anecdotes about gold doubloons turning up in this area during that same period years ago. And then there were the insurance records."

"On the Don Carlos Treasure?"

"Yes. Marge tried unsuccessfully to collect insurance on it a couple of times. And each time insurance agents and investigators came out and did a lot of digging."

"How did Carl get hold of that information?"

"You heard him. He practically panicked when I asked him if he worked for an insurance company. Obviously, he did. He might have seen some of the articles about the treasure and started rooting through the files, then decided to come on up and take a chance on finding it himself."

"That jerk! And here he had me believing he wanted to buy Shangri-La."

"That'll be the day."

She grew more somber. "Do you suppose any of them will buy it?" she asked him.

He shrugged. "Not if I can stop the sale," he told her.

She glanced at her jeans, draped across the back of a chair. She could just barely make out the outline of the journal in the back pocket. She was beginning to wonder if she would ever get a chance to take a real look at it. Right there in that little book were her father's words, and maybe the answers to her questions. She glanced at Marc. She should tell him she had it. She should show it to him.

But what if there was something in there that she wouldn't want him to see? What if her father had implicated himself in…something? She couldn't risk it. She had to read it first. And then, if there was nothing that needed to be hidden, she would show it to him.

She watched him, wondering.

And he was smiling at her, his head cocked to the side. "How are you feeling?"

"Fine. Really, I'm okay."

He reached out and touched her cheek and the warmth in his eyes made her heart stop. "You better be," he said gruffly. "I'm counting on it."

That Marc Huntington would look at her with such affection hardly seemed real. After all those years of thinking of him as an unattainable dream, here he was, acting as though he really liked her. Tears welled in her eyes.

"Hey." He frowned. "What's the matter?"

"Nothing." She covered his hand with her own and

tried to smile at him. "I'm just sort of wrung out, emotionally."

He searched her eyes, then nodded. "You're hungry," he said. "I've got something I've got to take care of, and then I'll be back with some soup for you. Okay?"

She nodded, wondering if she really dared to be this happy. "Okay."

He smiled and was gone, and she closed her eyes and tried to steady her heart. Here she was in Marc's bed. How had this happened? She smiled and settled in among the pillows, feeling as though she were on a cloud.

And then she remembered the journal. She listened. No sound of anyone approaching. Sliding to the edge of the bed, she reached for her jeans and grabbed the journal, with only a couple of twinges of real pain. But she had what she needed and she sat back and began to flip through it.

By the time she heard Marc coming back, she'd read enough to know her father was no thief. He'd started writing in the journal months before the treasure disappeared, and most of his entries had nothing to do with it. He made occasional notes about things that had interested him, the weather, who came to visit, discussions he and Hunt had had about politics or history. And then came the treasure and his anguish over being accused of taking it. She knew her father and she could tell that he'd had no part in it. What a relief.

Still, that didn't explain the little bag of gold coins she had in her suitcase. Where had it come from? Why? The first time she'd known anything about it had been when she'd begun packing up her mother's things. It was an emotional time. She'd finally had to admit she couldn't take care of her mother by herself any longer. She needed institutional care.

She'd found a very nice nursing home that she could barely afford. In fact, she'd had to start working at an extra job at a local restaurant, organizing banquets and setting up celebration parties, just to make ends meet. It had broken her heart to have to tell her mother she was going to have to place her in the home. Her sweet, dear little mother had looked bewildered, but she hadn't complained. Still, Torie hated to do it and she'd done a lot of the packing with tears in her eyes.

She'd been filling boxes with her mother's old clothes when she'd found the bag of gold. She'd never seen the Don Carlos Treasure with her own eyes, but she knew right away this was the same sort of thing—only smaller. When she tried to ask her mother where it had come from, she'd only looked frightened and turned away, biting her lip.

Torie could only think that her father had somehow ended up with some of the treasure—but how? Why? And that had started her journey back toward Shangri-La. She had to know the truth.

She didn't have time to read any of what Marc's father had written down. His handwriting looked like hieroglyphics and she was afraid she was probably going to need Marc to translate it for her. His writings came from a much later time period, probably just before he'd gone out on the sailboat with the treasure. Had he found out the truth? Did he know just what had happened?

She still didn't know that, but she knew from the entries in the journal that her father hadn't been guilty in the original disappearance of the treasure. Nonetheless, she still needed more facts.

When she heard Marc coming, she quickly shoved the journal under her pillow. She knew she would show it to him soon, but not yet. She needed to read what *his* father had written on those last few pages. She had a feeling that would answer some of the questions she still had.

"Hey," Marc said as he entered, a bowl of soup in his hands. "I was afraid you might be asleep already."

"No." She took the soup gratefully. It smelled wonderful.

He watched her eat for a moment, looking restless, then grimaced and raked fingers through his short hair, making it stand up like spikes on top.

"Carl's gone," he said shortly.

"What?" She stared at him. "Where did he go? Why?"

His gaze darkened and she realized he'd been curious what her reaction would be. Surely he didn't still think she might be attached to the man. She frowned, disturbed by that thought and not sure how to tell him how wrong that was.

"I told him to get out. He's not here for what he claimed he came for. No reason to let him stay."

"Oh."

"Don't worry about how you're going to get home. I'll take you."

She blinked a few times, thinking all this over. "But if Carl's gone, I suppose I might as well go back to my room," she said.

He shook his head slowly, warmth coming back into

his gaze. "Not a chance," he told her. "Now that I've got you here, I'm not going to let you go."

She laughed. She couldn't help herself. This was all so crazy. Somehow she had to assimilate this through-the-looking-glass present with the past she remembered and still had to live with. And that reminded her of something.

"Last night, didn't you bring my family photo album back from our attic adventure?" she asked him.

He nodded. "Ready to look at it?" he asked her.

Was she ready? It might not be easy and she was in a pretty emotional state as it was. She bit her lip and told herself to stop being a baby.

"If you've got it here, I'd love to."

"I've got it." He took it out of the closet and handed it to her. "Mind if I look at it, too?" he asked.

She smiled at him and he took that as an invitation to come in next to her on the bed. They leaned back against the pillows as they leafed through the album. There were pictures of her mother, looking young and happy in a way she hadn't been for years, and her father, tall and dignified, looking like a man you would put all your confidence in. How could anyone have thought he was a thief? Her heart swelled as she remembered how it had been.

And there she was as a shorter, rounder version of the current Victoria Sands. It made her laugh to see it.

Marc looked at the pictures and shook his head. "How did I miss the gorgeous creature you were preparing to turn into?" he teased her. "Good thing you came back. I needed to be hit on the head with this one."

She laughed and gazed up at him. He stopped smiling and leaned down to kiss her.

She opened to him, still amazed he might want her.
He said such great things to her but she was scared to
believe him. She couldn't let this go too far. She couldn't
risk being loved and left behind. Too much good had
already been snatched from her. She couldn't let it happen with him.

He pulled her up so that her body was molded to his
and she sighed with shivering pleasure. He was so hard
and strong it took her breath away. The thought of making love to this man sent her head spinning. But she felt
it. As his tongue explored her mouth, as her hands explored his skin, she felt the small, aching sweetness of
desire begin deep inside her.

She pulled back but he followed, turning so that he
was half lying on top of her, and the tiny desire leaped
into flame. She had to stop this now or she would be
burned away with the fire.

"Marc," she whispered, but he didn't seem to hear
her.

"Marc." She pushed hard against his chest. "Stop."

He groaned and rolled away, leaving her feeling
empty and alone. She closed her eyes and tried to get
her pulse rate down to normal.

And then he was back again, but this time sweetly,
kissing her eyelids, touching her cheek.

"I'm sorry," he told her softly. "I didn't mean to scare
you. Torie, listen to me. I would never, never hurt you.
And if you ever want me to stop, tell me and I swear,
I'll stop."

She smiled at him tremulously. "I didn't want you
to stop," she admitted to him. "But we have to. We just
can't…"

He nodded and took up her hand and kissed her fingers. "I know. You're right." He smiled and settled back beside her. "Okay. Just let me catch my breath."

She leaned her head against him, happier than she thought she'd ever been. Was she in love? What a question. She'd been in love with this man since she was about ten years old.

It took a few minutes, but they were back discussing their mutual problem very soon. They still needed to unravel the mystery that was the Don Carlos Treasure.

"You know, I was thinking," Marc said. "My father sent me a long, rambling letter just before he died. He didn't tell me just what he was planning to do, but if I'd read between the lines, I think I would have realized something was up. And he told me a lot of things I didn't understand at the time." He made a face. "I wish I had that letter with me. I have a feeling it might clear up a lot of this."

She hesitated. That, along with the journal, might fill in all the blanks for both of them. "Do you still have it somewhere?'

"I hope so. I'll have to look for it."

She should show him the journal. Of course she should. It was time.

"Marc," she began, steeling herself for the inevitable. He wasn't going to be happy that she'd kept it from him this long.

But a knock on the door interrupted her.

"Marc, you want to come down to the library?" It was Jimmy's voice. "Your mother has something she wants to talk to you about."

Marc groaned, but he answered. "Sure. I'll be right down." He dropped a kiss on her lips and rolled off the bed. "You get some sleep," he told her. "Your eyes are so dark they look haunted. You need some rest."

She nodded, half sorry she couldn't get the issue of the journal over with, half relieved to have it wait a bit. "Okay." She smiled at him. "See you in the morning."

"Sleep tight," he said, pausing for a moment to look back at her. His look was full of mysterious things she couldn't quite identify, but she thought she saw a warm sense of affection and a strong thread of hot desire in those eyes. It curled her toes to see it and she held on to that feeling for a long time after he went out the door.

CHAPTER ELEVEN

WHEN Torie woke up, sunlight was streaming through the room and Marc was coming in with a breakfast tray. "I've got coffee and eggs and toast and some news."

She stretched, feeling luxurious. "News first," she said. "Then we'll see if I can stomach breakfast."

"You're expecting it to be bad news?"

"Always," she admitted. "I always want to be prepared for that."

He set down the tray. "Well, it just happens that this time you are pretty much right." He looked straight at her. "The Texan has signed on the bottom line. He's buying the place."

"What?" she gasped. "Oh Marc, no!"

He turned away and she was sure he didn't want her to see how anguished he was over this. Or maybe just plain angry.

"What will you do?"

He turned back and she saw that her second guess was the right one. He was mad. There was no way he was going to let this happen without a fight.

"I haven't worked that out yet," he told her, his voice carefully controlled. "The problem is, my friend checked him out and he's for real. No baggage in his background. And he's got the money."

"Oh."

He shrugged. "But there's got to be something… some way. I just haven't thought of it yet." He smiled at her. "And I've got you on my side. Right? Maybe together…" He shrugged again.

She reached for the journal. She didn't even think about it. It was way past time she should have shown it to him. She held it out without a word.

He stared at it, then reached to take it. Just as his hand closed around it, a knock came on the door.

Jimmy again. "Hey Marc? Somebody named Billy is here to see you. He says he needs to tell you something about your father that you should know."

Marc glanced at the door, then at Torie. "How long have you had this?" he asked her, his voice rough and gravelly, his eyes dark with sudden suspicions.

"Marc?" Jimmy called again. "You in there?"

"How long?" he asked again, his eyes all intensity.

"Since yesterday. I found it in the car after we had the wine."

His gaze darkened. "Have you read it all?"

"No. Just what my father wrote. Your father wrote in it, too. I didn't read that."

Marc gave her one last long look, then shoved the journal into his pocket and turned to the door.

"I'm coming," he said.

And this time he didn't look back.

Torie groaned and fell back against the pillows. It shouldn't have happened this way. Now he thought she was keeping things from him—and he was right. She had. But there were reasons.

She had to go down and explain. Sliding out of bed, she pulled off her pajamas and quickly put back on her jeans and sweater. Going into the adjoining bathroom, she freshened up and combed her hair.

Looking into the mirror, she saw a familiar face, but there was a new light shining in her eyes. Determination. She was beginning to understand that she had something within her reach, something important, something to fight for. Finding out the truth about her father and the past was important too, but this wasn't about the past. This was about the future—her future. She'd never thought she would find someone like Marc to love. And now....maybe she would. Maybe. As long as she didn't mess it up.

She'd barely stepped out of the bathroom when the bedroom door swung open and Carl stepped in, closing the door behind him with a snap.

She gasped, and two seconds later wished she'd screamed instead, but by then it was too late. He had her in a choke hold and something made of cold steel was jabbing against her back.

"Just shut up and do what I say," he hissed into her ear. "I've got a gun. You don't want to find out whether I'll use it or not. I'm at the end of the road here, baby. If I don't get what I want today, I might as well put this gun to my own head and pull the trigger. So don't think I'll hesitate to use it on you."

She tried to talk but his hold was so tight, she could barely breathe.

"Shut up. We're going out to the caves. You're going

to show me where that treasure is or neither of us might come back."

"I can't…" she managed to grind out.

"I know. Your damn foot. Don't worry. I've got the golf cart at the back door. If we can get that far, we'll go all the way."

He yanked her toward the door and she tried to comply. She had to in order to keep from choking. He hurried her along the hallway, then down the stairs. She gazed around as much as she could with her head in his hammer-lock grip, but she didn't see anyone. A moment later, he thrust her into the golf cart and started it up, racing out down the hill and toward the beach. She sat back, gasping for air. He didn't have his hold on her any longer, but he did have a gun pointed her way. She stared at it, looking right down the barrel. She'd never been so scared in her life.

Marc went down the stairs and into the library with a dark scowl on his face. Every time he started to think he could trust Torie, she did something like this—hiding the damn journal from him.

Why? There didn't seem to be any point to it unless she was still trying to help Carl in some way. Maybe she felt like she owed him one. Who knew? But he didn't like it.

He stepped into the library, his gaze involuntarily going to the empty display case where the treasure used to be. And then he saw Billy waiting for him, looking nervous.

"Hey, Billy. What's up?"

"I've got something I need to tell you. I should have told you and Torie yesterday, but I wasn't sure…."

"Go ahead. I'm all ears."

Billy laughed shortly and moved jerkily. "I have to tell you the truth, man. I…I know what it's like to miss your father and…I just had to tell you the truth."

"What about, Billy?" Marc's voice was patient but only with effort. He wanted to shake the younger man and get him to hurry up and tell him what he had to say.

"About a week before your father…went out in the sailboat, he came to see me. I was still in high school, but I was planning to go to college in Oregon. He asked me how I was going to pay for that and I said I didn't know. Try to get a job on campus, I guess. Take out loans. Whatever." He looked down and shuffled his feet, then looked back up and smiled slowly. "When I told him I was going to study geology, because of all I'd learned from him on those rock-hunting trips, he was tickled. And he…" Billy's face contorted. "He gave me something he thought might help when the time came. But I wasn't supposed to do anything with it or tell anyone about it for at least five years."

Marc nodded. He knew where this was going. He'd already guessed at least a part of it. "How much did he give you?"

Billy shook his head. "It wasn't money. Exactly."

"I know. It was gold doubloons, wasn't it? Old Spanish treasure."

Billy looked guilt-stricken. "Yeah. A whole handful of them." He shook his head again. "They were worth a lot. I waited five years, like he said, and then…" He drew his breath in sharply. "Those coins pretty much paid my way through college."

Marc stared at him for a long moment, and then he smiled. "I'm glad. And thanks for telling me about that."

Billy hesitated. "Do you think they were part of the Don Carlos Treasure?"

Marc shrugged. "What do you think?"

Billy sighed, then spoke softly after looking around to make sure no one was in earshot. "I wasn't the only one, you know. He gave some to Griswold. And to my mother. And to a couple of other people who worked at the house over the years."

Marc groaned. No wonder the word got out that the doubloons were still being held on the property. He should have known.

He talked to Billy for a bit longer, then walked out with him toward where his motorcycle was parked. He heard the golf cart start up and looked back at the house casually, wondering who was using it. As it began to careen off toward the beach, he got a flash of the driver— and his passenger.

Carl. And he had Torie with him.

He stood frozen for a moment, trying to understand what this meant. Was Torie taking Carl out to the caves? Was she still that close to him that she would help him that way? No. He couldn't really believe that. And yet, hadn't she held out on him where the journal was concerned?

"Damn it, Torie," he muttered, clenching his hands into fists.

But what if Carl was taking her out there against her will? Either way, he had to stop it.

But how? He couldn't run fast enough to catch them. He whirled.

"Give me the keys to your bike," he ordered Billy. "Quick! I need to borrow it."

"What? Are you going to take it out into the sand?" Billy asked, horrified. "You can't do that."

"There's a compacted trail," he said. "Come on, man, I've got to get Torie away from that bastard."

"Oh. Well okay then." He handed over the keys and Marc ran for the bike, kick-starting it into a roar and taking off toward the caves. No matter what, he was going to make sure Torie was okay.

Torie tried to get her bearings. She still couldn't speak. It felt as though Carl had crushed her vocal chords. She looked ahead. The caves were coming into view. What was she going to do once they got there?

Her voice wasn't working but her mind was clear and focused. She'd known those caves well when she was a child and her visit two days before had reminded her of a lot. She didn't know of any current treasure hidden there, but she did know of a sort of secret area that you could only find if you were looking for it. If she could lure Carl into that, she knew how to get back out again and he wouldn't have a clue. That was it. That was what she would try to do.

The only sticking point was the gun. What if he shot her before she got him into the blind alley she planned to lead him to? What if he realized she was trying to trick him? Then she would be sunk. A shiver went down her spine and she glanced at the man beside her. His face was contorted with rage and hate. Just looking at him scared her. He might do anything at any moment. Would it be worth it to try to attack him right now and throw him off? No, probably not. That gun was just too dangerous. The man was just too dangerous. Fear quivered all through her.

And then she heard the motorcycle. Looking up, she saw Marc coming down the trail. Her heart leaped up and she glanced at Carl. He'd seen Marc too, and he raised his arm, aiming the gun at him.

"No!" she cried, throwing herself at his arm and knocking the gun out of his hand. At the same time, the golf cart hit loose sand and overturned, throwing her out as it tipped, smashing Carl beneath the steel frame. Marc arrived, stopping the motorcycle in a spray of sand and running toward them.

And she went out like a light.

She woke up on the couch with a blanket over her. She tested all her limbs. She seemed to be okay, except for a wicked headache. As she sat up, Lyla came into the room.

"Hey there, Torie," she said. "What a lot of excitement. I can't tell if you were the gun moll, the damsel in distress or the hero of this whole story."

"What whole story?" she asked, blinking and wishing her head would stop throbbing.

"I guess you did sleep through part of it, didn't you? Well, it seems Carl was not only not your husband, he was a complete crook. You helped Marc catch him. The cops have come and taken him away."

"Oh. Is Marc okay?"

She shrugged. "He looks fine to me. He went with Carl and the police to take care of the paperwork." She sighed. "But I'm leaving myself. Now that the Texan is buying the place, there's no reason for me to stick around."

Torie winced. "Where are you going?"

"Down to Los Angeles. Home."

Torie took a deep breath. More than anything, she wanted to go home. "Can I ride along with you?" she asked. "If Carl's in jail, I guess he won't be driving me."

Lyla laughed. "Sure thing, honey. I'll be glad for the company. But I want to get going in about ten minutes. Think you can make that?"

"Sure." Torie rose from the couch, only wobbling a little bit. "Just give me time to get my suitcase together. I'll meet you out at your car."

She went up the stairs carefully, then went into her room and pulled her suitcase out from under the bed. Reaching in, she drew out the bag of gold coins and looked at it. Then she hurried down the hallway and placed the gold on Marc's bed. Pulling out a pen and a piece of paper, she wrote him a note.

"I think this belongs to you. I found it with my mother's things when I had to move her to a nursing home. This was why I was afraid maybe my father had done something with the treasure after all. I had to come and find out the truth. Now I know that he didn't do it. But I still don't know why he had this bag of gold doubloons. So I'm giving it back."

And that was that. She threw her clothes into her case and headed for the parking area.

"Good bye, Shangri-La," she whispered, looking back at the house. She was surprised to note she didn't have tears in her eyes. "Good bye, Marc. Good bye dream."

And she headed home.

It was almost a week later and she hadn't heard a word from anyone at Shangri-La. She had heard from the police and she'd given a statement about what had happened with Carl. They'd told her she might have to testify. That wasn't a pleasant prospect.

But nothing from Marc. With every day that passed, her hopes grew dimmer, and she was actually getting a bit angry as well. After all, he could at least tell her what his father had written in the journal. She knew he was annoyed with her, but he could at least do that. Still, a part of her wasn't surprised. She'd known from the beginning that a relationship between her and Marc wasn't in the cards. She'd never thought of herself as the Cinderella type.

The bruises on her neck were still visible, but her ankle was doing fine. She'd gone to see her mother and had tried to explain to her that she had found evidence that her father was innocent of everything, but her mother didn't seem to understand what she was talking about. The visit was frustrating, because actually, she didn't have any proof to show her.

And there was still the mystery of the bag of gold. Why hadn't she heard anything from Marc? Maybe he'd given up as well. Now that the Texan was buying the estate, what was there for him to stick around for? He'd probably gone back to wherever it was he'd been over the last year since he got out of the Navy. It was so annoying that she didn't even know that about him. She hardly knew anything, and here she'd thought she might be building a bond between them. She'd been living in a fantasy.

It was Friday. She'd promised her mother she would take her out for ice cream. She pulled up in front of the home and walked to her mother's room with a heavy heart. She'd been so full of hope when she'd left the week before for Shangri-La. And she had nothing to show for it.

As she drew near, she could tell there was someone in the room with her mother. That was strange. The women in the home didn't do much visiting. Who could it be?

"Hi, Mom," she called as she came into the little room. She turned the corner and there was Marc, sitting beside her mother's chair, holding her hand. She stared at him, then looked at her mother. Her eyes were bright and her cheeks were pink. She looked almost like her old self.

"Hi, Torie," Marc said, as though they'd just seen each other somewhere in the last day or so. "I was just telling your mother how good it was to see you again. It was so good, in fact, that I decided I ought to come down and see her, too. Renewing old connections and all that."

Torie sank into a chair and stared at him. "Hi," she said weakly. She was grinning like a loon and blushing like a rose. She could feel it. The smile in his eyes sent her heart soaring.

It was okay. He didn't hate her. Tears welled in her eyes.

"Hey," he said, setting aside her mother's hand and reaching for hers. "Are you okay?"

"I'm fine," she said, embarrassed at how choked her voice sounded. "I'm just…oh, Marc!" Tears were spilling down her face and she was beginning to sob.

He rose and pulled her to her feet, holding her tightly and rocking her gently. "Torie, Torie, didn't you know I'd come and get you as soon as I could?"

"No," she said wetly. "I didn't know that at all."

He turned and smiled at her mother. "Excuse us, Mrs. Sands," he said. "Torie's been through a lot this last week and I've got to take care of her."

"You just go ahead, dear," the woman said, nodding approvingly. "I love her, too."

"Mother!" She hadn't heard that many words from her mother in years. Marc truly knew how to work miracles. She melted in his arms and cried until the tears stopped coming, and then he kissed her face and they all went for ice cream.

Sitting in the little ice cream parlor, he explained a lot to her. And later, when they took her mother back to the home and then went to Torie's apartment and sat on the couch together, he told her more.

"I found that letter my father wrote me shortly before he died," he said. "Now that I know what he was talking about, it was very clear he wanted to let me know about the writings in the journal without letting anyone else—such as Marge—know he'd told me where to look for it."

"So the journal was the key, just as I thought."

"You were right. Your father left it behind, and my father found it in the attic of your house. He realized there was no way he could hide the truth any longer. He'd done your father a terrible injustice and he felt it deeply. And yet, he wasn't strong enough to make Marge pay for what she'd done."

"And what had she done exactly?"

"From the beginning, she was looking for ways to get some funds together. She wanted to travel, wanted to renovate the house, wanted to have lavish parties. And my father was rapidly going broke. So she hatched a scheme to hide the Don Carlos Treasure in the caves and claim the insurance on it."

"That weekend when everyone was gone."

"Yes. She came back and took the treasure and hid it, then left and pretended she'd been gone the whole time, too."

"Then when the insurance investigators began to suspect as much…."

"She accused your father of having done it. There was never any proof, and when the investigators found the treasure in the cave, the whole thing fell apart on her."

"So your father felt guilty that he'd fired my father and acted like he might be the one who'd done it."

"Right." Marc shook his head. "And once he couldn't hide the truth any longer, he couldn't live with the guilt."

She frowned speculatively. "So he decided to take the treasure down to the bottom of the sea with him."

"Yes."

"Wow." She made a face. "So sad." Then she had another thought. "And yet, doubloons started appearing all over the place."

"Yes." He moved restlessly. "That's what puzzled me, because I knew my father wouldn't lie. If he said he was going to take the treasure down, he took it down."

"And where did our little bag of gold come from? Finding it made me so scared that my father might have been involved after all."

"He wrote about that in your father's journal. He brought it to your mother, hoping to help her after all she'd been through. He seems to have presented most of the people who used to work for us with at least a few of the coins. Sort of settling scores before he took his life."

Torie shook her head, truly bewildered. "But how…?"

"I'm getting to that. Here's the good part. The Don Carlos Treasure is safely at the bottom of the sea. But there's more gold in the caves. Lots of it." He said it slowly so it would sink in, then grinned at her. "A pirate's treasure trove of it. And my father's writings tell how to get to it."

"Oh." The entire concept of more gold took some getting used to.

"Even after reading his instructions, I wasn't sure if it wasn't just a fantasy of his. I had to work hard out there in the caves. It involved taking apart a whole ledge and getting to the space behind it." He smiled at her. "But I've got it now. And I've used it."

She gazed at him blankly. "What do you mean?"

"I outbid the Texan. I'm buying Shangri-La."

She gasped. "No!"

"Yes. Marge and Shayla are already headed to the Bahamas. I promised not to have her prosecuted for some of the things she's done if she would leave quietly. And she agreed."

"Oh, Marc!"

The look he gave her now was melting. "So now we're set."

"We?"

"We," he repeated. "You've always wanted to live at Shangri-La again, haven't you?"

She could hardly breathe. "Of course, but…"

He touched her cheek. "We'll get married on the patio overlooking the caves and the ocean."

"Oh!" Her head was spinning.

"And we'll bring your mother to live in the gatehouse. We'll hire full-time care for her there."

Torie sat and stared at him, studying every nook and cranny of his handsome face. She couldn't believe it. Was this real?

"Come here," he said, smiling at her.

She blinked at him. "Why?"

He touched her cheek again. "I haven't really kissed you yet."

She shook her head very slowly. She was still worried. "You're not supposed to kiss me."

"Why not?"

"Because we're not here for that. We have thinking to do."

He hooked his hand around her neck and began tugging her closer. "Change your plans," he told her earnestly. "Because kissing is definitely going to happen."

She blinked at him. "Really?"

He nodded. "The urge to kiss a beautiful woman is a powerful force. I've held it off as long as I can."

Now she looked truly worried. "Stop teasing me."

"I'm not teasing you. You're the most beautiful woman I've ever known. And you're going to be mine."

She searched his eyes. "Really? You really want me?"

"More to the point, do you really want me?" He smiled. "Don't you want to kiss me?"

She was melting again, and that was letting the joy in. "Marc Huntington, I've wanted to kiss you since I was ten years old."

"Then come here. We've got some time to make up for."

* * * * *

A PREGNANCY,
A PARTY
& A PROPOSAL

BY
TERESA CARPENTER

Teresa Carpenter believes that with love and family anything is possible. She writes in a Southern California coastal city surrounded by her large family. Teresa loves writing about babies and grandmas. Her books have rated Top Picks by *RT Book Reviews*, and have been nominated Best Romance of the Year on some review sites. If she's not at a family event, she's reading, or writing her next grand romance.

For Gabrielle, the younger twin,
pragmatic, dedicated, witty, and a very hard worker.
You're going to make a great pharmacist.
I love you, babe.

CHAPTER ONE

"'TWO LINES MEANS PREGNANT.'" Lauren Randall read the early detection instructions. "'One line, not pregnant.'"

Simple enough. Perched on the side of the bed in a long blue robe, heart beating a mile a millisecond, she scrunched her eyes closed—a cowardly act entirely unlike her—and then opened them to look at the stick.

Two lines.

She blinked. Looked again. Still two lines.

"Oh, boy." She blew out a pent-up breath. Her mind spun with the news. She was going to be a mother. Strolling to the bedroom's picture window, she stared unseeing at the Pacific Ocean.

Her hand went to her waist. She was expecting a baby.

Ray Donovan's baby. Mind-boggling. This type of thing didn't happen to her. She was too organized, too controlled. She didn't have unprotected sex. She *hadn't* had unprotected sex. But a broken condom might have changed her life…forever.

She glanced at the stick in her hand. Yep, still two lines.

"Oh, my." A baby.

A tiny part of her was thrilled at the knowledge. She was having a *baby*! Would he or she have Lauren's blond hair and light brown eyes? Or Ray's sandy, slightly darker locks and blue eyes?

Just thinking about it sent the more rational side of her reeling. A child was not in her current five-year plan.

Certainly not a child with a domineering man incapable of standing still for two whole minutes.

The sound of pounding drew her gaze down. Below her the lush garden of the Santa Barbara estate was being transformed into a wedding paradise. The day had dawned sunny and bright and, according to the meteorologists, might reach seventy degrees. Given it was Valentine's Day, they were lucky. February weather could be unpredictable in Southern California.

The event promised to be spectacular. On the edge of the property a white-columned gazebo stood against a backdrop of green hedges and long-standing trees, beyond which the vast Pacific Ocean flowed on forever, symbolic of the unending devotion about to be declared.

Short columns on which sat rose ball topiaries created the aisle. White chairs with silver sashes provided seating for the guests. A huge white tent graced the middle of the lawn and wood flooring had been put down. The tent-poles had been encased in columns to match the gazebo and thousands of white lights were being draped across the ceiling to give the impression of dancing under the stars.

More rose topiaries acted as centerpieces on the round tables at the dining end. Curved couches ringed the dance floor at the other end. The overall vision was elegant, yet understated, and *her* By Arrangement team had pulled it off beautifully.

Co-owners of By Arrangement, Lauren and Tori had both taken on new assistants at the start of the year. They were working the event, but the rest of the jobs had vendors in place, thus freeing their staff to attend as guests.

Shortly Lauren would be walking down the aisle toward Ray. Not as bride to his groom, but as maid of honor to his best man. Today was not her big day, but her twin's. Tori would marry the man she loved in a romantic ocean-view ceremony in a little over two hours.

If that gave Lauren a pinch of envy it was only because her sister was so happy. Difficult not to want that for herself.

But it was only a pinch. After a bad scare in college, she'd put her career in front of romance. So far she had few regrets. Lauren liked where she was in life. Of course she'd need to recalibrate now she was going to have a child to consider.

So, a wedding for her sister and a baby for her. The timing of the discovery was extraordinary. Was this some kind of karmic message? Or perhaps a spiritual nudge?

Now, *there* was a cosmic joke—because "marriage" and "Ray" were two words that didn't belong in the same sentence, or even paragraph. Heck, they wouldn't be in the same novel.

And if she hadn't been playing ostrich—again, totally unlike her—she would have known she was pregnant a week ago. She'd certainly suspected, with the nausea and the tenderness in her breasts. But she'd been busy and in denial—a slick combination for avoiding the inevitable.

There'd been too much to do, what with last-minute details for the wedding and family coming into town for the rehearsal. Seeing Ray again was what had prompted her to pick up the early pregnancy testing kit. She couldn't contemplate walking down the aisle to him without knowing the truth. Not that knowing the truth helped now that it was a yes.

Well, no time to brood about it now.

Tossing the stick in the trash, she moved to the closet to take down her dress. It was past time to join Tori and their mother in Tori's room to get ready.

A knock sounded at the door. Carrying the dress, she opened the door to her mother.

Like Lauren, her mom already had her hair and make-up done. Garrett, Tori's fiancé and owner of Obsidian Studios, had arranged for three professional hairstylists and make-up artists to come to the house to prepare the wedding party for the event. Her mom looked lovely, with her hair swept up in a sleek French twist and the expert application of cosmetics. But then she looked just as pretty with no make-up and her hair in a ponytail.

To Lauren, she was just Mom.

"Oh, Mom." She launched herself into Liz Randall's arms, letting the scent of lavender comfort her.

The news of her baby nearly tripped off Lauren's tongue. She pressed her lips together to prevent the words from spilling. This was Tori's special day. Lauren would never do anything to disrupt her twin's wedding day.

"Hey." Her mother's arms closed around her, careful not to crush the dress she held. "Are you okay?"

"Yes," she lied. She wouldn't be okay until this day was over and the certainty of running into Ray no longer existed. And, truthfully, the hug did make her feel better. She forced her mind to switch gears. "Our girl is getting married."

"I know." Liz gave her another squeeze before stepping back. "She won't be right next door anymore, but we have to remember we're not losing her—we're gaining a new son and brother." She tweaked the ends of Lauren's hair and studied her closely. "Are you sure you're okay? You're a little pale."

"I'm fine." Lauren hooked her arm through her mother's as they walked down the hall to the master suite. "I'll still miss her."

"She's your partner. You'll see her nearly every day."

"It won't be the same."

No, and their lives were going to change even more drastically than her mom knew.

"Different, yes, but in a good way." Liz was a glass half-full gal. "Especially when we start getting little ones to play with. You two will be twenty-nine in a couple of months. I've waited a long time to be a grandmother."

Yeah, well, her wait was nearly up.

"Oh!" Liz exclaimed. "Maybe she'll have twins."

Lauren's stomach did a little flip. She swallowed hard. Okay, she wasn't ready to think about having twins.

Down the way a door opened and Ray Donovan stepped into the hall. He wore jeans and a muscle-clinging green T-shirt. His shaggy dark blond hair had been trimmed considerably since she'd seen him last night. It was brushed back at the sides and a little wild on top. He looked entirely too yummy for her peace of mind.

He hesitated at the head of the stairs, his blue gaze traveling between her and her mother. He lifted his camera, aimed it in their direction.

"Ray, stop that. We're not dressed yet. Where are you going?" Her mother pointed to the car keys in his hand. "You should be getting ready."

He pocketed the keys. "I have an errand. I'll be back in plenty of time." With a last glance at Lauren, which she avoided, he headed downstairs.

For a wild moment she wondered how he would deal with twins. But her mind refused to wrap around the concept so she pulled her focus back to Tori.

"Mom, I think we should let her get through the wedding before we have her barefoot and pregnant."

"Sweetheart…" Liz patted Lauren's hand "…who are you kidding? Tori will be barefoot before the end of the night."

The statement was so true they were giggling when the door in front of them opened and Tori stood there in sexy curls, a silky white robe, and bare feet. "Where have you two been?"

Lauren met her mother's golden gaze, so like her own, and they both burst out laughing.

Ray Donovan shifted his wide shoulders in the custom-made tuxedo. Weddings gave him hives. *Been there, almost did that, never plan to do it again.* A fact not even his good buddy Garrett knew. It had happened so long ago Ray liked to pretend it had never happened at all.

Pacing the study, or "the groom's room", as Lauren's new assistant had corrected him, Ray twitched at his tie. He was slowly suffocating.

Thinking of Lauren didn't help at all. Contrary woman. The honey-eyed blond was the hottest armful he'd ever held, but way too stubborn for his taste when they weren't locked in a clinch. Their fling, for want of a better word, was over.

Until two days ago he hadn't seen her since Christmas, when she'd called time on their trysts.

How stunning to realize he'd actually missed her. But any hope of expending his nervous energy by reigniting the chemistry between them while they were hooked up for the wedding festivities had fizzled out when she had refused to meet his gaze at the rehearsal. Or any time since.

Okay. Message received.

All for the best. In spite of his hopeful initial reaction, he'd been truly unnerved as he'd watched her walk down the aisle toward him. The sight had been a punch to the gut. He hadn't stopped twitching since. Confirmation that he'd been smart to keep it casual, to let her end things between them.

He paused in front of a gilded mirror. He smoothed his short sandy hair back into place and straightened his tie. *Pull it together,* he silently chided himself. *You're sounding more like a wuss than a director known for going into the trenches with his stuntmen and actors.*

"Relax," Garrett said from his place behind the desk. "Anyone would think it was you getting married instead of me."

"I don't know how you can be so calm."

Ray dropped into the chair in front of the desk, picked up his camera and shot the groom. To occupy his hands, as well as his mind, he'd decided to give the bride and groom the gift of an insider's perspective on their wedding: pictures and videos no photographer would have access to.

"The waiting is excruciating. How much longer before this gig gets going?"

Garrett's gaze shifted to the mantel clock. "Soon. And it's easy to be calm when you're sure of what you're doing."

"Marriage is a trap for the unwary. Standing up there in front of everyone is a lonely place to be."

Okay, he knew that was warped even as the words slipped out. His memories had no place here.

"I won't be alone." Garrett laughed off the outrageous comment. "I'll be joined by the woman I love. Until then you'll be by my side."

Garrett opened the bottom drawer in the solid oak desk and pulled out a bottle of aged whiskey and a single crystal glass. After pouring a good dollop into the glass, he pushed it across the oak surface to Ray.

"Maybe this will help settle your nerves."

"No, thanks." Ray turned down the shot. Normally he'd accept and relish the burn. Today he'd remain stone-cold sober. The way he felt, adding alcohol was not a good idea.

"I don't understand you, dude." Garrett shook his head. "You're the one who told me I'd be safe with Tori."

"It's easy to see she makes you happy." Ray ran a hand over his jaw. Just because marriage wasn't for him didn't mean others couldn't benefit from the bond. "And of course you have that whole Spidey sense of approval going for you."

Apparently the twins were natural matchmakers and got a special "feeling" when they saw two people who belonged together. Lauren had gotten the feeling about Garrett and Tori, but hadn't said anything until after they were engaged.

Garrett arched a dark eyebrow. "Mock if you want. I'm reaping the rewards."

"Sorry. The truth is you deserve the best. Don't mind me—weddings make me twitchy."

"So you said when I asked you to be my best man. Thanks for doing this for me."

"You're the closest thing I have to a brother. Of course I'm here for you."

"What's your deal anyway?"

Ray shook his head. "Ancient history. Too depressing for the occasion."

Too depressing, period. He didn't talk or think about those times.

A knock sounded at the door and Lauren's assistant stuck her head in. "It's time, gentlemen."

"We'll be right there," Garrett assured her, and surged to his feet. He looked at Ray as he rose too. "Are you ready for this?"

Ray waved Garrett forward, then clapped him on the back when he passed. "Let's get you hitched."

Outside, Ray stood at his friend's side in the shade of the gazebo as music filled the air and the bridal party started toward them. Nick Randall escorted his mother to the front row. As soon as they were seated, Lauren began her journey down the rose-strewn runner.

Ray couldn't take his eyes off her. She wore a strapless, figure-hugging silver gown, showing her curves to sweet advantage. The fading sun gleamed in golden curls swept to one side, leaving one creamy shoulder bare. She grew more stunning the closer she got.

He completely missed the bride walking down the aisle as his gaze lingered on the maid of honor. Watching her, he remembered their first heated encounter in the laundry room of his home on Thanksgiving. Desire stirred.

Not wanting to embarrass himself, or his friend, he turned his attention—and his camera—to the ceremony. The officiate spoke, and then Garrett and Tori exchanged the poignant vows they'd written themselves. Weddings might make Ray itch, but as a film director he recognized powerful dialogue when he heard it.

He received the signal to hand over the rings. Garrett kissed his bride. The officiate introduced the couple as Mr. and Mrs. Black. And finally the time came for Ray to touch Lauren as they moved to follow the couple up the aisle in a reverse procession.

As before, she refused to look at him as he linked her arm around his.

"You look beautiful." He laid his hand over hers and squeezed. Forget her decree. He wasn't ready to let her go yet. Changing her mind was exactly the distraction he needed.

She bunched her fingers into a fist, but didn't look at him.

"You girls outdid yourselves with the decorations."

She rolled her amber eyes. "You could care less about the decorations."

"Not true. As a director, I admire a well-organized scene."

"I'm sure Tori will be glad you approve. It's her vision."

They reached the end of the aisle. Lauren immediately pulled free of him.

"Don't wander off. We'll be doing photos in a moment."

"Yes," he tossed out with droll humor. "I got a copy of the itinerary."

That drew her gaze as she narrowed her eyes at him. "Behave."

He lifted an eyebrow. "Where's the fun in that?" He leaned close, inhaled her sweet scent—honeysuckle and soap—and whispered, "Meet me in the laundry room in twenty minutes."

A blush added color to her rose-dusted cheeks. But, oh, such warm eyes weren't meant to give off chills. Her hands went to her shapely hips, but before she could speak she was drawn into a hug as friends and family descended on the wedding party.

"You're a piece of work," she managed in an aside between greetings. "What about your date?"

"I'm stag tonight." He shook hands and nodded as people stopped in front of him. In a short break between one guest and the next he sent her a sultry look over his shoulder. "There's been no one since you."

"What? I'm supposed to feel sorry for you?" She snorted, then had to paste on a smile when her grandmother gave her an odd look. "Spare me, please. You're a world-class director. You could have a woman on your arm with the snap of your fingers."

"I pine for you," he said, and lifted Grandma Randall's hand to his mouth to kiss her fingers. "So nice to meet you. It's easy to see where Tori gets her beauty."

The older woman twittered prettily and moved on.

"Flirt," Lauren admonished him.

He grinned. "She loved it."

"Only proves my point. You won't be alone for long."

"Come on—I barely know anyone." There were a few film industry people here, but the biggest portion of guests was made up of Tori's family and friends. "You're maid of honor to my best man. We're scripted to be together."

"Hmm. You've spent half the time behind that camera. I don't know why you need company at all."

Implying he was lacking at his duties? Why did he allow her to get to him? Yes, she was lovely, but he'd dated some of the most gorgeous women in the world. She was a bit of a brat, and she constantly challenged his authority. But one whiff of her scent and he could think of only one thing: getting her alone.

The thinning crowd shifted, bumping Lauren into Ray. He grabbed her to keep her from toppling. His fingers framed her hips as he drew her close.

He lowered his head and kissed the vulnerable curve

of her neck. "The laundry room door has a lock. We won't be gone long."

She melted against him. The corner of his mouth kicked up in satisfaction as he mentally tracked the fastest route to the utility room. They both had bedrooms inside, but the laundry room held sentimental value. Best of all, no one was likely to look for them there.

In the next instant she'd elbowed him in the gut and twisted from his grasp. "Hands off."

He immediately held his hands up in a sign of surrender. He looked at her more closely. "Are you okay? You're a little pale."

She looked away. "I'm fine. I just choose not to let my hormones rule me today. It's my sister's wedding. I'm not going to steal away with you."

Lauren's assistant appeared, ushering the wedding party back to the gazebo.

"No one will miss us after the photos are done."

"Just *stop*." She planted a hand in the middle of his chest and lifted a pleading gaze to him.

He stepped back. "Pardon me."

He'd never forced himself on a woman and he wouldn't start now. If she didn't care to act on the desire her stand-offishness couldn't completely disguise, he respected her decision. He'd only pursued her because she helped distract him from the wedding heebie-jeebies.

Shoulders back, he gestured her forward.

For the next twenty minutes he stood where instructed, smiled when told, and snapped his own shots when he wasn't needed. Finally the photographer released the wedding party. He trekked to the reception with Lauren's brother Nick.

They exchanged pleasantries. "How's work?" Ray asked.

"Busy. I know I shouldn't be happy about that." Nick ran the trauma unit at a Palm Springs hospital. "But I prefer

action to twiddling my thumbs. How about you? Is there
a new film I should be looking forward to?"

"I wrapped up *Gates of Peril* in December. It'll be out
over the summer. I'm still in the planning stages of the
next one."

"I'm going to hold you to that invite to a premier you
issued at Thanksgiving. Not only will I enjoy the movie,
it'll be serious chick points."

Nick introduced Ray to more family and he got some
nice group footage. Lauren had a large, fun family.
Grandma Randall did like to flirt. She snagged his arm
and showed him off. It made him think of his own family. He owed his grandmother a call. She had raised him
from the age of ten, when his parents had died in an auto
accident. Her birthday was this week.

Having delayed as long as possible, he wandered over
to the head table. Along the way a curvy redhead caught
his eye. She showed her interest with a come-hither gaze.
He kept on walking. He already had all the woman he
could handle tonight.

At the head table he slid into his seat next to Lauren.
Tori's parents sat on the other side of the happy couple.
Unwilling to sit in uncomfortable silence for the duration
of dinner, he turned on the charm.

He kept the conversation light and impersonal, which
put Lauren at ease. Stories from the set were always en-
tertaining, and he finally drew a laugh from his compan-
ion. It gave him almost as much satisfaction as when she
had melted against him earlier.

She'd been overly tense all day. Probably from having
to hand control over to her assistant. The woman was nothing if not bossy. The deejay announced the first dance: a
waltz to *When You Say Nothing At All*. Tori and Garrett
took the floor, and after a few minutes Ray led Lauren out
to join them and pulled her into his arms.

"Close your eyes," he bade her. "It'll be over in a minute."

She glanced at him through her lashes. "You're being very nice."

"Hey, I can take a hint when it slaps me in the chest."

"I'm sorry." She laid her head on his shoulder. "I've been such a brat."

He tightened his arm around her waist. "No more than usual."

She laughed. "You're just saying that to make me feel better."

"Is it working?" He laid his cheek against the silk of her hair. "Should I brave another invitation to move indoors?"

She pulled her head back, eyed him speculatively. "To the laundry room? There are more comfortable rooms available inside, if you're truly interested in tempting me."

"Hey, I have fond memories of you in a laundry room." He kissed a path to her ear. "Remember?"

She sighed. "I remember. It wasn't one of my finest moments."

"Oh, I disagree." He twirled her and brought her back against him. "You were more than fine—you were extremely hot."

"My parents were playing poker in another room!"

"You wild child, you."

She grinned. "It *was* rather naughty."

"Excellent." Blood surged hot through his veins. "Let's go."

With her hand in his, he started off the dance floor.

"Stop." She dug her heels in. "Fun as this is…" she waved between them "…there's no future to it. I can't keep dodging into closets with you."

"Why not?"

"I'm a responsible adult. I have to think of…my reputation. Eventually someone is going to notice if we keep disappearing together."

He scowled, positive that wasn't what she'd been going to say. "Dynamite, this is Hollywood—being seen with me can only up your reputation."

"Humble, much?" She shook her head. "Seriously, whatever was between us is over."

He stood watching her walk away, appeased only slightly by the look of regret he'd seen in the depths of her eyes.

This night was never going to end. Lauren gathered empties and carried them to the tray near the bar. And turned to be confronted by the bride.

"What do you think you're doing?"

"Nothing." Lauren fought the urge to hide her hands behind her back. She waved them instead. "See? Nothing."

"Uh-huh." Tori grabbed one of her hands and drew it close as she wrapped her arm around Lauren's. "Because it's *my* day, I'll pretend I didn't see you clearing the tables."

"Forgive me. Blame it on habit."

"Only because I had to stop myself from doing the same thing twice."

"Oh, that would never do."

"That's what Garrett said."

As they neared the dance floor Lauren demanded, "Where are you taking me?"

"Here." Tori drew her right into the middle of the dancers swaying to a soft ballad. "I've danced with all my favorite people today except one. You."

Lauren's stomach jolted at the idea of swirling to music even as her heart overflowed with joy. She stepped into her sister's arms and hugged her close. If she moved slowly enough she'd be fine.

"Be happy," she whispered. "More than anything, I hope for your happiness."

"I am. Happier than I've ever been," Tori assured her. "Garrett *gets* me."

"And you get him. It's why you click."

"I want this for you." Tori's eyes glittered with happiness, with a need to share her bliss with the world. Her gaze flitted to the head table, where Garrett and his best man lounged back with a couple of beers. "Maybe you and Ray?"

"Oh, no." Lauren automatically shook her head. "Sorry to disappoint, but that's ancient history."

"Why?" Tori challenged. "Because he causes you to act spontaneously? To have a little fun? I think he's been good for you."

"Good for me?" She laughed. Oh, he did wonderful things *to* her. But good *for* her? Not by a long shot. "Think about it. He's a master manipulator."

"He's a director," Tori reminded her. "It's what he does, not who he is. He's not Brad, Lauren. He'd never hurt you."

Easy for Tori to say. Lauren would rather not risk it. Something told her Ray's power to hurt would put Brad to shame.

"Ladies, you make such a pretty picture we had to come join you." Garrett smoothly stepped between them and brought their linked hands to his mouth, where he kissed the back of Lauren's fingers before twirling her around and passing her over to Ray.

Her world spun as he moved off with Tori.

"Hey." Ray's strong arms held her steady. "Are you okay?"

"Yes. No." She leaned her forehead on his chest, prayed for her stomach to settle. No such luck. "I'm going to be sick."

Lifting her skirts, she took off at a run. And, *oh, goodness,* she wasn't going to make it. But then a hard arm curved around her back and swept her along. She reached the bathroom off the kitchen with no time to spare.

Ray held her hair while she emptied her stomach. She

was mortified—and grateful. She wanted him to go but was also glad he was there.

"I'm so sorry." She flushed and slowly lifted her head. Wait—why was she apologizing? It was *his* kid causing this inconvenience! A fact he was sure to catch on to with this display.

"No need to be. We've all had a tad too much bubbly at one point or another." He pressed a damp cloth into her hands.

She lifted it to her face, reveled in the coolness. When she lowered the cloth he held a dripping bottle of water out to her. She gratefully accepted it.

"Oh, man, I could kiss you right now."

He smiled and tucked a loose tendril behind her ear. "Sorry, Dynamite. All trips to the laundry room have been cancelled for the night."

CHAPTER TWO

A TRILL OF BEEPS sounded from Ray's phone. And another, and another. He ignored them as he navigated the hill to his Malibu home. He'd skipped out on the post-wedding breakfast. With Garrett gone, Ray's duties were done. No need for him to linger. Nope, he was happy to put all things wedding-related behind him.

Another beep. Sounded like media alerts. He guarded his privacy, so he liked to stay on top of his media exposure. Such as it was. Better, in his opinion, to be on top of an issue than blindsided by it. With that in mind he had an assistant producer set to tell him whenever his name appeared in the news. Being best man at a major Hollywood wedding—an outdoor wedding, at that—would probably have the darn thing beeping all day long.

Once he reached his place, he dumped his garment bag at the bottom of the stairs, set his camera case on the foyer table, and wandered into the living room. He aimed the remote at his sixty-inch TV and powered it up. He'd barely tuned in to a basketball game before his phone beeped again.

He picked it up and started flipping through the alerts. Just as he'd thought, most were about the wedding. Pictures were already plastered across the internet. Distant and grainy, most gave a sense of the event but the people were unrecognizable unless you knew who they were—which would suit millions of viewers just fine.

A few obviously came from within the event. Garrett would have a fit about that.

Ah, crud. Just his luck—one of the up close and personal shots was of him bent over Lauren, kissing her neck. The look on her face spoke of wistful desire. So she hadn't been as indifferent as she'd pretended.

Too bad the knowledge wasn't worth the hassle it would bring. The photo had already gone viral. And, yep, right on cue his phone rang. The ringtone, an Irish ditty, announced that his grandmother waited at the other end.

"Hello, Mamó. How are you on this bright winter morning?"

"What do you know of winter? I saw on the news it's seventy degrees in Los Angeles. We've snow up to our knees. *That's* winter."

"I hope you aren't shoveling the drive again? I hired someone to keep the drive and walk clear."

"Wasted money." Annoyance flashed down the line. "We don't need it more than half the time."

"That's not the point." His brows drew together. It wasn't like Mamó to be grouchy. Thrifty, yes, but generally good-natured. He sought to distract her. "What do you have planned for your birthday?"

"Oh, they're making a fuss and I don't want it."

"They" being his aunt Ellie and his cousin Kyla.

"Nothing special about being another year older when I have nothing to show for it."

Knowing she meant great-grandkids, he dropped his head onto the back of the sofa. Lately she'd been more and more verbal about her desire for him to settle down and start a family.

"Are they taking you out to dinner?"

"No. They have a party planned at the community center. I keep telling them it's a waste of space and time."

"Everyone loves you, Mamó. I'm sure the place will be packed with your friends."

"It is difficult these days. My friends like to crow about their grandchildren and great-grandchildren. I have nothing to share."

"Mamó…"

"I know you don't want to hear this. But it is my life."

He frowned over the despair in her voice. He'd never heard her so depressed.

"I'm sorry—"

"Stop." A loud sigh blew in his ear. "Listen to me rant. Forgive an old woman her bitter babbling. I miss you, my boy. It would cheer me greatly if you could come to my party."

"A visit?" he mused. He might be able to manage that. A trip would help him to put Lauren out of his mind again.

Goodness knew there were a few harrowing memories waiting there for him. Perhaps it was time to put them behind him.

"Yes." Mamó showed a spark of life. "And you can bring your girlfriend with you."

Uh-oh. "Girlfriend?"

"Yes. I saw all the pictures of the two of you on the internet. You look so handsome." Her voice contained a world of excitement. "The two of you look just like a bride and groom yourselves."

In her stunning silver dress Lauren *had* looked like a bride. He remembered the stutter of his heart when she had started down the aisle toward him. In the midst of a harrowing day, she'd been the ideal distraction.

Now that played against him, giving Mamó unrealistic hopes.

"She's a lovely girl. I'm so excited to know you're seeing someone. Say you'll bring her."

This was going downhill fast. Mamó was setting herself up for disappointment if she believed a future existed for him and Lauren. "Listen—"

"You can't fool me. It's clear in the pictures you care for

her. Please, Ray?" Mamó beseeched. "You have to come
and bring her with you. It's my dearest wish. And this may
be my last birthday."

She was always saying things like that, but one of these
days it would be true.

Comfortable in yoga pants and a cap-sleeved tee, Lauren
sat on her beige sofa, feet kicked up on her ottoman coffee table, tea at her elbow, trying to focus on the mystery
book she'd been saving for her vacation. Her mom, dad and
brother had left for Palm Springs after breakfast, leaving
Lauren free to head home and officially start her vacation.

With Tori taking two weeks off for her honeymoon,
Lauren had decided to have a much needed break as well.
She saw it as a great opportunity to let their new assistants
take the lead on the two events scheduled for the coming
week. The women had done a great job at the wedding and
were ready for more responsibility.

Only a week off for Lauren, though. Hollywood's premier awards ceremony aired on Sunday, and By Arrangement was hosting Obsidian Studios' after-party.

The event represented a major goal for the company.
Yes, Tori was now married to the owner, but Lauren took
pride in the fact that By Arrangement had earned the contract *before* they'd got engaged. Their work for Obsidian at
the Hollywood Hills Film Festival had become legendary.

For the past two months they'd been getting more work
than they could handle. She'd gotten three new calls just
this morning.

Much as she loved her family, Lauren had been glad
to see them go. Being around her mom and not telling her
about the baby had just felt wrong. But Lauren wasn't ready
to confess her condition yet. Not just because she wanted
Tori to be there when she revealed the news, but because
Lauren needed to get used to the idea herself.

Which also explained why she wasn't ready to talk to Ray.

In a perfect world she wouldn't have to talk to Ray at all. She could dismiss him as a sperm donor and go about her life raising her child as she pleased. Unfortunately she possessed too much integrity for that option. Plus her work and his crossed paths too often for a pregnancy to go unnoticed.

A knock at the door drew her brows together in a frown. She couldn't think of a single person who might be calling. Setting her teacup on the ottoman, she made her way to the door. Where she caught sight of herself in the mirror over the hall table.

She skidded to a halt on the hardwood floor. She didn't have a lick of make-up on. After a bout of morning sickness she'd scrubbed her face clean and changed into comfy clothes. She'd barely run a brush through her hair before throwing the mass into a ponytail. She looked like a slightly hungover sixteen-year-old.

With any luck it would be a Girl Scout selling cookies. Lauren could buy a box of chocolate mints and send the child away without too much embarrassment.

A glance through the peephole proved she wasn't that lucky. Ray stood on the other side of the door. Geez, how did he even know where she lived?

Maybe if she didn't answer he'd go away. As soon as that thought registered she reached for the doorknob. It smacked of cowardice—something she refused to allow.

"Hey," Ray greeted her.

Of course he looked sensational, in black chinos and an olive lightweight knit shirt under a black leather jacket.

"Can I talk to you? It's important."

She'd bet her "important" beat his "important." But she wasn't ready to go there yet, so she really had nothing to say to him.

"I don't think that's a good idea." She blocked the door. "We pretty much said everything yesterday."

"Not this. I have a job for you."

Uh, no. "You'll need to call the office. I'm on vacation."

"I know." He kissed her on the temple as he pushed past her. "That makes it perfect."

Gritting her teeth, she followed him down the short hall to the open-plan living-room-kitchen combo. She had no doubt his "never take no for an answer" attitude had contributed greatly to his success as an award-winning director. On a personal front, she found it highly annoying.

"I don't think it's wise for us to work together at this time." She lingered in the opening between the hall and living area, watching as he made himself comfortable on her overstuffed couch.

"No one else will do for this particular job," he said, with such conviction it sparked her curiosity.

But she refused to be drawn in. She needed these next few days to herself, to re-evaluate and plan. To consider his part in her future.

"I'm sure that's an exaggeration."

"It's not, actually." He picked up her teacup and sniffed; he took a sip and nodded. "My grandmother's birthday is this week." He went to the kitchen and began opening cupboards until he found a mug. "I talked to her this morning. I've never heard her sound so down. All her friends are great-grandmothers and she's pouting because she doesn't have a baby to dandle on her knee."

"I'm sorry to hear that." Lauren took the mug from him and set it on the counter. "What does that have to do with me?"

"She asked me to come to her party. I'm hoping if I go it will cheer her up."

"Good luck with that." She did wish him luck, knowing how stubborn *her* grandmother could be when stuck on that topic. "I still don't see how By Arrangement can be of assistance. We have no connections in New York. If we'd had more warning we could have put something together for you, but at this late date—"

"I don't need your expertise as an event coordinator," he broke in. "I need a date."

She blinked at him; let her mind catch up with his words. "You want me to go to New York with you?"

"Yes. We leave tomorrow morning. I've already arranged the flight."

Of course he had. She pointed toward the door. "Get out."

"Lauren, I'm serious. I need your help."

"You're insane if you think I'm going to New York with you."

"I don't expect you to drop everything for nothing." He treated her to his charming smile. "I want to hire you."

The attempt at manipulation and the reminder that his request was a job offer only made the whole thing worse. Fortunately it had the benefit of reminding her he was a client and as such deserved a respectful response.

Drawing on her professional persona, she breathed deep, seeking calm. "As I already mentioned, I'm on vacation."

"Name your price." He would not be deterred. "I need you. Mamó saw that tabloid picture of us a couple of months ago, and now all the internet pictures of us at the wedding, and is excited about the idea of me having a girlfriend. All she wants for her birthday is for me to bring you with me."

"I'm not comfortable with the idea of deceiving your grandmother. If that's what you're looking for I'm sure there are any number of actresses who would be pleased to help you."

"It's not like that." He scowled. "It has to be you because you're the one in the pictures and because we do have a relationship."

"Did." She corrected him. "We had a fling." Calling

their frantic rendezvous a relationship seemed a stretch. "It's over."

He stepped closer, played with the ends of her ponytail. "It doesn't have to be. We could have fun on this trip."

Gazing into his cheerful blue eyes, she experienced the irrational desire to lunge for what he offered. She didn't think when she was in his arms—she just felt. An option that held huge appeal when her mind still whirled from the fact she was expecting his baby.

"No." She spun out of his reach, crossed her arms in front of her—protecting herself, protecting their child. "We couldn't. I told you, there's no future for us. I like to be in the driver's seat and so do you."

"I don't mind riding shotgun to a beautiful woman on occasion."

"Liar."

He laughed. "Okay, you got me. But we manage okay. What's wrong with having a little fun?"

"It's not me." Which was true—even if there wasn't a child to consider. "And I'm too busy. Don't forget the awards are this weekend. We're handling the Obsidian party."

"But you're on vacation. And we'll be back by Saturday."

"I prefer to be available in case the new assistants need help. And, believe me, I have things to keep me occupied." Like planning a new future. Making an actual doctor's appointment. Strategizing how she was going to handle him.

Ray stepped back, propped his hands on his hips. He appeared truly perplexed by her refusal. "Lauren, it's my *grandmother*."

Okay, he knew what button to push. She didn't wish his grandmother ill. She actually admired his attempt to help the older woman. But she couldn't let her sympathy lead her down a dangerous path.

"I'm sorry. She's going to have to make do with you."

"Right." His blue eyes turned cold. He turned away. "Sorry to have bothered you."

She closed her eyes rather than watch him walk away. A moment later she heard the front door close behind him.

Lauren's conscience niggled her all morning and into the afternoon. For all his forceful charm and pre-planning ways, Ray had genuinely been concerned for his grandmother.

And, though they were no longer and never really had been seeing each other, the tabloid and internet pictures gave the appearance they had. Ray's penchant for privacy—well known in Hollywood and no doubt by his family—only added credibility to his grandmother's assumption.

But every time she considered changing her mind her heart raced and she remembered how insane his proposal was. If she agreed to go with him she'd be the unbalanced one. The man rode roughshod over everyone. Case in point: he had bought her airline ticket without even getting her agreement first.

So arrogant, so controlling… She shuddered. So not a good combination.

Except her life was now irrevocably linked to his. The trip to New York would present the perfect opportunity to see Ray in the midst of his family. What better way to learn what family meant to him? His concern for his grandmother was already an eye-opener. How could she refuse to help him and then expect to have a harmonious relationship going forward?

Simple—she couldn't.

A child grew within her. Ray's child. Mamó's great-grandchild. Which meant Lauren had no choice but to go to New York.

She consoled herself with the knowledge that the trip

would provide the perfect opportunity to tell him the news of their pending parenthood.

She hated making spur-of-the-moment decisions. She liked to plan, set goals, make lists. Order prevented chaos, allowed her to be prepared, in control. She hadn't reached that point when it came to the baby. Or Ray.

If she was going to go to New York with him she wanted to lay down some ground rules.

Mind made up, she changed and drove to Ray's hill-side home in Malibu. It took close to an hour. She pulled in to his flagstone driveway and parked. He lived alone except for the middle-aged couple who took care of the house and gardens. Fred and Ethel lived in a small villa on the grounds.

Lauren smirked as always at the couple's names. They were poignant reminders of home. You didn't grow up in Palm Springs, rich with old Hollywood history, without being familiar with *I Love Lucy*.

She rang the doorbell, listened to it echo through the house. Given the size of the place, she gave it a few minutes before ringing again. Ray's home took up four acres and consisted of five buildings: the four-thousand-square-foot main house, a multi-level garage with a heliport on top, a guest house, a pool house, and the caretakers' villa. The grounds were terraced and included a tennis/basketball court, a pool, and two spas.

He also had top-of-the-line security with high-end electronic capabilities. Ray loved his gadgets. She didn't look into the camera above the door, but she knew it was there.

She frowned and glanced at her watch. Maybe he was out. But if that were the case why had she been let in the front gate? Lauren had allowed plenty of time for someone to respond to the bell, which meant he was here and making her wait or he was refusing to acknowledge her.

Now who was the coward?

"What do you want?" His disembodied voice came from no discernible source.

"To talk to you," she replied, keeping her gaze fixed on the ground. If he wanted to see her face he needed to open the door.

"I believe it was made clear there was nothing further to discuss between the two of us."

She crossed her arms over her chest. This was why they weren't compatible—the constant play for power. "I'm not having a conversation through a door."

"What?" he mocked her. "Am I lacking graciousness as a host?"

"Fine." She turned on her peep-toed heels. "Forget it."

All the better for her. No awkward acting required in New York, and she'd made the attempt, so he couldn't hold her earlier rejection against her.

The door opened at her back and a strong male hand wrapped around her upper arm. "Please come in." He led her inside to the large, open living room. "I wouldn't want you to come all this way and not state your business."

She walked past him and took a seat on an oval suede sofa in rich beige. *Shoot*, an already difficult discussion had just got harder. Because he looked yummy. He wore the same pants and shirt he'd had on earlier, but he was sexily disheveled, with his sandy hair mussed up, the start of a five o'clock shadow, and bare feet.

When she didn't answer he dropped into a chair across from her, knees spread, arms braced on muscular thighs.

She swallowed hard.

"No door, Dynamite." He gave her his full attention. "What do you want? If you'll remember, I have some packing to do."

Seeking composure, she straightened her shoulders and crossed her hands over her purse in her lap. "I've reconsidered my earlier decision. I'm willing to help you with your grandmother."

He considered her for a moment, his blue eyes assessing. "What's it going to cost me?"

Annoyed at the mention of payment, she seared him with a glare.

"By Arrangement is an event-oriented business. We do not get involved in family dynamics. I would be doing this as a favor for a friend."

Okay, that was stretching it. She'd be doing it to get to know her child's father better.

"So now we're friends?" He lifted one brown eyebrow.

She shrugged. She'd like to think they could be friends, but the chemistry between them made the ease of friendship a difficult prospect.

"The point is I'm willing to help. And it's not going to cost you anything more than a few common courtesies."

His eyes narrowed. "I knew there'd be something."

"Just a few ground rules so we don't get tripped up."

He sat back. "Such as?"

"Well, to start with I think we need to be as truthful as possible."

"Agreed."

"It'll be less complicated. And I prefer to be as honest as we can."

"No argument. What's next?"

"I want separate bedrooms."

He cocked his head. "It's my grandmother. I'm pretty sure that's guaranteed."

She relaxed a little. So far, so good. "No fostering false hope that our relationship will mature to the next level."

"'Mature to the next level?'" he repeated. "Who talks that way?"

"Nice." Her shoulders went back. "You know what I mean."

"Don't get her hopes up that we'll get married." He frowned over the words. "You really don't have to worry about that."

"I'm not expecting a proposal." A long-suffering sigh lifted her breasts, drawing his attention downward. How predictable. "I want you to promise you won't let concern for your grandmother sway you into implying something you can't deliver. She'll only be hurt in the long run."

"You can be assured I'm not going to do anything to hurt Mamó."

Uh-huh. She believed his love and concern were genuine. But she also knew his penchant for control, and that he had a compulsive need to fix things. She easily saw one emotion feeding into the other.

"The last is no unnecessary touching."

He threw back his head and laughed. "You've got to be kidding. The point is that we're a *couple.* How do we portray intimacy without touching?"

She understood his confusion. The man was very tactile —he couldn't *not* touch...things, materials, people.

"I didn't say no touching. Of course there will need to be public displays of affection. But you're a master director, brilliant at evoking emotion. I'm sure you can manage with the minimum of physical contact."

"So PDAs are okay?" His gaze ran over her as his mind connected the dots. He was to keep his hands to himself in private. "So businesslike. I thought you were doing this as a friendly gesture. Why so strict?"

How to answer that? The baby motivated her to help him, because she needed to maintain a position of power. But that wasn't the only reason. Before she'd known about the baby she'd fought her desires because they turned her into someone she wasn't. Reckless, abandoned, acquiescent.

She'd subjugated her will to a man once before. It had changed who she was—a mistake she'd never make again.

She considered telling him about the baby—just putting it out there. But, no. He was already dealing with a distressed grandmother. It wouldn't be fair to drop the baby news on him, too.

"I've put what was between us behind me. Yet there's no denying the sexual chemistry between us." She gave him the lesser truth. "I don't want to jeopardize the progress I've made. This is a deal-breaker, Ray."

"Okay, you win." He threw his hands up in surrender. "I promise to keep my hands to myself."

She knew she'd have to remind him of his pledge, but it would do for now.

"When is our flight?"

The limousine pulled to a stop in front of Lauren's home and Ray stepped out. He knew she co-owned the bungalow-style duplex along with her sister. The arrangement allowed the twins the proximity they enjoyed, yet gave each of them their privacy. Perfect for sisters who were both friends and partners, or so she'd told him.

Of course that would all change now Tori had married Garrett. Would the twins keep the property and rent out Tori's side? Or would they sell, leaving Lauren to find a new home?

In a flash he saw her at his place, bringing order to his chaos, watching daily edits with him in the media room, claiming the gaming loft as her home office.

He froze with his hand poised to knock.

His head shook along with a full-body shudder. Must be residual fallout from the wedding. His overactive imagination tweaking on domestic bliss overload.

He knocked. He still puzzled over why Lauren had changed her mind and agreed to accompany him to New York. Nothing really made sense except that family mattered to her.

He'd seen that first-hand last Thanksgiving, when he'd learned that Garrett was spending the day alone, with nothing to occupy him but memories of his father's passing and the shattering of his own body in a car accident the previous year.

Of course Ray had invited his buddy over for Thanksgiving dinner, and then made an emergency call to Lauren to see if By Arrangement could pull off a miracle.

She'd been about to sit down to dinner with her family, but had named a couple of restaurants he could try. He'd cut her off to invite her family to join him and Garrett. The home-cooked deal had appealed to Ray, and additional people would help to distract Garrett.

And, of course, thinking of Thanksgiving brought back memories of their laundry room tryst.

Luckily the front door opened, keeping him from remembering the details of their heated session on the washing machine.

"Good morning." Lauren came out, pulling a small suitcase. "Can you grab the garment bag?" She motioned to the blue bag hanging over the hall closet.

He stepped inside and grabbed it. "Just the two bags?"

"You don't have to be sarcastic." She glanced at her luggage with a frown. "I know it's a lot for a week, but you didn't mention anything except your grandmother's birthday so I have to be prepared for anything."

"I wasn't being sarcastic." He handed her bag to the driver, who also took the roller bag, then held the back door for her. "If you're prepared for anything I'm surprised you don't have twice as many bags."

She gave a small smile and slid across the seat. Her jacket dragged on the seat behind her and he swept it out of the way as he slid in after her.

"Is this your heaviest jacket?" He fingered the fleece-lined raincoat. "The forecast in Queens is for snow."

"I'm sure it'll be fine." She pulled the fabric free and tossed the coat over her purse on the other side of her.

"Fine for Southern California is not the same as fine for New York. You'll freeze if that's all you take." The car pulled away from the curb. "I'll have the driver swing by Rodeo Drive."

He reached for the intercom. Her hand intercepted his, pushing it down.

"Forget it. I'm not buying a coat I'll only wear for a week."

She quickly retracted her touch. The woman did like her rules.

"I brought sweaters and a warm scarf. I'll be fine."

He snorted. "Let me know when you change your mind."

She glanced at him over her shoulder. "Why? So you can say, *I told you so*?"

"So I can take you shopping." He trained his gaze on the muted TV monitor across the way. "The *I told you so* will be strictly implied."

Out of the corner of his eye he caught her grin. He relaxed back into his seat. The trip might not be the total cluster bash he feared.

"Please. Hold your breath," she advised, all sweetness and light.

He turned to address her sass, only to stop when she pressed a hand to her stomach. A glance at her face revealed she'd lost all the color in her cheeks. Concern tightened his chest.

"Lauren, what is it?"

She sat very still, slowly drawing in a deep breath. "I wasn't ready for that last turn. It sent my stomach spinning."

"What can I do?"

"Can you lower the partition?" She swallowed repeatedly. "I think it will help if I can see where we're going."

He picked up the remote and did as she'd asked. The additional light showed her color was returning. "If you're not feeling well we can delay our flight for a day."

"That won't be necessary." She dug in her purse and

pulled out a dry protein bar. "I should have eaten something earlier. I'll be all right once I have a couple of bites." She looked at him oddly. "You're awfully cavalier about our departure time."

"It's not a commercial flight. I called a friend and he's agreed to lend me his jet. Barring emergencies, it's at my disposal for the next week."

"Must be nice." She closed her eyes and leaned her head back as she chewed. Her hand lingered over her stomach.

"Rest." He ran a knuckle down her cheek. "I'll let you know when we get to the airport."

Instead of flinching away, she leaned into his touch. After another sweep of her silky skin he left her to rest. He took heart from the exchange. If she could take comfort from him, the connection between them wasn't entirely extinguished.

Strong enough, he hoped, to convince his family for a week.

And maybe to allow for one more hook-up?

Because Lauren might see them as over, but he wasn't doing well with the whole cold turkey approach. He watched the soft rise and fall of her breasts and struggled with the desire to pull her into his arms.

No, his feelings about their relationship didn't match hers at all. Sure, he believed in keeping things short and light, but *he* usually called the where and when.

And when he looked at her he saw unfinished business.

CHAPTER THREE

LAUREN ACCEPTED RAY'S suggestion to rest as an opportunity to avoid conversation for the rest of their trip to the airport. She shrugged out of the brown cropped jacket she wore over a cream sweater and jeans, then settled back against the seat and watched the road through the veil of her lashes.

Thank goodness seeing where they were headed had helped to calm her queasy stomach.

One thing was for certain. She needed to get this morning sickness under control or she'd be making explanations before she was ready. Ray was too intelligent not to put the pieces together with them living in each other's pockets.

And then there was his grandmother, aunt and cousin. Hopefully they'd be too caught up in Ray's visit and Mamó's birthday to pay much attention to her.

At the airport they departed from the commuter terminal. Expedited VIP service streamlined their boarding process and within minutes she climbed the steps to a mid-sized jet. The scent of fine leather hit her as soon as she entered the plane. Fortunately the baby had no objection to the smell.

Lauren made her way down the aisle between half a dozen armchair-style seats in creamy beige. The second half of the cabin contained two face-to-face couches of the same color in a soft ultra-suede fabric. At the end a door stood open on a full-sized restroom.

Just *wow*. This was totally going to spoil her for flying coach.

Pretending a sophistication she didn't feel, she turned to Ray. "Where do I sit?"

"Wherever you want." He indicated two armchairs facing each other. "Why don't we start here? I asked the attendant to bring you some tea once we're in the air. She'll also bring you something to eat. Do you want eggs and bacon? Bagels or muffins? Fruit?"

"I don't care for anything right now." She sank into the chair next to the window.

"A few bites of protein bar aren't much," he protested. "You need something more."

"Welcome aboard." The attendant, an attractive brunette in a gray pantsuit, appeared at her elbow. "My name is Julie. I'll be serving you today. If you need anything you can call me via the remote, or just push this button." She showed Lauren on her armrest. "I'll bring tea when we've reached cruising altitude. What more would you like?"

"Nothing for—"

"Thank you, Julie." Ray cut Lauren off. "Please bring a selection of bagels, fruit, and yogurt."

Lauren slammed him with a glare at his arrogant disregard for her wishes. She should know if she was hungry.

"May I take your things?" Julie offered. "There's a closet at the front of the cabin. You'll have full access during the flight."

Lauren handed off her purse and coat. She waited until the other woman had disappeared before addressing Ray.

"If you hope to get along on this trip you will refrain from treating me like a child."

"Then don't behave like one."

His gaze roved over her. She felt the weight of it everywhere it touched.

"You're still pale. Food helped in the car. I can only

assume it would be better if you had something more. It would please me if you ate. But the choice is yours."

She gritted her teeth. To argue further would only make her sound petty.

Luckily the pilot's voice filled the cabin. "Please fasten your seatbelts. We'll be departing momentarily."

Avoiding Ray's gaze, she glanced out the window as the plane began to move. His reasonableness did nothing to appease her. In fact it only annoyed her, putting her in the position of being unreasonable—an intolerable situation, which was totally his fault.

It would please him if she ate? Seriously?

Right this minute she felt fine. She hoped to stay that way through takeoff. And the thought of food...? Not helping.

As a view of the airport, planes, and air traffic personnel flowed by the porthole window she marveled once again at her current circumstances. The only explanation she could come up with was she must have royally ticked off Lady Karma in another life, because she should not be pregnant.

She'd started on the pill. Ray had worn condoms. Yeah, they'd been frantic for each other, but they'd also been responsible. Okay, there had been that once when the condom broke. Yet—hello?—still on the pill. Sure, her doctor had warned her that it took time for the body to adjust, but it had been a month. Well, almost.

The force of takeoff pushed her back in her seat as the plane began to rise. Her fingers curled into fists on the armrests, her nails digging into the soft leather. She closed her eyes, willed her stomach to behave.

"Are you okay?"

Ray's voice sounded next to her ear at the same time as a warm hand settled over her clenched fingers.

Her eyes flew open. When had he moved next to her?

More to the point, when had his touch become an instant soother?

It had to be the distraction, her logical mind asserted, but she didn't care. She turned her hand over, threaded her fingers through his and accepted the warmth and comfort he freely offered.

Tension eased away, taking the rising nausea with it.

"Thank you." She gave him a feeble smile.

"Nervous flyer?" he sympathized.

"Mmm..." She made a noncommittal sound. Poor guy. Her hormones were all over the place, her emotions likewise. Talk about mixed signals. *She* didn't know how she felt—how could he begin to guess?

"Not usually." She made an effort to participate in the conversation, hoping the resulting distraction would continue to work on her mind and stomach. "I guess I'm nervous about the whole trip. We haven't truly discussed how we're going to handle things. I'm not comfortable lying to your grandmother."

"Me neither," he said. "So we don't lie."

Eying his stoic expression, she felt the muscles in her shoulders begin to tense again. "If you're suggesting—"

"I'm not." He squeezed her fingers. "We're friends. At least I hope you consider me a friend. That's what we put out there."

Because his touch felt too good, she pulled her hand free of his. On another level she noticed the plane had leveled out. "But everyone has an expectation there's more between us."

"Exactly. We'll just be ourselves and they'll see what they want to see."

She tapped her fingers on the armrest as she considered his approach. "Still seems a little artificial."

"The power of illusion comes from a collective awareness. People believe what they want to believe. Directors use viewer expectations as a tool to manipulate the audience's emotions all the time. It doesn't make what they feel any less real."

"Do you hear the words you're using? *Manipulate... audience.* This is your family we're talking about, not a theater full of moviegoers."

She understood the concept he presented, and, yes, she expected it would work as well as he stated. The truth worked for her. Leaving his family with preconceived notions that went well beyond reality was more iffy.

"Look." His gaze earnest, he picked up her hand, swept his thumb over the pulse at her wrist. "I know the girlfriend front isn't ideal. Ordinarily I wouldn't even consider it. But you have no idea how upset my grandmother sounded." Concern darkened his eyes to a soft azure. "If this plan lifts her spirits, it's worth a little discomfort on my part."

"Okay," she agreed. And again removed her hand from under his. Bottom line: his concern was genuine. And, if she were honest, it wasn't as if she and Tori hadn't occasionally manufactured events to gain their mother's cooperation to get something they wanted.

His family—his call. She'd agreed to come, so she'd do as he wished.

"Teatime."

Julie had arrived with a cart. She reached past them to pull a table from a wall slot, trapping Lauren next to Ray. The sudden intimacy suffocated her. She wanted to protest. Of course she didn't.

She was too strong to give in to weakness, too smart to reveal it to the opposition.

Onto the table Julie slid a tray, artfully displaying an array of bagels, both toasted and non-toasted, along with a healthy heaping of cream cheese, butter, and jellies. There were containers of yogurt and a lovely selection of fresh fruit. Next came steaming pots of hot water and a small basket of teas.

A midsized plate and linen-wrapped silverware were

placed in front of each of them. "May I serve you?" Julie asked.

"We'll help ourselves, thank you." Ray's charming smile caused the poised woman to blush.

"Please buzz me if you require anything more," she bade them, and then disappeared to her niche in the front of the plane.

Lauren waited for her stomach to revolt. When it didn't she reached for the basket of teas, chose a soothing decaffeinated blend and steeped it in one of the pots. When it looked the right color, she poured the brew into a delicate teacup.

Ray slathered cream cheese on a cinnamon bagel and slid melon, pineapple chunks and a few blackberries on his plate.

"Can I fix you anything?" he asked, after she'd taken her first sip.

"Perhaps half a plain bagel, with a light spread of cream cheese."

He nodded and a moment later placed it on her plate. She cut it into quarters and picked up a corner to nibble on.

"You know, I'm all for sticking to the truth and all…" She set her cup back in its saucer. "But the details are still going to be a bit sketchy. You do realize we've never been on an actual date?" She stabbed at a plump berry on his plate and ate it.

His eyes narrowed in thought. He reached for a carton of peach yogurt, opened it and scooped in a few berries. He took a couple of bites before pointing his spoon at her.

"We've kept a low profile."

Her brows lifted. "You're a little too good at this."

He grinned and offered her the yogurt carton. "I'm a director. It's my job to invent and interpret."

"Convenient." Not even thinking about it, she accepted the yogurt.

The flavors, peach and blackberry, exploded in her

mouth. A few more bites finished it off. She sighed. A glance at her plate revealed he'd gotten his wish. She'd eaten all her bagel plus fruit and his yogurt. And she felt great. More energized than she had in forever.

"Finally you've a little color in your cheeks."

She gave him a cool glance. "Saying *I told you so* is unbecoming."

He shook his sandy head. "I'm just glad you're feeling better."

"Thanks." What else could she say without sounding petty? To his credit, he appeared sincere.

To break the moment she pushed the button on her armrest. Julie appeared within moments to clear the table. But all too soon she and Ray were alone again. It was all she could do not to twitch in her seat. How to get him to move away?

Turned out she didn't have to do anything. Phone in hand, he stood up.

"If you'll excuse me, I have some calls to make?"

She nodded and he moved across the aisle and up to another row of seats. Able to breathe freely, she refused to acknowledge she missed the heat and comfort of his proximity. Some alone time to think was exactly what she needed. She felt the best she had in days—make that weeks.

Maybe she'd actually be able to concentrate and come up with a course of action for this abrupt change in her carefully crafted life plan. So far she hadn't quite been able to wrap her mind around the enormity of the fact she carried a child within her. And that kept her from making sense out of the chaos in her head.

Which left her feeling out of control and desperate to get her life back.

Panicked, really.

The last time she'd given up control, she'd lost a part of her soul.

Lauren couldn't go through that again—especially

when she had a child to think of. She required her lists, her goals, her plans. She craved order, needed to be in charge. Only then could she cope.

She stared unseeing out the window.

Some things were obvious. Once Tori returned Lauren would tell her family. She would continue to work. She would tell Ray. It all sounded simple and straightforward. It couldn't be more complex.

Even telling her family. Sure, they would love and support her. She had no doubt of that. But there'd also be disappointment and concern. And questions. Personal questions, not easy to answer.

Continuing to work would require compromise and sacrifice. Deciding between daycare and a nanny was only one decision to be made requiring careful research. She also needed to consider housing—whether to sell the duplex and move to a bigger place in a family-friendly area. It didn't need to be done now, but it was already on her mind. A part of the mix keeping her from finding the necessary peace to deal with everything.

Telling Ray. Yeah, she'd been playing ostrich there. She knew she had to give him the news. Yet the where and when were still questions. She had no idea how to approach him, but she did know it wouldn't be before this deal with his grandmother played out.

It wouldn't be fair to distract him at this time.

And, truly, everything else hinged on his reaction. Any plans she conceived were contingent on how involved he'd want to be.

Her stomach roiled. The realization threatened the scant control she'd managed to muster.

She drew out her phone and powered it up. She had a couple of her own calls to make.

About forty minutes before they were scheduled to land Ray roused Lauren. Halfway through the trip she'd stretched out on one of the couches and slid into a solid sleep. She hadn't moved an eyelash when he'd dropped a blanket over her and stuffed a pillow under her head.

She was slow to awaken. He had no idea if that was natural or not, as they'd never actually slept together. He tended not to sleep with the women in his life. Too messy.

How fragile she looked. He traced the shadows under the fan of her lashes. She said she wasn't sick, yet she was tired and pale and a couple of times he'd caught an expression on her face that made him think she might be fighting off nausea. Perhaps it was the aftereffects of stress. Handling her sister's wedding during Hollywood's biggest party season must have been a challenge, even for a pro like her.

She was such a strong woman—quick and intelligent and in control—he tended to overlook the fact she was quite delicate.

"Lauren." He ran his hand up her arm, gave her shoulder a gentle shake. "Wake up, Sleeping Beauty."

"Hmm?" She sighed and shifted onto her side. "Gaway."

He grinned. "No, I'm not going away." Leaning over her, he pressed his lips to hers. "But I'll join you if you'd like." That ought to wake her up.

"Ray..." Her lips opened under his and an arm snaked around his neck, pulling him close.

The action put him off balance. He went down on one knee to keep from tumbling on top of her. He'd happily follow up on his offer to join her on the couch as soon as he knew her mind was as engaged as her body.

Meantime, he sank into the kiss.

Instantly the chemistry ignited between them. Angling his head, he slid his tongue past her lips to taste the honey of her mouth. Her sleepy response seduced him into a slow, deep exploration. The meandering journey pulled them down a path not yet taken. The softness of the moment was different but every bit as hot as their bolder encounters.

She sighed and shifted fully onto her back. The drag of her fingers through his hair was a dreamy caress, a subtle demand for more, for longer, for slow and sensual. He willingly set the pace, lingering over each touch, each taste, each smell, satiating all his senses. Her breath sighed over his cheek and he took satisfaction in each little moue and gasp.

Never had he burned for a woman like he did for her. And she was right there with him, her responsiveness inspiring him to new depths.

The gradual, sultry building of passion urged him to tenderness, to lengthy kisses and gentle insistence. He worked his hand under her sweater and glided up her silky skin, seeking the bounty of her breast.

She suddenly went very still and her hand came down on his, effectively pushing the stop button on his attempt to move their embrace to the next step.

"Not a good idea," she mumbled in a sleep-husky voice.

He groaned and tested her resolve, sweeping his thumb across the warm flesh of her stomach. She gasped and tightened her hold, but the knit of her sweater separating her grasp from his was a thin barrier to his persistence.

"Shh, Dynamite," he whispered against her lips, "you're dreaming."

"Liar." Her lips lifted in a smile under his and then she turned her head aside. "My body is too alive for me to be asleep." She pulled his hand free of her clothes. "We agreed no touching."

"You started it, wrapping yourself all around me." He kissed a path up her jawline to whisper in her ear. "Let me finish it. We can start the no touching when we get to New York."

She moaned deep in her throat—a sound he took to

mean she was tempted, if the look in her golden eyes meant anything.

"Uh-uh." She planted both hands on his chest and pushed. "I did not start it. You kissed me first. When I had no resistance. Unfair, Ray."

He let her up, slid onto the couch next to her when she pushed into a sitting position. "Spoilsport."

An arch glare came his way. "Really?"

The show of ire along with her mussed hair and just-kissed lips was too sexy for words. Made him want to take up where they had left off. Forget about apologizing. Besides, he still maintained she'd started it. His had been a mere peck on the lips; she had taken it to the next level.

Not waiting for a response, she rolled her eyes, then glanced back at him. "Why did you wake me?"

He checked his watch—much safer than contemplating her. "In ten minutes we begin our descent. I thought you'd like to freshen up before we buckle up."

"Oh. I would, thanks." She made her escape.

While she did her thing he went through his email and texts. The car service he used in New York advised that a driver was waiting. His meeting with the mayor was confirmed. And Mamó couldn't wait to see him.

With a sigh he slipped the phone into his pocket. This trip was long overdue. Sure, he saw his family regularly, stopping off in New York or flying them to him two or three times a year. But he rarely went back to the old neighborhood. Certainly not for any length of time. Too many memories he'd rather not deal with.

Lauren came back, looking as calm and fresh as when she'd first boarded the plane. Something he envied, considering he still ached from their recent bout of passion. He earned another glare when he settled in the seat next to hers, and those luscious lips opened ready to protest, but the pilot came on, demanding they buckle up.

The landing went well and soon Ray saw Lauren seated

into a sleek black town car. She promptly slid to the far side of the bench seat, leaving at least a foot between them, and pulled out her tablet, effectively shutting him out. Within a few minutes they were swallowed by the late-afternoon traffic headed through the borough of Queens to Queens Village.

His grandmother lived in a two-family, two-story pitched-roof house on a postage-stamp-sized lot. He'd tried to upgrade her to a bigger house on a larger lot in a better area, but she refused to move. She'd lived in her house since she'd moved in as a bride and intended to stay until the day she died. Rather than argue, he'd paid off the mortgage, bought out the neighbors so his aunt could move in, and made sure the house remained sound and safe.

"We're here," he said as the pale gray building with its white filigree fence came into view.

Lauren leaned close to look out the window. "Quaint house."

He explained his attempt to relocate her. "I told you she was stubborn."

Cars overflowed the driveway and street, forcing the driver to double park. Ray stepped out and turned to help Lauren. Leaving the driver to bring their bags, Ray threaded their fingers together, more for his benefit than hers, and climbed the brick stairs to the front door. It flew open before his knuckles connected with the wood.

"Ray!" Aunt Ellie pushed open the screen and pulled him into a big hug. "It's so good to see you. Come inside." She stepped back, dragging him with her, and by extension Lauren. "Everyone—Ray is here."

Pandemonium broke out. Women of all ages launched themselves at him. He barely recognized most of them but he hugged them anyway, one-armed. Because he was not letting go of Lauren. Behind him he heard her fielding greetings.

"Hello."

"Hi."

"Nice to meet you."

"I'm Lauren."

These were his grandmother's, aunt's, cousin's friends. He got that they were proud of him and wanted to show off. So he smiled and nodded and forged ahead.

He froze when he spied Mrs. Renwicki. The smug look on her face reminded him of her granddaughter, Camilla. And, *bang*, the past was right in his face.

Turning his back on it, he finally broke through the crowd of people and furniture, and there was Mamó. Short and plump, her white-gray hair woven into a braid and pinned in a bun on top of her head, just as he always pictured her. She rose from her floral wingback chair and framed his face in her wrinkled hands.

"Ray, my boy, I'm so happy to see you." She kissed him on the cheek.

"Mamó, you look great." He gave her a full-on hug. "I've missed you."

"Then you should visit more often." She admonished him. "But you're here now, and you've brought the beautiful Lauren with you."

"Yes." He met Lauren's guarded gaze as he wrapped his arm around her waist and drew her forward. She was a trouper for putting up with this gauntlet. "Thanks," he whispered before turning to his grandmother. "Mamó, this is—"

"This is Lauren!" Mamó broke in, taking Lauren's hands in both of hers. "Your fiancée."

CHAPTER FOUR

LAUREN BLINKED AT Ray's grandmother, the word *fiancée* echoing through the room. Or was it just through her head?

"Oh…" Lauren's smile froze in place while her mind scrambled for an appropriate response. Did she carelessly laugh it off, politely deny the allegation, or go along with the crazy suggestion?

This broke so many of her rules. What was Ray thinking? Was the tight grip on her elbow warning or encouragement?

She angled her head up and around, her gaze meeting his. The shock in his eyes reassured her that his surprise matched hers.

"Mamó—" he began, and Lauren sighed, willing to let him handle the unexpected claim. "We're not—"

"Forgive me," Mamó rushed in, cutting him off. She kissed Lauren's cheek, color high in her cheeks and a look of pleading in her pale blue eyes. "I know you wanted it to be a surprise, but I couldn't resist sharing the news with my closest friends." Her gaze flitted to an older woman across the room before lifting to meet her grandson's eyes. "Please say it's all right."

Behind her, Lauren felt Ray's chest expand in a heavy sigh. "Mamó, I don't know where you got your information, but—"

The hands holding hers shook as the older woman nearly crushed Lauren's fingers.

"Of *course* we forgive you," Lauren rushed to say. It was good to know Ray would uphold his promise to her, but she couldn't let him embarrass his grandmother in front of all her friends.

The way he suddenly relaxed told her it had been a difficult decision.

"Thank you," Mamó breathed in Lauren's ear as she hugged her.

A chorus of congratulations rang out and a few people rushed at them to offer a new round of hearty handshakes and some hugs.

Ray handled it like a pro, reminding Lauren of his short stint as an actor before he'd moved behind the camera.

"I want to see the ring," Kyla demanded, pushing to the front. She grabbed Lauren's hand, only to frown at her naked ring finger. Kyla turned the look on her cousin. "Where's the ring, cuz? I expected to see at least a couple of carats."

"We thought we'd ring-shop while we're in town."

Oh, he was good. He handled the crowd of women like a pro. He charmed them all. He was attentive, a little flirtatious, and slippery as an eel. But Lauren didn't relax. There were too many questions, too many people, too many opportunities to mess up.

"Food's ready," Ellie called out.

Lauren hid a grimace, the thought of food too much, but her stomach growled. She placed a hand on her belly, trying to decipher her body's mixed signals as the rest of the guests eagerly moved into the dining room.

"You okay?"

Ray appeared in front of her. It was the first moment they'd had alone since walking through the door.

"Listen, I'm sorry about the whole engagement thing. Especially after I promised nothing like this would happen. I'll talk to Mamó and see if we can't get it all straightened out."

Lauren shook her head. "I think it's too late for that."

"Yeah," he agreed, a frown pulling his golden-brown brows together. "She got herself into a pickle. Thanks for not embarrassing her."

"Of course." She sent him an arch glance. "She obviously wants to see you settled down."

"And bouncing a baby or two on her lap," he bit out. "It's no excuse for putting us in this position."

Mention of a baby put a tremble in her muscles. She locked her knees and tried for practical. "We knew she was hopeful of a deeper relationship when we headed east," she reminded him. "If we stick to our rules we'll be fine."

"I'm glad you're taking this so well." He placed a hand in the small of her back and directed her toward a table laden with food. "You can still expect an apology."

She sighed, seeing his persistence as a need to control the situation. But she also respected his desire to honor his promise and protect her. Then she reached the food table and all thought left her head as hunger took over.

Grabbing a plate, she filled it with salads, fruit, and meat. She reached for a roll as Ray handed her napkin-wrapped utensils.

"Good to see you have your appetite back." He kissed her on the top of her head.

Okay, she could take that as patronizing or affectionate—neither of which suited her. Deciding to ignore him, she took her plate and found a single seat next to his cousin Kyla. He frowned at her choice and ate standing up near the mantel.

Lauren smiled around a bite of potato salad and listened to the surrounding women talk about tomorrow's party. They were excited because there'd be dancing, but a comment about lack of partners had Lauren glancing around the room. Many of these same people would be guests at the party, and the ratio hit at about three women to each man. Hmm, maybe she could help with that.

A tall, gray-haired gentleman with a dignified bearing hovered around Mamó. A flare of awareness tingled through Lauren, signaling a connection between them. Interesting… Must be a strong link. She rarely experienced the matchmaking sensation without Tori nearby to bolster their shared talent.

The topic moved on to where she should shop for her wedding rings. She stiffened for a moment, then gave a mental shrug. What the heck? She could get behind a fictitious shopping trip.

Thirty minutes later Ray was standing chatting with Mamó's neighbor when Mrs. Renwicki joined them. She gushed over his engagement.

"I'm *so* happy you've finally put Camilla behind you."

Mamó's neighbor nodded and patted his arm as the other woman went on.

"My granddaughter is happily married, expecting her third child. It's time you found some happiness too."

The woman had some nerve, throwing Camilla in his face. He wondered if she knew of the great-grandchild her precious girl had thrown away. Having nothing to say to her, he excused himself and walked away.

The confrontation confirmed his worst fears. His most humiliating moment remained fresh in the minds of the community that had borne witness to it.

His faithful friend was at the ready, and he lifted the camera to his eye and took a few shots. He sought out Lauren with the lens. Seeing her soothed his ravaged nerves. She balanced a half-empty plate on her lap. Her honey-brown eyes blinking repeatedly spoke of her fight to stay awake. It was barely nine—six by west coast timing—but she couldn't keep her eyes open. Knowing her, she had started her day before six. And travel could be exhausting enough without suffering from a stomach ailment.

Ray strolled across the room to rescue her tilting plate. "Time for you to go to bed."

"The party is still going on," she protested as he pulled her to her feet.

"And it can continue without us." He handed her plate off to his cousin and led her to his grandmother. "Mamó, Lauren is exhausted. We're going to leave for the hotel."

"Oh, no." Mamó waved off his statement. "You're both staying here. I made up your room special for you, with new sheets and towels."

He gritted his teeth. He loved his family, but he preferred the privacy and autonomy of a hotel in the nation's largest city.

Plus, he hadn't missed the singular use of "room"—as in Lauren and him in the same sleeping quarters. He couldn't do that to Lauren. She'd already made a huge concession by allowing the faux engagement to stand. He wouldn't force her to share his room.

"We don't want to put you to extra trouble." Ray chose an explanation she'd understand. And it was true, too. "Plus I have appointments in the city."

"Oh…" Disappointment turned Mamó's smile upside down. "But we've already taken your things up to your room." Resignation rang heavy in her voice. She turned to Lauren. "Would you prefer your own room, dear? Is that it? There's a daybed in the sewing room. It's a bit dusty in there—I confess I haven't been in the room for several months—but it won't take long to spruce it up."

Drat. He should have had his assistant call her with his itinerary, but he'd been busy arranging siting plans with the mayor's office. Ray usually stayed in the city when he visited. He never stayed long, for precisely this reason.

He hated seeing his grandmother upset. A glance at Lauren showed her following the conversation with a slight frown drawing her delicate eyebrows together. Her sleepy eyes lifted to his and he saw the words forming on her tongue. He forestalled her so she'd know exactly what she was getting herself into.

"It's best if we go to the suite at the hotel. I did promise Lauren her own space. Plus, it's your birthday. You shouldn't have to be concerned about caring for houseguests."

"You know I don't mind. But if it's what you prefer…" All animation drained from Mamó's face. "I was so looking forward to cooking you breakfast, like old times."

Lauren reached for his hand and gave it a squeeze. "It's okay, Ray. I'm fine with staying here if you'd like."

Now he really felt torn. He'd much rather stay at the hotel, but the option of holding Lauren in his arms through the night brought a whole new element to the situation.

Generally he arranged his amorous adventures so he ended up alone in his own bed. He found it helped alleviate complications over the long haul. But for once a woman was less inclined for entanglement than he was.

In their month-long fling only one memorable encounter had occurred in a bed. He'd run into her at a hotel where she and her sister had been working a holiday party for Garrett. Ray had dragged her out a side door for a few heated moments. She'd quickly put the brakes on because she'd been working, but he'd sent a room key to her and after the event she'd met him upstairs.

It had turned out their stolen moment hadn't been as private as he'd thought, because the next morning a picture of a torrid embrace between the two of them had hit the tabloids. Who would have predicted that moment would have led to this one?

"If Lauren is okay with it, then I'm not going to say no to your pancakes."

In the end his purpose for being here motivated his decision. His worry had lifted during the party as Mamó had seemed like her old self. Watching the light fade out of her now tore at his gut. The fatigue stamped on Lauren's fine features added weight to Mamó's request. Staying here benefited both women at this point. And, truly, if he wanted to get Mamó out of her funk he needed to give a little too. Disappointing her on his first day was not a smart move.

"Excellent." Mamó clapped her hands together. "I'll show you up."

"No need." He kissed her cheek before pulling Lauren after him toward the stairs. "I know the way."

"It was a lovely party," Lauren said over her shoulder.

"Thank you, dear. I look forward to getting to know you better tomorrow."

"Goodnight, Mamó," he called.

Upstairs, he opened the door to his childhood room and ushered Lauren inside. He half expected the room to be the same as when he'd left for UCLA fifteen years ago. Luckily the movie posters, twin beds, and blue plaid bedspread were long gone. Instead the walls were painted a pale green and a queen bed stood in the middle of the room, covered by a sage comforter with brown swirls. A large rug in reverse colors was spread across the hardwood floor.

Well, most of it had changed. He grinned when he focused on the art. Movie posters, but instead of being tacked to the wall these were framed behind glass and they were posters for *his* movies.

"Nice touch." Lauren walked to the window and pulled the chocolate-brown curtains closed. "She obviously keeps up with your work."

"When I left for Los Angeles she asked me to send her memorabilia of all my work. I didn't realize it was going on the walls."

"She loves you. It was sweet of you to agree to stay."

He shrugged. It shouldn't be a big deal. It wouldn't be if his grandmother had agreed to move from this neighborhood. He felt powerless here.

"I'm not the one who wanted separate rooms," he pointed out, slowly stalking her into the corner of the room. When her back hit the wall, her hands hit his chest.

"Stop right there." She cocked her chin up and looked down her pretty little nose at him. "Nothing has changed."

He groaned and dropped his forehead on hers. "Please don't tell me I'm going to be sleeping on the floor."

"That won't be necessary." She kissed his cheek, then slipped away. Their suitcases sat at the end of the bed and she moved to lift one of hers onto the comforter. "We'll share the bed, but the no touching rule still stands. As much as possible, anyway. We'll sleep facing away from each other."

He laughed and picked up his camera. "You're joking, right?"

"I'm not, actually." She rocked on her heels, frowning at the lens directed at her. "I don't have the energy to joke."

With her confession he realized she was actually swaying on her feet.

She pulled a toiletries bag from her case along with a nightgown. "New rule: no nudity in this room. Including socks."

"Socks?" He got the no nudity—not that he liked it. But what was the deal with socks?

"Yes, socks. No stripping down to your socks and pretending you're not naked."

He cocked his head and tugged on the end of her pale ponytail. "It sounds like you've used these rules before."

"No," she denied. "But I know how men think. So don't bother pushing the limits. Not only would it be a cop-out, but let me just warn you: the socks alone look isn't sexy."

"Don't worry—it's not a look you'll ever see on me. Now, *you*…" he leaned close to whisper in her ear "…are free to prance around in stockings anytime you want."

"Not going to happen." She used the hand clutching her nightgown to push him back. "The rules are for both of us. So do you agree?" She scowled at him until he came out from behind the camera and nodded. "Good. Now, if you don't mind, I'd like to use the bathroom first."

"Go ahead." He pointed to a door in the corner. "You can use that door or the one in the hall."

"Thank you." She skirted around him. "Quit aiming that camera at me. The rules make this a safe zone. There's no need to hide." And with that she disappeared into the bath.

He set the camera down. How did she do that? See straight to his soul?

No one had ever questioned why he carried a camera. He'd picked up Mamó's small automatic camera not long after his parents had died. Happy to have him show an interest in something—anything—she had given it to him. For a long time he had hidden behind it. It was a world he controlled. He supposed old habits died hard.

Lauren wasn't herself tonight. Sure, she'd pressed her rules on him, but she lacked her usual sass and fire. The trip had obviously taken a lot out of her. Hopefully the faint shadows under her eyes and her low energy would go away after a good night's sleep. It unsettled him to see her out of sorts. At least her stomach seemed to have settled down.

While he waited for her to finish in the bathroom he checked the dresser and found the drawers were empty. Hiking his suitcase onto the bed, he swept the contents up in one arm and dropped them into the bottom drawer.

He eyed Lauren's open case and decided to help her out. Her stuff went in the top and middle drawers. Then he emptied her garment bag into the closet. Their shoes went on top of the stacked luggage in the bottom of the closet.

Once he'd finished the unpacking he settled in the lone armchair and tapped his fingers on the brown Pleather arm. He glanced at his watch: just after ten. No way was he sleeping anytime soon. Especially in that tiny bed with Lauren tucked up next to him. Not with a no touching rule firmly in place.

Hell. He scrubbed his hands over his face. It was bad enough being back in his old neighborhood, with all the memories waiting to trip him up, now he had to deal with a faux engagement.

He closed his eyes and just for a moment pretended it was real, that he and Lauren were on the brink of starting a life together. He saw the future spread out before him, complete with Lauren at his side and a beaming Mamó cradling a baby in her arms. The wonder of it felt so real he had to shut it down.

The shower was turned off in the next room. He walked over and gave a brief knock. A muffled acknowledgement came from the other side.

"Hey, I'm going to rejoin the party for a while."

The door opened a crack and one golden eye peeked at him. "Okay, thanks for letting me know."

"Leave space for me," he taunted her, hoping to spark some of her fire.

"I will," was her quiet response. "Goodnight."

"Night." He sighed.

The door closed. He pressed his hand to the wood and assured himself she'd be her old self in the morning. Then he grabbed his camera off the dresser and headed back to the party, the option of spending time with the matriarchs of his old neighborhood only slightly better than the torture of lying awake in a platonic bed with Lauren.

Lauren leaned against the bathroom door until she heard the bedroom door click. The door of the bedroom she shared with Ray Donovan.

What had she been thinking?

She'd been so careful to outline her conditions for accompanying Ray, with separate rooms right at the top. Plain and simple: Mamó had got to her. The pleading in her eyes, the resignation on her face… Until that moment Lauren hadn't seen the depression Ray feared, but seeing the loneliness in the older woman's eyes had made Lauren sad. No way could she deny her. Lauren loved her family, and couldn't imagine her mother's reaction if she tried to stay at a hotel when she visited.

Of course not every family was as close as hers. How she longed for a cuddle with her mom.

Wanting to take advantage of Ray's absence, she hurried to brush her teeth and slip into her nightshirt—an oversized T-shirt that fell to her knees and hung off her shoulder. It was the most comfortable and least appealing sleep garment in her wardrobe. She'd brought it for the comfort, but was glad for its lack of allure now she was sharing with Ray.

Yawning, she moved into the bedroom. The thought of unpacking filled her with dread. Her limbs felt so heavy she could barely lift them. The bed looked inviting. She wanted nothing more than to pull back the comforter and climb in.

Wait. She blinked at the empty spread. Where did her suitcase go?

She scuffed around to the other side, thinking Ray must have set it aside. *Nope.* Next she opened the top drawer of the dresser. She stared down at the contents, blinked, and stared a moment more, her mind slow to accept the notion of Ray unpacking for her. But there was the evidence.

Tears stung her eyes. How sweet. Seriously, she could kiss the man.

Good thing he wasn't around or she might break another rule.

The contents of the drawer needed straightening, but it was good enough for tonight. She tucked her dirty clothes into a corner and shoved the drawer closed. All things considered, Ray had been pretty decent today—taking care of her, sticking to the rules even when it upset his grandmother, unpacking her things.

Well, except for the kiss on the plane.

She pressed her lips together to squash the smile tugging at the corner of her mouth. She would *not* let the man seduce her again. No doubt he'd be back to his regular dictatorial self tomorrow. She'd be better able to deal with him then.

Giving in to her weariness, she burrowed into the queen bed, staying strictly to her side.

After all, rules were rules.

Mamó fell asleep in her chair as the last guests were leaving. Ray helped Kyla and Ellie on cleanup by carrying the dirty dishes to the kitchen while they put the food away and loaded the dishwasher. When he came back from taking out the trash, Aunt Ellie shooed Kyla off to bed.

Kyla folded her dishtowel and hung it over the stove handle. "Only because I have work in the morning." She stopped by Ray to kiss his cheek. "Welcome home."

He punched her in the arm. "Good to see you, too."

"Ow! That hurt." Rubbing her arm, she made for the door leading next door. "Bully."

"Girl."

"And proud of it. Night, Mom." Kyla stuck her tongue out at Ray just before she disappeared.

He grinned and turned to his aunt, slipping his arm around her shoulder. "It's good to be home." He nodded toward Mamó. "How is she doing?"

"Sound as an old horse. But she's been down a lot lately. It was good to see her so up tonight. You being here is going to be good for her."

"I hope so." His gut clutched at the concern in his aunt's eyes. "Don't they have meds for depression these days?"

"Yes, but she wouldn't take them even if she agreed to go to the doctor and get properly diagnosed. You know how she is about taking medicine. I've been checking out the internet to find natural remedies through diet and exercise."

"That sounds great."

"Of course the best thing would be—"

"For me to get married? Come on, Ellie, that's not fair.

And announcing it to the neighbors isn't going to magically make it happen."

Ellie groaned. "I know. I'm so sorry."

"Oh, I know where to place the blame. And we'll be talking in the morning."

"Don't be too hard on her. Mrs. Renwicki was being particularly obnoxious about Camilla—going on about her expecting her third child. Not only was Mom upset on your behalf, but I'm sure she was thinking those could have been *her* great-grandkids."

"Not in this lifetime."

"No, of course not. Obviously Mom lost it for a moment there."

All too familiar with Mamó's desire for him to marry and produce a great-grandbaby, Ray rolled his head over the hunched muscles of his shoulders. To keep from giving her false hope was one of the reasons he kept his affairs private.

"Yeah, well, it's not just me she's involved in her fabrication," he reminded his aunt.

"Gosh, you're right." Ellie's worried gaze went to the ceiling, towards where his room was situated. "Will Lauren try to take advantage?"

He barked out a laugh. "Not likely. But there were a lot of people who bore witness to Mamó's announcement."

"Oh." Ellie covered her mouth with her fingers. "You think someone will leak the news? But these are friends of the family."

"Who will see nothing wrong with sharing the knowledge with their friends and family. So, yeah, I expect word to get to the press within a couple of days."

Something he needed to warn Lauren about. She might not have been so quick to give in to Mamó if she'd realized the news would become public.

Which meant he owed her an apology as well as his appreciation.

"Ray…" Ellie fretted, regret in her hazel eyes.

"Don't worry about it. I'll call my assistant, get him started on damage control." He gave her a kiss on the cheek. "Do you need help getting her to bed?"

"No." She patted his hand. "I've got her. I just need to finish cleaning up. You head on up. I hope we weren't too overwhelming for Lauren?"

"No, she'll be fine. She's close with her family so she gets it."

"Good. She seems nice."

"She is." *To most people.* She liked to bust his chops, but he knew she'd get along with his family. If only to spite him. He actually looked forward to her giving him guff again. It would mean she was back to her old self.

"Why don't you take care of Mamó and I'll finish up here?"

"I can't let you do that."

"Sure you can. I'm on California time. I need to kill an hour before I'll be ready to sleep."

Begrudgingly she nodded. "It's good to have you home."

She shook Mamó awake and led his sleepy grandmother down the hall toward her bedroom.

Pulling open the dishwasher, he started loading in more dishes. Memories flooded in. Back in the day he and Mamó had had the routine down to a science and had been able to finish up in ten minutes or less.

He loved her. But she'd put him in quite a fix. He suspected that Lauren would be cool about the whole engagement thing, but in reality she could end up suing him for breach of promise when he failed to marry her. She knew he'd pay. Because no way would he humiliate Mamó by letting the whole thing play out in the news.

It had been a long time since he'd been able to trust a woman.

Fifteen years, to be exact—ever since Camilla had taught him that you never truly knew anyone. He couldn't bring himself to be happy for her. Not after what she'd cost him. So he was petty? He'd live with it.

Dishes loaded, he poured in dishwashing crystals, closed and locked the door, and set the machine in motion. Lauren thought of him as controlling and manipulative. He'd live with that, too. And place the blame right at Camilla's feet.

After drying his hands on the dishtowel, he wiped down the counter.

He'd never be caught unprepared again.

CHAPTER FIVE

LAUREN AWOKE SLOWLY. Her first thought was for the state of her stomach. When there was no immediate revolt her senses began to pick up on other elements. Like the large, muscular man she was snuggled up to.

Her eyes flew open to the yummy sight of smooth skin covering broad shoulders. She reared back, ready to scold Ray for taking advantage, only to find she'd been the one to encroach on *his* side of the bed.

Chagrined at being the one to break the rules, she rolled back to her side and immediately missed his warmth. Obviously she'd been lured by his heat during the night until she'd wrapped herself around him. With any luck he'd slept through her lapse, otherwise he'd razz her unmercifully for breaking her own rules.

She waited for him to move, to awake. When a few minutes passed and he didn't shift, she slid from the bed and fled to the bathroom. Several minutes later she stood brushing her teeth when the door from the bedroom opened and Ray strolled in.

"Morning." He gave her a peck on the cheek, then moved past her to the shower. Dropping his gray knit boxers, he stepped naked into the tub and pulled the curtain closed. Lauren choked on a mouthful of toothpaste.

She spit, rinsed, grabbed her make-up bag and escaped to the bedroom to dress before he finished showering. It didn't take long to pull on jeans and a lavender sweater. She tugged on thick socks and low-heeled boots, and then sat on the side of the bed to put her make-up on, consciously waiting for Ray to make his appearance.

Her stomach hadn't protested yet, but she snagged a soda cracker from her purse stash. Better safe than sorry. Yesterday's queasiness had been explained away with the travel, but it couldn't continue without serious questions arising.

Lauren preferred to tell Ray about his impending fatherhood on her own terms, at her own pace. Which might well be when they were back in California—not while she was half a world away from her support system. Or trying to keep up the pretense of a false engagement.

He wandered into the bedroom, a towel hitched around lean hips.

"Seriously?" she demanded. "You agreed to the rules!"

His bare shoulders were impossibly wide and the muscles in his arms and chest flexed as he rubbed a second towel over his head. The man was droolworthy, with his sculpted abs, tight gluteus, and long, hair-dusted legs. Just watching him walk across the room made her mouth water. Other body parts went straight to tingle.

This was exactly why she'd made the rules.

He glanced over his shoulder at her. "I've honored them." He stepped into a pair of boxer briefs before ditching the towel. "We never discussed the bathroom. Plus, let me just repeat how crazy I think they are. It's not like we haven't—"

"I know we've been intimate." Didn't matter. They'd never been naked together. Their encounters had been too hurried, too frantic. "But that's over."

"So you say." He grabbed a pair of chinos from the bottom drawer, along with a pale blue T-shirt. "I thought you might have changed your mind."

Her hands went to her hips. "What made you think that?"

"The way you cozied up to me in bed last night, for one."

Heat flooded her cheeks. So much for the hope he'd slept through her groping. "That was unintentional," she informed him. "It won't happen again."

"If it was unintentional..." he came to tower over her "...that means you had no control over your actions. What makes you so sure it won't happen again?"

She lifted her chin. "I was overly tired last night. That won't be a problem the rest of the trip."

"I hope you're right." He lifted his right hand, cupped her cheek, and traced the faint shadows under her eye. "Not that I'm complaining. I won't hold you to the rules. Feel free to cozy up to me anytime you please."

"I'm not going to hold you to a standard I'm not willing to uphold myself." She backed up until his hand dropped. "The rules are meant as a mutual show of respect. Is it too much to ask for your cooperation?"

"Not at all—but then I'm not the one trying to pretend our relationship never happened."

Her jaw dropped. "Oh, believe me, I'm well aware that our...fling...*happened*." Knowledge of their child ran deep within her. "And calling what was between us a relationship is pushing it, don't you think?"

"I don't generally say things I don't mean." He cocked his head, invading her space again. "Hurried and hot doesn't necessarily relate to lack of depth."

"Funny, that's exactly how I see it." She locked her knees, refusing to give him any more ground.

"Is that what bothers you?" he asked, all concern, and she was reminded again that he had started his career as an actor. "You doubt my commitment?"

"I have no doubt of your commitment..." she paused "...to getting your own way." She circled him and crossed the room. "Look, I admit the sex was hot. It was crazy and wild and fun. But it was totally lacking in emotional depth.

And that's not who I am." Hand on the doorknob, she met his gaze. "I smell coffee. We should go down."

Ray followed Lauren down the stairs, enjoying the sway of her hips in the well-fitting jeans. She had him in a quandary. She'd nailed his motivation dead-on, but she was also wrong.

His emotions were not as detached as she believed. He'd be a whole lot more comfortable if they were.

Instead he worried about the pallor in her cheeks and whether she had slept well the night before. Now he had her back in his life he wanted to explore the passion between them at a more leisurely pace.

When he'd finally joined her in the tiny bed he'd lain awake for a good hour, tormented by his promise not to touch. He'd stared into the dark while she'd shifted from position to position, as if unable to get comfortable. She'd seemed drawn to him, yet had jerked away if she got too close. Her subconscious was clearly on the job.

Her restlessness had added to his until he'd finally had enough. He'd rolled over and gathered her in his arms, tucking her into the shelter of his body. She'd sighed and gone limp in his arms. Despite the arousal intensified by her nearness, he'd soon followed her into sleep.

Thankfully she blamed their tangled bodies on their subconscious actions. Yeah, that was a confession he'd take to his grave.

In the kitchen Mamó stood at the stove, flipping pancakes. When she heard them on the stairs she turned with a huge smile.

"Good morning." She greeted Lauren and then Ray. "Sit. Sit. As promised, I have your favorite breakfast." She bustled to the stove and returned with a heaping platter she set in the middle of the table. "Blueberry pancakes."

"Mamó, this looks wonderful." Lauren helped herself to one pancake.

"They *are* wonderful." Ray added another to her plate. "Nobody can eat just one," he explained piling four onto his plate. He added warm syrup and dug in.

"He's right, dear." Mamó poured him a cup of coffee, then held the pot over Lauren's cup.

Lauren stopped her. "Do you have decaffeinated?"

Mamó grimaced. "Unfortunately, I do. But it's instant."

"That'll work." Lauren hopped up. "I'll get it. You sit with Ray. I'm sure you have a lot of catching up to do." Before his grandmother could protest, Lauren added, "That is if you don't mind if I make myself at home?"

"Of course, my dear." Mamó slid into the chair next to Ray as she directed Lauren to the proper cabinet. "I want you to be comfortable."

Ray silently toasted Lauren for the brilliant move. She met his salute with a smile and started the microwave. He turned his attention to Mamó.

"Great party last night. Thanks for the welcome."

"Everyone was so excited to see you." Mamó patted his hand. "It's been too long since you visited the neighborhood. They're so happy for your success."

"And apparently for my engagement." He eyed her over his coffee mug.

Mamó's chin lowered and her shoulders sagged. "I'm sorry," she apologized. Then she spoiled it by claiming, "It's your own fault—staying away so long, never giving me any news to share."

"The fact I haven't been back to the neighborhood for a while is not an excuse for lying to your friends."

She stared down at the table, twisted her mug between sturdy hands marked by age and wear. "I wouldn't have to lie if you'd make more of an effort."

He ignored that. Attacking her was not the way to bolster her up. But he couldn't let her get away with this behavior either.

"It's one thing if it were just me." He let the words hang

in the air for a moment. "But you've put Lauren in a difficult position."

A frown pulled Mamó's hand-drawn brows together. "Oh, but —"

Ray cut Lauren's protest off with a flick of his eyes and a shake of his head. "It's not okay, Lauren. When we start getting pestered by the press you won't feel so generous."

"Press?" She bit her pretty bottom lip.

"If it hasn't hit the social media outlets yet, it will soon." He hardened his heart. Soft-pedaling the news wouldn't help anyone. "Phone calls requesting confirmation won't be far behind."

She pushed away from the table. "Excuse me."

"Where are you going?" he asked.

"To text my family and warn them that rumors of my engagement are grossly exaggerated."

"You can do that from here." He looked at her plate, pleased to see she'd eaten both pancakes.

"I could, but my mom will be calling two seconds after she gets the message, so I'll take it to the next room. I'd be dealing with Tori, too, except she's halfway around the world on her honeymoon. No telling when she'll call."

"It's pretty early in California," Ray reminded her.

Lauren glanced at the kitchen clock. "Not early enough."

She took off, and Ray arched a brow at Mamó.

"It was just a few friends." Mamó avoided his gaze. Instead she fussed with the syrup pitcher, wiping the edge and replacing it in the middle of the table.

"Friends gossip," he reminded her.

"Doris Renwicki was the troublemaker." Mamó lifted contrite eyes to meet his gaze. "I really am sorry. She just got to me, with all her talk of babies."

"I know." He covered her hand with his. The woman had gotten to him, too. So, yeah, he understood. But that didn't mean he could let Mamó off the hook. His career was too public to have odd announcements like this popping up. Luckily he was here and could coordinate damage control.

"You've put Lauren and me in a difficult situation. If I were serious and had decided to ask her to marry me, you've stolen her moment of announcing it. And that's if she doesn't question my motives and agrees to accept my proposal."

"Oh, Ray, of course she'd accept you." Mamó covered her mouth, true distress in her pale eyes. "But you're right. I've ruined her moment. Do you think she can forgive me?"

Figured she would zero in on the injury to Lauren.

"What can I do?" She began to cry. "I don't want things to be difficult between the two of you."

Damn. This wasn't what he wanted. He pushed his empty plate to the side.

"Stop crying. Don't worry. I'll fix it."

"I'm sorry." She wiped at her eyes.

"I know, and I'm going to fix it. Just stop crying now. Lauren will think I'm being mean."

"It's not you, it's me." She hid her face in a napkin.

"It'll be okay." Her distress made his gut clench. He took her hand in his and squeezed.

"It won't. The press will come."

"I'll handle it," he promised, going around the table to pull her into his arms. "I love you, Mamó. Now, dry your eyes. You want to be beautiful for your party."

"I don't want to go."

"Of course you do. It's just the thing to cheer you up. Everything is going to be okay."

"No. I've messed things up for you and Lauren."

"When I'm done fixing things she'll think I'm a hero."

Mamó's body stopped shaking. "A hero, huh?"

A warm jacket was settled over Lauren's shoulders and she turned to give Ray a grateful smile. As expected, her mom had called right on the heels of Lauren's text. Wanting privacy for the call, she'd stepped outside onto Mamó's tiny stoop, only to discover it had snowed overnight. The overhang protected the stoop and some of the steps, so she wasn't standing in snow, but her sweater did little to ward off the freezing temperature.

"Don't worry. You'll be the first to know," she reassured her mother for the third time. "Ray's waiting for me. I have to go."

"Okay, but I want the whole story when you get home," warned her mom. "Say hello to Ray for me. Bye, love you."

"Love you." Lauren closed her phone. "Thanks for the jacket," she said to Ray. "It snowed."

"It does that here."

"Tori would be so jealous."

Making it snow at his Hollywood manor had been Garrett's Christmas gift to her twin. The romantic gesture had won Tori's heart and the acceptance of his proposal. Lauren still got choked up thinking about it. Here in New York she found the reality of the frozen landscape a bit overwhelming.

"So, did you haul Mamó over the coals?"

He cocked his head. "It felt like it. She cried."

"I'm sorry." She slipped her arms into his jacket. "But you needed to talk to her. It would be bad enough if you were an average guy. Right now you're the hottest director in the country. The press will be all over this. Is she okay?"

"Yeah." He flicked at a piece of paper. "I distracted her by asking after her 'to-do' list. Are you up for doing some chores?"

"Sure I'll help," she agreed easily. "I'm not about to pass up the opportunity to watch the great Ray Donovan at manual labor."

Just the notion had her insides tingling.

"Brat." He tugged on her ponytail. "Such wit. You should consider writing for the movies."

"Oh, no." Even though he'd joked, she literally backed

away at his suggestion. "That's your world, not mine. I'm happy staying in the background, thank you very much."

"You're good with details." He edged forward, eliminating the distance she'd created between them.

He always did that, and had done right from the beginning of their association. Even before they'd become intimate. It was intoxicating and unnerving at the same time.

"You'd make an excellent production assistant."

"I have a job, but thanks for the endorsement."

She inched back again, seeking the space she needed. Seriously, how was she supposed to keep a clear head around him while constantly inhaling the clean, male scent of him?

"What's on the to-do list?"

He consulted the paper. "A broken railing, changing some lightbulbs, and assembling a console."

"That's quite a list. We should get started if we want to finish before the party." Shivering, she tucked her hands in the pockets of his jacket. "Are there home improvement centers in New York?"

"Better. We have Chester's Hardware."

He invaded her bubble again, but a car pulling to a stop in front of the house distracted her. Had the press discovered them already?

A uniformed deliveryman emerged from the car, carrying a large box. He crunched through the snow, opened the gate, and approached the steps. "Delivery for Lauren Randall."

Her brows zinged up in surprise. She wasn't expecting anything—certainly not at this address.

"I'm Lauren Randall." She accepted the package, thinking she should tip the man. She glanced up at Ray. "My purse is inside."

"That's okay, ma'am," the delivery person assured her. "The tip was included. Have a nice day, now." He tipped his head and trudged back to his car.

She clutched the large package to her. "For a minute there I thought the press had found us."

"Actually, I see a fellow across the way with a camera." A hand in the small of her back urged her toward the door. "Why don't we take this inside?"

Her skin itched at the idea of being spied on, so she allowed him to direct her indoors.

She settled on the sofa and placed the large box next to her. "What did you do, Ray?"

"What makes you think it's from me?" He went to the fire and tossed on a log, then took up a spot at the mantel.

"Because nobody knows I'm here."

"Open it."

Eying him suspiciously, she worked off the bright red bow. Was it coincidence that the bow was her favorite color or had Ray asked for red? Coincidence, surely? She doubted Ray knew her favorite color.

She lifted off the lid and dug through mounds of tissue. Her heart began an erratic tattoo as she recognized the famous name blazoned on the inside of the box. Maybe he did know, because the paper parted to reveal a red leather coat trimmed in black fur. *Oh, my.*

"Oh, my…" Mamó echoed Lauren's thoughts. "What a beautiful coat."

Lauren held the garment up. The jacket was long enough to hit her just above the knee. A black asymmetrical zipper slashed across the front and the softest of faux fur lined the inside from shoulder to hem, including a shawl collar that converted into a hood.

"Gorgeous…" she breathed.

"Try it on," Mamó urged.

Lauren didn't need the encouragement. She had already unzipped the jacket and shrugged out of Ray's coat. She slid her arms in and sighed as softness and warmth surrounded her. The smell of rich leather teased her nostrils. Oh, she coveted it.

She turned to Ray, who smirked with quiet satisfaction.

"Thank you," she said as she shrugged out of the lovely coat. "But I can't accept it."

"Oh, but—" Mamó covered her mouth, turned around, and hurried toward the kitchen.

Ellie came through the connecting door to her unit and Mamó detoured to grab her arm and drag her along to the back of the house.

Lauren barely noticed. All her attention was focused on Ray's stormy expression.

"You need a warmer jacket. Your time on the stoop should have proved that."

"I'll manage."

For some reason her refusal seemed to hurt him. But accepting such an expensive gift implied an intimacy she was trying to avoid. She'd told him she didn't need a new coat, and yet true to his controlling nature he'd gone against her wishes and bought one anyway.

"It's too much."

"I can afford it."

"That's not the point."

"You just said it was." He raked a hand through his hair. "You're only here because of me. It's my responsibility to make sure you don't suffer for doing me a favor."

Silently she applauded him for the brilliant argument, but she saw right through him and chided him with a simple, "Ray…"

"As far as I'm concerned it's yours," he said dismissively. "If you don't want it, just borrow it while you're here and I'll have Mamó give it to the Salvation Army when we leave. Whatever you decide, I'm leaving for the hardware store in ten minutes."

He stormed off, taking the stairs two at a time.

Dang the man. By stating his intention to give the coat away to charity he'd taken the power of her refusal away from her. She stroked the silky black faux fur. Would it hurt to wear it during her visit?

Yes. She needed to stand by her principles—to show him she couldn't be bullied or bought. Regretfully, she folded the jacket back into the box. Sometimes being right really, *really* sucked.

CHAPTER SIX

OF COURSE THEY walked to Chester's. The neighborhood store turned out to be only three blocks away. It was easier to go by foot than to shovel the drifts away from the garage. Ray offered to call a cab, but Lauren refused. Not for three blocks.

She slid into her fleece-lined raincoat, borrowed Ellie's snow boots, and met Ray at the gate.

He scowled at her coat but refrained from saying anything. Instead he took her arm. "Be careful. The snow has been shoveled, but it can be slick."

At first they strolled in silence, but several people were out and Ray got hailed a number of times. He tried to keep them moving, which proved difficult when it was someone on the same side of the street.

Shivering as a light snow began to fall, Lauren admired his skillful ability to greet and go. Across the way she noticed the photographer Ray had spotted earlier. The man kept pace with them, yet seemed content to keep his distance.

All in all, by the time they reached the hardware store, she wished she hadn't been quite so quick to set Ray's gift aside.

"Here we are." He held the door for her.

Grateful for the promise of warmth, she stepped inside. She stamped the snow from her boots and faced Ray. Only to find he'd all but disappeared. A knit cap covered his

hair, his neck scarf had been pulled up to cover the bottom half of his face, and his shoulders were slumped forward. He'd gone from being a confident, dynamic man
who dominated any room he entered to a man most people
would overlook. Obviously that was the point.

Considering their trip here, she couldn't blame him.
On this Tuesday morning Chester's hopped with clientele.

"Hello, I'm Lauren." She offered Ray her gloved hand.
"Who are *you*?"

"Ha-ha." He took her hand and gave her a basket to
carry before leading her deeper into the store. "You're a
real comedian."

"Sorry, I couldn't resist. It's a very effective disguise.
Do you have to use it often?"

"No." He turned down an aisle and stopped in front of
an assortment of lubricating oils. He handed her a can and
took off again. "I'm not in front of the cameras anymore,
so I'm not as recognizable as celebrities on TV or in movies. Then there's the fact most people are too intimidated
to approach me. But this is my old neighborhood, so all
bets are off."

"Everyone seems happy for your success. And you're
very gracious with them. Yet you're also careful to keep
them at a distance." She followed him into the lighting
aisle. "Kyla said it's been years since you've visited Mamó
at home."

"Do you have a point?" His gaze roamed the shelves,
seeking three-way bulbs.

"I'm just wondering what you're running from?"

He went totally still.

Giving him time, she reached past him and selected
energy-saving three-way bulbs. She placed them in the
basket and waited for him to come back to her. His reaction confirmed her suspicion.

Ray hadn't willingly abandoned his neighborhood.
Something had sent him running.

Finally he shrugged. "We all have things in our past we'd rather forget."

"True." She hooked her arm through his. "But some stick with us more than others."

"Will you wear the coat?"

She rolled her eyes. Leave it to him to manipulate his own confession. Too bad she had him beat. "Oh, yeah. I already made that decision on the walk over here. I may be stubborn. I'm not stupid."

"Right." He grinned and reclaimed the basket. He held his other hand out to her. "Come on. Time to go play handyman."

"No touching," she said, reminding herself as well as him, and walked around him to the cashier.

Back at the house, Lauren gratefully released her end of the heavy box containing the mahogany console. They'd blown through the fix-it items on Mamó's to-do list and were about to put together the new console table.

Lauren read the directions while he went straight to sorting the nails and screws. When she caught herself staring at his bent head, she decided to press him a little more on his past.

She crouched down next to him. "So, about those things in the past you prefer to forget…sometimes it helps to share."

"I appreciate the offer." He stroked his thumb over the dent in her chin. "It's better left buried."

"I disagree." She blew out a breath. "I don't know if Garrett told you this, but Tori and I had a friend in high school who committed suicide."

"He mentioned it." His shuttered gaze met hers before he focused on lining up the planks by size.

She stood and squared her shoulders. This was never easy to talk about.

"Well, the school provided counseling for those that

wanted it, and because we were particularly close to him my parents continued it for an extra month. There was guilt and anger to deal with, as well as loss and sorrow. Mostly for Tori. I went more to support her. By talking about our experience we were able to gain perspective and work our way through the stages of grief in a healthy manner."

He slowly rose to his feet to stare down into her eyes. "And yet Tori's memories of that time almost cost her her relationship with Garrett."

"Talking about it doesn't take away the importance of an event. But it can minimize its power over you. Once you've shared with someone, the worst that can happen is over. Someone else knows. The fear of discovery is past, making it easier to deal with what follows."

"Really? Because having the whole neighborhood witness my humiliation, pain and disappointment didn't make it easier to bear. I call *liar* on that."

She flinched—more at what he had revealed than at the bite in his words.

"I once let a man control me to the point I almost ditched my family for him." Saying it out loud sent a cold wave down her spine. Her throat clenched. It was her biggest shame. And she had no idea why she'd just told him. Who knew being pregnant led to insanity? Worse, she couldn't seem to stop. "It was a form of abuse that I didn't even see happening."

"Oh, Lauren." He pulled her into his arms. The screwdriver in his hand bumped against her butt. He set it aside, then enfolded her in a tender embrace. "I just can't see it. You're so in control, so strong."

"In a way, that just made it worse. It was subtle and insidious and completely undermined who I was. Tori saved me."

And for a while Lauren had hated her for it.

"When I finally made the break from Brad I couldn't talk to Mom or Tori. I was too ashamed. That fear of discovery... But I remembered the counseling from high school and decided to see if my college provided counselors and I was able to talk to someone."

She'd learned only she had the ability to give her power away.

His hand stroked softly through her hair. Allowing him to hold her like this broke the rules, but she couldn't bring herself to care. Insanity aside, she'd started this in order to help him deal with whatever it was that had driven him away from Queens.

She eased away. "I can promise you nothing is as bad as you build it up to be in your own head."

He cupped the back of her neck, his intent gaze scrutinizing her carefully. "You're such a contradiction. You find it hard to accept a gift but now you've bared your soul for me."

A shrug was all she had to give him. "Different cost values."

He rocked his forehead over hers. "I don't know what to say."

"The point is your secrets are safe with me. You can say anything." She pressed her lips to his cheek before stepping back again. "And I have agreed to wear the jacket, so technically you owe me."

"I'll think about it."

"A little more your way," Ray directed, eyeing the entryway to gauge its center point. "Okay, set it down."

Lauren stepped back to view the finished results as Ray added baskets to the bottom shelf of the console. Thirty inches high and five feet long, it had three deep drawers across the front, with three rattan baskets going in the open slots below the drawers.

"It really is a lovely piece." She held her hand up for a high-five. "Well done, Donovan."

He slapped her palm. "I couldn't have done it without you, Randall."

"Seriously," she agreed, "that was one heavy beast."

He yanked on the end of her ponytail. "We make a good team."

"Hmm…"

She hummed the noncommittal response just to be contrary. Surprisingly, they had worked well together, making fairly quick work of the assembly. Still, after getting all touchy-feely with him it was best not to give him too much encouragement. The man didn't know the meaning of boundaries. Give him an inch and he'd take a mile.

Best not to encourage herself either.

More than once she'd caught herself staring at his hands. Remembering how they felt on her skin. Long-fingered, strong, and competent, his broad-palmed hands were sensual tools of torment, capable of sending her senses reeling.

Oh, yeah, he knew how to use his hands.

"Mamó will be thrilled." She forced her attention back to the moment.

"I think so." He glanced at his watch. "They should be back soon."

Ellie had whisked Mamó off to the hair salon after lunch. Her big birthday bash at the community center started at six and the women were off beautifying themselves for the event.

"Hair and nails for both of them?" She shook her head while stifling a yawn. Every time she slowed down sleep tugged at her eyelids. Must be jet lag. "It'll probably be another hour at least." She bent and stuffed plastic bags into a large cardboard box. "Why don't you grab us a couple of sodas and I'll finish cleaning up here?"

"I have a better idea." He took the box from her. "Why don't you sit down while I take care of this and get the sodas? It's the least I can do after all your help."

"I won't say no."

He headed outside with the box.

She checked her phone for messages, smiled at the

text from her assistant confirming all was set for the party tonight.

Curling into the corner of the sofa, she clicked on the TV. A reality show came on in which brides sought the perfect dress. A secret fan, she rested her head on a closed fist and watched as the bride and her mother clashed over a peek-a-boo corset dress.

She fought off a yawn. Earlier she'd stepped outside to make a few arrangements for tonight's big bash. Events were Lauren's "thing." She felt bad, sitting back and doing nothing for Mamó's party, so she'd reached out to a couple of local connections she'd met at national conferences and arranged for a little something extra.

Which reminded her—she needed to fill Ray in on her plan. Her eyes closed. She struggled to push them open. Hopefully Ray wouldn't object to her interference. It was all meant in good fun...

After disposing of the box and grabbing two cans of soda from the refrigerator, Ray joined Lauren on the sofa. The first thing he noticed was that Lauren was sound asleep. Jet lag, no doubt. Compelled by something bigger than his promises, he gave in to the urge to touch. He swept a silky blond tendril behind her ear, traced the oval curve of her jaw, stroked his thumb over the plump bow of her lips.

So strong, yet so delicate. His gut churned at the thought of her under another man's thumb. Never would he have suspected her of subjugating her will to someone else. Not with the grief she gave him.

An abusive experience sure explained her fierce need for independence.

His fingers curled into a fist as he fought the desire to smash something—preferably the abusive jerk's face. Too bad he was beyond Ray's reach. Slowly he unfurled each finger, because Lauren deserved tenderness and understanding. He wouldn't be responsible for bringing her any more pain.

Dropping his hand to her thigh, he turned his attention to the TV. His brows plummeted into a scowl. What kind of hot mess had she been watching? A woman in a robe was extolling the virtues of some man while a salesclerk waded through a forest of white gowns. Some sort of bride show.

Just kill him now.

He picked up the remote, ready to click it away. The picture changed to a young, dark-haired woman with brown eyes in a round face. His finger froze on the remote. For a moment he saw Camilla standing there. In a blink the resemblance disappeared.

He scrubbed at the back of his neck. He obviously had the past on his mind.

Hard not to when he was smack in the middle of the borough where it had all gone down. All he wanted was to put the past behind him. Yet everywhere he looked he stumbled across reminders of his darkest moment. And Lauren's probing didn't help.

Maybe he should talk to her. *No.* He appreciated her sharing her past with him, but he couldn't reciprocate. Exposing his shame would be like opening a vein. Better to leave it buried.

Aiming the remote again, he changed the channel, finding a hockey game to watch. He settled into the cushions, one hand on Lauren's thigh, the other wrapped around a cold soda. Now, *this* was more like it. An hour alone to enjoy a cold drink, a good game, and his girl. This was the way to relax.

"Here we are, ladies." Ray climbed out of the taxi and held the door for Mamó and Lauren. He escorted them inside, where the three of them checked their coats. Ellie and Kyla had gone on ahead of them. "May I say it's my pleasure to be accompanying the two most beautiful women at the party?"

"Thank you." Pleased with his compliment, Mamó twittered while patting her white-gray crown of curls. She glowed in a jacket dress of bright purple. A dusting of soft rose highlighted the natural color in her creamy cheeks. She looked lovely, and clearly ready to party.

He wrapped her in a gentle hug. "Make sure you behave yourself."

"Where's the fun in that?" She patted his cheek, giving him a wicked smile. "I plan to party hearty tonight."

"Mamó!"

"Leave her alone." Lauren hooked her arm through his. "This is *her* night. Let her enjoy it."

"Thank you, dear." With a flash of her diamond eternity ring, Mamó waved and walked into the hall.

"'Party hearty'?" Ray muttered. "She's seventy-six."

"She's still a vibrant woman with a huge capacity for love. I know of at least one gentleman attracted by her *joie de vivre*."

Lauren dragged her hand down his arm, over his hand, clung to his fingertips for just a second, then swung around and through the door behind his grandmother.

He was distracted by her touch, by the sheer grace of her in a sassy off-the-shoulder black dress, and her words didn't connect at first. He hadn't been paying lip service when he'd told them he was with the two most beautiful women at the party. Where Mamó was lovely, Lauren literally stole his breath. *Stunning* was the only word to do her justice.

The black dress clung to soft curves, its hem flirting with the silky skin three inches above her knees. The dark color contrasted sharply with her creamy complexion, giving the impression of delicate strength. Light shimmered in her blond hair, flowing like molten gold around her shoulders as she glanced back at him. A daring red lip gloss drew his gaze to her lush mouth.

He followed as if beckoned.

Only when she disappeared from sight did her words slam into him.

Wait—a "gentleman" was interested in Mamó? Not if *he* had anything to say about it.

He rushed through the door. And found Mamó and Lauren surrounded by a bevy of young studs dressed in tuxedos. Heavens, it was like a casting call for a Fred Astaire remake.

Oh, hell, no.

He waded through the throng to Lauren's side and heard the last of the introductions.

"And I'm Chad," a tall man said.

He had a square chin, brown eyes and dark hair. Ray eyed the other four. Not so young after all—which only made it worse.

"I hope you will save the first dance for me?"

"Oh, my." Mamó giggled as the man lifted her hand to his mouth. "I think I can do that."

Giggled. Like a girl. His seventy-six-year-old grandmother.

"What's going on here?" he demanded, making no effort to curb the edge in his voice.

"Oh. Everyone—this is my grandson Ray." Mamó beamed as she made the introductions. "Ray, these lovely gentlemen are here to dance with me."

"I beg your pardon."

"Now, don't be a grouch. Lauren arranged it. I love to dance, and with so many more ladies than men this ensures I'll always have a partner." She took the opportunity to give Lauren a huge hug. "Thank you so much. It's going to be the best party ever."

"You're welcome." Lauren kissed her cheek. "I might have to borrow one myself if Ray's going to be a party-poop."

"I won't blame you." Mamó stepped back and smoothed her hands over her hips. "I should find Ellie."

"May I escort you to the head table?" Chad offered his arm.

"You may." Mamó threaded her arm through his with another giggle. The two moved off and the other men melted away.

Ray crossed his arms over his chest, his gaze narrowed on Lauren. "*You* did this?"

"This?"

"Arranged for my grandmother to be groped by a gigolo." Her tinkling laugh grated over his taut nerves.

"They are *not* gigolos. They're dancers. I noticed a lot of Mamó's friends were single, so I called a friend of mine who arranged for a local dance studio to send over some men to act as stag dance partners."

Okay, it was a nice gesture. He still didn't like it.

"I didn't know you knew anybody in New York."

"I have contacts all over the world. We meet at conferences and trade shows. Events is a pretty small community, actually."

"I imagine you're a league above most of your colleagues."

She lifted one shoulder in a half-shrug. "No, we just have a more elite clientele than most."

"I've seen your work. I would argue you attract an elite clientele because of your above-par work." He looked around the room at the lush floral centerpieces and the billowing folds of white silk draped from the ceiling and cascading down the walls. "I can see your touch in more than the expanded guest list."

"Mamó has graciously opened her home to me. She, Ellie and Kyla have made me feel welcome. It was the least I could do."

He studied her for a long minute. She was wrong. She was a guest. Nothing had been expected of her. Not even a gift, as they were optional. In fact, in a very real way *she* was a gift—from him to his grandmother.

"I'm not sure I approve." He pulled her close and pressed a light kiss to her lips. "But Mamó is happy, so thank you."

"You're welcome." She swiped a thumb over his lips, removing a light layer of red. "Shall we join Mamó at the head table?"

"Sure." He settled a hand in the sweet spot at the small of her back. "On the way you can explain your comment about a gentleman being interested in Mamó."

"I noticed a connection between her and a gentleman at the welcome party the other night—"

"No." He cut her off. "No noticing anything between her and any gentleman. Just turn your Spidey senses off."

She stopped abruptly, blocking his path. He almost tripped over his own feet to prevent himself from running into her.

Hands on hips, she slowly swung to face him. "You just can't help yourself can you?"

"What?"

"There you go, trying to control me. Worse, you're trying to control your grandmother, who deserves any chance at happiness fate hands her."

"I don't want you interfering."

"It's not 'Spidey senses,'" she informed him in icy tones. "It's a very real feeling about a connection between two people."

"Well, aim it elsewhere. Mamó is not interested."

"That's for Mamó to say, not you."

"I'm saying it for both of us." He stepped into her space, let her see he meant business. "Turn it off."

A flash of hurt went through her eyes before they frosted over in a blink. One red-tipped nail poked him in the chest, pushing him back.

"One: don't disrespect the matchmaking." Another poke. "Two: I'm here as a favor to you. Under protest, if you'll remember." Two pokes this time. "Three: you're just mad because I didn't run the idea by you first. I'd never do anything to hurt your grandmother. You're the one who will do that when she finds out our whole relationship is a sham and has been since the beginning."

She twirled on her stylish black heels, obviously planning to leave him in the dust.

He caught her arm. "Don't even *think* about telling her."

She glanced from his hand on her arm to his face. "It's good to know exactly what you think of me, Ray. For a while there you almost had me fooled that you were a decent guy. I thought I'd learned to see beyond a man's act."

He watched her throat work as she swallowed hard.

"Thanks for the reminder."

Stung, he dropped her arm. "Don't put me in league with that monster. I'm nothing like him."

"No?" She rubbed her arm. "You always have to be in control. You want to tell me what to do, who I can talk to, and what I can say. At least I can see it this time." A slight shiver shook her small frame and a hand went to her stomach. "Tell Mamó I'll be along in a few minutes. I'm going to talk to the facility director."

Again, she began to walk away. It struck him that he'd handled this badly. He'd never meant to hurt her. He just wanted to protect his grandmother.

"Lauren, wait." He moved quickly, blocking her escape. "I forgot four."

She nailed him with cold eyes. Who knew gold could cut so sharp?

"We're already done. I've been telling you that for days."

This time he let her go, his mind ticking over ways to fix this. He'd give her a few minutes to cool down. Let her do her business thing. It would help restore her sense of order. At least he hoped so.

Because he still saw that flash of raw hurt in her eyes. And it made him sick to his stomach that he was the one to put it there.

CHAPTER SEVEN

THE ARGUMENT WITH Ray sent her scurrying for the restroom, the bitter taste of bile rising up her throat. Funny how her nausea often coincided with high emotions.

After she'd emptied her stomach, she liberated a few crackers from the buffet. Perched at a table on the edge of the room, she nibbled away and soon felt better. Well, her stomach felt better. Her emotions still felt thrashed.

Ray's behavior hurt. Did he really believe she'd put Mamó at risk? That she used her matchmaking gift to manipulate people?

That was his talent, not hers.

Wanting to avoid the aggravating man, she went in search of the facilities director. She thanked the plump brunette for allowing the last-minute additions to the decorations. The woman waved her off, saying she'd never seen the room look so pretty.

Lauren heard the same message again and again as she slowly made her way to the head table. And the cost had been minimal, as the flowers were recycled from a wedding earlier in the day. The five gentleman dancers accounted for the biggest expense, but it thrilled her to be able to add to Mamó's day.

Spending the night chained to Ray's side...? Not so enchanting.

He tried to pretend nothing had happened. She responded to his attempts at conversation with the briefest of responses. She wouldn't have responded at all except for Mamó. No need to draw her attention to their tiff.

After a while Ray excused himself and took off with his camera.

She didn't know who was more relieved to have him disappear behind the lens—him or her. Kyla slid into his vacant seat.

"You're my favorite person in the whole wide world." She squeezed Lauren's hand on the table. "The room is just stunning. And all the matrons are atwitter about the studs you lined up as dancing partners." She glanced over her shoulder at a couple of the men at the next table. "I'm kind of aglow myself."

Lauren laughed and nudged her new friend's shoulder. "The night's paid for. I say have fun."

"Really?" Kyla nibbled her bottom lip. "You wouldn't mind? You hired them for Mamó and her contemporaries."

"Of course I don't mind." Lauren assured her. "I want everyone to have a good time." She paused and pointed to the ninety-year-old woman chatting up Chad. "But you might not want to get between the men and Mrs. Harris."

Kyla snorted, then quickly clapped a hand over her mouth. "You're wicked." She leaned close. "To return the favor I'll warn you to stay clear of Old Man Tanner. He has wandering hands."

Pink-cheeked, Lauren asked for a refresher course on the names of the people she'd met the night before. "I'm usually good with names, but I was a tad distracted."

"I suppose news of your engagement might do that." With an understanding smile Kyla complied, adding bits of harmless gossip designed to help Lauren remember names.

Ellie broke in to steal Kyla away, muttering something about the cake.

When the music started Ray reappeared and asked her to dance. She declined. But she gladly accepted Chad when he returned Mamó to the table.

Ray's scowl as she walked off with Chad soothed her ravaged heart.

On the dance floor Lauren swayed lightly to a slow tune. Chad was charming and undemanding—two traits she particularly appreciated tonight.

Relaxing, she smiled at him. "You and your fellow dancers are a big hit."

"It's nice to be appreciated." He winked. "Actually, this is the first gig of this type I've heard of. I wouldn't mind if it caught on. It's nice to put a smile on a grandma's face. Is it true her grandson is *the* Ray Donovan?"

Lauren controlled a grimace. "Yes, he's the famous director. And it will thrill her to pieces if you ask her just like that."

"I like his movies. He's not afraid to take on hard core issues." His gaze traveled past her shoulder. "But obviously I'm a bigger fan of him than he is of me."

Lauren felt the weight of Ray's regard and knew Chad had just clashed gazes with her nemesis.

"Don't mind him. He's being a jerk, but it's not personal."

His gaze shifted past her again, then back down to her. "Do everyone a favor. Have pity. The guy is bringing the party down."

He'd barely finished speaking when a hand appeared on his shoulder and Ray asked to cut in.

Chad stepped back, bowed graciously, and disappeared into the crowd.

Lauren shifted her frown from one man to the other. *Men.*

"What's wrong?" Ray demanded as he pulled her close. "What did he do? Should I go after him?"

"No." She arched her eyebrows at him. Ray was the one who needed to apologize. The music stopped. She dropped her arms. "I want to return to the table."

Another ballad started. His arm tightened around her waist.

"Dance with me," he said. When she simply stared at him, he added, "Please. I want to apologize."

"Okay." She relented, sliding her arms up his hard chest to link her hands behind his head. "But only because your tantrum is marring Mamó's enjoyment of the party."

He made a rude noise in the back of his throat. "Hardly! Mamó barely knows I'm here. She's too busy dancing. Besides, I'm not the one walking away, dancing with other men."

Lauren closed her eyes. *Oh, goodness.* The very lack of emotion in Ray's voice revealed the depth of his upset. And it dawned on her that she was showing him up in front of the neighbors he already felt looked down on him. *Dang.* She wasn't ready to give up being mad yet. But he didn't deserve another fifteen years of misery either. She relaxed in his hold and let him turn her around the floor.

"You're right. I'm sorry. I forgot your situation for a few minutes. I'll behave myself. But that doesn't mean you get to tell me what to do or mock my talent."

"Oh, I believe in it. Mamó has the same weird juju when it comes to babies. I just wish you could make it go away."

A hot tide of dread ran down Lauren's spine and a hard knot lodged in her throat. Praying that it didn't mean what she thought it meant, she gulped, then cleared her throat. "Mamó has a talent? Regarding babies? What? She can tell the sex?"

"The sex—and she's a walking early pregnancy test. She'll know someone's pregnant before they do. Made for some awkward moments growing up." He shook that off. "But we're talking about your talent. So, can you make it stop?"

A walking early pregnancy test? Nothing to worry about there…

Lauren propped her hands on her hips. "You're not usually so dense, Ray. I know you love your grandmother, and you're concerned. But you should be happy for her, not thinking of yourself." Enough. She'd let this go on too long. "If I'm not going to get my apology I'm returning to the table."

His hands tightened on her. "So hard tonight." He lifted her chin on the edge of his hand until she looked him in the eyes. His held regret. "I hurt you. I'm sorry."

The simplicity of his words arrowed right to her heart.

She lowered her eyes, unable to hold his gaze. Confronted with his sincerity, she was forced to face the truth. Her anger acted as a shield. Otherwise she'd too easily fall into his arms again. Especially at the party.

Every time they'd hooked up it had been at a festive event of some sort, starting with Thanksgiving at his Malibu mansion last November.

She'd gone with him to set up the poker table in the loft. They'd started arguing over nothing, he'd kissed her, and the electricity between them had flared out of control. The open loft overlooked the living room, where her father and brother had been watching football, so Ray had dragged her around the corner into the first room they stumbled across—which had happened to be the laundry room.

To this day she couldn't do the laundry without blushing.

"Lauren?" He breathed her name against her temple. "Am I forgiven?"

"Oh. Of course." She bowed her head. "I may have overreacted a bit."

"No." He pulled back to see her better. "I'm the one at fault. I know you'd never hurt Mamó. And you have no control over the attraction you sense. It's just—"

Suddenly he swung Lauren around until they had a clear view of Mamó, dancing with an older gentleman with a full head of gray hair, a Van Dyke beard and mustache. "It's George Meade, isn't it? He's been sniffing around her all night."

Her stomach took longer to catch up than the rest of her. Lauren leaned against Ray and drew in some deep breaths.

"Hey…" A big hand cradled her head to him. "Are you okay?"

"Just a little dizzy," she assured him.

Regaining her composure, she created some distance between them.

"I know it freaks you out, thinking about her with a man, but having someone to focus on in her life besides you and your potential offspring might be the answer to your problem."

"Huh," he responded, his gaze focused across the room again. "I'm right, aren't I? It's Meade."

"I'm not saying." Lauren refused to throw the poor man to this predator stalking him. From the corner of her eye, she saw Mamó circling the floor in George Meade's arms. The faint glow of their connection reached Lauren across the distance. "Let Mamó have her evening."

"So it *is* him." Ray released her, his intent clear.

She grabbed his arm before he took two steps. "If you interrupt them I'm leaving."

He froze. "You said you'd behave."

"How I behave won't matter if I'm gone."

Taking her hand, he drew her to the edge of the dance floor. "I just want to talk to him. I'll only be a minute." He turned toward his quarry.

"I won't stop until I'm back in Hollywood," she warned him.

He pivoted in his Italian leather shoes to face her. "You wouldn't?"

She crossed her arms and pinned him with a glare.

"That's just mean."

"You have no idea." Her fingers bit into the fabric of his jacket as she pulled him further away from the dancing. "This is your grandmother's birthday party. I'm not going to let you embarrass her in front of her friends."

"You mean her *man* friend." He scowled.

"Him most of all." Aware of the hard muscle under her fingers, she dropped her hand.

Turmoil roiled inside him. She felt the surge of emotion as much as she saw it storm across his features.

"Just because I sense a connection it doesn't mean anything will come of it. It's up to them to act on it. Or not. But if you interfere you'd better believe I will be on the next plane out of here."

For just a second panic flared in his blue eyes. "You wouldn't really leave me alone with these people?"

She blinked at him, totally unprepared for his reaction even though it confirmed her earlier revelation. The flash of vulnerability exposed how difficult this trip was for him.

She took his hand. "Ray, these people are your family, your friends. They all care about you."

His face shuttered. "They like to claim they know me." He glanced around. "But none of them really does. They care because I'm famous and because of Mamó."

"They could hate you for the same reasons, but they don't."

She debated for a moment about her next move. Her confession might freak him out more than reassure him. She straightened her shoulders and went for it.

"Listen, the same vibe that allows me to see a connection between a couple also lets me pick up on high-level emotions. And the overall feeling in this room is positive—to the point it overwhelms everything else."

He stared at her for a moment, then cupped her cheek and drew her to him for a brief kiss.

"What you're feeling is for Mamó," he said.

"Yes," she agreed. "But I haven't noticed any malice or envy around you. And I think I would." She laid her head on his chest, felt the steady beat of his heart. "Just because they don't know all your secrets it doesn't mean they don't care."

And, oh, how she wished the sentiment didn't strike so close to home.

"Ray...Lauren." Kyla joined them. "Look who I have. This is Lulu, my goddaughter—isn't she beautiful?"

Lauren pulled back, but Ray kept his arm around her waist. She focused on the baby in Kyla's arms.

She held a tiny little girl with dark button eyes, pink bow lips, and short dark curls. Lulu couldn't be more than five months old and she melted Lauren's heart.

Her throat closed up at the thought she'd soon hold a baby of her own.

"Oh, my goodness. She's so sweet." She itched to hold the baby, but Ray beat her to it.

"She's a heartbreaker." He plucked the infant from his cousin. "Aren't you, my beauty?" He held her with confidence and ease, his comfort in handling the child obvious.

Lulu grinned, her bow mouth a perfect O, flashing toothless gums and innocent joy.

"Ah..."

Lauren and Kyla echoed each other, which caused them to laugh.

"She likes you." Lauren ran her finger over the petal-soft skin of the baby's hand. Lulu promptly wrapped her fingers around Lauren's digit.

Kyla snorted. "*All* women love him. Not even a five-month-old is immune to his charm." She held up a camera. "Her mama wants a picture." She stood back and clicked a shot of Lauren, Ray, and Lulu. "Thanks."

"What about Mama?" Ray asked. "We should get one with her, too."

Kyla beamed. "She would totally love that. I told her you'd go for it— Oh, my lord, *no*! Those little stinkers are going for the cake. Be right back." She took off at a trot, a fierce glint in her eyes.

"Oops." Ray's gaze followed his cousin's retreat. "Wouldn't want to be one of those boys."

"No."

Lauren couldn't take her eyes off Ray. Watching him with the little girl had charmed her more than she would have believed. He was so natural with the child. Actually, it surprised her. She would have expected just the opposite.

"You're very good with her."

"I'm into kids," he confessed. "I'm godfather to my assistant's one-year-old boy. I love when he brings him to the house. We play catch."

"Catch with a one-year-old?"

"Okay, you got me." He grinned. "We play chase the ball. But it's fun."

Lulu waved her arms and yammered a mouthful of noises. Ray bounced her in his arms.

"Don't worry, sweetness, we haven't forgotten you. Do you want to hold her?"

Lauren nodded and he passed the child to her. She gathered the tiny girl into her arms. How light she felt, yet warm and cuddly. "Well, hello, Lulu."

She received a big grin just like Ray had got. The precious moment lifted her spirits. She held a miracle in her arms. And soon she'd hold her own miracle.

Lulu waved her plump arms and latched onto Lauren's hoop earring. "Oh. Ouch!"

"I've got it." Ray gently held Lulu's arm and worked her fingers free of the gold hoop. His eyes were laughing as he looked down at Lauren. "For someone so small, she's got a good grip."

"She's perfect." Lauren bounced her gently. "But we really should find her mother and return her."

"Just one dance first." Ray wrapped his arms around her waist, swung the three of them onto the dance floor, and set up a mellow sway.

"You really need to learn to wait for an answer," she chided him. But her reprimand lacked heat. "I think she's tired. Her eyes are closing."

"Oh, yeah, she'll be out soon." His unreadable gaze lingered on her and the child. "You look good with a baby in your arms."

"Hmm?" She stalled, her mind flashing to his child in her womb.

It took all her concentration not to miss a step. She'd envisioned a life with just her child and her—based on his single jet-set lifestyle she'd figured he wouldn't want a child in his life. Certainly not disrupting his home. Seeing him with Lulu had put those notions into question.

"You looked pretty good yourself. Surprised me, really."

"They're just little people."

Not really...

"So, you plan to have a few kids of your own someday?" She held her breath, waiting for his answer.

His body tensed and he didn't respond right away, his gaze focused over her left shoulder. "Maybe," he finally allowed. "Never say never, right?"

Breath rushed back into her lungs. What kind of non-answer was that?

"I want kids," she shared, watching for a reaction. "At least two...maybe three."

He zeroed in on her, heat flaring in his pale eyes, moving over her face and then over the child in her arms. Her body reacted to him, warming under his regard. He lowered his head and she angled hers, anticipating a kiss.

"She's asleep," he whispered.

"Asleep?"

Lauren blinked. In the space of those two seconds her mind had shut off and her body had taken over. It took a moment for her brain synapses to start firing again.

"The baby. Oh, right."

"We should get her back to her mother."

"Yes. You definitely owe her a picture for taking her child hostage."

"I'm putting the blame for that right where it belongs."

He directed her through the other dancers with a hand at the small of her back. "Squarely on Kyla's shoulders."

Lauren shook her head. "Is anything *ever* your fault?"

"Rarely."

"Ha!" *Of course not.* "Why do you say that?"

"Mostly because I don't play the blame game. It's not constructive. I plan and I fix. I provide good directions, and when something goes wrong I come up with a new plan. It's pretty close to the way I've seen you run your events company."

It was *exactly* the way she and Tori ran By Arrangement.

"I'm always excited when an event comes together without a hitch. But I confess it's exhilarating when we pull off an event that's been problematic."

"Right. It's more about the process than the end result."

"Exactly."

Listening to him made her realize how alike their careers were. He created movies and she created events. His were caught on tape and hers were more in the moment, but they both required careful direction and the ability to adjust. "That's what I enjoy most about being an event coordinator—it's an organic experience."

"You've discovered my secret. Now I'll have to kill you." He waved at Kyla, who stood beside a larger version of Lulu. "Or marry you."

"What—? Huh?" She clutched the baby so hard she woke up and squealed. "Shh, baby. I'm sorry." She glared at Ray. "That wasn't funny."

"Oh, but it was." Laughter danced in his eyes. His lips softly touched hers. "Remind me not to propose again while you're holding a baby."

CHAPTER EIGHT

"MMM. IT SMELLS wonderful in here." Mamó strolled over to a lush chair in soft teal and sat. "I might have to take some of whatever that is home." She indicated the seat next to her. "Come. Sit. Ray said he'd see us here at eleven. We're a few minutes early."

Lauren took in the elegant reception area of the exclusive day spa. Ray had swept them away from Queens early that morning, treating them to breakfast at the Plaza before dashing off to a meeting with the mayor. The spa had been a short walk up Fifth Avenue in the thirty-four-degree weather. Mamó had called it pleasant.

Pleasant? Wasn't thirty-two freezing? Thank heavens for the red leather coat.

"Good morning. Welcome to Nouveaux Vous."

A beautiful redhead appeared at the front desk. She wore a classic black dress that contrasted with her milky complexion. Her make-up was flawless, not a freckle in sight. Her serene expression fit perfectly with the elegant pale teal and cream decor.

"Fern Donovan and Lauren Randall?"

"Yes. We're meeting my fiancé here."

How odd did that sound? Apparently they did have an appointment, though Lauren was surprised to hear her name. She and Ray were supposed to be going siting for a movie scheduled to start filming toward the end of the year. Finding out Ray had made an appointment for her was disappointing. She'd been jazzed at the prospect of seeing some of this famous city.

"We have you both listed for a massage, facial, and glamor. Mr. Donovan arranged for you to have your sessions together. Rene and Kim are available when you're ready. May I get you coffee or water while you wait?"

Mamó shook her head.

"No, thank you." Lauren checked her phone. "No message from him. We're going to wait for a few minutes," she told the receptionist.

Aware this was the moment she'd been dreading, Lauren settled next to Mamó in a lobby chair.

Since learning of Mamó's ability to tell when a woman was pregnant, Lauren had anxiously anticipated a confrontation with the older woman. Until now they'd been in company or on the move. She could put it off no longer.

The other woman spoke first, patting Lauren's hand on the armrest between them. "I want to thank you for your gifts. There was no need for you to bother—just having you here is such a joy to me. But the extra decor and having the gentlemen there to dance with was a treat beyond telling."

"I'm happy it added to your day," Lauren responded honestly.

"Oh, it made my year. My friends had such a grand time. No one will top this event for years."

"I'm glad you had a good time." Lauren smiled at Mamó's joy. Then she sobered. "You know, don't you?" She didn't look at Mamó but at the placid seascape on the far wall.

Mamó didn't respond right away. Then her hand covered Lauren's and she squeezed. "It's your news to share. I respect that."

"Ray doesn't know," Lauren said.

"I've gathered that." There was no judgment in Mamó's voice, just curiosity.

"It's hard to see him as a father."

Or it had been before she'd watched him cradle little Lulu in his arms. The sight of the big, strong man confidently holding the precious infant had changed everything. Or it could change nothing. She needed time to re-evaluate.

"He's always been good with kids. I think that's what hurt him most in the breakup." Mamó's hand shook and she pulled it back into her lap. She twined her fingers together until the knuckles showed white.

Lauren stilled. This must be the incident Ray had referenced. "The breakup?"

"He must have told you? It's the one time I truly regretted my talent. But I couldn't let him say his vows without knowing the truth."

"No, of course not," she soothed.

Vows? Questions ricocheted through her head. She wanted to press Mamó for answers but refrained. The older woman was already distressed by the conversation. Better to calm her down before Ray arrived. She'd put the questions to him at a more appropriate time.

Mamó's unusual talent might have pushed up Lauren's agenda to tell Ray, but it didn't change her concerns over his emotional availability to his child. She needed to know about the past before she could make a decision about the future.

"Honesty is important to Ray," Lauren reassured her.

"That's what I told myself even though I knew he'd leave." Mamó wrung her hands. "It was for the best. He's an important man now."

"I have the feeling Ray would be important whatever he did."

"Probably." Mamó nodded. "But he saw no future for himself here. I had to tell him."

"It was the right thing to do."

Curiosity was killing Lauren, but it wouldn't be fair to

pump Mamó. The story needed to come from Ray. Just as the news of their child needed to come from her.

"I'm going to tell him."

"Of course, dear. I won't say anything," Mamó assured her. "Unless I'm asked, I've learned to keep what I know to myself. Well, most of the time."

The shop door opened and Ray walked in on a blast of "pleasant" air. His presence filled the space along with his broad shoulders. Lauren hopped up and he greeted her with a kiss on the cheek. And then he bent to kiss Mamó's powder-dusted cheek. For a man who prized his privacy so strongly he was demonstrative. She'd pretty much given up on the no touching rule. The man just couldn't keep his hands, or his lips, to himself.

And apparently she couldn't keep to her side of the bed. She'd woken up wrapped around him again this morning. This time she'd got caught—literally—while she'd been trying to unfurl herself from him. He had turned over and met her nose to nose.

She'd refused to admit to disappointment when he had merely wished her good morning with a brief peck on the forehead before bounding from the bed to hit the bathroom first.

Oddly, sleeping with him seemed to suit the baby, because her morning queasiness had all but disappeared.

She'd always considered his bid for privacy to have stemmed from arrogance, but now she knew him better she thought it might be more a matter of self-defense. It was something to think about.

"Listen, babe, there's been a change of plans. The master of the Port Authority isn't available tomorrow, so I'm meeting with him today and viewing the docks. That's going to be a cold, dirty trek I'm sure you have no interest in. Instead I booked you matching spa treatments with Mamó. Is that okay?"

Dirty docks or a facial? No-brainer. "Sure."

"Good." He kissed her again, this time on the lips, a gesture of simple affection. Clearly his mind was elsewhere. "I'll pick you up at three and we'll go shopping."

"Shopping?" She was not letting him buy her another thing.

"Yes, the mayor invited me to a black tie reception tonight. I told him I'd be escorting my two best ladies."

"Ray—" The protest had barely passed her lips when a well-attired man with black hair opened the door and nodded at Ray.

"Sorry, Dynamite, I have to go. We'll talk later."

And then he was gone and the redhead was back. Lauren sighed and shared a glance with Mamó, who shrugged.

"He's a busy man."

Yeah, right. But Lauren didn't push it. "Shall we go get pampered?"

"Yes—and we should buy some of that lovely-smelling lotion. I'm sure Ray would want us to have some."

A smile tugged at the corner of Lauren's mouth because she had no doubt he would. "Yes, we really need some lotion."

Four hours later Lauren followed Mamó from the spa feeling refreshed and revitalized. The massage and facial had worked all the toxins and tension from her body. The beauty regimen had pampered her in a whole new way, leaving her feeling beautiful and eager to show off her pretty new look.

She really must schedule a spa day for her and Tori post-honeymoon.

Mamó had a real glow about her, too. Though some of that might have been due to the call she'd taken from Ellie. She'd made plans for dinner back in Queens and Lauren got the impression George Meade might be involved. Seemed Mamó wanted to showcase *her* new glamor, too.

Lauren didn't push for details. What she didn't know she couldn't spill to Ray.

Bright shafts of sunshine fought through the cloud cover and high-rises to warm the afternoon pedestrians. A limousine stood double-parked at the curb. Ray stepped out as they approached.

He flattered Mamó on how lovely she looked, accepted the news she wanted to bow out of the reception with good grace, and sent her off in the limo, suggesting she use the car service to collect her friends for dinner.

"She always gets a kick out of her neighbors' reaction when she comes and goes in a limousine. She'll be extra excited to give them a ride."

Enchanted with his obvious affection for his grandmother, Lauren hooked her arm through his. "Today she feels beautiful and special. You did good."

Satisfaction showed in the form of a smirk. "Good. There's still a sadness about her, but Ellie says she's been better the last few days." He waved down a passing cab. "How was she today?"

"Fine. It was a mellow day. And she seems excited about tonight."

"Good." He nodded and helped her into the waiting taxi. "Bloomingdales," he directed the driver.

Lauren settled into her seat without argument. She'd already decided to treat herself to a new dress for the reception and as a souvenir of the trip. By Arrangement's success over the past year certainly allowed for a little extravagance—which reminded her: the designer of Tori's wedding dress had a loft in New York. Lauren loved her work.

She scrolled through her contacts, made a quick call, and then asked Ray to change their destination.

"I'm glad you're getting into the spirit of tonight's adventure." He swept a loose tendril of hair behind her ear.

"Hmm?" She relaxed against him. "Are we having an adventure?"

"Yes. This is our first official date."

"So it is." Tipping her head back, she eyed his profile. He appeared pleased with himself. "There's likely to be press at this event. How do you want to handle it?" she asked.

"Word of our engagement is out. I already got asked about it a couple of times today."

"What did you say?"

"That I wasn't answering questions. But I'll make a brief statement tonight." He picked up her hand, threaded his fingers through hers. "I'm sorry you got dragged into a lie."

"Thank you, but it's not your fault."

"I had my team put together a news release. I'll show it to you at the hotel. It includes who you are, when we met, how long we've dated and details currently known about the wedding."

"You have a team?"

"I do. Besides my assistant there's my manager, a publicist, a project manager, an accountant, and—to my shame and at my assistant's insistence—a stylist."

She laughed and slapped his knee. "You do *not* have a stylist."

"Only during awards season. Which reminds me—will you be my date for the awards ceremony this weekend?"

"Walk the red carpet with you?"

Her eyes popped and she sucked in a breath before she got herself under control. The awards were a big deal for Ray this year. They were equally important to her career.

"I'm working that night."

"If we make an announcement, everyone will expect you to attend with me."

"By Arrangement is handling Obsidian Studio's afterparty." She rubbed her thumb over his knuckle. "It's been our goal since we focused our business in Hollywood to cater a post-awards ball."

"And I'm betting it will be *the* party to beat this year. People are still talking about the job you ladies did for Obsidian at the Hollywood Hills Film Festival. Couldn't you keep an eye on things from the perspective of being my date?"

His request went totally against her work ethic. She shouldn't even be here this week, but preparing and overseeing the biggest event of her career. Work had become her savior, her solace. She took comfort in the discipline and control necessary to pull off a spectacular event.

But with a baby under her heart and a major life decision to make regarding her child's future her mind couldn't focus on work. She owed it to herself, to her baby, and to Ray to take the time to make the most informed decision she could. In the meantime, twice daily updates from her assistant kept her sane on the work front.

She recalled Mamó's mention of vows and realized there was so much about Ray she didn't know. Dates were meant to help a couple get to know each other better. So that was what she would do. Enjoy the night, learn more about Ray, and maybe get some answers about his past.

Whatever his reservations about his old neighborhood, he hadn't deserted his community. On her way to the restroom at the community center last night she'd spied a plaque posted in gratitude to Raymond Patrick Donovan for the donation of a gymnasium and pool.

Dated seven years ago, the timing of the donation matched his first huge success—a film about a wounded veteran saving a small town from a corrupt mayor. He'd blended drama and action into a brilliant display of bravery, sacrifice, and justice that had provided moviegoers with an emotional and visually satisfying experience. The film had made Ray's name a household word—he'd swept the awards that year, and gone on to become part of the Hollywood elite.

And Ray had handed a cool million to his old neighborhood.

"I'll think about it. Let's get through tonight first."

"Deal. We're here." He climbed from the cab, glanced up at the building. "She's stretching the limits of the garment district, here."

"That doesn't really mean anything to me," she said as she joined him. "Did you see Tori's wedding dress? Fabulous. She found it at a small boutique on Rodeo Drive, and of course she had to call the designer to rave about it. The two of them are now email buddies."

Inside, the receptionist directed them to the third floor. Eve Gardner met them at the door.

"Lauren, I'm so glad you called." The slim blond greeted them in her showroom. "I've seen pictures of the wedding. Tori was absolutely stunning—you must share all the details."

"I will, but first let me say your dress was the jewel in her day. I've never seen her look more beautiful."

"As a designer I can promise you *she* made the dress—not the other way around. My phone hasn't stopped ringing all week." She laughed lightly, looking a little shell shocked. "I should have paid her to wear the dress!"

Lauren squeezed her hand. "You deserve the recognition. It was a stunning dress. I'm hoping you might have something for me." She introduced Ray. "We're going to a reception for the mayor tonight."

"Tonight?" Eve's eyes widened as she recognized Ray, but she quickly recovered and pulled Lauren further into her shop, introducing the two of them to her assistant, Christy. "What type of affair is it?"

"Black tie."

"Hmm, what are you? A size five? I think I have a couple of items you might like."

Eve invited Lauren and Ray to sit and then disappeared into the back. Christy offered them refreshments and then followed Eve.

Lauren sat on a dove-gray tufted sofa while Ray roamed the showroom. The white walls provided an excellent showcase for the life-sized framed prints of celebrities and models in Eve's designs. Several racks around the room held vibrantly hued garments.

"Nice." Ray stopped in front of a print of a high-profile actress in a midnight-blue dress on which the bodice consisted of strategically placed bands artfully woven across the breasts and throat while the skirt fell in a straight sheath to the floor.

"That's showing too much skin for me."

He turned back to her, arms crossed over his chest. "You'd be stunning in something like this."

She shook her blond head. "I should have told her something conservative would be best. Preferably in black."

"Absolutely not. Tonight isn't a job. It's fun. You need a dress to play in."

"I won't be working this event," she agreed, mimicking him by crossing her arms over her breasts. "But you will. I need to respect that."

"Dynamite, in my business the more skin you show the better."

"Yes, but I'm only visiting your world. In my world I can wear the dress again at an event I *will* be working."

"If you don't have the guts all you have to do is say so." He strolled over and dropped down beside her, his arm resting on the back of the sofa behind her.

"I don't have the guts."

No need to bluff. And she wouldn't let him dare her into wearing something she couldn't be comfortable in. That was Tori—not her. Classy and conservative suited her just fine.

"Okay," he said easily, tracing a finger over her ear,

making her shiver. The man was always *touching*. "But you have the body for it. Just so you know."

"You're not supposed to be thinking of my body. Remember? It's one of the rules we discussed."

"I thought you gave up on those rules?"

"No. What made you think that?" She should never have let him get away with the constant touching. It gave him the wrong idea.

"I don't know. Possibly the fact I've woken up with you curled around me the last couple of nights."

Heat rose in her cheeks. The hope that he'd slept through her nighttime wanderings ended at this embarrassing revelation. Of course she knew it had been a futile hope.

"That doesn't count," she bluffed. "We can't control what we do while we're sleeping."

He leaned close, bringing the scent of man and spice with him. He whispered in her ear. "That's not what you said the other night."

"Yes…well…" He smelled so good she'd lost her train of thought. *Oh, yeah.* "The point is the rules are in full force. And you're breaking them."

"Wrong. The rules say no unnecessary touching. I can admire all I want."

No. He had to stop. His admiring and his touching were chipping away at her resolve. She'd agreed to their date tonight, to get to know him better. But already she felt her control slipping. Being the sole focus of his attention might be more than she could handle.

"Your admiring is making it hard to breathe." She put a finger in the middle of his chest and pushed. "Behave yourself."

"Okay." He settled back into his place, but didn't remove his arm from behind her. "But you're forgetting the security cameras. Touching is totally within our limits."

Of course he'd be aware of the cameras. Short of pleading, she only had one other option. A good threat.

"Go ahead—have your fun now. Risk putting me in a bad mood for tonight, when I'll be wearing a sexy dress and sipping a nice wine."

"Good point."

His blue eyes narrowed, showing her he'd caught her meaning. The gleam in those eyes sent a message too. He knew he bothered her. And he planned to put that knowledge to good use later.

He gave her ear a tug and pulled out his phone. "I'll just return a few texts."

"You do that." She reached for her purse. Actually, it was a good time to check her own messages. All was well at By Arrangement. Her mom was still waiting for a full explanation. And no word yet from Tori.

"Here we go." Eve returned, Christy on her heels, with a handful of dresses in her arms. "Come with me. I found a lovely cobalt gown perfect for your skin tone."

"Wait." Ray waved his phone. "How long will this take?"

Lauren stared at him blankly, then turned to Eve.

The designer shrugged. "As long as it takes."

Lauren nodded.

He stood, looking back and forth between them as if expecting something more. "Right. I have something to take care of. I'll be back for you."

"No."

"You want me to wait?" He lifted his phone to impart his response.

"No."

He went still and lifted a brown eyebrow, waiting for her direction.

Okay, she had to admit it was heady stuff. Except for her rules, she'd been following his lead for this whole trip. It was nice to have a little power. It might only be over travel plans, but she'd take it.

"You go ahead. I'll catch a cab and meet you back at the hotel."

They had decided to stay in the city for the night, in the suite Ray had originally booked for them.

"Okay." He advised the person on the other end of the phone he'd be there shortly. Then he came over, kissed her hard, and headed out, taking her hard-won power with him.

But not for long.

She turned to Eve. "I hope the cobalt is sexy."

CHAPTER NINE

THE BLUE FABRIC clung to Lauren's curves. A fitted bodice flowed into two straps that both went over one shoulder, creating an asymmetrical keyhole. The straps narrowed to two-inch strips spanning her bare back. The skirt hugged her hips before falling in a straight line to the floor.

Ray sipped a well-balanced whiskey as he half listened to the mayor talking about the summit underway at the United Nations. Undoubtedly it was a worthy endeavor, but Ray found his attention held by two blue straps—or, more specifically, by the creamy skin they didn't cover. His fingers itched to touch.

A few members of the society press were covering the event out front. They'd lit up like kids on Christmas morning when they'd spied him and Lauren. Made him glad he had the press statement ready.

Lauren had handled the congratulations and intrusive questions well, but her poise had failed to disguise the tremors running through her body—especially when an idiot had demanded to know if she was pregnant.

Ray had wanted to plant his fist in the man's mouth. Instead he'd shut the questions off and moved her inside. They'd made it through the informal procession line with no further incident.

He enjoyed having her at his side. She neither preened nor disappeared. Nor did she defer to him, but treated him as he imagined she treated all her dates—as an equal.

Which influenced those around them, easing the burden of his celebrity.

It was a treat he took full advantage of for over an hour. Difficult to enjoy an event when people feared approaching you or made the conversation all about you. This room held important men who wielded real power. Even casual discussions rippled with nuances of bigger things.

It was almost enough to engage his whole attention. But there was always a part of him aware of Lauren, whether she stood at his side or had wandered a few feet away in a breakaway discussion.

Something about the woman got to him.

He'd earned a reputation for being a hardcore bachelor long ago because he guarded his privacy and made it clear to all his companions that they could expect nothing more from him than a good time and a fond farewell.

Generally he stuck to two dating pools when he wanted female company: women in the industry but behind the camera, because they were familiar with what it meant to be in the limelight, or women unconnected with the industry, because he didn't have to worry that they were trying to further their careers.

Lauren straddled the line, giving him the best of both worlds. He was comfortable with her—which might freak him out except for the sizzling chemistry between them.

He wouldn't be used because of his occupation. He wouldn't be used, period. Being seen as a meal ticket and an escape out of the neighborhood had taught him that harsh lesson before he'd ever made it big.

And the price had been the life of his child.

On his wedding day he had truly understood that anybody could be driven to kill. If not for Mamó he might well have crossed the line.

He shook off the memory. Not the time. Not the place. His fingers itched.

Lauren thought she was safe, standing in deep discussion with the mayor's wife. But she'd set the rules. He could only touch her in public. So, actually, she'd chosen the place. It was only fair he should choose the time.

He'd been very restrained so far. From the stunning moment when she'd stepped from her room at the hotel, through the limo ride to the reception, to having her by his side through the barrage of introductions.

His patience was at an end.

"Are we boring you, Ray?"

Bob, the governor of New Jersey, clapped him on the back, drawing his attention back to the group.

"I know you're not working tonight, but I'll admit I was hoping for a chance to talk to you about using the great state of New Jersey in one of your films."

"I'm afraid I'm not very familiar with New Jersey, other than flying into the airport."

"Well, I'm happy to rectify that. I can arrange a tour at your convenience."

"Thanks, but my time is limited on this trip, and I have several locations to site tomorrow. I expect it to take most of the day."

"I've put an aide and a limousine at his disposal for the day," the mayor interjected.

"A helicopter would be more efficient, and then you could add a couple of Jersey sights."

"A helicopter?" Ray mused, liking the idea. Liking the idea of smoothing his hand over lotion-scented skin even more. Lauren might get a kick out of an aerial tour.

"Have your assistant contact my office with your schedule." Bob pulled out a card. "And I'll have a bird ready and waiting."

"Come on, Bob," the mayor interposed. "Are you trying to steal my revenue stream?" He was only half joking.

Lauren's laugh tinkled on the air, the sound energizing Ray.

Bob shrugged big shoulders. "I just want to show Ray,

here, the diversity of my beautiful state so he can keep us in mind for future ventures."

The mayor harrumphed.

"Thanks, Bob," Ray said. He flicked the card. "My assistant will be in touch. Gentlemen, it's been a pleasure."

"Running off so soon?" the mayor protested, then followed Ray's gaze to where the women chatted a few feet away. A look of admiration chased away the touch of irritation in his eyes. "Ah. I understand. Congratulations, by the way. You're a lucky man."

"Indeed."

He nodded to the men and strolled the short distance to Lauren's side, shaking off the odd combination of pride and anger at the way the other man had eyed Lauren.

He wasn't usually territorial. Then again he didn't usually have a temporary fiancée either. That had to be it.

His fingers connected with the skin of her lower back and he sighed. Satisfaction and desire replaced all other emotions.

Lauren instantly acknowledged him, looking up and back. She continued her conversation but settled into his touch.

"It's really not that difficult to up the interest factor of an event," she explained to the cluster of ladies. "It can be as simple as having a signature cocktail or adding visual props."

"These affairs always look the same," a white-haired matron said, while fingering the diamonds at her neck.

"That usually happens when it's left up to a hotel. Understated elegance is a classic, so it's often the default mode." She responded calmly, as if her audience wasn't sending furtive glances his way.

"What would you have done differently tonight?" the mayor's wife asked.

"We often work with the client to come up with a theme. Lacking that, I'd switch things up. Flowers are a standard, but instead of roses I might have gone with something more exotic. A tropical feel in the middle of winter would be welcomed by most. And I might have replaced a few of the round tables with a conversation area of sofas and chairs."

A hum of approval came from the group.

Lauren shrugged gracefully. "My sister is the truly creative half of our team."

"Ladies," Ray broke in, "I'm going to steal Lauren away. We have reservations for a late supper."

"How romantic," the matron announced. "Enjoy these early days, dear. It's never quite the same once you've said your vows."

"And Marian should know," one of the others volunteered.

"Yes," Marian agreed with a trill of laughter. "Walter is my third husband."

"Let's give Walter something to think about, shall we?" Ray lifted Marian's diamond-laden hand to his mouth and pressed a kiss to the back of her fingers.

Marian flushed pink, her delight in being singled out bright in her smile.

"Ladies…" He winked and led Lauren away.

Watching the world spin away before her sent Lauren's stomach rolling. Not because of the baby this time, but the dizzying ride in a glass elevator. Placing a hand on her belly, she turned away from the rising view.

"You okay?" Ray wrapped an arm around her waist and pulled her close.

"Vertigo." She leaned against him, took comfort in the caress of his hand on her back. "Better now. Thanks."

The elevator opened on the forty-seventh floor. Ray gestured for her to exit. She did so, but questioned him.

"You said we had reservations for a late supper. I thought we were headed for the rooftop restaurant?"

"It's been a long day. I ordered in." He used a card key to let them into the lounge area of their suite. "I hope you don't mind?"

"No, but I'm disappointed. I was looking forward to relaxing while taking in the rooftop view. New York keeps beckoning, yet I've only seen a slice of the Big Apple."

This was exactly the type of highhanded behavior she found annoying.

"Sorry." Loosening his tie, he bent to kiss her on the top of her head. "I've had enough of being a spectacle today. I had them set the table up by the window, so the view should be nearly the same."

"Oh…" Now she felt bad. She hadn't considered how being "on" all the time must get tiring for him.

Feeling the quiet of the room embrace her, she admitted it was a stellar option.

"Good thinking. What did you order for us?"

"Lobster, steak, a full range of sides and desserts." At the dining table he began lifting lids on dome-covered dishes. "I wanted you to have a choice."

"How thoughtful." And it was. Her mood improved. "This looks delicious."

Ray handed her a plate, took one for himself, and they served themselves. She chose both lobster and a small piece of steak, with asparagus and tender red potatoes.

"How's the vertigo?" Ray's concerned gaze ran over her features as he held her chair. "Would you like me to pull the table away from the window?"

Touched, she smiled her appreciation. "No, I'll be fine. It was the motion combined with the view that got to me. Here the table blocks the feet-to-skyline view, so I should be all right. But I think I'll skip the wine, just to be safe."

Finding ways to decline alcohol and caffeine were getting harder and harder.

She set her plate down and allowed him to seat her. "This is lovely."

New York in all its glistening glory was spread out before them. High-rises and bridges threaded together with streets of lights. She recognized the Empire State Building and Ray pointed out several other landmarks.

"Where's Queens?" she asked.

"You can't see it from here. Wrong angle." But he pointed out the boroughs they *could* see amidst the myriad buildings. Even from this height and distance the city's flow and movement reached her. New York was a living, breathing metropolis unlike any place else she'd ever seen.

He told her about his day at the docks, making her laugh with his dry sense of humor. She refrained from boring him with details of her day at the spa, assuring him instead that it had been relaxing. "Not as relaxing as this, though."

A gleam appeared in his eyes. He reached over and threaded long fingers through her smaller ones. His touch soothed and aroused.

"I know what you mean. It feels like forever since we've been alone."

Yes. She got that. And the fact she'd missed him was as surprising as it was true.

She felt as if she'd been on edge for days. They'd been together almost constantly, but rarely on their own. To all intents and purposes they were truly alone for the first time since leaving Hollywood. Well, except for the time they spent together in his small bedroom—which was not relaxing in the least.

Baby might enjoy sleeping in Daddy's arms, but Mama found the whole experience nerve-racking.

Tonight the mood was intimate, yet mellow. The amazing view and the delectable food were too good to ruin with bad vibes. The ease between them presented the perfect opportunity to address something bothering her.

Mamó had mentioned vows in connection with Ray, and something to do with a pregnancy. It wasn't hard to connect the dots, but she didn't work well with supposition. She liked solid facts. Much less room for misunderstandings.

The one time she had allowed herself to have faith in her emotions she'd sunk deep in an emotionally damaging relationship. Some—Tori—might call it abusive. Lauren's pride argued that she'd pulled out before it had reached that stage.

The point was she'd learned a tough lesson: not to let her heart lead her head. Especially now she had a child to think of.

"Can I ask you a personal question?"

"Sure. We're engaged—at least for a few more days."

Uh, no, they weren't. But they *were* going to be parents. She figured that gave her a right to know. So she'd run with his permission.

"Have you been married before?"

He stared at her with an unreadable expression for a long moment, until she wondered if he'd answer her after all. Then he stood, pulled her to her feet by their joined fingers and led her to the large, plush couch.

"If we're going to get into something deep, let's get comfortable."

He sat and drew her down next to him, never letting go of her. And still he didn't elaborate. He played with her fingers, his gazed locked on their entwined digits, their hands perched on his hard thigh, because he'd allowed no space between them.

"I suppose someone mentioned it to you at the party?" Bitterness edged his response. "Fifteen years and four major industry awards and I *still* haven't lived it down."

Okay, that didn't sound like a denial. Then again, she'd never heard of marriage referred to as "it" either.

"So you *were* married?"

"No."

An odd sense of relief slid through her.

Ridiculous, of course. And unfounded. It would be unhealthy for a man his age never to have been involved in a committed relationship. So he preferred to be discreet? That didn't mean he didn't have a private life. Or that he didn't care for the women he spent time with.

Okay, so their interaction had been purely physical, with nothing more than a fake engagement to indicate any sense of depth. She'd be a fool to assume all his relationships were so shallow.

But he hadn't cared enough to get married. She supposed that meant something. She hoped hearing his history might give her the answers she needed.

He'd been quiet while she stewed. Brooding himself?

"Painful memories?" She squeezed his fingers and leaned her head on his shoulder.

"Yeah." It was almost a grunt.

"You don't have to talk about it if you don't want to," she offered. She'd be disappointed if he changed his mind now, but she couldn't force him to share. Not when she had secrets she wasn't prepared to reveal yet.

"It was a lifetime ago. Feels like it happened to someone else." He scrubbed his free hand over the back of his neck. "I was just a kid."

"If it happened fifteen years ago, you *are* a different person. We all change and grow. I know *I'm* not the same person I was when I started college."

He flinched, and she knew he was thinking about what she'd gone through. His jaw clenched. But he started talking.

"I was headed for college, with a scholarship to UCLA in my grasp, when my world fell apart. My girlfriend, Camilla, informed me she was pregnant."

Lauren's hand clenched around his. Even though she'd expected to hear a child had been involved after Mamó's earlier comments, Lauren still took the news like a shot to the gut.

Another woman had carried Ray's child.

The knowledge made her raw. She couldn't squeeze a word past the constriction in her throat. She shouldn't care. Theirs was not a romantic connection. Being so cozy these last few days had given a false sense of intimacy. Nothing had changed.

Ray rubbed his thumb over her wrist. "We had one of those on again, off again relationships—mostly because she wanted constant attention and I was wrapped up in making movies. Neither of us was thinking long-term. At least I didn't think so. She knew I'd planned to go to Los Angeles whether I got the scholarship or not. The University of California Los Angeles is arguably the best school for film and television in the world."

"I remember reading an article stating that you won an award for a documentary on homeless runaways that had scholarship money attached to it."

"The Stahling Award. That's when I knew I had a good chance at going to UCLA. The award carries a lot of prestige. Along with my other awards and a short film, it was the complete package."

He hadn't been wrong. He'd gone to UCLA and become one of their biggest success stories. But something wasn't adding up. Something must have happened with the baby. Or maybe there hadn't been a baby at all?

"Was Camilla lying when she said she was pregnant?"

"No. Mamó would have known."

He got up and poured another glass of wine. He held the bottle up, silently asking if she wanted some. She shook her head. Sipping, he stared out the window.

"My world shattered. The last thing I wanted was a kid. But I'd been raised by my grandmother and my aunt—two widows, basically single mothers. I knew the hardships they'd faced. They raised me to take responsibility for my actions. I couldn't walk away from my kid and everything they'd taught me."

"You proposed?" she guessed, feeling for the young Ray who'd had all his dreams disrupted.

"I didn't love her. We'd only hooked up in our senior year. But the kid was mine, so, yeah, I proposed. Camilla and her mother started making rush wedding plans. She told me she wanted the ceremony right away, so she wouldn't be showing in her gown. I was committed. When didn't matter to me. Providing for my family did, so I started looking for a better job."

"You didn't consider taking Camilla with you to Los Angeles?"

"I considered it, but the scholarship was for dorm housing, so I'd have needed to work. And probably Camilla, too, which would be difficult with a newborn. At least in Queens we'd have family support nearby. But I wasn't giving up. I might have to do night courses, but I started putting in applications to New York film schools. Camilla had a fit when she realized."

"She thought she'd be going with you to Los Angeles?"

"Oh, yeah. She said if I could be a director she could be an actress. I laughed at her."

"Uh-oh." The word escaped without thought. Never a good idea to laugh at a woman—certainly not a pregnant one. The fact her aspirations had been somewhat misguided would only have made it worse.

"Not my shiniest moment," he confessed. "But my tolerance was stretched thin by then. I explained my reasoning. She didn't care—said I was jealous of her and insisted we go. I refused. Said I wasn't taking a child to California. She left in a huff."

Lauren closed her eyes, briefly shutting out his pain. She saw the train wreck coming. His stoic delivery as he relived the tragic memory was not fooling her for a moment. Aching for him, she stood and went to him. Wrapping her arms around his waist, she laid her head on his back and just held him. A fine tremor shook his body, re-vealing the hurt he tried to hide. He laid his hand over hers.

"I'm so sorry," she whispered.

"At that time we were only days away from the wed-ding. I should have figured out something was off when she stopped yammering at me over details I couldn't care less about. And she'd begun avoiding Mamó. I didn't no-tice. Hell, I couldn't even put a good face on it at that point. The less time I spent with her the better."

"Oh, Ray."

"I was at the church, dread heavy in my gut, and Mamó came into the little room where I was waiting. She knew how hard everything was for me."

"She never encouraged you to go?"

"No. She supported my decision to stay and raise my child. But she couldn't let me go through with the cere-mony when she no longer sensed a child."

"What did you do?"

"I challenged Camilla. At first she refused to see me. Then she tried to deny it. But I knew. When I demanded someone go for a pregnancy test she broke down and claimed she'd lost the baby. She said she still loved me and now we could go to Los Angeles together. It made me sick to my stomach."

"She aborted the baby?"

"She denied it. Still does, as far as I know. But she was lying. She got pregnant to hook me and got rid of the baby when it threatened her plans."

The muscles in his back flexed as he braced his body to control the shaking. To disguise what Camilla's betrayal had done to him.

"You don't believe she ever intended having the baby."

The breath left his body and he unlinked her hands to turn and study her. He cupped her face, stared into her eyes. "How can you know that?"

"I'm beginning to know *you*. Camilla's perfidy was

painful, but having an innocent life trivialized made it worse."

"It wasn't just an innocent life. It was my child. Her treachery crushed me. Her total disregard for my child's life—that destroyed me." His jaw clenched as he fought for composure. "She stole seed from me and tossed a life away as if it meant nothing. All for a trip to Hollywood. How could I go to UCLA when I knew the lure of Hollywood was what had caused my child to lose his life?

"Ray..." Her heart broke for him.

"For about a week I punished myself. Pulled all my applications from the local schools, grabbed my camera, and hit the streets. I found destitution, despair, disassociation, defeat. These weren't the teenagers I had filmed before. They had been survivors. These people had given up entirely. After three days I couldn't stand it and I dragged myself home. Mamó was waiting for me. She embraced me, fed me, scolded me and shamed me. In the face of all I'd seen, her steadfast love humbled me. The next day she told me to get over the self-pity, pack my bags, and leave for Los Angeles, already. I'd seen what defeat did to a person. Damned if I was going to let Camilla steal my soul. So I followed Mamó's advice and never looked back."

"I'm glad you did. None of what happened was your fault."

"I made a child with her. I let her talk me into unprotected sex. *Stupid.* I was an eighteen-year-old boy, and she'd teased me past the point of control. But that's on me."

"The fact that you accept the responsibility makes you a good man. If you'd walked away unscathed you would be no better than her. But you cared. You mourned. You went on to be a brilliant film-maker. Truly, the world would be a sadder place if you had turned your back on Hollywood."

"Thank you." He pressed his forehead to hers. Tension drained from him. "Most of the time I can bury the memories. But being back has brought up a lot of those old emotions. It doesn't help that the gossip continues."

"Do you ever see Camilla?"

"No." A simple yet harsh statement. "I rarely come to the neighborhood."

"You shouldn't let the past keep you away. Mamó is so happy to have you at the house. A few stray comments amongst friends are nothing to some of the stuff I've seen in the tabloids. If you were around more the gossip would fade away from natural attrition—which would be good, because you're going to want to visit Mamó when you find a real fiancée."

Okay, that was too much. She stepped back. No doubt Camilla's escapades would dwindle when news of Ray's impending fatherhood got around.

Should Lauren tell him now?

No. It wasn't the right time. She didn't want him associating her news with the loss he had suffered in the past.

"I'm not interested in another fiancée."

An arm at her waist didn't let her go far. Long fingers traced the keyhole in her bodice. "Did I tell you how lovely you look tonight?"

"You did." And the desire in his eyes had repeated the message over and over throughout the night.

She'd wanted to make him notice her, and she had succeeded, all right. To the point it had almost backfired on her. The searing weight of his gaze had followed her all night, and her body had responded with heightened awareness until she could barely concentrate. There she had stood, rubbing elbows with the rich and powerful, and she'd struggled to put together coherent sentences. Fortunately the fact that a friend of the mayor's wife had heard of By Arrangement had caught her attention and grounded her in the conversation so she didn't actually embarrass herself.

The desire was back in his eyes now, burning brighter

than ever, making her nerves tingle and her body heat. She much preferred seeing passion over pain in his sea-blue eyes. And, oh, he smelled good.

She missed being held by him. So, with luxury surrounding her, New York lit up at her feet, and a hard man pulling her close, she surrendered her control.

Rising on her toes, she kissed the hard line of his jaw. "Are you just going to look? Or do you plan to do something about it?"

CHAPTER TEN

RAY NEEDED NO further urging. He swept her into his arms and carried her to his room. Towards his bed. *Oh, yeah*. Satisfaction roared through him.

The thought of Lauren in his bed touched off something primitive in him.

Probably because it had taken so long to get her there. From the very beginning their sexual encounters had been steamy, exciting and clandestine. They were like flint and paper—sparking off each other until antagonism flashed to passion and they rushed to find the first private space available.

He'd never had better sex.

And it should have been enough.

He wasn't a possessive man when it came to women. Generally he preferred to keep things as unencumbered as possible, going to a hotel or to her place. He didn't trust easily. Women were a pleasure, not a commitment.

Rehashing his past had been like opening a vein: painful and potentially hazardous. What good could come of it? None, in his regard. He never talked about himself. Yet he'd felt compelled to share with Lauren. Bringing her to New York had probably been a mistake. Their closeness gave a false impression of intimacy.

Tonight he didn't care. He couldn't get too close.

Setting her on her feet, he sought out the side zipper

he'd spied during his frequent perusals of her throughout the night.

His hadn't been the only eyes on her during the reception. The attention she'd drawn had caused a low level animosity to burn under his skin.

She was *his*, damn it. Yet he'd also been proud to be with her. Smart, beautiful, poised—she was the total package.

He kissed her, hard and deep, then stepped back. "Take this off for me."

A shy smile greeted his request—unusual for the confident woman he knew her to be—but her delicate fingers went to the alluring blue straps that had tantalized him all night. Enchanted, he perched on the edge of the bed, prepared to enjoy her performance.

With a flick of her fingers the straps were loosened. A shimmy of her hips and the cobalt fabric pooled at her feet.

Sweet, merciful angels.

He sucked in a breath. It lodged in the back of his throat. She stood in nothing more than a black lace thong and mile-high shoes so sexy they made her pretty legs look like they reached clear to heaven.

Being in her arms was as close as he'd probably ever get.

"You should breathe," she advised him, her confidence fully restored.

She walked to him, all creamy skin and soft curves. Wedging herself between his spread knees, she started undoing buttons.

"Your turn."

"I've never seen anything more beautiful than you." He urged her down to him, kissed her lips, her chin, the side of her neck, working his way to luscious bounty.

She hugged his head to her and he felt her mouth against his hair. In that moment he felt cherished. She always brought intensity to their encounters. This was different—slower, softer.

They were different—no longer acquaintances scratching a passionate itch. She'd met his family, they'd traded secrets, slept together without making love; it was more than he'd had with anyone since leaving New York.

And it was more than he wanted to think about. Time to stop thinking and start touching.

Lying back, he took her with him and then rolled over so she lay beneath him, flushed and dewy-eyed.

"You're not usually so shy." She linked her arms around his neck and smiled at him. "This is going to be difficult to accomplish unless you remove these clothes."

"I don't want to stop touching you."

"Excellent argument. But it doesn't solve our problem."

"We have all night, Dynamite, a soft bed, and no need to rush. Short of being evacuated, I plan to make love to you all night long."

"All night? You *are* feeling frisky."

"I've spent the last few nights with this lovely little tush tucked up next to me. But because of your rules I couldn't do anything but hold you." He surged to his feet and stripped off his clothes. In less than a minute he'd joined her back in bed. "Until now. Frisky? Oh, yeah."

"So…oh…you're saying…uh…you cheated?"

Lauren arched under Ray's talented touch. He knew all her hot buttons and stroked them to maximum effect. True to his promise he took his time, building sensation on sensation, his touch in equal parts tender and demanding.

He smiled against her cheek. "Every chance I got."

He did something with his fingers that stole her ability to speak.

She tried to reciprocate, but all she could do was surrender to his erotic assault. She understood that he sought to escape the demons he'd revealed earlier. It had hurt to see him struggle through his vulnerability tonight, but no sign of it remained as he urged her with mouth, hands and body to mind-blowing responsiveness.

He bit her earlobe, nuzzled behind her ear, sending tingles sparking over heightened nerves. *Yesss*. She happily sacrificed her body to help him through the night.

Lauren lay with Ray curled around her and stared out the wide picture window into the predawn sky. Even at this height she saw lights in surrounding buildings, heard sirens and other city chatter. New York really never stopped.

And neither did her mind.

True to his word, Ray had pleasured her well into the night. Her body was boneless with satisfaction. And still Ray's story kept repeating in her head. What a tragic introduction to adulthood. How did someone *do* that to a person?

She rubbed her belly.

How did someone use another life with such capriciousness, such cruelty? It was unconscionable. And it made her question her own decision to withhold news of their child from Ray.

No doubt he'd be upset.

And he had every right to be.

She might be carrying the baby, but he or she was as much a part of Ray as Lauren. It shamed her to remember how easily she'd dismissed his interest in the child because she hadn't wanted to deal with her child's father. How arrogant of her to think he wouldn't want to be a part of his child's life simply because he had a demanding career and a high-profile lifestyle.

He said he loved kids, and the confidence and care with which he'd handled young Lulu proved his claim. Most men were afraid to hold a child that young. Not Ray. He had reached for her with genuine affection.

Suddenly she longed for the day he held their child.

The time to tell him had come.

In fact she worried that she should have told him last night, but she stood by her decision to wait—to give him distance from the misery he'd relived. She couldn't prevent the past from rising up when she told him he was going to be a father, but she could make sure he was in a better frame of mind.

Today they would tour the city. They'd be playing tourist, but Ray would also be working. She'd be careful to give him his space, to watch his mood. And when the time was right she'd share her precious news.

A helicopter! Lauren wavered between being thrilled and terrified. Dressed in jeans and a black sweater under the red leather jacket, she let Ray strap her into her seat. Once he'd settled in his own seat, and they both had headphones on, she reached for his hand.

"Don't let go," she implored him, not caring if the mayor's aide heard from his seat up-front.

"I won't." He brought her hand to his mouth and kissed her knuckles.

"What are you looking for today?"

"I'm doing a futuristic police procedural. The story is set fifty years in the future. I'll be looking at parts of the city with modern elements."

"Oh."

Well, *boo*. She'd hoped to see more than just architecture. So much for playing tourist. Still, it would be fun to see some of the other boroughs. And they were flying. Surely she'd catch a glimpse of something interesting.

"Can we at least fly by the Statue of Liberty?"

He squeezed her fingers. "We're starting with the statue. What would a film in New York be without a shot of the famous landmark? Don't worry. You'll see plenty of sights."

The helicopter lifted off, the world dropping away beneath her. Lauren clutched Ray's hand. They were leaving from the roof of their hotel, so they already had some elevation. For a moment the surrounding buildings seemed too close, but as the helicopter gained height they grew smaller.

Her breath caught. The panoramic view stunned her senses with the sheer vastness of the city. She waited for the vertigo, but it never came. The wristband the pilot had given her must be working.

"We have to land at Ellis Island." The mayor's aide, Felton Smith, a balding Asian American, addressed them through their headsets. "Helicopter landings are restricted at Liberty Island. A National Park representative will be there to greet us and take us over to the statue."

"National Park?" Lauren asked. "So it's not run by New York?"

"No," Felton confirmed. "Coolidge declared the statue a national monument in 1924, and in 1933 Franklin Roosevelt transferred jurisdiction to the National Park Services. You probably aren't going to want to film right on the island. Unless it's integral to the plot, the view is better from a distance."

Ray nodded. "We'll probably replicate the parts we need at the studio, but I like authenticity and it's been years since I've been to see the statue."

Within minutes the helicopter began to descend on Ellis Island. Having the earth rise to meet them got to Lauren, so she closed her eyes, taking comfort in Ray's hold on her hand. The bump of their landing was so skilled she barely felt it.

A park ranger in a crisp green uniform stepped forward to greet them. Ranger Paceco had graying brown hair and a military demeanor. After introductions, he gave a curt nod.

"Ms. Randall, Mr. Donovan—welcome to Ellis Island. How can I be of service today?"

Ray explained his mission as they walked toward a pier where several boats were moored.

Ranger Paceco stopped next to a speedboat. "Let's take you over. We'll give you the full tour."

Lauren looked longingly over her shoulder at the huge brick building housing so much American history. "Will we have time to take a peek inside when we come back?"

Ray wrapped an arm around her waist. "We'll see if we can find some time." He glanced significantly at the mayor's aide, who looked down at his tablet with a frown.

The speedboat made short work of the trip between islands. It seemed longer because of the cold. Lauren snuggled next to Ray on the bench seat, thankful for his body heat and the red leather coat.

From the shelter of his arm she watched the statue grow bigger and bigger, until she towered over their approach, a symbol of welcome and freedom. She was awe-inspiring. Lauren could only imagine how emotional it would have been to see her at the end of a cramped ocean voyage—the embodiment of a new beginning.

The manicured grounds were immaculate—a sign of the respect and pride the rangers took in their care of the lady. The stairs spiraling upward seemed never-ending. But, oh, the view was worth it.

The ranger gave them ten minutes to themselves. Ray whipped out his camera and started shooting, climbing right up to the glass.

No way was she leaning forward to look down. Her heart was already pumping out adrenaline. But she could still see the city in the distance. And New Jersey on the other side. Spectacular. She took a few pictures with her phone.

She admitted to being a homebody. She liked the comfort of having her things around her. Yet standing in a piece of history, with the world literally spread out before her, she acknowledged the appeal of traveling. Especially when you got VIP treatment.

Thinking of Ray, she sought him out. Her heart jumped into her throat when she saw him pressed right up against the glass, filming straight down.

"Ray." She took a step toward him, then stopped.

She wanted to leap across the space, wrap herself around his leg, and demand he come down from there. But the element of adventure was so much a part of him. She couldn't hold him back by placing her fears on him.

To ground herself she wrapped an arm around a newel post and eyed him anxiously.

"Just a minute more, Dynamite." His balance shifted as he bent even further forward.

"Ohmigoodness."

The man had a death wish. If he didn't fall to his death, she'd do it for him. She might anyway. And suddenly the world was spinning—not because he was falling, but because *she* was. Falling hard. For him.

She loved this crazy, thoughtful, manipulative, brilliant, stubborn, funny man.

Seeing him poised on the brink of a two-hundred-foot fall shot that knowledge home like nothing else. And— oh, goodness—the enormity of the emotion dwarfed all previous relationships. Including that dork in college. His name wouldn't even come to mind.

Ray filled her to the exclusion of everything else.

"Hey." Suddenly he stood in front of her, lifting her face to him. "I'm fine. With the glass, there's no chance of falling."

"Tell that to my racing heart." She wrapped her arms around herself.

"It's perfectly safe." He held his camera out to her. "And I got an incredible shot."

She didn't bother to look. "Oh, that's all right, then."

She pushed past him toward the stairs. He'd just become her whole world and he was doing things like testing the weight factor of the glass in the crown of the Statue of Liberty. He was going to get himself killed before he met his child.

His child. Oh, heavens. She had to tell him. To wait

another moment just seemed wrong. Except for the ever-vigilant Felton Smith and Ranger Paceco. You didn't tell the man you loved he was going to be a father in front of an audience.

"Hey, hey, hey." He caught up to her, swung her into his arms. "I'm sorry." He kissed her softly. "It's so amazing I got carried away." He tucked his camera in his backpack. "Here, come with me. Let me show you what I see."

He climbed up next to the glass and held out his hand.

She shook her head. "I don't think I can."

"I'll have you."

He caught the hand she'd instinctively raised to meet his and pulled her up next to him. Vertigo rose, but he wrapped both arms around her. His firmness and strength surrounded her.

"Okay?" he whispered in her ear.

She nodded, her body tense in his grasp. "Don't let go."

"I won't." Holding her close, he pointed. "That's Queens. And over there is Manhattan. See the spire? That's our hotel."

Cradled in his arms, she listened as he brought his world to life for her. Slowly she relaxed against him, enjoying his enthusiasm. He told her about his movie and she saw the wonder of his vision through his eyes.

Paceco finally signaled it was time to go.

Ray carefully helped her down. "Maybe it'll cheer you up to hear that Felton has made time to visit Ellis."

She blinked up at him. She always focused on his need for control, but the truth was he could also be incredibly giving. He was sacrificing part of his siting agenda to let her play tourist. And the timing would work out perfectly. When they got to Ellis Island she'd pull him aside. As soon as she had him alone she'd give him the news.

The ride back to Ellis Island seemed twice as long as the trip over. On the other hand she barely felt the cold, because she was trapped in her head.

Excitement and anxiety played tug-of-war with her emotions.

She didn't know what she wanted his reaction to be. Excitement, of course. But with his history she knew that was a lot to expect. She wanted him to be pleased, to start thinking of a future together.

Heavens, did she *want* a future together? Until yesterday she'd still been contemplating sole custody.

Don't get ahead of yourself, girl, her head warned her heart.

Finally the boat arrived at Ellis Island. As the group neared the building Lauren turned to their guides and upped the wattage of her smile. "Would it be okay for us to just wander around on our own for a few minutes?"

"Of course." Ranger Paceco offered his hand. "I'll leave you to your wanderings. If you need me, just have one of the rangers call me."

"You've been very helpful." Ray shook his hand. "I should have come over more when I was a kid."

"Sometimes we need age to appreciate things. Take care, now." He nodded and took his leave.

"I'll meet you at the chopper in forty minutes," Felton said. He already had his phone in his hand as he walked toward a bench.

"Nice move, Randall." Ray draped an arm around her shoulders. "I was beginning to feel crowded." He nuzzled his nose into her hair. "Mmm. You smell good." Moving toward the building, he asked her, "So, do you have family that came through Ellis Island?"

"My great-great-grandfather on my father's side. He was six when he came over from England in 1908."

"Cool. Mamó's grandmother came over from Ireland. Hey, I'm pretty sure that was 1908. Maybe they stood in line at the same time?"

"It's a romantic notion." She eyed his profile through her lashes. "And I can see a story brewing in that head of yours. This trip is getting to you. You don't usually do relationship movies."

"It's good to stretch yourself. What are you doing?" He stopped when she tried to direct him toward a bench in the sun. "The entrance is that way."

"I know. I need to talk to you."

At the bench her knees gave out and she gratefully sank down on the stone seat.

"I have something to tell you."

"Are you okay?" Dropping down next to her, he tucked a wisp of hair behind her ear. "You've gone pale."

"I'm fine." She gathered his hands in hers, hoped he wouldn't feel the tremors through her gloves, and looked at them rather than at him. This should be easier. Shouldn't it be easy to tell the father of her child?

"Lauren, what is it? You're shaking." He wrapped her hands in both of his and rubbed them to generate warmth.

"You'll be shaking in a moment."

"Now you're scaring me. Just tell me."

Deep breath…slow release. She looked into his concerned blue eyes. "I'm pregnant."

Shock knocked him back. A flash of joy, and then his expression closed down. His eyes narrowed and he looked out over the water.

"A baby."

His flat tone revealed nothing.

"That explains your upset stomach. And your refusal of wine and coffee. How long have you known?"

"S-Since the wedding." Hating the shake in her voice, she cleared her throat, tried for more confidence. "I did an early pregnancy test that morning. I would have confirmed it with my doctor this week, except I've been here."

He stood, thrust his hands in his pockets. "So you've known for four days and you haven't said anything?"

He made it sound unreasonable. "It was unexpected. I needed time to think."

Anguish flashed across his face.

"No!" Her heart constricted in a punishing vice, she jumped to her feet, rushed to him, placed a reassuring hand on him arm. "Not about aborting the child. I'd *never* make that choice."

"Then what was there to think about?" he demanded. "What was more important than telling me I'm going to be a father?" He pinned her with a hard gaze. "I'm supposing I *am* the father?"

Wow. She retreated a step, then two.

"Yes, of course." Offended, she fisted her hands at her sides. "Are you questioning your paternity?"

"I remember the broken condom." He turned away, ran a shaking hand through thick hair. "Though my attorney will want a paternity test. I can't believe this. I must have super-swimmers. You should have told me, Lauren. All week we've been together. On the plane, at Mamó's." He scrubbed his face. "Hell, last night I poured my heart out to you about the child I lost."

"Right—and I was supposed to break into the middle of that story with *By the way I'm pregnant*?" She wrapped her arms around herself, trying to hold herself together as his words tore her apart. "It wasn't the time. This week hasn't been the time. You've been worried about your grandmother, dealing with the whole fake engagement thing, as well as this siting business. I didn't even know about the trauma of confronting your past."

This was a mistake, she thought. *I should have waited.*

The backs of her knees hit the stone bench again. She sank down. She'd known after his revelation last night that he'd have a hard time with her news. She hadn't expected him to be thrilled, but after their time together here in New York she hadn't expected him to be hurtful either.

He came to stand over her. "If you're expecting a proposal, think again. I'm not eighteen anymore."

"I'm not expecting anything from you." A slide to the

left gained her some breathing room. "I'm a successful, professional woman. Don't worry. I can take care of myself and my child."

"*Your* child." He dropped down next to her, but half turned away. "I get it now. You weren't going to tell me."

"Don't be so dramatic. Hollywood is too small to hide a pregnancy. Of course I was going to tell you."

"When?"

"Why do you care?"

"What?" He pinned her with an astounded stare over his shoulder.

"You've made it clear you're not interested in the baby." No need to cast a feature film to get that point across. "Fine with me. Consider yourself uninvited to the party."

"Seriously? You're going to pout because I didn't get down on one knee?"

"No, I'm going to live my life around my child. I'm not a self-important prima donna, too worried about protecting myself to know if I'm happy about being a parent or not."

She needed to get away from him. *Now.*

On her feet, she faced him. "Keep your ring. I never wanted it anyway." She hiked her chin toward the helicopter. "You should go on with your tour. I'm going to hang out here for a couple of hours."

Gaze locked on the entrance to the huge brick building, she put one foot in front of the other. She just needed to get inside before she broke down. No way was she giving him the satisfaction of seeing her cry.

After a few steps he grabbed her arm. "I'm not leaving you here alone."

"You don't have a choice," she informed him. "I'm all grown up, Ray. I can make my own decisions and get myself home." She glared pointedly at his hand on her arm.

He released her. "Why?"

"Because you're not responsible for me."

"No, why did you tell me now when you had no plan to do so?"

"You scared me." Giving him half the truth, she waved toward the statue towering in the distance. "I thought you should know you had a kid before you did something foolhardy and died."

"Listen, come with me." His hand dropped away. "I'm not handling this well, and I'm sorry. I need time to process everything."

"And we both know you'll process better without me. I'll see you back at Mamó's."

"Okay." He gave a gruff nod. "I'll arrange for a car to pick you up at Battery Park. I'll text you with the information. They'll take you wherever you want to go."

Home. Could the driver take her to Hollywood?

It was where she longed to be—curled up on her couch with her grandma's quilt tucked around her, surrounded by familiar things, with her sister next door and her mother on the other end of the phone.

The fantasy burst, an impossible dream.

"Thanks," she said, for once happy with his need to manipulate every situation. Then she continued toward the entrance, not wanting to watch him walk away.

She needn't have worried. She barely saw the doors through the tears blurring her vision.

CHAPTER ELEVEN

Staying over in the suite tonight.

LAUREN STARED AT the text, numb both inside and out. Apparently she was supposed to process the fact she was pregnant immediately and then go on to share the news with him, but he needed most of the day and the night, too.

"Ray isn't coming home, is he?" Mamó set a tray on the coffee table and settled into her chair next to the couch, where Lauren sat trying to reproduce the image of home she'd created earlier.

"No. Business is keeping him in the city, so he's going to stay at the hotel again."

"You don't have to cover for him, dear." Mamó leaned forward to pour steaming liquid into a sturdy mug. "I made hot cocoa." Heaping spoons full of whipped cream followed. "I thought you could use the pick-me-up."

It was just the thing. "Thank you." Lauren accepted the mug, drank a small sip. The heat and the chocolate sent warmth and comfort rolling through her. "Mmm. Perfect."

"You told him, didn't you?"

"Mmm," Lauren hummed. She had too much pride to bad-mouth the woman's grandson in her own home. "He's processing."

"He didn't take it well." It wasn't a question.

"Let's say he was shocked." The truth, and yet far short of everything.

Mamó nodded. "Which translates to being a jerk."

"I'll stick with shocked." Lauren sighed. "Now I've calmed down I recognize I was a tad hormonal and perhaps overly sensitive."

"All the more reason for him to take care of you." Sadness tugged at the corners of Mamó's eyes and her lips trembled as she sipped from her cup. "He's never cared much for surprises. I blame losing his parents at such a young age."

Lauren remembered the shock and horror of losing her high school friend to suicide in their senior year. It had consumed her whole world for months. How much worse would it be to lose family? To lose both parents at the same time?

"I don't even want to imagine the pain he must have experienced. And then Camilla pulled her heartless stunt. It's understandable he dislikes surprises."

Unfortunately she knew of no other way to deliver news of a baby. Especially an unplanned pregnancy.

"He told you about Camilla?" Surprise chased despair from Mamó's face. "He's never told anyone, as far as I know. Not even Ellie. I had to piece parts of it together myself."

"It's not a pretty story."

"Far from it. I was so proud of him. I knew how much he wanted to go to UCLA, how hard he'd worked for the Stahling Award. But he set aside his future in Hollywood for a future with his family. It was the smart thing, the responsible thing to do. It shattered him when he realized Camilla had murdered his child to mortgage her own career."

"Murdered…?" Lauren murmured. He hadn't used the word last night, but it sounded like Ray. It was very telling.

"His word." Mamó unknowingly confirmed it. "Most men would have been happy to get out of a forced marriage. Ray was committed from the beginning. I know my boy. I read all those tabloids where they call him a confirmed bachelor, and say how he prizes his privacy. They've got him all wrong. The truth is he has a big heart. He's just learned to guard it carefully."

"He's afraid of being hurt again." Lauren related to that sentiment. Better to be alone than to give up a part of your soul.

"You're different."

That caught Lauren's attention. "What do you mean?"

"The way he is with you. It's different from when he's with other women. He doesn't just look at you—he watches you as if he can't look away."

"Really?" She cringed a little at the hope in her voice.

"This isn't an easy time for either of you. I implore you to give him a chance. Your little ones deserve to have both parents in their lives."

"Lives?" Lauren croaked.

"Yes, dear. You're having twins."

Mamó says twins.

Ray read Lauren's text over and over. Twins. *Hell*. This was news he could have waited to hear. He couldn't stop thinking, wondering, worrying. Any minute now his head would implode.

When he couldn't take another second he went on the move. He rented a car, took the 87 in the Bronx and headed north. Blowing by Albany, he chased the Catskills, his mood black.

He took a curve, low and tight, and came out on a straightway. Punching the accelerator, he raced through the night, going faster than he should in an act Lauren would no doubt consider foolhardy.

His foot lowered, squeezing out a little more speed.

He was an adult. The last thing he needed was a woman telling him how to act.

The rental handled well, but his plan to go for a drive

in order to get away from his thoughts wasn't working out. Okay, it was a flawed plan. Where his head went, his thoughts followed. And, no matter how hard he tried to focus on something else, his mind kept wrapping back to Lauren and the babies she carried.

He tried thinking about his upcoming film and the sites he'd seen today, but honestly he didn't remember much after the bomb she'd dropped.

Mamó's condition couldn't even hold his attention. And the industry awards scheduled a few days away barely blipped on his radar—which peeved him, because he really wanted to sweep the season and this was the biggie. Not since his first film had he hit the trifecta of awards. To do so again would prove he had staying power.

Was it just yesterday he'd asked Lauren to go with him? This week stretched out forever in his head.

He ground his teeth, mad at the world, mad at himself, mad at Lauren, mad at life.

Mad at the world because, seriously, why him? The first time had completely undone him. He might not survive a second time.

Mad at himself because of the way he'd managed to muck things up. He wasn't handling it well, but he couldn't get a grip.

Mad at Lauren because she was the one doing this to him. No matter how cockeyed that thinking was. Which only added guilt to the mix as well. *Hello.*

Mad at life for the whole mix.

And now twins.

It only made the situation worse to hear the news here in New York, after spending half a week mired in memories he'd spent fifteen years burying skull-deep.

He slowed for another curve, flinched as headlights hit him in the eyes. It was the first traffic he'd encountered in a while—not surprising, considering the late hour on a work night. Soon he'd have to think about turning around and heading back to the hotel.

It might be a cop-out, but no way could he face cuddling up in his old bedroom with Lauren. At the same time he'd miss having her in his bed. It didn't make sense, yet it was one of the loops his head kept tracking.

That and memories of that horrific summer. He'd been shocked and devastated when Camilla had broken the news. He'd tried to hold it together, but in the end he'd bolted.

It had crushed his spirit to give up on UCLA, but he'd seen no other choice. The kid had to come first. How idealistic he'd been. But even in retrospect he couldn't see playing his hand any differently.

Except to wear a damn condom.

Resentment festered. Why did this keep happening to him?

He felt victimized, and yet there was no fault here. They'd had protected sex. Hell, *he'd* been the one to provide the condom that broke.

Fighting off weariness, he rolled his neck, stretching muscles, working out kinks. He owed Lauren a better apology. More, he owed her his support. She was just as much a victim as him. Yet deep down he couldn't help feeling as if she'd done this to him.

Because she'd kept the news from him.

He'd deserved to know as soon as she knew. The babies might be in her body, but they were as much a part of him as they were of her. He had *rights*, damn it. Being the last one to know, having no say in decisions, didn't sit well with him. How could he protect his children when he didn't know what was going on?

Anger lashed at his nerves.

Back to being mad at himself, because he couldn't stop being upset with Lauren. She might have been blameless in the conception, but she had withheld the news, taken the power of knowledge from him. Tried to push him away. Still was, come to that. Who knew how long she would have taken to tell him if Mamó's depression hadn't pushed them together?

Well, Lauren needed to adjust her thinking. He might be a perpetual bachelor, but he was damned if he'd be a sperm donor. If he'd fathered a baby—babies!—he'd be a part of his children's lives.

And, no, he didn't doubt the babies were his.

He knew Lauren—knew her integrity and the value of family to her. Never in a million years would she play false with the paternity of her child.

And she'd never hurt her child. *Children.* He believed that completely.

Yet he took little comfort in the thought.

Never would he have contemplated it of Camilla either. He couldn't conceive of it himself, so he had a hard time putting the unconscionable act in anyone's head. Then again, for Camilla the baby had been a means to an end—a tool to get what she wanted, never meant to see life.

And he had to put that aside.

The past had no bearing on the current situation. He needed to get past it and move on.

Desperate for a break, he took the next exit and pulled into the parking lot of an all-night diner. The waitress gave him a choice of the many empty booths. He slid into one next to the window, a distance away from the other two occupied tables.

"Coffee, please."

"Anything else?" the waitress asked. Young, slightly plump, with a high ponytail and pretty features, she waited patiently for his response. Her name tag read "April."

Had he eaten? He scrubbed his hands over his face, barely able to string two thoughts together. Whatever. He had no appetite.

"That's all, thanks."

She nodded and wandered away.

Ray turned his gaze to the window and got smacked with his own reflection. He looked haggard, but otherwise the same as he had this morning. That was just *wrong*. His life had changed; surely his appearance should show it?

April returned. She set down a big mug of steaming coffee and slid a plate with a large slice of chocolate cream pie in front of him.

He looked up at her. "I didn't order this."

"I know, but we're known for our chocolate cream pie. And you look a mite troubled. Pie always helps me when I'm troubled."

Looking at the whipped cream piled high, he felt his appetite come rushing back. He tipped his chin up. "Thanks."

"You want to talk about it?"

He tasted the coffee, hummed his approval as he shook his head. "Anything but."

"Okay, then." She leaned against the facing booth. "You're that director guy, aren't you?"

"I've made a few movies," he acknowledged. Usually he'd politely shut her down, but she'd brought him pie and he welcomed the distraction. "Are you interested in movies?"

"I like a good flick, but my passion is fashion design."

He recalled his trip to Eve's and seeing Lauren's transformation. *Passion* summed it up. "Well, April, that's a fine profession."

A huge smile lit up her face. "Let me know if that family gets too loud." She winked. "I'll bring you another piece of pie."

She wandered off and he glanced at the family: a mother, father, and three kids somewhere between the ages of five and eight. They chattered and laughed as they ate. The oldest, a boy, was telling the story of some ride where he'd been scared but his dad had been there so he'd felt brave and lifted his arms and felt like he was flying.

"And then *I* got scared," the dad said. "Because I thought you were going to fly away."

At that point the mom sent the kids off to the bathroom. Once they'd trooped off, she murmured something to the dad and they shared a laugh and a kiss.

Their unity got to Ray. Their love and camaraderie at the end of a long day. It shouted family with a capital F. And he realized he wanted that—the love, the togetherness.

April brought him a full to-go cup along with his bill. He left her a hefty tip. Time to head back. Running only worked so long before you had to step up and face what you were running from.

"Mamó." Lauren's voice shook. "I'm bleeding."

"Oh, my dear." Mamó came from the kitchen to take Lauren's hands and lead her to the couch. Sitting next to Lauren, she held her hands over her belly. "May I?"

Lauren nodded.

Mamó laid her hands on Lauren's belly and concentrated. Heart tripping wildly, Lauren waited breathlessly.

"I sense no distress," Mamó announced, and Lauren allowed herself to breathe. "Is it heavy bleeding?" Mamó asked. "Are you in pain?"

"Spotting, mostly. No pain. But it's not good, is it?" Lauren squeezed the words through a sand-crusted throat. She wished she'd been to the doctor, had some indication of what this might mean. "I've always heard bleeding is bad when you're pregnant."

"Some things are natural. But much has been learned since I had my babies. You will feel better if you see a doctor."

Lauren squeezed Mamó's hands. "I will, yes."

"Then we will go. You have been through much these last few days. I'm so sorry for my part in causing you distress."

"Mamó—"

"No." The older woman shook her head, swiped at a tear. "Ray was right. It is not okay. I've worked myself into a state, wanting great-grandbabies, but it's not fair of me to pin my happiness on Ray's life. Seeing the problems I've caused, I realize it's not healthy for either of us." She patted Lauren's fingers. "You stay here. I'll get Ellie and your purse and we'll be on our way." She bustled off.

Lauren wrapped her arms around her babies and sat perfectly still. If she didn't move, nothing could happen to them. Where was Ray? She longed for his strength and support—could really do with some of his take-charge attitude right about now.

Mamó returned with Ellie and her purse and jacket. Ellie was dragging Lauren's luggage.

"Hey, I'm thinking positive. In case you're good to travel you'll have to leave from the hospital."

Oh, right. Lauren had made a flight reservation after her assistant had called with an emergency. Lauren had handled it, but she'd decided she needed to go home. Ray didn't want her here and she was needed in California. It was after she'd finished packing that she'd noticed the spotting.

She'd hoped to see Ray before she left, but she really couldn't think about all that right now. She was too worried about the twins to focus on anything else.

Mamó and Ellie bundled her up. And they were off. Lauren tagged Ray with a text. Yes, it was cowardly, but she didn't feel like fielding a lot of questions she didn't have answers for.

And he should *be* here, damn it.

Suddenly chilled, she shivered. All night she'd lain awake, wondering what his "processing" might result in. Would their children—oh, goodness, she still reeled at the reality of twins—would their twins bring them closer or drive them apart?

Perhaps that was her answer. Never had she felt so alone

as she had sleeping by herself in his bed last night. Not that she'd slept much.

She should be more understanding. Recalling her own shock and her struggle to adjust to the life-altering news, she should have a clue what he was going through. And she did. But it didn't stop her from resenting his continued silence.

It might be unfair of her to think so, but there was a difference in being uncommunicative when the other party existed in blissful ignorance than when they waited in breathless anxiety. He'd been the one to pull back. The way she saw it, he needed to be the one to come to her.

Now would be good. She really needed him.

I'm bleeding. Mamó is taking me to the hospital.

Fear punched into Ray's gut as he read Lauren's text. He immediately tried her phone, but she didn't answer. *Damn it.*

He dialed his grandmother. She answered on the first ring.

"Mamó, how is she?"

"I don't get any sense of distress from the babies. And I believe I would if they were in true danger. But to be safe we're taking Lauren to Emergency."

"Let me talk to her." Muffled voices rumbled on the other end of the line.

"She doesn't want to talk to you."

Damn it. Add anger to the fear and dread forming a ball in his chest. His fault. He shouldn't have put her off with texts last night and this morning.

"Put her on."

"She's not shutting you out," Mamó assured him. "She doesn't want to talk because she doesn't have any answers. She's holding it together, but she's scared. It doesn't help that she's out of her element here in New York."

"Ask her what I can do."

This time he heard Lauren answer clearly. "Just tell him to get here."

"She said—"

"I heard," he cut in. "Text me the address. I'm on my way."

Ray explained the situation to the major's aide, thanked him for his assistance, and hopped in the car waiting for him. He gave the driver the address and instructions to hurry. As the car raced toward Queens he kept his mind off worrying about Lauren and the babies by looking ahead.

He'd need to get Fred and Ethel to baby-proof the house and grounds. Maybe they'd have a recommendation for a nanny. Or perhaps Lauren knew someone.

No doubt she'd want to be a hands-on mom, but he wanted someone available to help so she didn't get worn out. It was a given she'd continue to work.

Calculating dates, he figured Lauren would be due in seven months, give or take a week or so, which put him a month into filming here in New York. Maybe he should chuck the location shots?

His shoulders tensed at the notion. There was an authenticity that came with location filming that couldn't be captured on a back lot or in a substitute spot. He'd figure something out.

Because he wasn't missing the birth of his children.

And this—whatever it ended up being—was just a blip. Mamó would have sensed it if something were wrong. Battling another surge of fear, he clung to the fact she hadn't felt any fetal distress. Everything would be all right.

The car hit the bridge, and he made a proclamation and a prayer. He had to believe.

The alternative just wasn't acceptable.

The driver changed lanes, cutting off a delivery truck with inches to spare. Ray gritted his teeth and held on. They couldn't move fast enough for him. He hated not knowing. Hated not being there for Lauren. How he longed to have her safe in his arms right now.

Again, his fault. He'd been punishing her for...what? Thinking of herself first? Adjusting to the fact she was going to be a mother? Letting him deal with his grandmother and his past before learning he was going to be a father?

What a hero he was.

Finally he spotted his destination. The driver pulled right up in front of the emergency room at Queens Hospital and Ray hopped out. He spoke briefly with Mamó and Ellie, then waved down a nurse. He recognized the woman from the neighborhood, and for once he was happy for the connection as she personally escorted him to the cubicle where Lauren was being treated.

"How is she?" he asked, his heart running a marathon in his chest.

"The doctor has seen Lauren and she's fine. The bleeding was due to some natural adjustments of the uterus. Nothing to worry about. But to be on the safe side he ordered an ultrasound. The technician is in with Lauren now."

"Thanks." Relief left him breathless.

"No problem." Arriving at a cubicle, she pushed the curtain aside. "Mr. Donovan," she announced. She patted him on the arm, said, "Congratulations, Daddy," and left.

"Ray." Lauren gave a glad cry of relief and reached for his hand.

He stepped forward, wrapped her fingers in his. "The nurse said you were fine."

She lay on a gurney while the technician ran a scope over her belly and monitored the machine next to her.

"That's what they tell me. More important, the babies are fine. Look."

First he leaned down and kissed her on the top of her head, disguising his huge relief. Seeing her animation, touching her, reassured him more than any medical niceties could.

He glanced at the picture she indicated on the screen but failed to make out anything until the technician directed his attention to two little heads and two sets of feet, showed him the two beating hearts.

He slowly sank down on the side of the gurney next to Lauren, overcome by this visual evidence of his children. The twins were no more than a couple of inches big, but they packed a big wallop.

The picture blipped as Lauren scooted over, making more room for him. "Pretty awesome, huh?"

"Yes." The word *terrifying* came to mind. "I want to be involved."

It was a bald statement.

Her gaze flew to the technician. "We don't need to talk about that now."

For once he didn't care who heard his business. He'd never been more certain of anything in his life. "I've been an ass. I'm sorry."

"Stop." Lauren tightened her grip on his hand.

"I'll just check with the doctor." The technician handed her a couple of tissues for the gel on her tummy and made a discreet exit.

Ray took the tissues and wiped her clean, his touch warm after the chill of the gel. "Lauren—"

"No." She laid a finger on his lips. "Before you go on I need to say something."

Needing to feel more in control, she tugged her sweater down and sat up.

"Yes, I thought you were being a jerk, but I was wrong. And so were you. This is huge." She waved at the blank screen that had so recently held images of their children. "We're going to be parents. It's important, and it's not something to rush. I already made that mistake. And I'm sorry."

"I shouldn't have yelled at you."

"You were in shock. So was I. We need time, both of us, to come to grips with this change in our lives. And I mean more than a few hours—possibly more than a few days. And that's okay, because we have another seven months to figure everything out."

He lifted a sandy brow. "Ms. Clipboard? You're not going to be able to wait seven months for anything."

The corner of her mouth kicked up at that. "Probably not. But I know I want to do this right. And rushing isn't the way to do that."

"No rushing around for you, young lady," the doctor said, entering the cubicle. "You're carrying precious cargo."

He introduced himself to Ray.

"How are the twins, Doctor?" Ray asked. "Anything we should be concerned about?"

"Everything looks normal." The doctor included Lauren in his answer. "You'll want to see your doctor when you get home. In the meantime try to keep stress to a minimum—which means no rushing. But you're healthy...the babies are healthy. I see no reason why you can't fly."

"Thank you, Doctor." His assurances finally allowed her to relax.

"Congratulations to the both of you." He shook Ray's hand and departed.

"Well, that was good to hear." Ray helped her up. "Now, let's get you home."

"Listen, I'm not going back to Mamó's." She stood and looped the strap of her purse over her shoulder. "Something came up at work so I booked a flight earlier. I can still make it, so I'm going to go. It's for the best. It'll give both of us the extra space we need." She kissed his cheek.

"Wait, you can't go." He followed her out into the hall, pulled her to a stop. "We're just starting to actually communicate."

"We'll communicate better in Hollywood, when we're both back in the real world."

"You can't leave. You just got out of Emergency.

"And the doctor said I'm okay to fly."

"Come on, Lauren," he implored her. "It's not like you to pout."

"I don't pout."

Moving around him, she moved toward the lobby, where Mamó and Ellie waited. His arguments made her more determined to leave. She pulled her phone out and texted the cab company she'd called while waiting for the technician.

"What would you call running away? I thought you were done playing games?"

Serene mood shattered, she swung on him. "This isn't playtime for me, Ray. I'm not a paper doll. I've been there, done that, didn't like it. I won't apologize for making my own decisions." Not wanting to go there, she dropped her head on his chest, leaned on his strength. "You need to finish your visit with your grandmother, and I just want to go home."

His arms came around her, his hand fisting in her hair. "I don't need more time, Lauren. This scare has confirmed my feelings. I want to be a part of my children's lives. I'll let you go now. But factor me into your thinking—because I'm not going away."

CHAPTER TWELVE

RAY STOOD IN THE middle of his room, surrounded by emptiness. All evidence of Lauren's presence was gone. Only her scent lingered. Honeysuckle and soap. He stared at the too-small bed where even she had defied the rules she'd set down, curling so sweetly into his arms.

He didn't spend the night with women. And he didn't bring them home. Those two steps prevented any misguided sense of intimacy from developing between him and his companions. Those two decrees were the bedrock of his rigidly practiced relationship controls, followed by:

Never let sex control a decision.
Never get personal.
Never have unprotected sex.

Those few restrictions had helped him live an uncomplicated life for the last fifteen years. Yet from the very beginning Lauren had slipped past his shields. She'd blown through the first two in one night.

You couldn't get any more personal than having family over for Thanksgiving. He should never have invited them...her...not even to drag Garrett out of his funk. But, hey, he'd figured he had his attraction for her under control. Heck, she'd irritated him as much as she'd turned him on—if not more. And her family on the premises should have guaranteed nothing was going to happen.

Best sex he'd ever had.

It hadn't mattered that they'd been in the laundry room, or that her parents had been down the hall. One smart remark too many had sparked the flame of passion, incinerating the barrier of restraint, creating an urgency not to be denied.

He'd only meant to quiet her with his mouth.

The taste of her had ignited his blood.

It was the last coherent thought he'd had until, heart racing, he'd collapsed against her and let the washing machine absorb his weight.

At the end of the night he'd shaken it off. Okay, it had happened. Lesson learned. He'd keep his distance in the future.

Right.

It should have helped that she was having the same discussion with herself.

It hadn't.

Twice more they'd hooked up. The urgency just as strong. The sex just as good. The broken condom should have been deterrent enough to prevent a third session—but, no. He'd just been glad he'd had condoms on him when the mood had struck, because the passion was so overwhelming he couldn't claim he would have stopped.

Add sleeping with her to his list of violations. He'd taken just as much satisfaction in holding her as she slept as he'd taken in pleasuring her lovely body. The last rule broken. The contentment he'd felt waking with her in his arms had overridden any thought of self-preservation.

He'd always been a rule-breaker, but not about this. The way he'd blown through his own rules should have warned him against asking her to accompany him to New York. Arrogance again. He'd missed her, so he'd thought he could give Mamó what she asked for while seducing Lauren into a vacation fling. A win-win for him.

And now they were to be parents.

He yanked his bag out of the closet and started empty-ing the drawers into it. With Lauren gone he felt a need to follow her to Hollywood. He stopped packing to text his friend's pilot and got an immediate response that the plane would be prepped and ready within two hours. His flight set, he tossed in his remaining items and zipped the bag.

To the pit of his soul he detested the need to alter his life for another unexpected pregnancy. Yet the one clear thing he'd taken away from the last two days was the de-sire to be a part of his children's lives.

The juxtaposition twisted him up inside. Deep down he knew he had to get past the resentment or he'd poison any relationship he established with Lauren and his kids.

Still he lingered, his thoughts in turmoil.

He dropped down on the bed, dragged Lauren's pillow from under the covers and buried his nose in the softness. The heady honeysuckle scent went to his head. Through all the uncertainty the one thing he did know was she'd touched him in ways no one else ever had.

"Ray." Mamó appeared in the bedroom doorway a little winded from her trip up the stairs. She carried something red clutched under her arm.

"Mamó." He hopped up and led her to the bed to sit.

She patted the bed beside her and he sat too.

"I'm sorry Lauren felt the need to leave early. Such a nice girl. I'm so glad you brought her with you."

"Yeah, it turned out to be more of a trip than I ex-pected."

"I apologized to her and now I'll apologize to you. I'm sorry for my meddling, for letting my emotions get the better of me, for causing you so many problems."

"You may have caused a few complications. I managed the problems all on my own." There was a fine truth. In the scheme of things Mamó's preemptive engagement an-nouncement had turned out to be a minor development. Hard to trump twins.

"I guess I don't have to tell you my news."

"Dear boy, I won't deny I'm pleased." She patted his knee. "I do regret my gift has been such a trial for you. To this day I mourn the part I played in ending your wedding."

"Don't." He draped an arm around her shoulders, took comfort in the strength of her thin frame. She was tougher than she looked. "None of what happened was your fault. I'm glad I learned the truth. If not for you, I would have married a woman I didn't love under false circumstances. The marriage would have ended anyway, because the child was the only reason I was with her."

"And will you propose to Lauren?"

A denial sprang to mind, yet he hesitated. "Truthfully, Mamó, I don't know how I feel. It's hard to unwrap the events of today from the events of the past."

"It shouldn't be. You were a boy then, just starting out. You're a man now, well established and successful in your field. Your feelings for Camilla were mild at best, your decisions based on honor and expedience. And she was using you. Your feelings for Lauren are deeper, stronger. She's successful in her own right. She's with you because she chooses to be, not because she needs you. You'll be partners in whatever manner you elect to go forward."

She made it sound so simple. But she didn't know the whole truth.

"Lauren came to New York as a favor to me." He explained the circumstances. "So, you see, we aren't actually romantically connected."

"Hmm. I think you're wrong. And you just proved my point. There was no need for her to help you. You may feel like you're caught in the same situation, but these women couldn't be more different. My advice is to stay focused on the present. Don't let the past cause you any more misery than it already has. Here."

She held out the red item she'd been carrying and as it unfolded he saw it was the coat he'd given Lauren. The one she'd refused. The one she'd looked so beautiful in when the weather had trumped her stubbornness.

His jaw clenched as he took it. Obstinate woman. He started to hand it back, to demand Mamó donate it to charity as he'd threatened Lauren he would. But he couldn't. He hated the thought of another woman wearing the coat.

A honk from the street announced the arrival of his taxi.

"There's your ride. Give me a hug." She wrapped him in her arms and for a moment he felt like he was ten years old again and she was his whole world.

He kissed her cheek. "You take care of yourself."

"I'll be good." She patted his cheek. "No more feeling sorry for myself. Besides, I have great-grandchildren to look forward to."

Well, *there* was an upside to the situation.

He helped her down the stairs, and then he was out the door and on the road.

A short while later he boarded the plane. He tossed his backpack and the red jacket into a seat and dropped down in the leather chair beside it. Soon they were in the air. The six-hour flight stretched ahead of him.

Leaning forward he stabbed his hands into his hair. Heck, he couldn't stand to spend any more time with himself. If he didn't find something besides his life to think about, he'd go insane.

"Good afternoon, sir." The flight attendant appeared. "Would you care for refreshments?"

Ray shook his head. "No thank you, Julie."

"May I secure these items?" She gestured to the backpack and jacket in the seat next to him.

"Leave them. That will be all for now."

The woman disappeared and Ray reached for his bag, drew out his camera and laptop. He'd organize his photos and video shots. That should occupy him for a while.

To start he sorted the work into three categories: family

and Mamó's birthday, the siting trip, and others. He soon
noticed a commonality in all three. Lauren.

Grr... The point of this was to get away from thoughts
of her. He began dropping all the photos of her into a separate file. It didn't take long to discover the problem with
that plan. He lost nearly all his photos. Easily two-thirds
of his pictures went into the "Lauren" file.

She'd obviously been a primary target for his lens.

Curious about what had drawn him, he went back and
started looking from the beginning.

There were shots of her sleeping on the plane, pale and
exhausted. He should have had a clue something was off
right then. He called her Dynamite for a reason—because
he never saw her going less than full out. She'd given him
some excuse and he'd bought it, chalking her frailness up
to pulling off her sister's big wedding, right during awards
season, which would knock out any normal person.

Then came shots of her at the welcome party, surrounded by strangers, yet smiling and poised, all while
under the duress of supporting a fake engagement. She
really had been a good sport.

He grinned at the less than patient expression on her
face in his bedroom as she tried to lay down her new rules.
As if they could sleep in any sized bed without touching.
He'd taken great delight in letting her break *that* rule.

Lauren at Mamó's party, looking elegant and feminine. He wanted to delete the picture of her with the hired
dancer. But he left it as penance for the one of her with her
head bent, hurt and sadness evident on her face and in her
posture. His fault for insulting her matchmaking talents.

Not his best moment.

To make up for it he'd tried to tell Mamó he knew about
her admirer before he left. She'd twittered and waved him
off, saying she knew all about George's hot crush. And that
someday she might do something about it.

Appalled all over again, he'd turned, looking for Lauren, and immediately realized his mistake.

Damn, he missed her.

Seeing her coat next to him, he curled his hand into a fist on the leather. Then he forced his fingers to loosen the fabric. He'd already sniffed her pillow today, like some lovesick pup. Besides, he could smell the honeysuckle from where he sat.

He wished she were here.

More shots of Lauren—in the hardware store, coming out of the spa, on the streets of New York, at the mayor's reception, stunning in that blue dress, flying over the city, on the boat to Liberty Island, in the crown... He'd even caught one of her when she'd wrapped herself around that newel post.

The fear on her face was stark. Real. Telling.

He looked into her eyes and adrenaline shot through his body as if he was prepared to defend, to protect, to battle— whatever it took to remove the anguish staring out at him.

Problem was he'd be fighting himself.

Lauren cared about him. It showed in every smile, in every indulgent look, in every censuring grimace—and she'd nailed him a few times—in every sultry glance.

His gaze landed on the one boudoir shot. He grinned, remembering he'd snapped it before she'd realized he held the camera.

She'd beat him back to bed after a steamy shower and sprawled half under the sheet, half on top, so the camera had caught the naked length of her back. Her blond hair was a messy knot on the top of her head, damp tendrils clung to her face and neck, and she looked directly into the camera, anticipating his return.

His blood heated and—

His breath caught.

He leaned forward. Blew up the shot. And stared right

into sleepy eyes, molten gold and shimmering with soft emotion.

Love.

He'd missed it at the time—damn camera—but there was no mistaking the intensity of emotion.

Satisfaction and something more filled him up.

Lauren loved him.

The question was what to do about it?

CHAPTER THIRTEEN

LAUREN SAT AT her desk, carefully scrutinizing the event schedule, shifting people around, hiring more where necessary. It was the biggest Hollywood awards ceremony of the season, and By Arrangement would be hosting Obsidian Studio's huge after-party. She expected it to go on way into the next morning.

Usually they wouldn't attempt two events on such a big day, but a valued customer had called two days ago, requesting they handle a brunch for twenty on the day of the awards. Lauren hadn't been able to refuse. So she'd shuffled and shifted, authorized overtime, and wrung miracles out of vendors.

When her phone rang she lifted it to her ear, eyes still on the schedule. "This is Lauren."

"I leave for a week and you run off to New York and get engaged. To *Ray*. I knew there was more to that fling than you were admitting."

"Tori!" Lauren hopped up and closed her door. "I didn't expect to hear from you until you got home."

"I am back—well, in New York anyway. We'll be flying home later today." The second half of her honeymoon she would be attending the awards, and then settling into her new home with Garrett. "And I see I just missed you here. It would have been fun to spend the day together in New York."

"Honeymoon so boring you need company?"

"Uh, that would be *no*." Tori's merry laughter rang over the line. "France was fabulous. We had dinner at the top of the Eifel Tower the night before we left. It was breathtaking."

"So is New York from the crown of the Statue of Liberty. You should check it out if you have time."

"Hmm... So, are you going to tell me about Ray?"

"Oh, Tori. I miss you so much." Lauren forced a calming breath. "But I'm not going to intrude on your honeymoon."

"The only way you're going to do that is if you leave me hanging."

"I'm serious."

"So am I. Garrett went to the gym for a few minutes. Spill, already."

Lauren spilled everything. Taking the pregnancy test at Tori's wedding, Ray's request to go to New York with him, Mamó's announcement of their non-existent engagement, falling in love, Ray freaking at the news of the baby— which, hey, turned out was twins.

Tori let her talk, except for shrieking over news of the twins. In the end she went right to the heart of the matter.

"You've been through a lot in such a short amount of time. I heard you blow by that mention of love. I know you're hurt by his distancing himself, but do you love Ray?"

"Yes. No. I do, but—"

"No buts. Yes or no?"

"It's not that easy," Lauren protested. "I can't, Tori. I thought yes once before, and it was an illusion."

"Love isn't meant to be easy. I almost lost Garrett because I was afraid to trust him. Afraid to trust myself. I let a piece of my past stop me from seeing beyond the surface. I needed to open my eyes and my heart and take that final step into the present."

Lauren remembered. Watching her sister suffer and not

being able to help had been excruciating. But Lauren's situation was different.

"You don't understand. What I feel for Ray is so much more than what I felt for Brad. His reticence *does* hurt. It makes me worry I've given too much of myself away. I can't be in another relationship where I care more than my partner. If it goes wrong with Ray I'm not sure I could find my way back."

"Sis, you're stronger than you think. Brad was able to influence you because you believed you loved him and naturally wanted to please him. You never conceived of someone taking advantage of you in such a way. You're aware now. You need to trust yourself and trust Ray."

Lauren paced in front of her desk. "I don't know if it can work. He's manipulative and he likes his own way."

A snort sounded in her ear, and then Tori demanded, "What man doesn't? Let me ask you this: has he ever coerced you into doing something you didn't want to do?"

The whole New York trip came to mind. But, to be truthful, he'd accepted her refusal. She'd been the one to change her mind. He always seemed to be making plans she had issues with, but when presented with challenges he adapted well.

"Uh-uh." Tori finally cut off Lauren's search for an example. "You told me after we were engaged that you'd seen Garrett and I belonged together."

"I remember. You obviously cared for him, but I didn't want to unduly influence you. If you'd continued to be stubborn I probably would have said something eventually."

"I'm glad to hear you say so. I get the same feeling about you and Ray."

Lauren froze. "You're just saying that to get me to act."

"Maybe, but it's also true. Don't dismiss the significance of the bond just because it's not what you want to hear."

"He's back in town," Lauren volunteered. "Before things blew up between us he asked me to go to the awards show with him."

He'd called and texted every fifteen minutes for the past hour and a half. *Now* he wanted to talk. Finally she'd texted back that she was busy with work and she'd contact him on Monday. His response was that he'd leave a ticket for her at Reception.

"Wow. You've got to go. It would be perfect if we're both there, and then we can go to the party after. It's everything we've been working toward."

"Except for the pre-event work and the estrangement between me and Ray."

"Yeah, well, you need to get over that. You belong together, Lauren."

A deep male rumble sounded in the background. Then Tori's muffled voice.

"Give…minute…talking to Lauren."

A giggle.

"Always…that thought…shower…"

Then she was back.

"Lauren, think about what I said. Trust yourself, girl. The risk is worth the reward."

The happiness in her twin's voice reinforced her claim. She'd given Lauren a lot to think about.

"Hey, don't worry about me. Go take care of your man."

"I do believe I will. See you soon. Oh, and Lauren? If you don't allow yourself to love again, then Brad is still controlling you. And that's just sad."

Unsettled by the call, Lauren returned to her desk and the spreadsheet. Mouse in hand, she stared at the screen.

"If you don't allow yourself to love again, then Brad is still controlling you."

Tori's proclamation echoed through Lauren's mind again and again. The concept of him still having any influence on her raked across her senses like fingernails over a blackboard.

Neither did it sit well with her that he might triumph over Ray in any way. It wasn't true. Yet that was what Tori's words implied. Lauren's blood chilled at the very notion of anyone getting that impression, including her. *Especially* her.

She blinked and the schedule spreadsheet came back into view. By sheer strength of will she finished it and handed it off to her assistant, deliberately leaving Tori and herself off the assignment delegation. They'd both be there, but this way Tori got to enjoy herself. And Lauren could be wherever she was needed.

After the success of Obsidian Studio's event at the Hollywood Hills Film Festival, Obsidian's after-party was being hyped as the event not to miss. It was the pinnacle of By Arrangement's achievements. Not even her current heartache could steal her pride in their accomplishments. This party signified everything she'd been working for.

Logistics-wise, there really was no reason she couldn't attend the awards with Ray. With the adjustments she'd made, her assistant and Tori's should be able to handle both events without the company's owners. Plus, the two of them would be attending the Obsidian Studio party and could step in if needed.

But it was to be *her* night, *her* success, and she needed to be in the midst of it…

Still, she remembered the thrill when he'd asked her to attend the awards with him—the longing to go. Not because it put her closer to her career goals, but because she wanted to support him. His brilliance deserved to be honored and something instinctual in her demanded she be by his side.

Except the day had to belong to *her*. If she gave it up, did that prove she was right back to putting a man's desires before her own?

Not forgetting the fact that the world believed her to be his fiancée. How could she walk the red carpet at his side, pretending all the time they were together, when in truth they'd never been further apart?

By Sunday morning Lauren still hadn't made up her mind. Her emotions rode a teeter-totter ride—up one moment, down the next. She went from wanting to support Ray to needing the validation of self-worth that would come with working the party. Giving it up would diminish her power. Which was exactly what she feared happening.

Of course Ray completely ignored her attempt to put him off until Monday. At ten a courier arrived in her office with an envelope. Inside was her ticket to the award ceremony and a note:

> *It'll be a crush at the theater. I wanted to save you the trouble of going after the ticket. I'm hoping you'll be my lucky charm.*
> *Ray*

His lucky charm. No pressure there. And he didn't fool her—he wanted to make it easy so she had no excuse for not doing what he wanted.

Yeah, *that* was going to work. But along with annoyance came a little thrill of flattery. He really had no need for her to join him. He usually walked the red carpet alone. With her along the attention would flip from the potential of his movie winning to their faux engagement. She would literally be stealing his limelight.

An hour later another courier arrived, carrying three large stacked boxes tied with five-inch-wide red ribbon and a huge red bow.

"No. N. O. I'm not accepting this," she told the wiry teenager in a gray tee and jeans. "Take it back."

"Sorry, ma'am."

Ma'am? Seriously? Okay, yeah, she'd be a mother soon, but she was way too young to be called "ma'am."

"There's a no return flag. I'm not allowed to take it back." He gave her a big grin. "Got a *nice* tip, though. You enjoy, now."

He practically ran out the door. No doubt in a hurry to spend his "*nice* tip".

Hands on hips, body and soul at odds, she sighed, eying the stacked boxes. Her fingers itched to tear into the ribbon to see what the white boxes hid. A dress, for certain, and possibly shoes. A weakness of hers. But if she saw, she'd want. And he was manipulating her. Seducing her with niceties and beautiful things into going with him instead of working.

And he was getting to her. But she lacked the skill-set to spend hours in his company pretending there weren't unresolved issues between them. If nothing else the New York trip had proved that beyond all doubt.

She tore into the boxes. *Temptation, thy name is Ray.* And, yes, the biggest held a dress. An Eve Gardner. Oh, he was good.

She'd tried this black gown on in New York and it had fit like a dream, with a fitted bodice with narrow straps and a square neckline low enough to display the rising swell of her breasts. The dress had clung to her curves, the material flowing over her body with a soft sheen. Too daring for the mayor's reception...tame by Hollywood standards.

The smallest box held shoes—strappy silver heels, with rhinestones and a lifted sole that made her drool.

No fair. He knew her too well. And he'd hit her weaknesses dead target.

The last box surprised her. It held the red leather jacket he'd bought her in New York. The one it had broken her heart to leave behind. She clutched it to her like she'd found an old friend.

A note slipped to the table.

Something to wear. And shoes, because a special dress deserves new shoes. Or so Kyla assured me. No lingerie, because frankly I don't care if you wear any. And the jacket because I plan to buy you many things through the years. Best to get used to it now.
Ray

She folded the jacket and put it back in the box. Tucked the dress and shoes out of sight too. His reference to "through the years" yanked at her heart strings. A master at setting scenes, his message today hinted at a future together. But she didn't dare assume.

She fingered the phone in her skirt pocket, longing to call him.

But, no. Their conversation, when they had it, needed to be in person. If she called he'd try to charm her into going to the awards and all her progress would be lost. Best to tough it out.

A task made more difficult when the staff spied the boxes and demanded to see their contents. Oohs and aahs echoed through the room, but what really cut through her resolve was when her assistant, Maria, pulled her aside and assured Lauren she could handle the party.

"I've learned so much from you. I can do this. You should go to the awards—have fun."

"This is a big event. It's not fair to ask you—"

"You're not asking. You've trained us to be a well-oiled machine. You should take advantage of what you've wrought and live the life the rest of us only dream about."

"Thanks, Maria. I'll think about it." An easy promise to make as her thoughts revolved around little else.

Just before noon Lauren stood at her desk, gathering her things to move over to the Lowes Hotel—the venue for tonight's party. It was adjacent to the theater which was the home of the awards ceremony.

She glanced up at the sound of the bell to see two men in their display showroom. One wore an expensive suit and the other a security guard's uniform.

Smoothing her hands over her blue skirt, she went to greet them. When they saw her they advanced to meet her. On closer view, she noted that the guard was armed and the man in the suit carried a metal case handcuffed to his wrist.

Good gracious, Ray, what have you done?

"Gentlemen, I'm Lauren Randall—how can I help you?"

"Yes, Ms. Randall. I have a delivery for you. Might we go somewhere more private?" asked the suited man.

"This will have to do." Her office wouldn't hold the three of them.

"Very well." He set the briefcase on the nearest display table. "May I see some identification, please?"

"And if I say no…?"

"I've been instructed to stay with you until I've made the delivery."

"Of course you have." She went to her desk, grabbed her purse, returned to show him her ID.

Suit Man opened the case and lifted out a long, flat velvet jewelry box. With practiced ceremony he opened the hinged case and displayed the dazzling contents.

"The Sabina of the Claudia Collection, House of Brandia."

Diamond layers about an inch wide formed a pattern that reminded her of leaves. The avant-garde neck-piece was designed to flow around the neck and almost meet at the front. One point, formed of three oval rubies, would hit the center of her chest above her breasts, then the collar would wrap around her neck and the second ruby-tipped end would stop two inches above the first point, leaving an inch of skin between the two points. Matching earrings completed the set.

Speechless, Lauren simply stared. The set had a name— the Sabina. She loved the avant-garde design of the pieces.

But she couldn't wear them. Not in a million years. Not if its delivery required an armed guard escort. This went so far beyond the red jacket it was ridiculous.

What was Ray *thinking*?

"And there's this." Suit held out a small box.

Lauren's heart jumped into her throat. A tremble revealed her state as she reached for the ring box. It shook in the palm of her hand.

Suit reached into his front breast pocket. "Mr. Donovan also sent a missive." He offered the envelope with a flourish.

Missive? The dude clearly liked his drama.

As did Ray.

"You need to take this back," she informed Suit, and included Security Guard just to cover all bases. "I can't be responsible for this."

"May I suggest you read the letter, Ms. Randall?"

The hefty guard nodded.

Of course they'd stick together.

Turning away from the two men, she tore into the envelope.

Dynamite

Don't freak out. The jewels are on loan. Just a few baubles to add to your enjoyment of the night. I hope you like them. When I saw the necklace I thought of you. A special piece for a special woman.

The ring is my grandmother's wedding ring. She gave it to me fifteen years ago to give to the woman I would marry. Camilla didn't deserve it. I couldn't give it to her.

Will you wear it tonight? With you by my side I'll be a winner regardless of the results revealed on stage. Afterward we'll go to your party and I can watch you work. So sexy.

I love you, Lauren. I want to live my life with you

and our twins and our future children. I admit it took me a while to get to this point. But it feels right.

We have much to talk about. Much to look forward to.

Tonight our journey begins.
With all my love,
Ray.

Lauren opened the ring box, drew in a sharp breath. Stunning—just stunning. An oval of small diamonds framed three raised round diamonds, the middle one bigger than the top and bottom gems. Two rows of diamonds flowed off each side into a platinum band.

It fit perfectly on her finger.

She was so lost.

From the vantage point of the Panorama Suite of the Lowes Hotel Lauren watched the frantic activity down below as the Hollywood elite started to arrive for the big night. The limo line would be non-stop for the next four hours as the five-hundred-foot red carpet and then the theater filled. The people filling the seven hundred bleacher seats had been in place for hours.

Behind her the thirty-five-hundred square foot suite, complete with baby grand piano, was ready except for the food and servers—but this was just the escape route, or more accurately the end-game.

Downstairs her team was putting the final touches on the transformation of the main ballroom into an upscale club with a sexy edge. Music, dancing, and live performances would take the party into the wee hours.

Along with the Panorama Suite, Obsidian had taken a full floor of rooms. Some were for performers, others for executives, and half were set aside as changing rooms. Many stars liked to change after the awards. Lauren had convinced Obsidian to offer them a place to do so.

Her own finery was spread out on the bed in her room.

The problem? She still ping-ponged about whether to go with Ray or stay and work.

She'd texted him not to send a car for her; said she was working at the Lowes. Vague, much?

He'd proposed, sent her a beautiful ring she had yet to remove, had been the first to admit his feelings. Pretty brave, considering she hadn't spoken to him since leaving New York. She owed him a real response.

More importantly, she owed herself an honest response.

"Hey." Tori's heels clicked on the hardwood floor. "We're heading out. Garrett wants to get a quick bite to eat before we meet up with Ray in an hour."

"Have fun," Lauren urged without turning around.

"I'm still hoping you'll join us." Warm arms enfolded her in a hug. "I wish it were as clear to you as it is to me. You love him, he loves you, you're having twins. You belong together."

Lauren curled her arms over Tori's, savoring the familiar touch, the unconditional love.

"I wish it were that simple, too."

Suddenly bigger arms, stronger arms, enveloped the both of them as Garrett added his support. His deep voice sounded close to her ear.

"He's the best man I know."

"Of course you think so." Tears welled up. A half-sob escaped as her breath hitched. "He's your best friend."

"Yeah, but you're my sister now," Garrett said. "I wouldn't tell you something I don't believe to be true."

"Thank you."

His support touched her. A loving family was a new concept for him, so she knew what reaching out cost him. She turned around and hugged them both.

"I love you." She pulled free. "Now, go. I'll see you later."

After a last hug from Tori, they left.

At the door, Tori looked back. "Get out of your head. As long as you're replaying the same loop you're going to get the same answer." She waved and was gone.

Get out of her head? If only she could. Unbidden, Tori's words from yesterday came back to Lauren.

"If you don't allow yourself to love again, then Brad is still controlling you."

She clenched her hands until her nails bit into her palms. No way was she letting that happen. So enough, already. No more internal fighting. She needed to let go of what she *should* do and focus on what she *wanted* to do. In other words: get out of her head.

Eyes closed, taking deep breaths, she let it all go. Counting…ten in, ten out. Three times. It was the most peace she'd had in hours. Days.

Her hand found her stomach and she focused on the twins growing within her. She imagined holding them in her arms, guiding them through their first steps, trying to decipher twin-talk, taking them to preschool, ballet classes, T-ball, puppy dogs, high school drama and graduation.

She stopped there because she had her answer.

Through all her visions of laughter and chatter, pirouettes and proms, doggies and dugouts Ray stood by her side, guiding, dancing, scooping, and beaming: a family.

By her side. Not leading or directing, but sharing—a partner in life.

Tension drained out of her as she accepted the truth.

She'd been doing to him what she'd feared he'd do to her: punishing him for another's sins. She'd worried she'd lose herself to Ray's dominant personality as she had to Brad's. *Not going to happen.* As Tori had said, Lauren was aware. She knew what to watch for. The problem was she hadn't been paying attention.

Ray was a self-confident, take-charge kind of man, used to getting his way and directing events to his liking. Yes, he manipulated—but he did it in your face. No snarky, sneaky moves for him. And he'd never guilted or maneuvered her into doing something she didn't want to do.

That had been Brad's style. Always using faux understanding or disappointment as a tool to make her do as he wanted. He'd made it seem as if she were deciding to do something when he'd actually used her emotions against her to get his way. Her desire to compromise had eventually become habit, until she'd always deferred to his will.

In truth, the two men couldn't be more different.

She loved Ray. There was nothing wrong with wanting to be with him on this exciting day in his career. In fact it was normal.

With her decision made, she felt the anxiety surrounding her work disappear. Yes, this event represented everything she and Tori had been working toward. But just because she wasn't overseeing every little detail it didn't take any of the responsibility or success away from her. She'd built the business into what it was. And she'd be there. Available to assist if needed. The best of both worlds.

Ray knew how important her career was to her. He'd never try to get in the way of it. In fact he'd written something in that last note. What was it? She'd read right over it, too stunned by everything else in the message.

She found her purse and the note tucked inside. Now she was free of conflict the romance of it struck her anew. He'd honored her request not to contact her until Monday while completely disregarding it at the same time.

Here it was:

Afterward, we'll go to your party and I can watch you work. So sexy.

Her heart swelled even fuller. He was the best man *she* knew, too.

A glance at the clock revealed an hour had passed since

Tori and Garrett had left. They'd be starting on the red carpet soon.

She reached for the zipper on her dress, yanked it down as she kicked out of her heels. *Hurry!* Thank the angels her hair and make-up were already done.

The beep of her phone announced a text. From Ray.

Lauren. I'm at the theater and you're not with me. I understand. We have a lot to talk about. This changes nothing for me. I hold you in my heart, so you are with me even when you're not. It just means we'll have one more thing to celebrate tomorrow when we do get together. I'll see you at the party. You couldn't keep me away. Fair warning, Dynamite: Monday starts at midnight. I love you. Ray

Incorrigible.

Grinning, she wiggled and her dress hit the floor. Seconds later her underthings joined the dress. Naked, she slipped into the sexy gown. So naughty—but, oh, yeah, Ray deserved a thrill for the silent treatment she'd subjected him to all day long.

Ten minutes later she rode the elevator down and walked over to the theater. The crush of people grew thicker as she neared the red carpet. The public pressed against the barricades while the press jockeyed for position and Security tried to maintain control.

She finally reached the entrance and found more chaos. Someone took her ticket and sent her to the aisle that led directly into the theater. She was tempted to meet him inside, but he wanted her by his side. And she wanted to be there, too.

Just then she spied a friendly security officer she knew from events they'd both worked. Waving, she caught the plump African American woman's attention.

"Ms. Randall—wow, you are *rockin'* that dress. You need to be on this side of the carpet."

"Thanks. That's why I called you over. My date has already started down the carpet. Can you take me to him?"

"So it's true? You're engaged to Ray Donovan?"

"Yes!" Lauren held out her hand, flashing her ring. "I really need to get to him."

"You sure do, girlfriend." The woman ran a hand over her red dreads. "How can I help?"

"Can you take me to him?"

"Hmm. I really can't leave my post."

"Oh." Disappoint bit deep. "Okay. I guess I'll wait for him inside."

"Can't have that. You need to get to your man. Hang on."

The officer stepped away and spoke into her radio.

Seconds and then minutes ticked by. Lauren chafed under the wait. Finally a man the size of a linebacker came along, clearly someone with authority, and talked to her friend. He glanced at Lauren, then approached her.

He looked at the necklace she wore, consulted his clipboard. "Is that the Sabina?"

"Yes." Her hand flew to the jewels at her neck. "From the Claudia Collection, House of Brandia."

He nodded. "Ms. Randall, we're going to get you through." He unhooked the rope barrier and let her pass. "Bonnie will lead you to Mr. Donovan. He's about a quarter ways up the carpet."

"Thank you." Lauren followed Bonnie as she started up the carpet.

The red carpet worked efficiently by having the press and cameras on one side and the stars on the other as they strolled from photo point to photo point. To keep from photo-bombing half of Hollywood, Bonnie led Lauren down the press side, which involved evading cables, cameras, and lampstands as well as many members of the press.

Threading their way through, they caused a bit of disruption. A buzz started behind her and moved forward with them as she was recognized.

"We're causing a spectacle," Lauren told Bonnie. "Maybe I should just meet him inside."

"This is Hollywood, girlfriend. Everyone loves a good spectacle."

"Then let's hurry."

Picking up her skirts, she took off as fast as her heels allowed.

Ray stepped up to the next microphone in a long line of microphones. He greeted the host by name and complimented her on her dress. Gave silent thanks she didn't ask who he was wearing.

No, she went right for the kill.

"Ray Donovan, you have a chance to sweep the season with *War Zone* tonight. And we got news of your engagement this week. Where *is* the lucky woman? With the stakes so high for you, we were hoping to see her on your arm."

"Of course she wants to be here. But, as owner of the hottest event company in Hollywood, today is a busy day for her."

"I imagine." The woman turned to the camera. "We're talking about Lauren Randall of By Arrangements, which has been applauded for great premier productions. Her sister just married Obsidian Studios owner Garrett Black. These lucky twins are snapping up Hollywood royalty."

"I don't know about royalty," Ray demurred. Mention of the newlyweds had him looking around, hoping for a save. They were stuck one mic back. "Garrett is a good friend." He kept it simple. "Now we'll be family."

Or so he planned.

He hoped he hadn't put Lauren off with his persistence today. No lie: he had freaked when she'd refused to talk to him. Not that he didn't deserve it. Now he knew what *she'd* gone through while he'd kept her waiting in New York.

He'd hoped the ring would sway her, because he really wanted her by his side—now and forever.

"Well, good luck tonight." The woman waved, then put a hand to her ear. "What's that?"

Ray got the sign to move on, which suited him fine. He turned away, rolled his eyes when he caught Garrett's stare.

"Wait. Ray!" The woman caught Ray's arm. Then quickly dropped it as she flushed red. "There's a disturbance on the red carpet. It seems Lauren is trying to catch up with you. Why don't you wait…?"

Joy swelled up, lending Ray height as he leapt off the dais and backtracked to reach Lauren.

Progress moved at a snail's pace. He traveled against the flow of humanity, causing a commotion, and making it worse were all the friends and colleagues who wanted to greet and congratulate him.

All he wanted was to get to Lauren.

He picked up his pace.

And then he saw her. He came to a dead stop, awed by her beauty, by her grace, by her radiance. The dress hugged her curves, displaying her delectable cleavage, while the jewels drew attention to her uniqueness.

His soul shouted, *Mine!*

She looked up, saw him, and her face lit up.

Lauren looked up and there was Ray. Finally. Her heart sang. Feet moving with grace and balance, she danced her way to him and launched herself into his arms.

Applause broke out around them. She barely heard it, too busy kissing her man.

"You made it," he said against her lips.

"I wouldn't miss it for the world."

Neither spoke of the awards show. "I love you," he breathed into her ear, arms locked around her in an embrace meant to last forever. "I was punishing you for so many reasons. All wrong."

"Me too." She couldn't let him go—never wanted to let go ever again. "I was afraid to give you too much power because I gave too much to Brad. But you've never taken from me. You've always empowered me to be more, better, sexier. I love you, Ray Donovan, with all my heart and with all my head."

Lights and clicks flashed and binged from every direction.

He pulled back to frame her face in hands strong and sure, his love on full display. "Will you marry me? I'll get you your own ring—"

"Shh." She pressed a finger to his mouth, held up her hand so Mamó's ring flashed in the afternoon light. "This ring is perfect. It comes with a history of love."

His jaw clenched and then he was kissing her again, long and soft, with tenderness and devotion. She sighed inside, seeing the caress as a testament to his hope for the future.

He lifted his head, stared into her eyes, his eyes promising everything his kiss had just declared. "I wish we were alone."

"Not me. The world is watching, and I want everyone to know you're mine. Time to say goodbye to your bachelorhood, Mr. Donovan."

His eyes lit up at the challenge. "My pleasure, Mrs. Donovan-to-be."

He took her hand, kissed Mamó's ring, and turned them both toward the waiting crowd of spectators and press.

"Congratulate me, everyone. Lauren Randall has agreed to be my bride."

EPILOGUE

LAUREN REACHED THE DOOR, checked in both directions down the hallway and slipped inside. She flipped on the light and grinned at the spread she found already set up on the counter next to the washing machine.

Holding her extended belly, she waddled over to inspect the goodies. Cheese and fruit, some roast beef from last night's dinner. And—oh, yeah—pickles. She stole one and popped it in her mouth. Such a cliché craving for a pregnant woman—but, hey, clichés got to be known for a reason.

She started when the door opened behind her. Just Ray, sneaking in. He carried a bottle of sparkling apple juice and two glasses.

He came to her, bent over the twins, and kissed her softly. "Hello."

"Hello. Did anyone see you?"

"Nope. Tori and Garrett just got here. That'll give Mamó and your mother someone else to focus on for at least half an hour."

The newlyweds had announced that they were expecting at the last family get-together in July. Lauren's mom was in heaven, with both her girls married and starting families. She and Mamó had become best friends. Everyone was gathered at her and Ray's place now because she was scheduled to have the twins in two days.

"This was a great idea." She settled into the chair he

pulled out and opened for her, shifted trying to get comfortable. Her back had been bothering her all day. "I love the support and having everyone about. But I have to say I miss having you all to myself."

With so many people in the house, alone time had become impossible. So when Ray had suggested a laundry room tryst she'd jumped at it. The small room had become their little hideout whenever the house was full. Nobody looked for them there.

He sat next to her and she leaned against his strength. She rubbed her belly. "Two girls. Are you ready?"

"No." A touch of panic sounded in the one word. "Maybe we can put it off for another week. Maybe a month."

She laughed, then winced as a twinge rolled up her back. She groaned. "You wouldn't do that to me, would you?"

"I guess not." He watched her carefully. "Are you okay?"

"Just tired. You may not be ready, but I am. And so are the girls."

"They were restless last night."

"Tell me about it. I wasn't able to get comfortable all night. Two more days. I can hardly wait." She sympathized with his nervousness, but she'd moved on to the *I want them out of me* stage.

"Are you hungry?" He served her food and juice, watched over her every move. His care showed his devotion to her and their girls.

"You take such good care of me."

"Not too controlling for you?"

"Marrying you was the best decision I ever made," she answered, without looking up from the tray he held for her perusal.

It scared her sometimes, how close she'd come to walking away from him. Thank goodness for his persistence.

She picked up a thin piece of provolone, but almost lost her hold when the tray was yanked away. "Hey!"

"Hey, back." He took the cheese, tossed it toward the tray, kissed her long and deep. "I love you. Marrying you was the best thing I ever did."

She was so lucky, so loved. "Oh."

"Oh, you love me too?"

"No. I mean yes. I love you. But *oh* because my water just broke."

She watched him carefully, waiting for the hint of panic from earlier to take hold. It never came.

Ray went into director mode, herding her downstairs, putting the family to work gathering her suitcase, getting the car, the baby gear. Never once did he let her go. She relaxed and let him do his thing, confident he had everything under control.

Four hours later she cradled her first daughter in her arms. Looking down into her tiny features, she felt such love flowing through her she didn't think it could get any bigger, be any stronger. Then she looked up and saw Ray next to her, cooing at a second little girl bundled in pink, and her emotions doubled in an instant.

The doors opened and family flowed into the room to admire the new additions.

Amid the chaos Ray lifted blue eyes to hers and mouthed, *I love you.*

And her love grew even bigger.

* * * * *

HIS PROPOSAL, THEIR FOREVER

BY
MELISSA McCLONE

Melissa McClone has published over thirty novels. She has also been nominated for a romance Writers of America RITA® Award. She lives in the Pacific Northwest with her husband, three school-age children, two spoiled Norwegian elkhounds and cats who think they rule the house. They do! visit her at www.melissamcclone.com.

To Margie Lawson and the Wonderblue Wordsmiths:
Allie Burton, Linda Dindzans, Amy Mckenna Rae,
Megan Menard, Laura Navarre and Sarah Tipton

Special thanks to Amy Mckenna Rae, Lisa Hayden,
Terri Reed and Kimberly Field

Chapter One

The hourly chime of tower bells rang through the Piazza del Duomo. Bailey Cole raised her face to let the Florence sunshine kiss her cheeks.

Glong. Glong. D-ding-a-ting-glong.

Not bells from the famous tower, her cell phone ring tone.

Bailey opened her eyes. Not Italy. Home.

Her home. Haley's Bay, Washington.

She rubbed her face, trying to wake up.

The phone kept ringing.

A glance at the digital clock made her blink: 5:45 a.m. Too early for a social call. Something must be…

Flynn. Bailey's heart slammed against her chest. Air whooshed from her lungs. Her brother in the navy had mentioned going somewhere in his email last week.

Please let him be safe.

She reached for her phone on the nightstand, read "Grandma" and her phone number on the screen.

Bailey's chest sank with the weight of a flag-draped coffin. She fumbled for the talk button. "Grandma? Is everything okay?"

"Your aunt Ida Mae called. Told me the craziest thing. Said there's a construction crew set up in front of the Broughton Inn."

Not Flynn. Bailey released a breath. "Did you say a construction crew?"

"They've been moving things out of the inn and loading them into a big truck since late last night." The words flew out of Grandma's mouth faster than her homemade molasses cookies disappeared from the jar. "Equipment is parked on the street. A bulldozer and a crane with a wrecking ball."

Bailey sat straight, the covers falling to her waist.

"What's Floyd Jeffries trying to pull? I just saw him two days ago. He didn't mention any construction, and a wrecking ball sounds more like demolition. He knows owners can't touch a historic building without approval." She scrambled out of bed. "He practically wrote the preservation laws."

"Maybe he forgot."

"No way." She turned on the lamp, waited for her eyes to adjust to the light. "I took over the historical committee from him. He knows every single rule and regulation."

"He could be expanding the owner's apartment now that he's in a relationship."

"Floyd didn't mention his girlfriend moving here. She's half his age and most of their relationship has been online. Something's going on. I need to find out what. Fast."

Bailey pulled her nightshirt over her head and took a step. Her foot twisted, then slid, jamming into the bedpost.

A sledgehammer pain sliced through her big toe. She sucked in a breath. Tears stung her eyes. The phone slipped from her hand. She swore.

"Bailey?" Her grandmother's voice carried from wherever the phone had landed. Lilah Cole had been a widow for the past fifteen years, and her grandchildren had become her focus. "Are you okay?"

Hell, no. Bailey was naked, her mangled toe throbbing. She picked the phone off the bed. "I'm getting dressed. Trying not to panic over the twenty-five thousand dollars' worth of artwork inside the inn."

She hit the speakerphone button and placed the cell phone on the dresser. She opened the top drawer. Panties and bras. Second drawer—pajamas. Third drawer, *empty.* She had been so into her new painting this week she hadn't done laundry.

She wiggled into a pair of underwear, then put on a bra, trying not to cry out and worry Grandma. "Floyd might be struck stupid by Cupid, but he loves the inn."

"So do you. I know you'll straighten him out."

"Gotta go. I'll call you later."

Bailey bunny-hopped on one leg to the bathroom. Clothes overflowed from the hamper. Paint-splattered white, long-sleeved coveralls hung on a hook. She gave the fabric the sniff test. The cotton smelled of paint and solvents. Oh, well, this was what she'd planned to wear today while she worked. She dressed.

Clean panties and bra. Dirty coveralls.

Could be worse, right? A glance in the mirror brought a tell-me-I'm-still-dreaming cringe. Nope. This was pretty bad.

She didn't look sleep-rumpled sexy. More like bizarre, deranged scarecrow. Her wild hair stuck up every which way. Bet she'd freak out folks around town if she carried a broom this morning.

Okay, maybe not, but she would likely scare them, broom or not.

She combed her fingers through the tangles and twisted her hair into a messy bun. A slight improvement, but get-

ting to the Broughton Inn was more important than looking good. So what if she ended up being tonight's gossip at
the Crow's Nest, the local dive bar? Wouldn't be the first
time or the last. Bailey took a step.

"Ouch, ouch, ouch." She stared at her aching foot turning blue. Her toe was swollen. Not bee-sting swollen—
hot-air-balloon swollen.

Forget regular shoes. Her monster toe would never fit
inside. Her oversize fuzzy slippers would have to do.

She shoved on the right slipper, then maneuvered her
aching left foot inside the other. A jagged pain sliced
through her toe, zigzagged up her foot.

Bailey hopped to her desk, using the wall and doorways
for support. She grabbed the Broughton Inn files in case
Floyd wanted to argue about what he could do to the inn,
shoved them and her purse into a yellow recyclable shopping bag covered with multicolored polka dots. The colors
matched the paint splatters on her coveralls. The newest
trend in low fashion. Yeah, right.

Bailey hobbled to the door, walking on the heel of her
bad foot. Not easy, but she had to get to the inn. Driving
was her only option. She rehearsed a quick strategy.

Don't panic.

Don't burst in, acting as if she owned the place.

Most of all, don't piss off Floyd.

Logic and common sense, not to mention laws, would
prevail. But she was prepared to do battle. No one was
touching the Broughton Inn or the artwork inside.

Bailey was a Cole. Stubborn, unrelenting, ready to fight.

Early Thursday morning, Justin McMillian stood outside
the Broughton Inn, McMillian Resorts' newest acquisition.
Slivers of sunlight appeared in the dawn sky like fingers
poking up from the horizon, wanting a piece of the night.
He wanted to take what was his today.

This past winter's remodeling fiasco in Seaside on the Oregon coast had destroyed his parents' confidence in Justin and his two sisters' ability to take over the family company. The project had gone over schedule and over budget due to hidden foundation issues. His parents had blamed Justin, Paige—one of the company's attorneys—and Rainey, an interior designer, when two different inspectors hadn't seen the problem. That fact hadn't stopped his parents from threatening to sell to the highest bidder and firing their three children if the next project didn't run smoothly.

But today, Justin's mouth watered with the taste of success. His parents would be apologizing long before the new Broughton Inn opened next year. This project would be different from the Seaside one. His parents would see how capable he and his sisters were, and McMillian Resorts would show Haley's Bay what luxury and first-class service were about. Something his family had perfected over the years with both small and large properties.

"Loaded and ready to go, boss." Greg, Justin's driver, motioned to the semitruck parked on the street in front. "Never seen so much junk. Loads of outdated furniture and way too much artwork for such a small inn."

"Floyd Jeffries didn't have a clue how to run a boutique hotel."

"Good thing we do."

We. McMillian Resorts. Unless his parents followed through on their threat. That was not. Going. To. Happen. "Text me when you reach the warehouse."

"Should take me three hours or so to reach Lincoln City, depending on traffic."

"Drive carefully. I don't want the artwork broken. We can sell the better stuff to local galleries."

Greg adjusted the brim of his Seattle Mariners cap.

"Raw eggs could be loose in the cab and wouldn't break when I'm driving."

"Let's not test that theory."

Greg stared at the old inn. "Quaint place. Suz and I honeymooned here."

"Cozy, maybe, but a dinosaur. With those million-dollar views, the new inn will be the crown jewel in our hotel portfolio."

"Hope so." Greg took a picture of the inn with his cell phone. "Better hit the road."

Greg glanced at the inn again, then he headed to his truck.

Interesting. Justin had never known the driver to be sentimental.

Wyatt, the site foreman, walked up, adjusted his gloves. "We're ready. Say the word and we'll fire up the engines."

"It's time." Nothing beat the first morning on a new job, except the last day. Justin rubbed his hands together. "Tear her down, boys."

With whoops and hollers, his crew jogged to their equipment. Engines revved, filling the early morning air with noise. The crane hopped the curb and headed for the inn. Next came the bulldozer.

Finally. Over the past year, Justin had spent every free moment developing plans for a new Broughton Inn, even though he'd been unsure whether Paige could pull off the deal with Floyd Jeffries. They'd approached him last year with an offer that Floyd turned down. But Paige had achieved the impossible by not giving up and closing the deal.

This project would prove he and his sisters could run the company as well as his parents. Better. The three of them had grown up living in hotels. They knew the business inside and out.

A dog barked.

Huh? Justin shouldn't be able to hear a dog. Except the equipment had stopped moving. Engines had been cut off.

"What the hell is going on?" he yelled.

Wyatt pointed to the inn's porch where someone stood by the front door, hands on hips and a pissed-off frown on her face. "That woman."

Was that a woman with a yellow shopping bag hanging from her shoulder or an escapee from the circus? She wore painter's coveralls, but the color splatters made her look as if she'd been caught in a paintball battle.

"Where'd she come from?" Justin asked.

"No idea."

"The woman must be some sort of nut job. A disturbed bag lady or a history fanatic. I'll see if she has demands."

"Demands?" Wyatt asked.

"A woman doesn't step in front of a wrecking ball unless she has a death wish, or wants something. Given the crazy way she's dressed, my money's on the latter. Call the police in case I'm wrong and she'd rather meet the Grim Reaper."

Justin walked toward the porch. He didn't want his crew near the woman.

"Stop. Don't come any closer." Her voice sounded more normal than he'd expected. "You can't tear down the inn."

Her hands moved from her hips to out in front of her, palms facing Justin, as if she could push him away using The Force.

Demands. Justin knew a few things about women, though his ex-wife might disagree. He kept walking. Given the crazy lady's appearance, he knew how to handle her. He flashed his most charming smile, the one that got him what he wanted most every time, whether for business or pleasure.

"Hello there." In two steps, Justin stood on the porch. He softened his voice. "Can I help you?"

A jade-green gaze locked on his. Wow. Talk about a gorgeous color. Her warm, expressive eyes made him think of springtime.

"I'm looking for Floyd." Her voice rose at the end; her words weren't a question but had a hint of uncertainty.

Hell. She must not know about Floyd selling out. Not Justin's problem. Eyes aside, he didn't know why he kept looking at her. Clothes, hair, demeanor. *Not his type* didn't begin to describe what was wrong with the woman.

A brown dog barked and ran figure-eight patterns around the bulldozer and crane. Where had the animal come from?

"Oh, no. That poor dog is so skinny." Her compassion surprised Justin. "Catch him. He looks like he's starving."

Oh, man. The guys still ribbed him for the time he shut down a demo for a missing ferret. Stupid thing took five and a half hours to find.

"Please," she said, her eyes clouding.

Demands and a plea. Tropical-storm-strength pressure built behind his forehead. Easy jobs must be handed to worthier men. "Have you seen the dog before?"

"No." Her gaze remained on the animal. The dog ran around and barked. "But I don't see a collar. Could be a stray. Or lost."

Justin wasn't about to chase the dog on open ground, but he couldn't have the thing running around the site inside the safety fencing. That would be too dangerous.

He glanced at Wyatt, who stood on the grass between the porch and the equipment. "Give the dog a leftover donut."

"No chocolate." The words exploded from her mouth like a cannonball. Worry reflected in her eyes. "That's bad for dogs."

Justin didn't know that. He'd never had a dog or any kind of pet. His parents allowed guests to bring dogs and cats to the hotels, but had never let their children have an animal, not even a goldfish.

"Fine. Nothing chocolate. A sandwich, maybe," he said to Wyatt. Justin wanted to get back to work. These stupid delays were killing him. "Then get the dog out of here."

While he got rid of the woman. A McMillian team effort. That was the way things got done at their company. Each person did his or her part. The effort led to success. But when one didn't do what was expected, like his ex-wife, the result was failure.

He faced the woman. "Where were we?"

"Floyd Jeffries. Do you know where I can find him?"

"Belize."

Her nose crinkled. "Floyd never mentioned a vacation."

"Floyd might not share his personal life with customers."

"I'm not a customer." She raised her chin. "I'm his partner in the gallery."

Gallery. Justin's headache ramped into a cyclone. That explained the artwork on its way to Oregon, the splattered coveralls and Green Eyes' odd smells. "You're an artist."

"Painter." She gave him a strange look. "If Floyd's away, what are you doing here?"

"I'm the inn's new owner."

She flinched as if his words punched her. No clown makeup was needed to make her eyes look bigger. Any larger and they would be twins to her gaping mouth. The caricature was complete. All she needed was a dialogue bubble over her head to star in her own comic strip.

She took half a step back. "Floyd sold the inn?"

"We recently closed on the deal."

"Where's the artwork?" Her words shot out as if catapulted. "The textiles, paintings, sculptures?"

"Gone."

Her face morphed into a look of horror, a worst-news-ever-face. "Where?"

The raw emotion in the one word drew him forward. She looked desperate. Of course she was. Junk or not, the art pieces he'd seen must have taken hundreds of hours to make. If someone made off with a set of his blueprints that took half that long, he'd go ballistic. Ridiculing the woman no longer seemed cool. If anything, he wanted to give her a hug.

He forced himself not to step closer. He…couldn't. She was a stranger, a nuisance. "The inn's contents were part of the purchase agreement."

She bit her lip. Trying to decide what to say, or buy time? For what, he didn't know. She blinked, then wiped her eyes.

She'd better not, not, not cry. His sisters always pulled that stunt. His ex-wife, too. Taryn had blamed him for their marriage failing, saying he loved his work more than her. She hadn't understood that his job paid for everything, including their house, her shopping sprees and the numerous trips she took to Portland and Seattle while he was away at a site.

His sympathy well was drained. Not a drop of compassion remained. No way would he let this woman manipulate him. Time to send overwrought clown lady on her way. He handed her his business card.

"Talk to Floyd. Call my office for his contact information." Justin's voice sounded distant, unemotional, as intended. "You need to leave now so we can get back to work."

She grabbed the porch rail, gave him a this-isn't-over look, then sat. "I'm not going anywhere."

Of course not.

Justin should have known she wouldn't make this easy, but a one-person sit-in? "We have a schedule to keep. It's time for you to go."

"You can rephrase your request over and over again, but my answer will be the same. I'm not letting you touch the inn, let alone destroy the second-oldest building in Haley's Bay."

Attitude poured from the woman as easy as milk from a carton. Too bad hers was sour. "I've called the police."

Neither her gaze nor her facial expression wavered. If he wasn't on the receiving end of her stare, he might have been impressed by her backbone.

"Good." That attitude of hers wasn't letting up. "Because you're stealing."

Justin laughed. The woman had nerve. He had to give her that. "I have a contract."

"So do I. You may have bought the inn, but not the rest."

"Okay, I'll bite."

"The artwork doesn't belong to Floyd or the inn. He sold the pieces on consignment for local artists like me."

"The inn's contents belong to us per the deal—"

"The artists had contracts. Nontransferrable contracts."

She talked faster as if her nerves were getting to her, and her words were making him wonder what the hell was going on here.

"I see the Oregon plates on your equipment. I hope whatever truck you were loading earlier isn't headed across the bridge toward Astoria." She leveled him with a stare. "Given the value of the artwork, the theft qualifies as a class-B felony. But I'm sure the police can place blame where it's due and make the necessary arrests."

The woman could be telling the truth or she might be delusional. Could this be nothing more than a ruse to stop the demolition? "Floyd never mentioned the art didn't belong to the inn."

"Due diligence, Mr.…?"

"Justin McMillian." Her vocabulary told him she knew something about business. Her know-it-all manner annoyed him like the sound of nails on concrete, but her point made his hope sink. Had Paige cut corners in a rush to get the deal closed? Their parents had put so much pressure on them it was…possible. He held out his arm to shake hands. "Mc-Millian Resorts. And you are?"

The woman pursed her lips, making her look haughty and naughty, a dangerous combination. This one was trouble.

After leaving him hanging a moment too long, she shook his hand. "Bailey Cole."

Warm, rough skin. Not unexpected, given that she worked with chemicals. Up close, she was kind of pretty with her pink cheeks and full lips. She might look halfway decent cleaned up.

Bailey removed the bag from her shoulder. "I'm happy to provide copies of the contracts to prove rightful ownership of the art. I have the information right here."

Paperwork? Crap. So much for her being delusional. The foundation mess in Seaside wasn't looking so bad now. At least they'd finally completed that project and had a viable hotel in a desirable market. But if what she said was true, he and his sisters were in trouble. His parents would never let them run the company. Hell, his mom and dad would probably refuse to pay bail.

Time to regroup. Get Greg back with the truck. Call Paige to find out if this Cole woman's story checked out. Justin glanced around but didn't see any of the crew. He texted Wyatt.

"I'll call the artists to pick up—"

Justin cut Bailey off. "The artwork will be back shortly."

Her jaw jutted forward, hard as granite. "You do know that transporting stolen property across state lines carries additional charges."

She might be an artist and the poster child for *What Not to Wear*, but this woman was no delicate flower swaying in the wind. She was a tree, solid and unmoving, firmly rooted in the earth, a sequoia. A good thing they had chain saws in the truck.

"The artwork is in Washington." He hoped.

Sirens sounded. Blue and red lights flashed.

Good. The police would get her off the property—no chain saws needed—and his team could get back on schedule.

A young, tall uniformed officer got out of his police car and straightened his hat. He took long, purposeful strides toward them.

Justin smiled at the guy who would save his day.

The officer stopped on the walkway in front of the porch. His attention, including a narrowed gaze, focused solely on Bailey Cole. The woman must be a known troublemaker in town to receive such scrutiny from a cop.

"What the hell are you doing, Bailey? And what's wrong with your foot?"

Justin noticed her knee was bent so her foot didn't touch the porch. No wonder she'd wanted him to go after the dog.

"You're not here to give me a hard time." She stood. A grimace flashed across her face. "I'm not the one who called you. This guy did, even though he stole the artwork from the inn."

The officer looked at Justin. "Is this true?"

Justin's smile hardened at the edges. He should've known she'd try to pin this on him, but he needed to keep his voice respectful. "My company, McMillian Resorts, bought the inn from Floyd Jeffries. The contents of the inn were included in the property's purchase. She's trespassing."

"What part of consignment don't you understand?" Bailey's hands returned to her hips, elbows pointed out. "The artists retain ownership and Floyd only received a commission if a piece sold. The artwork wasn't his, so it couldn't be included in the sale. Thus, it's been stolen."

The pursed lips returned, distracting Justin from her accusation. He needed to focus. She hadn't called him a thief exactly, but she was walking the line. She was still on *his* property. Her violation was clear. They needed to move this along.

He glanced at the officer whose face looked skeptical. Strange, but the guy had similar coloring to Bailey. Dark hair and green eyes.

On the lawn, Justin's crew gathered within listening distance. No sign of the dog. The donut or sandwich must have worked. Progress. Time for more.

"We can discuss the return of the art—if necessary—once she's escorted off my property." Justin might not know the whole story behind the gallery, but he trusted his sister to have negotiated a legally binding contract on the building and its contents.

"Not yet," Bailey said. "I'm here to protect my property and the inn, Grady. His construction permit did not go through the historical society's approval process."

She knew this how? Justin looked from Bailey to the cop, noticed the "Cole" name tag on the officer's chest.

"I'm Grady Cole. Bailey's my sister. She knows more about the approval process than anybody in town except Floyd Jeffries."

Siblings. This was not Justin's day. No matter. This project was *not* going to hell on his watch.

The crew moved closer, cutting the distance in half from where they'd stood before. He couldn't show any weakness or worry. Not in front of his guys.

"No problem." Justin removed the paperwork from his back pocket. "I have a permit."

"We'll see." Grady flipped through the forms, not once, but twice before frowning. "This permit is from Long Beach. The approvals, too."

"Yes, that's where I was told to go." Justin's headache throbbed. Holding back sarcasm was becoming harder. How long was this going to freaking take?

Bailey's smile widened. If she'd been a cat, canary feathers would be hanging from the corners of her mouth.

A knot formed in Justin's stomach. Crap. She knew something he didn't. "I checked the paperwork myself. We're good."

"You used the Long Beach zip code, not the one for Haley's Bay." Grady returned the papers. "This permit isn't valid. The town's municipal office must be used for projects within the city limits. You're also missing an approval stamp from the historical committee, since this property is on its registry."

The knot wrapped around the donut Justin had eaten for breakfast. "No problem. Floyd told me to go to Long Beach to get the permit. I'll head over to your town hall and get that and approvals right now."

"I'm sorry, but it's not that simple," Grady said.

Warning lights flashed. A cement roller pressed against Justin's chest. A vise squeezed his brain.

Bailey opened her mouth as if to speak.

He raised his hand, cutting her off. He didn't want Miss Know-It-All telling him why his must-succeed project was grounded. He wanted her gone; more than that, he wanted her to tell him this was a giant misunderstanding and they could work it out in the next two hours. And then smile.

Not gonna happen. "Once I have the permits, I'll be free to work on my property."

"Not exactly, Mr. McMillian." Her gaze remained on his, unwavering. More sure of herself with every passing minute, but maybe—if he wasn't stretching it—she was sympathetic, too. "Broughton Inn is on the Federal Register of Historic Places."

"I know. I also know private owners are not bound by any restrictions if they want to improve the property."

"Not bound by restrictions only if federal money—

grants—haven't been attached to their property." The confidence in her words matched the determined set of her chin.

The knot-entangled donut in his stomach turned to stone. He had spoken to the former inn owner, taken notes, confirmed each detail about what being on the historical register meant for improvements and teardowns. The ticking-clock time frame of Floyd Jeffries wanting to close the deal was looking suspect. "We were assured—"

"Floyd lied. You got taken, Mr. McMillian." Bailey pulled out files from her bag and handed one to Justin. "If you don't believe me, check these papers. They'll prove federal and state monies are attached to the Broughton Inn. Some are old, before Floyd's time as owner."

Justin noticed his crew creeping closer to the porch. The men had cut the distance in half twice, no doubt curious. He didn't blame them. This was their livelihood, too. He wouldn't let them down or allow Bailey Cole to screw up this project any more than she had.

He opened the folder, eager to prove her wrong. Except...

The first page listed the inn's grant awards. Not one, several. Federal and state funding had been provided to the inn.

His neck stiffened, the cords of muscles tightening and coiling like electrical wire. He turned the pages, one after another. Each was a death knell to his plans for the inn, smothering his hope for success, throwing the resort company's future ownership in doubt.

It now made sense why Floyd gave them only forty-eight hours to make a decision about purchasing the inn. The man had been trying to pull a fast one. Not trying, succeeding. Damn.

Talk about a crook. Paige, everyone at McMillian Resorts, had been duped. If Justin couldn't fix this, his parents would sell the company and ride off into retirement without a second thought to their three children who had spent their lives living and working at the family's hotels.

Not about to give up, Justin straightened, handed back the papers. "We were not provided this information. I would appreciate copies at your earliest convenience."

"I'll get those to you as soon as I can," Bailey said.

Grady took the file out of his sister's hands. "I'll have copies made. You need to get off your feet."

"I will." She ground out the words as if clenching her back teeth. "I have to return the artwork first."

"So, what's the approval process so we can begin our project?" Justin asked Grady.

The officer looked at his sister. "That's Bailey's expertise."

Great. She was the last person who would offer help, but too much was at stake for Justin not to ask. "Care to enlighten me on the steps?"

"Gladly." She leaned against the railing, but her casual position didn't match the sharp, predatory gleam in her eyes. "First the intended project plans must be presented to the Advisory Council on Historic Preservation."

Not insurmountable. Justin released a quick breath. "That doesn't sound so bad."

"No, but that's only the federal portion of the process." Bailey flexed her knee with the injured foot, then straightened her leg. "After the feds check off on the plans, you need input from the State Historic Preservation Office."

Each approval would take time. Not good. He scratched his chin. Too bad he couldn't itch away the problems with the inn. Or her. Bailey explaining the process without prodding worried him. She might have a hidden agenda. Or maybe she liked knowing more than he did. "Is that all?"

"After state approval, you'll need to present the plans to the Haley's Bay Historical Committee in order to receive your city permit."

"Seems straightforward." Except the timing would impact the schedule, possibly change their plans completely. His parents wanted the inn to open before the busy summer season next year. He needed to talk to Paige ASAP and figure out not only damage control but also a plan B.

"My sister is head of the committee," Grady added. That wasn't the cherry on top that the officer's voice seemed to imply, but a grenade with the pin pulled.

Justin's hands curled into fists. He wasn't into violence, but he wanted to punch Floyd Jeffries. The man had told Justin tearing down the inn would be as easy as crushing a sand castle. Going through three groups could take days, weeks, maybe even months. Who knew if they'd allow the old inn to be torn down so a new one could be built? He had a feeling Miss Bailey Cole would be readying her troops for a battle.

Bailey's I-know-something-you-don't smile suggested she could read Justin's mind. "You realize if you do anything without getting approval—"

"I understand what's at stake, Ms. Cole." His words sounded harsh, but he'd lost patience. He couldn't keep his cool any longer. This so-called diamond in the rough, aka the Broughton Inn, was nothing more than a piece of fool's gold. He and his sisters looked like amateurs for not thinking the inn's fire-sale price came with strings of steel.

Ones that might handcuff them for months, maybe years, in a web of approval procedures. Ones that might destroy their lifelong dream of running McMillian Resorts.

He gave a nod to Wyatt and the crew. "Pack it up, boys."
For now.

Bailey Cole might be smiling, but he would show her who was in charge. His parents, too. This approval process delay wouldn't change the inevitable. The old inn was coming down. A luxury five-star boutique hotel would be built on this spot.

No one, including Bailey Cole, was going to stop him. McMillian Resorts would succeed. No matter what Justin had to do to make that happen, including charming the silly slippers off the mess of a woman standing in his way.

Chapter Two

An hour later, Bailey eyed the dark, ominous clouds gathering over Haley's Bay. The approaching clouds carried big fat raindrops, ones that could turn this already horrible morning into a complete catastrophe. But cracking jokes and drinking coffee seemed to be the construction crew's priorities this morning. Unloading the artwork from the semitruck parked on the street and carrying the pieces back into the inn, not so much.

She half hopped, half hobbled to the truck's ramp. Her left foot was swelling like the water at the mouth of the bay. But she had more things to worry about than her injury. "Hurry. We need to get the art inside before the storm hits."

"We're going as fast as we can, miss." The foreman, Wyatt, used only one hand to carry Faye Rivers's four-foot-tall sculpture composed of driftwood and colorful glass floats collected from the beach.

"Hey, that's glass." These bozos had no idea what they were doing. "Be careful."

"I've got it." Wyatt stepped off the ramp, snagged a cup of coffee from the hood of a pickup truck, then glanced her way. "Want some coffee?"

The scent of French roast teased. Her sapped energy level longed for a jolt of caffeine. But forget about asking for a cup. No fraternizing with the enemy.

"I'll get one later." After the artwork was safe.

Wyatt juggled Faye's sculpture with one hand and his coffee with his other.

"You guys are going to pay if anything gets damaged." Bailey sounded like a Harpy, but she would keep nagging until they finished the job. Too much was at stake to play nice.

"Nothing has been damaged, and nothing will be." Justin came around the end of the truck. His scruff of blond stubble could be called bad-boy sexy, except his shorter hair looked too corporate. It was messy at the moment, but a sweep of a comb would have him looking a little too neat, even with whiskers. "Relax."

"Wish I could." Bailey was rethinking turning down the cup of coffee and not bringing a chair to take weight off her throbbing toe. "I'll relax when the artwork is inside."

He hopped on the ramp with the ease of an athlete and walked into the trailer. His steel-toed boots would have come in handy when she woke up this morning. Brown pants hugged muscular thighs, and the tails from his light blue button-down peeked out from beneath his tan jacket.

He leaned his right shoulder against the truck's wall and stared down at her. The casual pose contradicted the hard look in his eyes. He definitely had that I'm-hot-and-know-it demeanor. Sexy, if you liked that type. She didn't, but he was easy on the eyes. A good thing she was immune to men like him.

"Patience." His tone wasn't condescending, but she

couldn't tell if he was teasing or not. "You wouldn't want us to drop anything."

"Of course not." Now he was being a jerk. This wasn't a gallery of painted rocks. "But there's no need to move in slow motion. Unless the crew is following orders."

"Be careful." His voice contained a hint of warning. "Or you might find the guys going in reverse."

Grrrr. "I bet you'd enjoy telling your crew to do that."

A grin exploded like a solar flare, making her forget to breathe.

"Just give me a reason, Ms. Cole. That would be the bright side to this dark day."

"This isn't my fault. Blame Floyd."

She wasn't about to let Justin McMillian's threats get to her. The rest of the crew was on its way to the inn or already inside the building. None of them wanted to be caught outside when the rain hit. She would have to take care of this herself.

"Unload the truck faster. There may not be damage yet, but the weather—"

"Don't lose your purple slippers over this."

Justin's you-know-you-want-me attitude annoyed her. Yes, the man was attractive. She appreciated the way the features of his face fit together. Rugged, yet handsome. Her fingers itched for a pencil to capture the high cheekbones, the crinkles around his eyes and his easy smile when he joked with the crew. But she wasn't here to admire the eye candy.

She pinned him with a direct stare. "The rain will be here in five minutes. That's my concern."

He raised an eyebrow. "You the local rainmaker?"

"Not maker. Predictor."

"Artist, history buff and the town's weather expert."

"I'm from a fishing family. We learned to read the clouds

before we could count to ten. Predicting rain is a necessary skill when you're out on a boat trying to earn a living."

"But you're a…"

"Girl?" Bailey finished for him with a tone she would call "ardent feminist."

She knew his type. The last man she'd dated, a wealthy guy named Oliver Richardson from Seattle, hadn't been a chauvinist, but was just as arrogant. He'd thought his job, condo, city and artistic tastes were better than everyone else's, including hers. Turned out her greatest dating asset to him was her oldest brother, AJ, a billionaire computer programmer. Since then, she hadn't felt like dating any man—rich or otherwise. Who needed that crap?

"Haley's Bay might be small and full of old-timers with big fish tales, but working women thrive here, Mr. McMillian. One day, my younger sister Camden will be the captain of her own boat."

"You might be a rain predictor, but you're not a mind reader." Justin laughed.

The sound made Bailey think of smooth, satin enamel paint, the expensive kind, no primer required. She'd used a gallon on her kitchen walls. Worth every penny and the peanut butter sandwiches she'd eaten to stay in budget.

"I was going to say 'artist.' That has nothing to do with your gender. I'm not a chauvinist, as you quickly and wrongly assumed." Justin sounded more annoyed than upset. "I have two sisters. Smart, capable, hardworking women, but without the smarter-than-you attitude."

"You think I have an attitude?" Maybe she did, but so did he. The guy was full of himself.

"I don't think. You do."

Standing on the trailer bed, he towered over her, but she wasn't intimidated.

"Your attitude is entitled," he said. "You assume you're correct. You assume I'm an idiot. That I can't recognize rain clouds. Hell, I live on the Oregon coast. Let me do my job, and we'll get along fine."

Bailey's muscles tensed, bunching into tight spools that weren't going to unravel any time soon. He might have a point, but she didn't like Justin McMillian, and she wasn't good at faking her feelings. "How we get along isn't important."

"You're the head of the historical committee. We'll be working together."

"I sure hope not." The words flew out faster than a bird released from captivity. "I mean… Oh, who am I kidding? That's exactly what I meant."

His surprised gaze raked over her. "You're honest."

"Blunt. Like my dad."

"I'll go with honest. For now." Justin picked up a painting, one of hers.

Bailey reached up for her piece. She loved the seascape, sketched on the beach early one morning, a morning like this one with a sky full of reds, pinks and yellows bursting from the horizon and a sea of breathtaking blues. But turbulent and dark clouds were moving in, matching the mood at the inn. She longed for the return of the calm, beautiful dawn.

"I'll take that one." She trusted herself more with one leg than him with two.

He kept hold of the frame. "I've got it."

"Be careful."

"This one more special than the others?"

"They're all one-of-a-kind."

Bailey pressed her lips together to keep from saying more. She should stalk off into the inn and check on the artwork that had been unloaded, but something held her in place. Something—she hoped not vanity—made her want him to notice her painting, to like her painting, to compliment her painting.

His studied the work in his hands. "Not bad if you like landscapes."

She bit her tongue to keep from uttering a smart-aleck remark. No way would she piss him off with her painting in his hands.

He looked at her. "It's one of yours."

"Yes."

The colors in the painting intensified the brightness and hue of his eyes.

Bailey's breath caught. The man was arrogant and annoying, but his Santorini-blue eyes dazzled her. She thought about the tints she'd use to mix the exact shade. Not that she would ask him to model. His ego was big enough. But she would paint those eyes from memory.

He lifted her painting slightly to keep the frame out of her reach. "This is the last one."

"Good." The dark clouds came closer. The scent in the air changed. She knew what that meant. "Get inside now. The rain's going to hit."

"How can you tell?"

"The smell." She reached forward. "Give me the painting."

"I've got it. You can barely walk in those slippers." He carried her painting down the ramp.

"There isn't much time."

He walked past her. His long strides and her bum foot made keeping up with him impossible. He slanted the canvas so any falling rain would hit the back, not the painted side. Nice of him, but she wanted her piece indoors before drops fell.

Wyatt came out of the inn. "Any more?"

Justin handed over the artwork. "Last one."

The spool of yarn in her stomach unraveled. She exhaled. Her muscles relaxed. Bailey's painting and the oth-

ers were safe. If only saving the inn would be as easy…
"Thank you."

Justin stood near the porch. She was just reaching the
walkway. "Told you I'd beat the rain."

Dumb luck, but she wasn't about to complain.

A step sent pain shooting up her foot. She squeezed her
eyes shut to keep from crying out. Darn toe. She needed
ice, ibuprofen and a barista-poured fancy cup of coffee with
a pretty design made in the foam. Who was she kidding?
She'd settle for black sludge at this point. She needed to get
the artwork back to the rightful owners first.

"Hey there," he said. "You okay, Anubis?"

Her eyes popped open. "Anubis? The Egyptian god?"

"Protector of Egyptian tombs from raiders and destroyers. Fits, don't you think?"

The edges of her mouth twitched upward. She managed a nod, just barely. That Anubis was half jackal didn't
seem to matter to him. A drop of water hit her cheek, followed by another.

Bailey took a step. Pain, jagged and raw, ripped up her
left foot. She hopped toward the inn like a human pogo
stick. Big, fat raindrops fell faster and faster.

She stumbled.

Strong arms swept her off the ground. "Hold on."

She stared into Justin's concerned eyes. Her heart thud-
ded. He carried her to the inn and looked down at her as
though he cared.

Maybe there was more to Justin McMillian than she
realized.

She should tell him to put her down. But a part of her
didn't want to say a word.

Rain pelted her face, but she wasn't cold. Not with
his body heat warming her. The pain faded. Her insides
buzzed. Something she hadn't felt in…forever. She closed

her eyes, trying to remember the last time she'd been in a man's arms like this.

Too long ago.

"What did you do to your foot?" he asked.

Her eyes opened. This wasn't any man carrying her onto the porch and into the foyer, but the guy who wanted to destroy the inn. "I'm not sure if it's my foot or toe or a combo."

"Did you hurt yourself here?"

"At home." Water dripped from her hair. Two minutes ago, she didn't think she could have looked any worse, but now she was a wet Medusa. "Worried I might sue you if I'd injured myself here?"

"Nope. I was wondering if you normally strut around town in fuzzy slippers."

"They were the only shoes my foot would fit. And just so you know, I don't strut. Sauntering or sashaying is more my style."

"You seem like the strutting type."

"If anyone struts, you do."

"That's right." He carried her into the dining room, right off the entryway and lobby. "I wasn't dissing you. Can you stand?"

"I've been standing all morning."

"Which is why your foot is hurting. You should have stayed home and done first aid."

He sounded like one of her five overprotective brothers, telling her what to do and who not to date. Didn't matter that two were younger than her. "I jammed my toe. A sprain. That's all."

"Looks like you may have broken something." Justin placed her feet on the floor, causing her to suck in a breath. "Hold on to me until you're steady."

She dug her fingers into his jacket. The padding couldn't hide his muscular arms. His chest was solid, too. Fully dressed, he was hot. Naked, he would be a specimen worthy of a master sculptor, Michelangelo or da Vinci.

She imagined running her hands over the model to get the right curves and indentations in the clay. Her pulse skittered, and her temperature rose. His body shouldn't impress her, not after she'd sketched and painted male models who were as good-looking, if not more classically handsome.

Uh-oh. Time to go on a date if she was getting worked up over a guy like Justin. His company's name shared his last name. That meant he likely had money—Oliver Richardson all over again. Wealthy men wanted more money or connections, such as with her brother, and would use women to get them. No, thank you.

So what if he knew a little Egyptian mythology and carried her out of the rain without getting winded? She saved historic sites. He toppled beautiful old buildings. Someone like him would never be right for her.

She let go of his arm. Looked around. Fell over.

He grabbed her. "What?"

"Gone. Everything's gone."

A dozen dining tables gone. Over fifty chairs gone. Antique buffets, rugs, draperies gone.

"It's all in the truck," Justin said.

His words brought zero relief. Seeing the empty room hurt worse than her toe. Only the scent of lemon oil and memories remained.

Oh, Floyd. Why? Why would you sell the inn?

"For over a hundred and forty years, guests have eaten meals here." She stared at the empty room where she'd dreamed of having her wedding reception someday. "That will never happen again."

"Guests will be back when the new Broughton Inn opens. We'll have a café, a bar and a restaurant with a view of the bay."

Her lungs tightened. She took a breath, then another. "It won't be the same."

Bailey rubbed her tired eyes, trying to keep their stinging from turning into full-blown tears.

"Sit," Justin ordered.

Getting off her feet sounded wonderful, but she had a job to do. "I need to inventory the artwork."

"You look like you're about to pass out." He pointed to the floor. "Sit. Five minutes won't kill you."

She hesitated. A Cole never shirked responsibility. Even AJ, who had left town eleven years ago and moved to Seattle, had done what he could to help their family when the economy soured and they were on the verge of losing their boats.

But Justin was right. Five minutes wouldn't change anything. Bailey slid to the floor, careful of her foot, and stretched her leg out in front of her. She leaned back against the wall.

Oh, wow. This felt better. "A couple of minutes."

The construction crew seemed to have disappeared. Maybe they were off in another part of the inn. Maybe they'd left. She didn't care. Fewer people around meant fewer chances of bumping and damaging the art.

Justin sat next to her. He stretched out his long legs. She waited for his thigh or shoulder to touch hers, but that didn't happen. Thank goodness he understood the meaning of personal space. She was too tired to deal with anything more this morning.

"How long until the artists pick up their stuff?" he asked.

He was calling her life's work "stuff." How quickly her fantasies about an intelligent man who worked Anubis into a discussion were dashed. But then again, he wanted to tear down the inn.

"While you were taking your time unloading the truck,

I called and left messages. The artists have jobs and families. They'll be here as soon as they can."

He glanced at his cell phone, but she couldn't tell if he was checking the time or a text. "Can you be more specific as to when?"

"Got big plans, like working on the approval process?"

"Something along those lines."

"I'm here. You don't have to hang around."

"I do. I own the inn." Justin motioned to her foot. "Besides, you're hurt. You can't do this on your own. You need help."

"Resting is helping." Not really, but she wouldn't admit how much her foot ached. "I'll stay off my feet. There's no reason for you to stick around."

"I need to lock up when you're finished."

"I've got a key."

"Floyd gave you a key to the inn?"

Justin's incredulous tone matched the look in his eyes. He and Oliver could be twins separated at birth.

"No, his late father, Clyde, did." She shouldn't feel the need to explain, but she did. "I started working here when I was sixteen."

"Front desk?"

"Kitchen." She glanced to the doorway on the right where she'd spent so many years. The imagined smell of grease was as strong as if the fryers were going. "I was a cook until a few years ago. Then I partnered with Floyd to open the gallery. We hold art events here. Held them, I mean."

The gallery no longer existed. The inn, either.

The truth hit her like a sneaker wave, knocking her over on the beach and dragging her out to sea. The coast guard couldn't rush in and save the day. No one could. The inn as she knew it was gone.

The news devastated her. This was the place where

she'd figured out how to bring artist and art lovers together. Where she'd worked in the kitchen and grown up amid a staff that treated her as an equal, not a kid. Where she planned on getting married… She struggled to breathe.

Returning the art was only the first thing she had to do today. She needed to find another venue.

"What kind of events?" Justin asked.

She flexed her fingers. "Shows, exhibits, classes. I'm supposed to hold a Canvas and Chardonnay class here tomorrow."

"Canvas and Chardonnay?"

"That's what I call my paint night. The class appeals mostly to women, though a few men join in. People socialize, drink wine, eat appetizers, and I show them how to paint."

"In one night?"

"Everyone paints the same subject. We go step by step. It's fun and easy. And the inn was the perfect location for the gathering." She leaned her head against the wall. "The results are amazing. Each person leaves with a smile and takes home a finished canvas."

Bailey didn't know why she was going on about her painting classes. He didn't care what she did. She would sit for sixty more seconds, then get things done, not chit-chat with her nemesis.

He glanced at his cell phone again.

"You need to go," she said. "Work. I'm fine here by myself."

"It's Wyatt, seeing where things stand." Justin typed on his phone. "I'm staying."

His words meant only one thing. She reached into her pocket and pulled out her key ring. The ache in her heavy heart hurt worse than her toe. "Then I don't need my key."

A part of her wanted to hear the words *keep it*. Wishful thinking. He said nothing.

Bailey's fingers fumbled. She worked to remove the key that she'd carried with her eleven, almost twelve, years. She managed to unhook the key. "Here you go."

Her fingers brushed the skin of his palm. An electric shock made her drop the key onto his hand. She pulled her arm away. Must be static electricity in the air.

"Thanks." He stuck the key in his pocket. "Thought you'd put up more of a fight."

"You own the inn."

"I do, but you act like I've done something wrong."

"Architectural and historical preservation is vital, but you've ignored basic—"

"This architecture isn't anything special." He made a sweeping gesture with his hand. "The renovations over the years have nothing to do with the original design. It's a hodgepodge of trends over the past century."

"Hodgepodge? Thought was put into every change." Red-hot heat flowed through her. She should have known he'd never understand. "Did you know the materials used in the renovations have been salvaged from all over the Northwest, the United States and Europe? Each piece has a history aside from the inn. Stained glass and lead glass windows from old churches. Beams and flooring from nineteenth-century buildings."

"Don't romanticize being cheap." His tone made tearing down a historic landmark sound like a public service. "The inn has lost its appeal over the years. What character remains isn't enough to make up for everything else that is lacking. Don't get me started on structural concerns or electrical issues. The wiring is a mess, as is the plumbing."

She scooted away from him to put distance between them. He might be a pro at justifying his plan, but that didn't make him right. "If you feel that way, why did you buy the inn?"

"To turn the place around. Make a profit."

"By flattening the building with a wrecking ball?"

A muscle twitched at his neck. "Given the low sale price, if we hadn't purchased the inn, someone else would have."

Maybe, but something felt off here. She didn't know if it was Floyd or Justin. "Someone else might not have torn down the inn."

"I'm not the bad guy here." His voice sounded sincere, but he would never convince her that he and his company had the inn's best interest at heart. "I'm just doing my job."

"That makes two of us." Or she wouldn't be sitting here hurting and looking so frightful. "As head of Haley's Bay Historical Committee, I'll do everything I can to make sure this inn remains in all its hodgepodge, character-lacking glory."

Three hours later, Justin walked another lap around the inn's dining room, ignoring the urge to check the time on his cell phone again.

Bailey leaned against the wall on the other side of the room, talking with a gray-haired artist who introduced herself as Faye. The two women had been chatting for over twenty minutes. Not that he had anything better to do than wait for them to finish.

The older woman had been the last to show up, and he was stuck until she left. He'd never spent this much time anywhere unless he was working or sleeping. Sure, he'd sent texts, made calls and done what research he could on his smartphone, but he needed Wi-Fi and his laptop. The two things Justin had achieved this morning were memorizing every inch of this room and every inch of Bailey Cole.

She laughed. The sound carried on the air and drew his gaze to her once again. Her coveralls were finally dry, no longer clinging to her body. Okay, her chest.

Yeah, he'd looked. What man wouldn't? More than once, her shift in position gave him a better view and rendered him mute. Not his fault. He was a guy, one who'd been too busy working to date regularly.

Her feminine curves sent his body into overdrive. Looking made him think of holding her. Carrying her the short distance through the rain had felt so right. Too bad he wouldn't be touching her again.

Bailey's sharp glances and pursed lips suggested she wouldn't mind punching him once or twice. The thought of her getting so worked up, the gold flecks in her eyes flashing like flames, amused him.

She was driven, cared about things other than herself. The opposite of his ex-wife, Taryn. Passionate beat dismissive any day. Not that he was interested in a relationship. Marriage wasn't for him. Too much work and compromising.

Plastic crinkled. The other woman covered her sculpture.

"Thanks for coming on such short notice." Bailey bent her knee so her foot didn't touch the floor. "I'll let you know about tomorrow night's painting class."

Faye picked up the sculpture. "You'll find a place."

"Would you like help carrying that to your car?" Justin asked.

"Heavens, no. But thank you." Faye smiled at him. "This is light compared to the driftwood I drag across the beach. Bye." She walked out of the dining room.

Bailey slumped against the wall, her eyelids half-closed. Slowly, as if exerting effort hurt, she pulled out her cell phone. Her shoulders sagged, the worry over the inn seeming too much for her now. "Darn. The battery died."

"You can use my phone."

"Thanks. I want to text my family. I'm going to need help getting out of here."

Justin nearly flinched. Why was she calling someone else when he was right here? He'd carried the painting. Hell, he'd carried her. He had this. "I'll help you."

"Thanks, but…" She rubbed the back of her neck.

"What?"

"It's not getting the paintings or me to the car." She looked down at the floor. Her energy had drained like her cell phone. "My foot. I don't think I can drive myself home."

He'd only spent the morning with her, but she had a backbone and strength. She had to be hurting badly to admit she couldn't drive.

Bailey sat without being told. That worried him. She leaned her head against the wall. That concerned him more.

He walked toward her. Her face looked pale compared to earlier, her eyes sunken. "This isn't only about your foot. You don't feel well."

"My fault."

Her reply surprised him as much as her admitting she couldn't drive herself.

"I haven't eaten," she added.

"Since breakfast?"

"Um…since lunch yesterday."

"You haven't eaten in over twenty-four hours. Why not?"

"When I get into a painting I lose track of time. That's what happened yesterday. I don't think I went to bed until two. And then my grandma called me early this morning."

"I've done that myself when I'm working on a new design. I'll drive you home in your car. One of the crew can pick me up."

"No, you don't have to."

Take the out. Walk away. That was the smart thing to do. Except she looked as if she might pass out. "I'm taking you home now. You need to eat. Sleep."

"And shower."

Justin imagined how she would look naked with water dripping from her hair and down her skin. He tugged at his collar. Getting a little warm in here. Time to turn off the video in his mind. A full view of her strange outfit would do the trick. His gaze ran the length of her. "So this isn't your normal style?"

Bailey framed her face with her hands. "What? You don't like the psychotic nutcase look?"

"I've never been a big fan of nutcases or clowns."

"Me, either. I'm glad there aren't any fun-house mirrors around. I'd scare myself."

"You don't scare me." He hadn't meant to flirt with her. Maybe she didn't notice. "I'll help you to your car, then come back for your artwork."

Her wary look changed to resignation. "I can carry a painting."

"It would be easier if I carry you."

Bailey might be on the fashion police's Most Wanted List, but if he got to carry her out of the inn, this day would rank up there with a Seattle Seahawks' Super Bowl win.

"What do you say?" he asked.

Chapter Three

So much for carrying Bailey.

Outside the inn, Justin adjusted his grip on her framed painting. Plastic wrap crinkled beneath his fingertips. He could tell this piece meant more to her than the others, so he would be extra careful. But the woman herself...

He should have known better than to get worked up over *her*.

Passionate, yes, but stubborn to the nth degree.

He'd offered to carry Bailey to the car, then go back for the artwork. She hadn't wanted to do that. He'd then suggested getting her car and picking her up in front of the inn. She'd said no again. Mules had more sense than Bailey Cole.

She moved at a snail-pace wobble, her steps unsteady on the wet sidewalk. Any second, she might go down and hit the concrete. She would probably want him to let her fall than risk damaging her art.

She might be one of the most annoying women he'd ever met, but she worried him. "You okay?"

Bailey shot Justin a glare, one he'd become familiar over the past few hours. Her lips should thin in three... two...one...

And they disappeared. A line of chalk was thicker than her mouth. As easy to read as the Sunday comics. Too bad her lone-wolf act didn't make her curves less appealing.

"I told you." Her know-it-all voice grated on his back teeth. "I'm fine."

Sure she was. And he had complete control of the Broughton Inn project. What a pair they were. Well, a pair for however long this situation took to get resolved.

He supported the canvas between his far arm and body, in case she needed help. "You're back to looking like you're going to fall over."

"You have bigger things to worry about than me."

True, but he needed to get rid of her before he could deal with the rest of the mess. "Until I get you home, you're my biggest concern."

"It won't be for much longer. Five-minute drive, max. I'll be home long before I come close to losing it."

Whoa. His gaze ran the length of her. Maybe he hadn't figured her out. "Did you just admit you're on the verge of a meltdown?"

She didn't shrug or shake her head. "Maybe."

That was more than he thought she'd admit. Bailey Cole had ruined his day, but given her injury, she was a trooper—make that a general—who had defeated him. He couldn't wait for a rematch and to come out on top. Still Justin had a strange desire to comfort her, a feeling not only due to her killer curves.

She shortened her stride again. "If you don't mind add-ing a couple of minutes onto the drive to my house, I'd be grateful if you swung by the Burger Boat."

"They sell burgers on a boat?" he asked.

"Nope. Local fast food place. On land, not water. They have a drive-through, so we won't have to get out of the car. Not that I could." She glanced at her foot with a want-to-start-the-day-over look. "But it's past lunchtime. I'm starving and my cupboards are bare."

Her words reminded him of the "Old Mother Hubbard" nursery rhyme. Not that they had a dog to feed. Thank goodness the mutt was gone.

Thinking about a rhyme should seem odd, but wasn't given the way she was dressed and how strange today had been. "No eating. No food at home. You don't take very good care of yourself, Miss Cole."

"I take good care of myself." Her tone was an interesting mix—defensive and honest. She inched toward the curb. Exhaustion creased her face. "Except when I'm wrapped up in a project. Then my plans, like grocery shopping, get pushed aside. Most days bring a surprise or two."

Surprises, indeed. She'd surprised him.

"You might find a healthy meal and sleep a boon to your creativity."

"I'll remember that the next time."

"No, you won't," he said.

"I was trying to be polite."

"You sound annoyed."

"I'm that, too."

"Because you're hungry." He didn't wait for a reply. "A burger sounds good. I need to pick up lunch because Wyatt gave the dog my turkey sandwich."

Bailey stopped. "Where is the dog?"

"No idea. Dined and dashed. Probably headed home."

A look of concern returned to her face. "He could be a stray."

Nope. Justin wasn't going there. She might want to drive around and try to find the damn thing. Then they'd have to call Animal Control and wait. Again. He'd wasted his morning. He wasn't about to lose the entire day.

Time to change the subject. "Which car is yours?"

She pointed toward a four-door hatchback with a bright yellow exterior and black upholstered seats parked on the street.

"Looks like a bee." Tiny cars were annoying to drive, but this one was the color of a hot rod. He might not mind the leg cramps headed his way.

Bailey nodded, then stumbled.

He grabbed her with his free hand. "I've got you."

"Thanks."

He should be thanking her. Warmth and softness pressed against Justin, making him think of lazy autumn weekend mornings spent in bed, the brush of flannel sheets against skin, the feel of someone else's heartbeat and the sound of another breath.

Yes. He needed to get out more. Nothing serious, just for fun.

He helped her into the car, closed the door, then walked around to the hatchback and loaded the painting. "Tell me about this burger place. Good food?"

She turned and leaned between the front seats. "Best fries in town, thanks to a special seasoning mix. A little spicy, but not too much."

"I don't mind a little heat."

His words came out more suggestive then he'd intended. But what could he say? That image of a bed and tangled flannel sheets was burned on his mind.

She faced forward. "There are bungee cords, if you want to secure the painting."

Justin battened down the frame, then slid into the driver's seat. His right knee crashed into the steering wheel. "Knowing that was coming didn't help."

He expected her to laugh at him, tease him at the least, but no mocking laughter appeared in her eyes.

"That had to hurt." Her nose crinkled, her forehead, too. "You okay?"

"That's supposed to be my line." He didn't like being on the receiving end of her seeming to care. She was the enemy and would lose this fight to save the inn. "I'm fine."

"That's my line."

"Now we're even." He adjusted the seat so his legs half fit, then saw the stick shift. "You managed to drive a clutch with your injured foot."

"You're changing the subject."

"Damn straight I am." The woman was unbelievable. But he knew that. "Did you even consider staying home or at least off the roads?"

"I had no choice. If I hadn't come, there wouldn't be an inn."

So much for a truce. "If you'd been bleeding with your foot torn to shreds—"

"That's what rolls of gauze and bandages are for."

"You're either dedicated or insane."

"A little of both."

Her admission surprised him. "Seriously?"

"No one completely sane chooses to be a full-time artist. The market's as fickle as the economy, creativity comes and goes and making a living is hard. But I give lessons, put on events and sell an occasional piece. Somehow things work out."

Her car sat lower to the road than any car he remembered driving. Not a bumblebee. More like a battery-powered toy. He fastened his seat belt. "You must be doing okay, given this car."

"I'm not a starving artist, even if I look like one. I travel back and forth to a gallery in Seattle. I need a reliable vehicle. This one fits the bill."

From crazy to practical in less than thirty seconds. She must drive her boyfriend to the brink of insanity.

But what a way to go, a voice in his head whispered.

Justin ignored it. He drove up the block to the inn and parked at the curb. "I'm going to bring out the rest of your artwork. Won't take me long."

Five minutes later, he was back behind the wheel. "Which way?"

"Follow Bay Street until you reach Third Avenue. You can only turn right. You'll see the Burger Boat on the left."

He glanced at the digital clock on the dashboard. "Think you'll be able to hold yourself together that long?"

"Guess we'll find out."

He couldn't tell from her tone if she was joking or warning him.

Justin drove past the marina. Many of the slips were empty. The fishermen and charter-boat captains who made a living on the sea must be hard at work. People like Bailey's family.

Across the street sat stores and cafés, one after another. The buildings looked newer, not just with a new coat of paint, but updated facades to add to the quaint, coastal feel of the town. One restaurant had a crow's nest, but no drive-through window.

People, dressed in shorts or sundresses, filled the boardwalk running the length of the Bay Street shops. The little town of Haley's Bay was a big draw with Cape Disappointment and Long Beach nearby.

A boat-shaped building with a giant plastic hamburger for the ship's wheel caught his attention. Must be the Burger Boat. The blue-and-white paint job looked new, as did the windows. But the architecture screamed early 1970s tacky and retro-cool.

"Follow the anchors painted on the pavement to get to the drive-through window."

He did and stopped behind a silver minivan. There was no intercom system with a digital screen to display an order, only a window. "What do you recommend besides the fries?"

"The pirate booty burger is good if you have a big appetite. The hazelnut chocolate shakes are amazing."

"You know the menu well." He expected a shrug, but didn't get one.

"I eat here once a week. Have since I was a kid. They add seasonal shake flavors like pumpkin in the fall, and occasionally change up the Catch of the Day burger, but pretty much the menu has stayed the same for as long as I remember, a lot like Haley's Bay until they put in new shops on Bay Street."

"You don't like the changes."

This time she shrugged. "They are tourist spots, necessary for a service-oriented town, but not practical shops for those who call this place home. I miss the old places like the hardware store and pharmacy."

"The familiarity?"

"Consistency."

"To balance the not-always-stable life of an artist?"

"I guess. Maybe I'm just stuck in my ways."

The minivan pulled away from the window. Justin released the brake and drove forward.

"I'll have a dinghy burger, fries and root beer." She dug through her yellow shopping bag and pulled out a twenty-dollar bill. "Lunch is on me. I appreciate the ride home and not having to wait for my family."

Justin had two choices. Accept her offer or say no, thanks. He weighed both options. One would piss her off. Both might. But she was tired, and they were hungry. No sense aggravating the situation more. And she had ruined his day. A free lunch wouldn't make up for the mess she caused.

He took the money.

Loose strands of hair curled around her face and caught the light. The color looked coppery like a shiny new penny. His stomach tightened. That had nothing to do with being hungry.

She wasn't sweet or nice. She was a pain in the ass.

Still, he couldn't take his eyes off her.

The fast-food place's drive-through window slid open. "Ahoy, matey. Welcome to the Burger Boat." A man in his early twenties with a chipped front tooth and a sailor cap grinned. "What can we reel in for you today?"

Justin gave their order and paid with Bailey's twenty.

A foghorn blared inside the restaurant, the nautical sound effects matching the place's boat theme.

"Here's your change. I'll bag up your catch." The window slid closed.

"Did you ever work here?" Justin asked her, trying to fill the silence in her car.

"No, I thought being under a chef would teach me more than how to grill burgers and blend milk shakes."

"Smart thinking for a teenager."

"I like learning as much as I can about what I do."

She had more going on in her head than what subject to paint next. She hadn't known what she'd faced this morning, but she'd arrived prepared with files and paperwork.

Unlike him.

The window opened again. The man passed over the drinks. "Here's your order."

Justin put the drinks in the cup holders between their seats, then handed her the bag of food. She gave him directions to her house. He pulled forward and turned out of the parking lot.

The scent of burger and fries made his stomach grumble. "Smells good."

"Tastes better." Bailey opened the bag, removed a couple of fries and lifted them to his mouth. "Here."

"Thanks—"

He hit the brake to let pedestrians cross the street.

Her fingers bumped into his chin, then slipped away, leaving a trail of heat.

A blush rose up her neck. Sexy.

Easy, guy. Justin needed to add "fingers" to the list of her lethal body parts, along with her breasts and her brain.

"Sorry," she said.

He reminded himself to swallow. The spice hit the back of his throat. "Eat. We're down to the final thirty seconds until you lose it."

Bailey ate French fries, then a bite of her burger. "I feel better already."

On her street, a man dressed in cargo shorts and a stained T-shirt stood next to Officer Grady Cole in front of a blue-painted cottage. Colorful flowers filled every space that wasn't covered by grass, including the basket of a rusted bicycle leaning against the outside of a white picket fence.

The house looked surprisingly normal, though Justin hadn't known what to expect. A run-down shack? A padded room? "That looks like your brother."

"Two brothers. Grady and Ellis." Bailey leaned forward. "Both should be at work."

What now? Justin gripped the steering wheel. "How many brothers do you have?"

"Five, and one sister."

"Where should I park?"

"The driveway is right past the police car." She dragged her upper teeth across her lower lip. "I hope nothing's wrong."

He reached out, touched her forearm. A gesture of comfort, except he wasn't 100 percent certain that was all. "Hey.

I'm sure everything's okay. Grady knew you injured your foot. They're probably checking up on you."

She nodded, but doubt remained in her gaze.

Justin switched on the blinker, turned into the driveway. Her brothers glared like wolves protecting their pack. His fight instinct kicked into high gear. He parked the car. Two against one. He'd faced worse odds and come out ahead.

"My brothers don't look happy," she said in an understated voice.

Justin recognized their don't-mess-with-my-sister expression. He pulled the key out of the ignition. "Let's find out why."

Seated in her car, Bailey sipped her root beer. She needed one more fortifying drink of sugar to face her brothers. Ellis and Grady's body language suggested they wanted to take someone out. They'd looked the same way when they found out she'd lied about going to a sleepover and snuck down to Seaside during spring break to hang out with college boys from the University of Washington.

No worries. She needed to stay calm and settle her brothers down. Fast. Or someone—namely, Justin—was going to get hurt.

Ellis, the second-oldest and married with kids, opened her car door. "Where have you been? We've been calling."

"The inn." She unbuckled her seat belt. "Grady knew where I was. Grandma, too."

"Grady told me you were at the inn, but you didn't answer my texts. When I called, all I got was your voice mail." Ellis sounded like their dad, only more caring.

"Long morning. My cell phone died." Bailey moved her legs out of the car. Her fingers dug into the seat fabric. She sucked in a breath. Oh, boy, that didn't feel good.

"You're hurt. And you look a mess." Ellis touched her shoulder. He turned to Grady. "You're right about her foot."

Grady nodded. "Told you."

"Excuse me." Justin pushed forward, moving her brothers out of the way, and picked her up. "Bailey's injured. Whatever you're here for can wait until I get her inside."

"Who are you?" Ellis asked.

"A Good Samaritan helping your sister," Justin said. "Out of my way."

Ellis grabbed the shopping bag from her hands. "Do you need anything out of the car?"

She nodded. "The artwork and our lunch."

"On it," Grady said.

Uh-oh. Her brothers were being too nice and not giving Justin a hard time. Something was up.

Justin carried her toward the front door. His strong arms cradled her. Her pulse quickened.

She didn't like what Justin McMillian intended to do to the inn, but her heart melted a little. No guy had ever stood up to her brothers. Not that Justin had caused a confrontation. But he'd shown concern for her without worrying about the repercussions. That was new. And seeing Ellis and Grady get out of the way was funny. They were as stubborn as she was.

What Justin did for a living stole a building's soul. But she was glad he was here. Pain and hunger must be softening her standards. "I appreciate the help."

"I figured you needed to get inside. Not answer a lot of questions."

Justin handed her the keys.

She pretended to unlock the door, not wanting another lecture from any man, brother or stranger, about forgetting to lock the front door, then opened it.

He carried her inside. "Is the couch okay?"

"Perfect."

He set her down. Being horizontal felt good. If only her foot would stop hurting.

"Put your leg up on the back of the couch." He eyed one of her paintings on the wall. "Nice artwork. You're talented."

Tingles filled her stomach like a flock of swallows. She wished his words didn't mean as much as they did. "I love what I do."

"You work here."

She glanced at the paint-covered drop cloth and easel with an unfinished painting. All she'd wanted to do today was complete the piece, wash clothes and grocery shop. So much for plans. "Yes."

Ellis set her yellow bag and lunch on the coffee table. He helped himself to some fries. "I'm Ellis Cole."

"Justin McMillian."

Ellis kneeled next to her. "How ya doing, sis?"

"My foot is killing me, but the inn is in one piece." She smiled, proud she'd saved the structure from demolition, then grabbed more fries. "A good day."

"Depends on your perspective," Justin said.

Grady set a painting against the wall. "I texted Mom. She's picking up Grandma. They'll be right over to take you to the hospital."

"Urgent Care will be fine." Bailey eyed her brothers. "Why aren't you guys at work?"

"Tyler called. He wanted me to find you," Grady said in his no-nonsense police voice. A world away from the wild kid he'd once been.

"Tyler is my cousin," she told Justin. "He's the only lawyer in Haley's Bay." She looked at her two brothers. "If this is about me introducing him to one of the girls in my painting class—"

"It's not." Grady's gaze ping-ponged from her to Justin. "I'm here on official business with news about the inn."

Justin rocked back on his heels. His face tightened. "What news?"

"I'm sorry, Mr. McMillian, but your company is the victim of a fraudulent real estate transaction," Grady said.

"Fraudulent?" Justin asked.

Ellis nodded. "You got conned."

Bailey sat up. "What are you talking about?"

"Floyd Jeffries sold the inn to two buyers on the same day," Grady said. "One buyer was McMillian Resorts. The other was represented by Tyler."

Justin swore. "You're joking, right?"

"I wish I was," Grady said.

Justin's face contorted, turned red. He started to speak, then stopped himself.

She didn't know what to say to him. But the news made her dizzy. She leaned back against the sofa pillow. "That's not the kind of person Floyd is. The man drives ten miles an hour below the speed limit. He's no criminal."

"Was," Ellis said. "He changed after he met that girl on the internet. I heard he canceled all the upcoming events at the inn."

Bailey's body stiffened. "He didn't cancel my paint night tomorrow."

"You ran the art events, not Floyd," Ellis said.

"I don't know him as well as your sister does, but there must be a mistake." Justin paced the length of the couch. The lines on his forehead deepened, more like canyons than wrinkles. "We have a top-notch team of lawyers. We might have misunderstood the permit process, but they're professionals. They'd never fall for a scam deal."

"Well, I heard Floyd gave the employees three days off with pay. Never told them the inn had been sold or they'd lost their jobs." Ellis sat on the sofa arm. "That's why no one was there last night or today."

Oh, no. The staff. Bailey had been so worried about the inn itself she hadn't thought about the employees. Floyd had worked with some of those people since he'd been a kid.

None of this made sense. "That doesn't sound like Floyd. He cares about those who work for him. He bought my senior prom dress when Dad wouldn't pay for one without sleeves."

"I know the guy was good to you." Ellis's voice softened, his tone compassionate. "Floyd bought fish from us for all these years, was often our biggest customer, but he's not the same person. He's changed."

Justin shook his head. "Floyd might not have disclosed everything about the inn, but my sister negotiated a legal deal. She would never have paid cash otherwise."

"Tyler's client was a cash buyer, too. Part of Floyd's requirements," Grady said.

Ellis whistled. "That's a lot of money."

"No." Bailey didn't care what Grady said happened. "Floyd wouldn't do that to me—to this town—and all the people who trusted him."

"You're right." Ellis rolled his eyes. "Floyd headed to Belize with his twenty-five-year-old internet girlfriend and a suitcase of cash because of the good weather down there."

"Floyd is fifty-five and he's never married. He's been lonely." Bailey knew him better than her brothers did. "He's been wanting to settle down for years."

"With a woman less than half his age? The man has more money than common sense," Ellis countered. "But now he's added another zero or two to his net worth and he's laughing all the way to some tropical island paradise with no extradition treaty."

"Innocent until proven guilty," Grady cautioned.

"Guilty, bro. You know it." Ellis sounded convinced. "Tyler will prove Floyd is nothing more than a two-bit criminal. His parents and grandparents must be rolling in their graves."

Justin stopped pacing, pulled out his cell phone and

looked at Grady. "I have to speak to our attorneys. Is there anything you need from me right now?"

"No," Grady said. "But don't dispose of anything you took from the inn. I'll need you to return everything."

Justin's face paled. "The truck's here in town. I'll have my crew unload the contents."

The on-edge tone tugged at Bailey's heart. The day had gone from bad to worse for him. Justin might want something completely different for the inn than her, but that didn't matter right now. The guy looked as if he'd been knocked over with his own wrecking ball. She wanted to reach out to him, but she didn't dare in front of her brothers.

"Thanks for driving me home," she said instead. "I'm sure Ellis or Grady can give you a ride back to the inn if you don't want to walk."

"I will," Grady offered.

"Thanks," Justin said, sounding anything but grateful.

Grady waved. "See you later."

"Wait." Bailey looked over the back of the sofa. "You never said who else bought the inn."

Ellis and Grady exchanged a knowing glance. Both shifted their weight.

Uh-oh. "What?"

"We were hoping you wouldn't ask," Ellis said. "But since you did, AJ said it was okay to tell you."

"What does AJ have to do with this?" she asked.

The lines on Justin's forehead deepened. "AJ?"

"He's our oldest brother," she said.

"AJ Cole?" His voice matched the dumbstruck look on his face. "Your brother is the internet guy?"

Ellis nodded. "He's the buyer Tyler represented in the second deal."

She straightened, ignoring her foot. "Why would AJ want to buy the Broughton Inn? He's never talked about owning a hotel."

"AJ didn't buy the inn for himself." Grady looked as if he was about to jump out of a cake and yell surprise. "He bought the inn for you. Happy early birthday, sis!"

Huh? She blinked, Grady's words echoing in her head as if she were standing on the edge of a canyon. *Bought. Inn. For. You.* She tried to make sense of the words, but failed as if this were a precalculus test and not a simple conversation she was trying to understand.

"Say what?" she asked.

Ellis beamed. She hadn't seen him smile so brightly since his son Maddox hit a home run at a T-ball game last week. "The inn is yours."

"Not so fast." Justin raised his hands. "McMillian Resorts purchased the inn."

"There are two owners for now," Grady said. "The lawyers and the court will have to decide the true owner."

Her gaze met Justin's and held it for a long moment.

He looked away.

Bailey rested her head back against the sofa. She wanted to be independent, make her own way, not rely on her billionaire brother, but he'd come through in a way she never could have expected. The last thing she wanted was anything to take her away from her art, but at least now she could save the inn and jobs of everyone who worked there. *Way to go, AJ.*

"What do you have to say?" Ellis asked.

Ideas swirled through her brain, but first things first. She looked at Justin. "I want my key back."

Chapter Four

Two days later, Justin stood outside Tyler Cole's law office on Bay Street. A breeze rustled the leaves in a nearby tree. The cool morning air made him want to walk back to the B and B where he was staying and crawl in bed. He yawned, stretching his arms overhead.

A horn honked. Kids in a passing car waved at him. He gave a mock salute. That was all he could manage at the moment.

Worry over gaining possession of the inn was messing with his sleep. Random thoughts about Bailey Cole in her rain-soaked coveralls weren't helping. This quaint little town and its residents could be his ruin.

Cell phone against his ear, he popped another breath mint into his mouth. Should have picked up antacid tablets instead. But he doubted anything in a bottle would lessen the unease in his gut.

The unanswered ringing plucked his patience. "Pick up, Paige."

The line clicked.

"About time," he said.

"Ready for the big meeting?" His sister sounded way too cheerful under the circumstances.

"I was about to ask you that question. You're supposed to be here." Justin had better lower his voice. Kent Warren, one of McMillian Resorts' buttoned-down, Brooks Brothers–wearing lawyers who worked with Paige, was nearby. If Kent went running to Justin's parents, this whole thing would turn into a bigger mess. "Where the hell are you?"

"The office."

He pictured Paige sitting behind the impressive mahogany desk, her brown hair pulled up in a French twist, manicured nails tapping impatiently and her face puckered with an annoyed look. A hundred bucks said his annoyance level was higher.

"The meeting starts in five minutes." He didn't hide his anger. "Unless you've discovered a way to magically transport yourself, you're going to be late."

"I'm too busy. Mom and Dad have no idea what's going on. I have to keep them in the dark. That means staying in Lincoln City."

Paige acted as if she ran the company already. Not far from the truth. He and Rainey—their twenty-five-year-old younger sister—worked off-site much of the time. That left the hamster wheel of meetings, negotiations and fires needing extinguishing to Paige, but she thrived on pressure. Looked forward to it.

"You should be here in Haley's Bay," he said.

She clicked her tongue. "You don't need me. Kent knows everything about the deal. All you need to do is represent the McMillian name and reputation while we try to fix this deal before Mom and Dad find out."

She might be twenty-nine and the opposite gender, but

her tone and word choice sounded exactly like their father. Too bad she hadn't developed the same sixth sense their dad had to know that Floyd had been scamming them.

"You tried to make me the fall guy with the Seaside remodeling fiasco. I'm not going to let you do that again." The misadventure with foundation issues had cost them big money and made their parents question their capabilities. If Justin and his sisters lost the company, he wasn't going to be the only one they blamed.

"No reason to bring up the past."

"It's the perfect reason. Both places were your deals." Justin wished he'd never supported buying the Broughton Inn, but the bay view from the inn had captured his imagination, and any issues they'd found in the inspection didn't matter in a teardown. "You should be here cleaning up the mess."

"One for all, bro. Suck it up and represent." Her attempt at joking fell flat. "Stay in Haley's Bay. Make sure we end up with the inn. Otherwise…"

"I know what's at stake." The big reason behind his sleepless nights. "If we lose the Broughton Inn, we lose McMillian Resorts. You, me and Rainey will be out."

Out of the company. Out of a job.

Out of the one thing that mattered most to him.

The business was as much a member of his family as his parents and sisters. Without the company, they would never see each other, let alone talk. Everything would be different. His family would be forever changed. And not for the better.

A lump the size of the ugly, outdated chandelier hanging in the inn's foyer formed in his throat. His entire life had revolved around McMillian Resorts. Working for their parents wasn't easy, but the siblings' dream had been to run the company themselves, to pass on their legacy to a future generation of McMillians. Not possible if their parents cashed out by selling the business and firing them.

"Don't fail," Paige said. "Rainey and I are counting on you."

"Doing my best. We're up against deep pockets."

"AJ Cole doesn't care about the inn. Focus on his sister. She's the one we need to make give in."

Bailey. He pictured her warm green eyes, the look of pure delight when she bit into a French fry.

"Use your infamous charm on her," Paige continued. "You have a way with the ladies."

Kent cleared his throat, flashed the time on his cell phone.

"Gotta go," Justin said. "The meeting's about to start."

He disconnected from the call and entered the law office, located in a small, converted house and decorated with quilted chairs and black square tables. A metal magazine rack hung on the wall. The smell of coffee filled the air.

A thirty-something brunette with an easy smile greeted them, motioning down a hallway. "They're in the conference room. First door on your left."

"Thank you." The carpet muted Justin's footsteps.

"Smile," Kent ordered in a courtroom defense attorney voice. "You look like your dog died."

"I was never allowed to have a pet because we lived in hotels."

Kent's gaze hardened, making the lawyer look like a beady-eyed shark about to bite off a limb. "Those hotels will belong to someone else unless you pull yourself together. This morning, you're the face of McMillian Resorts."

Justin stopped at the conference room doorway, glanced back at Kent. "Fine. Sucking up on demand."

Two people sat at an oval table—a man in his early thirties and a woman who looked as though she belonged in a Renaissance painting. Copper corkscrew curls. A close-mouthed smile. Gorgeous face. Striking green eyes.

Justin smiled at her. Being stuck in this meeting didn't seem like a chore now. Was she Tyler Cole's paralegal or personal assistant? Another lawyer?

Justin searched for something witty and charming to say. He took a closer look. Familiar-looking. The laughter in her eyes matched her grin and reminded him of...

"Looks like we're all here now." Her voice was instantly recognizable.

Bailey. His pulse accelerated like an electric drill switched to the fastest speed. Man, she cleaned up well.

"Hi." Eloquent, no. But the two-letter word was safer than the others coming to mind. Sweat dampened the back of his neck. His collar shrank an inch, maybe two.

The man seated next to Bailey stood, then shook Justin's hand. "I'm Tyler Cole. I represent Bailey and her brother AJ, who couldn't be here today."

"Justin McMillian." The firm grip suggested the opposing counsel worked out. "This is Kent Warren, one of our company's attorneys."

Kent shook Tyler's hand, then Bailey's. "Nice to meet you."

Justin tried to think of more than one or two words to say to Bailey. "How's your foot?"

"Not broken. I got lucky."

He wouldn't mind getting lucky with her. His gaze met Bailey's. Something churned, then settled, in the pit of his stomach. Too much breakfast or too little coffee? "Glad you didn't break any bones."

"Me, too."

Kent cleared his throat.

Damn. Justin was staring. An artist or a siren? Right now he'd go with the latter. Not good. He couldn't let himself be distracted. One of them would walk away from this situation empty-handed.

Not him.

He sat on the opposite side of the table.

She drummed her metallic-blue short fingernails on the table, drawing his attention once again. Cuts and scars marred her hands. Working hands, like his. But her life seemed to be a contradiction, given she'd received an inn for a birthday present.

"Let's get started." Tyler handed out half-inch-thick documents. "Police reports have been filed by both parties. According to an update this morning from Detective Hanson, Floyd left the United States on Tuesday evening, but he never entered Belize. His whereabouts are unknown. AJ Cole has hired a private investigator."

"So has McMillian Resorts." Kent scanned the documents.

Bailey leaned forward over the table. The gap in the neckline of her pink blouse provided a glimpse of lavender lace and creamy, soft skin.

Justin's mouth went dry. He forced himself not to leer, but took another look. Not a good, long look, more like a glimpse.

"Have you spoken to Floyd, Justin?" Concern tinged each of Bailey's words.

His gaze flew up to meet hers. He wasn't sure whether she'd busted him or not, but his cheeks warmed, something that hadn't happened in...years. "I spoke with Floyd on Tuesday afternoon. I haven't heard from him since. His phone goes straight to voice mail."

Tyler jotted a note. "Both properties closed on the same day. Different title companies were used. No financing was involved in the private contracts, Floyd waited three days, then took the money and ran."

Bailey's nose crinkled. "This is so out of character for Floyd. I don't know why he'd do this."

"We believe an individual who recently came into Mr.

Jeffries's life may provide his motivation." Kent removed a file from his briefcase. A photo of a beautiful young blonde was clipped to the front. "Our investigator turned up information on Mr. Jeffries' girlfriend, Sasha Perry. Not only does she date older, wealthier gentlemen, she has been investigated for fraud four times over the past three years. The various DAs lacked evidence for any indictments."

Tyler squinted, reached for the picture. His face paled. "That's the woman who handled AJ's closing."

"Ours, too," Kent admitted.

Tyler swore. "So we both have a title and what appear to be legal copies of the signed documents."

Kent shuffled his papers. "Yes."

Lines creased Bailey's forehead. "What does that mean?"

Justin wanted to reach across the table and squeeze her hand, an inappropriate response under the circumstances. *Focus, McMillian.*

"Good question," he said. "We both can't own the inn."

Kent removed another legal-size file full of paperwork. "You both hold titles and own the inn. For now."

"So, will the court decide ownership?" Bailey asked.

"Yes, but a ruling will take time," Tyler said. "That leaves the inn closed and staff unemployed."

Bailey's face pinched. "The employees and vendors rely on the inn."

"We have other options such as mediation, relinquishing rights or a buyout," Kent offered.

"Wouldn't a buyout mean one party ends up paying more money?" Bailey asked.

Kent shrugged, but that sharklike look returned. Justin didn't like that Bailey was the intended prey.

"Paying more isn't an issue if someone wants the inn badly enough," Kent said.

"Only forty-eight hours have passed since we discovered what Floyd did," Tyler said. "We need to understand the extent of the fraud and legal implications before any settlement options are decided upon."

Kent didn't flinch. Of course not. The guy dressed as if he stepped off the glossy pages of a magazine, with his hair supergelled into place. He was the one who'd taught Paige to be cool and calm before she went in for the kill during negotiations. Justin wondered how being scammed made Kent feel. The guy never showed weakness or emotion.

"Just putting one possibility out there," Kent said.

"I don't want to sell," Bailey said, to Justin's surprise. "I want the inn."

He leaned back in his chair. Bailey didn't need the inn. Not when space for her art events and classes could be found elsewhere. But the determined set of her jaw reminded him of when she told him she wouldn't move away from the wrecking ball. This could be a tough battle.

"So, what happens next?" Justin asked.

"You first, Kent," Tyler deferred. "You're more experienced in these matters."

Kent's expression didn't change, but he tapped the end of his pen against the table. The less their adversaries knew, the better. "We've filed a civil claim with the court, but getting restitution from Jeffries is unlikely with his whereabouts unknown. The police are investigating criminal charges. You and Miss Cole need to decide how you want to proceed."

Bailey dragged her upper teeth over her lower lip. "Can't we temporarily open the inn so people can have their jobs back?

Kent shook his head. "There would be liability issues to deal with and money needed to fund temporary operations."

"From a legal standpoint, it's not something I recommend," Tyler added.

"So we just wait? And the inn remains closed?" Bailey's

frown matched the frustration in her voice. "What about the employees?"

Kent smiled. "They are eligible for unemployment benefits."

Her lips thinned. "That's not the same as a job with pay."

Kent's smile vanished. "Miss Cole. If you are close to the inn's staff, I suggest you not raise their hopes of the inn reopening any time soon. Looking for new employment will be in their best interest."

She looked at Tyler. "Is that true?"

Her cousin gave a slight nod. "We need more information before we can proceed."

Her lips drew into a thin line. Anger flashed across her face as clear as the lights on a fire truck. The opposite of her poker face when she'd hid her pain at the inn the other day. Which was the real Bailey?

"How long are we talking?" she asked.

"It's hard to say," Tyler said.

She blew out a breath. "So this meeting was only a formality."

Another nod from Tyler.

"Is there anything I need to know or do right now?" she asked.

"No. Not today." Kent looked at Tyler. "But I'd like a few minutes of your time, counselor."

Tyler straightened his papers. "I'm free until ten."

Bailey rose. "I'll be going home, then."

All three men stood. Tyler pulled out her chair. "Do you need help out?"

She looked up at her cousin, adoration in her eyes. The Coles seemed to be a close family. "Thanks, but I'm good."

She walked out of the office with only a slight limp. A gray walking brace covered her left foot. She wore a flat sandal on her right. Her floral-print skirt flowed back and forth with the sway of her hips.

Let her go.

But Justin didn't want to. Not yet.

"I'll wait for you outside." Justin ignored the startled look on Kent's face and quickened his steps to catch Bailey. "Wait up."

She stopped in the hallway, glanced over her shoulder. "I didn't mean for everyone to leave."

"I got tired sitting at the grown-ups' table."

The concern in her eyes remained, but she smiled. Her curved lips looked soft and tasty. Yeah, he wouldn't mind a nibble. Anticipation thrummed to his core.

He motioned to her brace. "You're walking better."

"Staying off my feet. My family has been hovering, not letting me do anything."

"Annoying you?"

"You have no idea."

Being around Bailey made him want to forget everything but her. "I might. I have two sisters and we work for my parents."

"Then you do know." She blew out a puff of air. "I love my family, but I'm not used to being around people all the time. Talk about exhausting."

Justin bit back a smile.

"What?" she asked.

"You're different."

She struck a pose. "Crazy-clown-lady different."

"Not today." In the time he'd spent with Bailey Cole, two things were clear. Honesty and integrity defined the woman. He glanced around the parking lot. The sun was shining, but no sign of her yellow bumblebee car. "Did you drive?"

"My grandmother dropped me off. My family has taken to chauffeuring me around."

"You can't drive?"

"I can. They think I shouldn't."

He remembered when his younger sister, Rainey, needed surgery on her knee. Her parents had been busy with a resort's grand opening. He and Paige had rotated caring for their youngest sibling. Bailey was lucky to have a family who cared about her.

Bailey removed her cell phone from her purse, a colorful, summery bag with circular designs in pink, lime green and yellow. "Better text for a pickup."

"Have a cup of coffee with me first." The offer tumbled from his mouth, driven by intrigue and attraction. Fraternizing with an adversary was not on Paige's to-do list. Probably shouldn't be on his, but he'd asked. No reason to take back the invitation. "There's a place across the street. If you can't walk, I'll carry you."

She eyed him warily. "Thanks, but I can walk."

"Let's go, then."

She gave him a look. "I didn't say yes."

"You didn't say no."

"True, but..." She glanced back at the law office. "Given the circumstances, do you think us hanging out is a good idea?"

Her question surprised him. She didn't seem like the cautious type. "One coffee. No big deal."

She looked at the coffee shop across the street. "I guess."

"Don't worry, I'm not trying to woo the inn away from you," he teased, though the thought had crossed both his mind and Paige's.

"Good to know, but I'd never fall for that tactic."

Bailey sounded jaded. He didn't like the idea someone had hurt or taken advantage of her. Maybe he was reading too much into her tone.

"Come on," he said, wishing they could call a truce. "Let's get some coffee."

Bailey grabbed a table for two by the front window at the Java Cup while Justin waited for their drinks. The scent of roasting beans, brewing coffee and baking treats filled the air. Normally the small shop felt like an extension of home, thanks to the friendly greetings from familiar faces, but not today.

Justin leaned against the counter. His black shoes screamed *Italian leather*. He wore gray slacks and a blue button-down tucked in. His hair had been combed into place and the stubble shaved from his face. The result... dazzling—if she liked that kind of dressed-up guy, but she'd had enough of sharp-dressing men who flaunted their wealth and acted as if they knew everything.

She hadn't seen that side of Justin yet, but she preferred his work clothes to business attire. Not that what she liked mattered where he was concerned, except she seemed to be the only woman here who felt that way.

A twenty-something blonde barista batted her eyelashes as if she were a butterfly, trying to show off beautiful wings. She said something to Justin.

He laughed. The deep, rich sound filled the air and drew attention to him. More female gazes turned his way.

The barista's cheeks turned pink, but she kept looking at Justin.

Bailey didn't blame the woman for wanting his attention. Men like him didn't walk into the corner coffee shop every day. Especially in a town the size of Haley's Bay. Her type or not, she couldn't deny Justin was good-looking. Gorgeous, really.

She needed to be careful around him for the sake of the inn and its employees. They were in a fight for ownership of the Broughton Inn. One of them would win; the other would lose. He might not be trying to charm the inn away from her, or so he claimed, but she couldn't let him distract her.

Justin looked over at Bailey, smiled. "Be right there."

Her tummy did a double twist as if she were a high diver. Nerves knocked against her insides like trick-or-treaters at her door on Halloween. This morning's overcast, windy skies and sense of foreboding in the air were better suited to late October than early July.

She should have said no to coffee. *N-O.* How hard could saying two letters be? Not that she'd said *Y-E-S.* Yet here she was.

Stupid, stupid, stupid.

She massaged her temples, trying to quell the headache threatening to erupt.

Justin might not be planning to "woo" her out of the inn, but he must have an agenda. To mine her for information or plant doubts that she could run the inn. This wasn't a date, because Justin wouldn't be interested in Bailey if he lost his bid for the inn. Or if he won, for that matter. He was only interested while the inn was in limbo; she had to keep that in mind.

Well, two could play that game. Maybe she could plant some doubts of her own.

"Hey, Bailey." Mrs. Caldecott, the wife of the town's butcher, stopped at the table. A pink baseball cap covered her white hair. She carried two coffees in a drink holder and a small brown bag. "Sorry to hear about your foot, but good to know you're looking out for the inn. I know you'll make sure everything turns out right."

"Thanks." More than one person had called or texted yesterday to lend support. Added pressure, yes, but that only firmed Bailey's resolve. "I'll do my best."

Mrs. Caldecott smiled warmly, the wrinkles on her face deepening. "You've always been a good girl, Bailey Cole. Just a little…different."

With that, Mrs. Caldecott left the coffee shop.

Different, huh? Bailey supposed that was a step up from odd. She'd been called that, too.

"Here you go." Justin placed a large white mug in front of her. "One cappuccino with a pretty flower."

"Thanks." Bailey studied the rosebud in the foam, complete with a stem and a leaf. "The baristas personalize their drink creations here. Bart, who works weekends, makes animal faces. He's a volunteer at the local rescue shelter. Puts out a jar for donations."

Cup in hand, Justin pulled out his chair. "I'll stop by on Saturday."

Her spine went steel-beam rigid. "You're staying in town?"

"For now." He sat.

The small, round table made for close quarters. His scent, soap-fresh and enticing, tickled her nose. She raised her cup to smell her coffee so she wouldn't want to sniff him.

Bailey's foot ached. She stretched her left leg and brushed his. She stiffened. "Sorry."

"My fault." He scooted back in his chair. "You need more room."

No, she needed distance from him. "I'm fine. We won't be here long."

Bailey drank her coffee. The warm liquid did nothing to help her growing unease.

"I'm putting together an improvement plan for the first approval committee." Justin raised his mug in her direction. "I appreciate the handy list you put together on the city's website to help approach the groups. Very thorough. Thanks."

"You're welcome." She chewed the inside of her mouth. Great. Her work would lead to the inn being torn down.

Okay, not really, but she needed to drink her coffee and leave before she gave him more helpful hints. "That's a requirement of my position."

"You're not anti-remodel."

"Not at all, but improvements need to be carefully considered so the historical significance isn't remodeled out of the property. Integrity of the architecture and intent of the design must be protected. Floyd..."

Saying his name squeezed her heart. She stared at the pink lip gloss mark on the rim of her cup.

Justin reached across the table, covered her free hand with his. The touch filled the empty places inside her with surprising warmth.

"What about Floyd?" Justin asked.

She stared at their hands. A sketch formed in her mind with lines and shadowing falling into place. The rough and calloused skin on his hands contradicted his style of dress. Her late grandfather and father and brothers—AJ, Ellis, Flynn, Declan and Grady—had similar hands. Her sister, Camden, too. Bailey's weren't much better.

"Floyd created the historical committee." She set her mug on the table. "He put together the committee to oversee property improvements. Wrote most of the rules and regulations. I took over for him a year ago."

For such large, scarred hands, Justin's touch was solid, safe, comforting. So what if pulling her hand from beneath his was the smart thing to do? She liked the feel of his skin against hers to deal with the consequences and rumors.

"His choice to leave the position or someone else's?"

"His. He wanted me to take over."

"Doesn't sound like the same guy I talked to. He was all for tearing down the old and making way for the new."

"Floyd was raised at the hotel. Loved that old building. Cared about the employees. His girlfriend must have pressured him to do this."

"You keep surprising me, Bailey Cole."

She glanced up, meeting Justin's gaze. "Why?"

"Most people want Floyd to rot in jail."

"I've known him my entire life." Bailey expected Justin to lift his hand off hers. He didn't. That surprised her, but in a good way. "Floyd let me open a co-op gallery at the inn and use the bar for my classes. I'm not about to condemn him without a hearing. I just wish I knew why."

"You might not ever hear his side or get the answers you want, but his reason could be as simple as falling in love with the wrong person."

"Yeah, his girlfriend sounds like a loser. That relationship has been full of red flags from the beginning."

"Lust can be addicting and dangerous. Powerful enough to make people change, not always for the better."

Something about Justin's tone piqued her curiosity. She leaned forward. The table pressed against her rib cage. "Are you speaking from personal experience?"

Bailey waited for Justin to answer her question. His taken-aback expression told her she'd crossed the line. Wouldn't be the first time.

The bell on the coffee shop door jingled. A young couple—tourists, based on the camera bag one carried—walked in holding hands and gazing lovingly into each other's eyes. Sweet.

A part of Bailey longed for a partner, one in the truest sense of the word. She stared at Justin's hand still on top of hers. Oliver had never comforted her with a touch. He was too worried about the solvents on her hands ruining one of his expensive manicures.

Why had she gone out with him? Oh, yeah, her sister-in-law Risa had set her up. The guy had been wrong for Bailey from the start, but she had liked having someone to go out with when she was in Seattle—AJ was always too busy—but as soon as Oliver began spouting his opinion about what she should be doing with her money or talking about his newest client and wanting to be introduced to AJ, the fun ended. Being on her own was so much easier.

Still, she found herself drawn to Justin in a way she hadn't been before. The little things he did, like having a hand ready if she stumbled or a kind gesture when she needed one most, were thoughtful, and she liked hearing what he had to say, even when she disagreed. But nothing would change their situation with the inn. No reason to complicate matters. Or chase heartache.

She pulled her hand from beneath Justin's. "So…"

Justin did a double take at her hand at the edge of the table, as if he hadn't realized he was still touching her. Maybe he'd enjoyed the contact as much as her.

Best not to go there.

He put his hand under the table.

Then again, maybe not.

With his other hand, he ran his thumb along the cup's handle. "We're talking about Floyd, not me."

"Didn't mean to pry."

"Yes, you did."

"Okay, I did." Bailey nearly laughed. "Subtlety isn't my strong point. But I'm trying to understand."

"Floyd?"

"And you."

His thumb continued moving up and down, up and down. "I wouldn't waste any time trying to figure out Floyd's actions. Sometimes those we think we know turn out to be complete strangers."

"Sounds like some woman did a number on you."

He flinched. "Excuse me?"

His shocked expression made her want to giggle. She'd caught him off guard. Again. "From what you're saying, I'm guessing it's not all about Floyd."

"I'm…divorced."

Interesting. Most women wouldn't catch and release such an attractive guy with a stable job who seemed relatively charming. Though she hardly knew him. He could be a weirdo for all she knew. Or a cheater. "Should I say I'm sorry or something else?"

"Sorry works. My ex wanted the divorce."

His voice held zero emotion. Over the woman or in denial? Hard to tell. Not that his past was Bailey's business.

"And no, I didn't cheat." He stared into his coffee cup, then met her gaze. "That's what everyone assumes."

"The thought may have crossed my mind."

"Our expectations of married life were different. She wanted to live in Portland. My work was on the coast, and job sites weren't always close to home. We grew apart."

"That's happened to a few people I know." But not Bailey's parents. They had been married for thirty-five years, through good times and bad times, and some horrible, want-to-forget ones, but they'd stuck together. That was what commitment—and saying "I do"—was about. But she'd never dated anyone for more than a few months, so what did she know? "You don't have to tell me this."

"You wanted to know."

"Yes, but that's small-town life for you. Hard to break the butting-your-nose-in habit, even though I don't like when people do it to me."

"Any more questions?"

"Are you still in contact with your ex?"

"No, she remarried and had a baby. She's happy now." A mutual friend had told Justin the news. "No reason for us to be in touch."

"Would you get married again?" Bailey asked.

"Hard to say, but unless I found a woman who either liked being on her own or traveling to job sites with me, probably not. I thought marriage would be easier, but it's a helluva lot of work. I have enough of that with my job."

How sad. Having to work at a marriage might be hard, but she believed the rewards would be worth the effort. Maybe Justin would realize that someday.

The conversation around them rose as silence took over their table. A man typed on his laptop. A woman stared at her smartphone. An elderly couple sat on a love seat and read the paper together.

A longing to grow old with someone rose within Bailey. She tapped it down.

"So my turn to ask the questions," Justin said. "How does an artist living in a small town end up on the historical committee?"

"Painter, and I love old buildings."

"What do you love? The design, the materials?"

"Those things are interesting, but for me it's all about the history." She wrapped her hands around her mug. The heat from the coffee warmed her palms, but she preferred Justin's touch. "The buildings are living memorials to the people who have been there before."

"Some are."

"Every single one." She thought back. "When I spent a semester in Europe, I climbed so many bell towers. The stone steps were worn smooth. You could see the paths people took, and that made me think of everyone who had climbed before me. Were they local or from far away? Recent or from centuries ago? What had they wanted to see when they reached the top? Were they with someone special or getting over a lost love?"

Justin leaned back in his chair. "You don't hesitate getting in someone's face, but you're also a romantic."

"I don't know about that." Bailey ripped the edge of a napkin into a symmetrical fringe. She couldn't believe he'd figured out that side of her. "My family would disagree. They call me hard-nosed."

"You're that, too," he teased.

He studied her like a scientist looking to identify a new virus. She forced herself not to move. "I wouldn't disagree, but hard-nosed and romantic don't exactly go together."

Maybe her brothers weren't the only reason she was

still single. Maybe she was as much to blame for driving men away.

"The traits go together in their own way." Justin's flirty smile raised her temperature ten degrees. "You know the past and see a future. You won't be bullied, but value artistry."

She sat taller, buoyed by a sense of purpose and pride. "I take my position on the historical committee seriously. And the inn…" From the time she was a little girl, she'd imagined getting married there someday. "…means a lot to me personally."

"Your actions are proof of that. The self-declared Guardian of the Broughton Inn."

"Thanks." Satisfaction bubbled inside her.

"You would take that as a compliment."

"I do." Her gaze met his. "You realize no matter how much you and your family want the inn, I plan on living up to that title. And winning."

"I have no doubt we'll fight to the end." His respectful tone held a challenge. "I'm up for it."

She raised her chin. "So am I."

Chapter Five

Bailey had thrown down the gauntlet, and Justin had taken it up. He leaned back in his chair at the coffee shop. He didn't want to think about the damage that would be done by the time he won this battle. "Enough about the inn."

She eyed him warily. "That's the only reason we're here."

Not him.

He'd never met a woman like Bailey Cole and wouldn't mind getting to know her better. Smart, attractive, she would prove a worthy opponent, but no matter how determined she was, she would lose. At the end, she would hate him, if she didn't already. He couldn't tell. That bugged the hell out of him.

"Doesn't mean the inn's all we have to discuss." The coffee shop door jingled. From his peripheral vision, he saw people entering, but his attention remained on Bailey. Justin rested his elbows on the wooden table. "Tell me about—"

"I'm boring."

"Haley's Bay," he said a beat after she spoke.

She blushed.

Hmm. Maybe she liked him a little or maybe she was egocentric. Either way, she amused him, but he kept his smile neutral rather than a blatant I-see-you're-interested-in-me grin.

Justin raised his cup, only to realize no coffee remained. He took a pretend sip. Bailey would be none the wiser, and that would keep them from saying goodbye too soon.

"Didn't you do a market analysis of the town before you purchased the inn?" she asked.

"For an artist and former cook, you know how business works."

"Common sense. And art is a business if you want to make a living with your work."

He liked her answer. Brains had always been a turn-on to him. "A market analysis was performed, but you live here. I want to hear what you think."

Bailey gazed into her mug, then looked up at him. "Haley's Bay is a typical Pacific Northwest small town. The name comes from a trader who anchored his ship in the bay. Fishing used to drive the local economy, but now tourism brings in the money. Population nearly doubles in the summer, thanks to tourists wanting to hang out at the beach or sightsee. The Lewis and Clark Interpretive Center appeals to the history buffs. And who doesn't like lighthouses?"

"Sounds like you gave me the Chamber of Commerce robot spiel."

A smile lit up Bailey's face. "Guilty. I'm biased, so I gave you the vanilla, glossy trifold brochure version."

"I want to hear the Rocky Road version."

"With nuts?"

"Of course." Some whipped cream would be nice, too. And a cherry. He undid the top button on his collar.

"Well…Haley's Bay is a small town with lots of history.

A couple of families like mine have lived here forever. Gossip is rampant. The women at the Cut, Curl & Dye Salon are the worst. I drive to Astoria if I need a trim, or do it myself. The guys who hang out at the Crow's Nest aren't much better. Conformity is applauded here. Being different means no one will even try to understand you, except family. And that's not always a given. High school was brutal for kids like me. Most grew up dreaming about leaving for the big city, but many of us stayed or came back. "

"You came back?"

"I never left except for college. My family, except for two older brothers, lives here. For all the town's faults, there's a sense of paying it forward in Haley's Bay I haven't found elsewhere. This is the only place I want to live."

At least she was honest about that fact, unlike his ex, who swore she wouldn't miss living in Portland. But Taryn had gone into the marriage thinking she could change his mind about staying on the coast. "You mentioned driving to Seattle."

Bailey nodded. "I oversee AJ's gallery. I'm up there a few times each month."

"More opportunity for art sales in the big city?"

"In the off-season, most sales happen through the Seattle gallery. I'm grateful for the extra exposure. So, you live on the Oregon coast?" She downed what remained in her cup.

"Lincoln City. My sister Paige works with my parents at our headquarters there. She's an attorney. My younger sister, Rainey, is an interior designer and spends her time at whatever resorts we're renovating."

"You oversee construction."

"And design. That's my favorite part."

"You're an architect who wears different hats."

He nodded. "Keeping the work in the family. All we're missing is a chef."

"Your parents should have had four kids."

"We joke about that."

Bailey glanced out the window to her right. She leaned toward the glass. "The stray dog from the inn is out there. He's so skinny."

Justin followed the direction of her gaze.

The thin brown dog sat on the sidewalk staring into the coffee shop. Mud covered the animal, but Justin saw the outline of the dog's bones beneath the dirty fur.

Bailey stood, took a step toward the door. "That dog needs medical attention."

He rose. "Where are you going?"

"To get the dog."

"Stay off your feet. I'll get the dog."

Her gaze narrowed. "You sure?"

Helping the dog might put him on Bailey's good side. "Positive."

How much trouble could a dog be? Justin stepped out of the coffee shop. The sun was brighter, the temperature at least five degrees hotter since they'd entered the coffee shop.

"Hey, dog." He looked at the pathetic, filthy animal that hadn't moved. "Hungry?"

The dog panted.

"You must be thirsty, too." Justin knew nothing about animals and couldn't believe he was having a conversation with a dog. But anyone with half a heart could see this one needed help. "Come here so we can get you fixed up."

The dog scratched himself with a hind leg.

"You know you don't want to be on your own out there. Let's get you some food. A bath. Flea medicine."

The dog tilted his head. Two brown eyes watching Justin.

He took a step closer. "Make me look good for the pretty lady looking out the window, and I'll get you a bone."

The dog didn't move.

"And a ball." He came closer. At least the dog didn't

seem to be afraid of him. "That's fine. Just sit there. I'll come to you."

Justin wanted to show Bailey he had this, even if he'd never owned or even walked a dog. He stood less than an arm's distance away. "Let's get you fed and cleaned up, buddy."

He reached for the dog, felt fur under his palm, then air. The dog bolted.

Justin lost his balance and hit the sidewalk, flat on his ass. So much for impressing Bailey.

"Oh, no," Bailey's voice sounded from the door to the coffee shop. "Are you okay?"

He sat on his butt, brushed off his hands. "Ego's bruised, but that's about it."

She joined him on the sidewalk. Her lips curved upward. "Not very experienced with dogs, are you?"

"You could tell."

A smile graced her lips. "Just a little, but nice try."

If she was trying to make him feel better…

She extended her arm. "Let me help you up."

He took her hand and found himself standing so close to her he could feel her breath on his neck. Her eyes locked on his. Her pink, delicious-looking lips parted.

Oh, yeah. He wanted a taste. A nibble would do.

If he angled his head slightly, he could kiss—

A bark cut through the air.

Bailey took a step back. "The dog."

Justin glanced around to see a flash of brown trotting away from them along the sidewalk. Not too fast, but a catch-me-if-you-can pace.

Bailey's nose crinkled. Concern filled her gaze.

Justin had a feeling he would regret this, but what the hell. Anything he had to do could wait until later. "Want to go after the dog?"

* * *

Bailey waited outside the coffee shop for Justin to return in his truck. Her stomach twisted like a glass-blown piece gone wrong. A part of her wanted him to take his time, except she wanted to find the dog. But she needed to cool herself down. Heat continued to burn her cheeks. She must look like one of Titian's blushing virgins.

How embarrassing. She'd thought Justin was going to kiss her when he stood up. Worse, she'd wanted him to kiss her. This was becoming more complicated by the second, and she wasn't the type for complications. Life was hard enough. She should say goodbye and not see him until their next meeting about the inn.

And she would.

After they found the dog.

Bailey scanned the street for a glimpse of the stray. Tourists packed the sidewalk, but no sign of the pup who needed food, water, medical treatment and to know someone cared.

She did.

If only her foot wasn't hurt, she could have run after the dog instead of being forced to wait for a ride. But she'd been standing too long this morning, and her entire leg ached. She sat on a nearby bench.

Glong. Glong. D-ding-a-ting-glong.

The bells chimed on her cell phone. She glanced at the screen. "Hey, Grandma."

"Hello, dear." The sound of waves could be heard in the background. "I'm in Long Beach. Do you need a ride home from Tyler's office?"

"I'm good." Justin would probably offer to drive her home after they found the dog. "Don't rush back for me."

"Okay, I'll bring lunch by later. I baked brownies this morning."

"Yum. My favorite. Thanks." Her grandmother loved

cooking for her family, especially her grandkids. "But I'm going to gain five pounds if you keep feeding me so much."

"Men like women with curves."

Did Justin? The thought flashed in Bailey's brain. She shouldn't care, but the more time she spent with him, the more she did.

A large black pickup stopped at the light caught her attention. Justin sat in the driver's seat, looking like a cross between a CEO and a cowboy. Her pulse stuttered. A totally inappropriate response when *not* seeing him again was her smartest move.

She rose, swung her purse onto her shoulder and walked toward the curb. "I've got to go, Grandma. Justin is here."

"Who's Justin?"

No. No. No. Bailey cringed. Had she really mentioned a man's name to her grandmother? She hadn't opened a can of worms; she'd released a vat of them.

"Bailey? Are you there?"

She swallowed around the lump in her throat, wishing she could have a do-over. "I'm here."

"Is Justin your new beau?"

The hope filling Grandma's voice sliced into Bailey's heart with scalpel-like precision. Having her grandchildren marry had become Lilah Cole's driving goal since AJ fell in love with nanny Emma Markwell last August. A big, billionaire-worthy wedding was in the works and that delighted Grandma. At least her matchmaking was subtler than Risa's, but Bailey wouldn't be surprised if the two were in cahoots, along with her great-aunt Ida Mae.

Bailey knew she had to say something, but as little as possible. "I hardly know the guy. He's the one who wants to tear down the Broughton Inn."

"Then why is he picking you up?"

At least she had a good reason. "We're looking for a stray dog."

"Is that a sex term?"

Bailey stiffened. "Grandma."

"What?"

"We're looking for a brown dog, covered in dirt and malnourished. Most likely a stray."

"Oh." Grandma sounded disappointed. Hard to believe the woman would be eighty-one in August. She acted much younger. "I suppose it's easier to keep your enemies close if they're good-looking."

"Have you met him?"

"No, but he's staying at Ida Mae's B and B. She said he was handsome."

Bailey was not going to discuss Justin's looks with her grandmother. Bad enough her great-aunt Ida Mae had mentioned him.

"Don't keep your young man waiting," Grandma added.

"He's not…" Bailey blew out a puff of air. Best not to go there when the truck was pulling up to the curb. "I'll talk to you later."

Justin jumped out of his truck and held open the passenger door. "Need a hand?"

"Thanks, but I'm fine." She climbed up using her good leg, but sensed him right behind her in case she fell. "It's okay."

"I'll move once you're buckled in."

"You don't have to play big brother to me."

"Trust me, my feelings for you aren't brotherly."

Her heart stumbled. He might not be her Mr. Right, but she was still female. Of course he could mean the exact opposite of what she was hoping—no, thinking. "Does that mean you're taking the term 'enemy' to heart?"

"I didn't say that."

But she didn't want to think of the alternative—that he might find her attractive. Something, maybe even desire, flashed in his eyes, as if he was imagining her naked and liking what he saw, made her feel pretty and wanted, and totally not in control of the situation.

The man was not only trouble, but also dangerous. The hair on the back of her neck stiffened, each one screaming to get the hell away from him. And she would. Once they found the dog.

Justin couldn't believe they'd spent an hour and a half driving around town with no dog to show for it. Not even a glimpse of dirty fur. He pulled into Bailey's driveway behind her car, the bee with tires.

"I'll keep my eyes out for the dog," he said.

"Thanks. I really thought we'd be able to track him down. I'll let Grady know so he can contact Animal Control. They take the animals they find to the local shelter." She yawned.

"Tired?"

"A little."

More like a lot. He turned off the ignition. "You haven't said much."

"I'm worried about the dog. And this is my first time out of the house since I went to the doctor. I'm not used to being vertical this long."

"Then let's get you inside."

"I can take care of myself."

"I know that, but if you fall, guess who'll get the blame? Don't you think being known as the man who wants to destroy the inn and got put into his place by Bailey Cole is enough infamy for one week?"

Her smile brightened her face. So pretty, though her look that other morning at the inn was endearing in hindsight. "People are saying that?"

"I might be exaggerating, but I don't want your brothers blaming me if you fall."

She reached up and touched Justin's cheek, surprising

him, but in a good way. "Oh, that would be bad. They'd mess up your nice face."

His chest swelled. "You like my face?"

Bailey jerked her hand away. Her shock widened his smile.

"I'm speaking as an artist." She looked everywhere but at him. "Your features are aesthetically pleasing and fit well together."

"You must have a good memory since you're not looking at me."

Her Mona Lisa smile hit him hard in the gut. He wished he could taste those lips. He grinned at the thought of doing just that.

She opened the front door. "What's so funny?"

He didn't dare tell her about wanting to kiss her on the sidewalk earlier. Not unless he wanted her to slam the door in his face. "This is the last place I expected to be again. Not that I mind. Your company is better than Kent's. The guy reads judicial briefs for entertainment."

Bailey stepped inside. He followed, closing the door behind him. "Kent's going to think you've gone missing."

"I texted him."

"Does he know you're with me?"

"I left that part out. Self-preservation."

She raised an eyebrow. "Sounds like a line I'd use with my family."

"Don't forget I have sisters. Paige routinely goes ballistic over less, but in this case she'd be firing words faster than bullets fly at a SWAT team's target practice."

"We have something in common."

"You sound surprised."

"Maybe I am." Bailey plopped onto the couch, resting her foot on a coffee table with designs burned into the wood and painted bright colors. "We're...different."

"Not really. We just happen to be on different sides with

the inn." Justin hadn't noticed the decorative table when he was here the last time. He touched one of the etch marks. "I like this."

"Bought the table at a garage sale for five dollars. A few doodles, wood-burning and paint…good as new."

Her modesty was endearing, but misplaced. "I'd say better than new. You could make an entire line of refurbished tables like this one and sell them for a shabby chic fortune."

"Listen to you." She held a pillow on her lap. "Tough guy resort developer talking shabby chic."

"We furnish every place I build or renovate." He pulled an overstuffed patchwork ottoman over and sat. "My sister might be the interior designer, but I know a thing or two about style. I also know you're a painter, but you have talent for furniture, too."

"Thank you," she said. "We're even for compliments."

He tugged off the sandal from her good foot. She hadn't asked, but his helping her felt strangely natural. "But I can hear in your voice that you're not interested in starting a business."

"It's not that. I sell what I make all the time, but I like to choose what I work on unless someone commissions a piece. I'd rather not be locked into making tables or anything else."

"Free-spirited."

"Sometimes. Other times not. Truth is, I'd let orders wait if I was inspired to work on a painting. I'd let everything wait, actually, which makes me wonder—"

Justin's hands still held her good foot. His fingers longed to rub her skin, soothe any sore muscles. He let go of her foot. "If you want to run the inn?"

Bailey frowned. "The inn has a staff to run it. I'm talking about, well…life. I'm different from my sister-in-law, whose life is her family. She volunteers, works out, cleans, cooks and gets mani-pedis. She's very happy, but I'm…"

"You worry whether you want a husband and family."

"*No.* Not at all. I worry I won't be good at it. That I'll put my art before everyone else, and then need to stop working altogether because I can't figure out how to balance the two."

The emotion behind her words startled him. He didn't understand her trusting him with something so personal when he was supposed to be the enemy, the rival for the Broughton Inn, the guy she stopped by standing in front of his wrecking ball. Or why he had the urge to move to scoop her into his arms and tell her she could handle marriage and a family.

He needed to get a hold of himself. She was a stranger, not his friend. But he'd tried the marriage route and failed. Maybe he could help her.

"Trust me, Bailey. Being a good wife has nothing to do with whether you work or stay home. It's difficult, no matter who you are. So is being a good husband. But you care about people and that's what matters." Reassurance came naturally, because the words were based on his experience. "That's my ounce of wisdom for the day."

"More like sixteen ounces of good advice." Gratitude filled her voice and her eyes.

He wouldn't swear an oath, but he glimpsed what might have been a tear. For the first time in a long while, he felt like a hero. Which made no sense, because he'd done absolutely nothing to earn the title, and had no right to give advice, given his divorce. "Do you want a glass of water or something to drink?"

"I could use some ibuprofen and water." She looked relieved at the change of subject. Well, join the club. He wasn't sure why the topic had come up. "The pills are in a white bottle on the counter. The glasses are in the upper cabinet right off the sink."

"Be right back.

"I'm not going anywhere."

Bailey's kitchen was like her—unique and comfortable. The Dutch-blue walls complemented the white cabinets with fused glass handles. Colorful pottery sat on top of the kitchen cabinets. Small seascape canvas paintings hung on the walls. The area was neat and tidy, except for two coffee cups in the sink. She must have had company this morning. Who?

He took a closer look and noticed lipstick stains. Not a guy. Then he remembered she'd said family members had been taking care of her. Her sister? Bailey talked more about her brothers.

Justin filled a glass with water and grabbed the pills. He stepped into the living room. "I've got your…"

Bailey's eyes were closed, a soft smile on her slightly parted lips. He took a step back. Okay, three.

Beautiful, yes. He'd been surrounded by attractive women his entire life. Hell, Taryn was gorgeous. But something about seeing Bailey like this took her appeal to a new level.

Her expression wasn't vulnerable. Nothing about her was needy, but at that moment, all he wanted to do was take care of her. Not in a caveman type of way. She was the last woman who needed protecting, with such a strong independent personality and surrounded by family as she was. But he wanted to make sure she had everything she needed and was…happy.

Happy.

Crazy and illogical, given the inn. He'd better get out of here before Paige found out. But first he wanted to do something.

Justin placed pills on the table and set the glass on a coaster. He covered her with an afghan from the back of a rocking chair. She didn't stir.

Okay, now he could leave. But a part of him wanted to stay to make sure she didn't wake up and need something.

He glanced around the living room. Seascapes with lighthouses. Landscapes with mountains. Photographs in hand-painted frames hung on the walls and sat on shelves, a glass jar full of painted rocks on one corner of the mantel, a bowl with seashells on the other and a colorful flowerpot with colorful, swirly lollipops sticking out on the windowsill near the front door.

Easy access for visiting kids, old and young?

He took a closer look at the photographs. One with Bailey and another woman on the beach caught his eye. The two resembled each other—her sister, Camden?—but their looks were the only similarity. Bailey was the image of femininity in a blowing skirt, tank top and no shoes. The other woman wore rubber waders held up with suspenders and a cap worn backward on her head. Bailey was the image of Mother Earth, while the woman next to her defined *tomboy*. He recognized Ellis and Grady in several of the pictures. The other men must be her brothers. Not identical facial features, but you could tell they were related. The lengths and shades of brown hair varied, but their heights only slightly so. He moved onto the next photograph, then another and another, making his way around the living room.

A slight knock sounded; then the front doorknob turned.

He'd closed the door, but hadn't turned the lock.

A short, white-haired woman entered, then closed the door. He'd seen her picture on the wall. She wore a green tracksuit and carried two bags. Her eyes widened. "Well, hello." She didn't look worried or surprised.

"Hi."

A welcoming smile deepened the wrinkles on her face. "You must be Justin."

How did she know his name? "Yes, I'm Justin McMillian." He motioned to Bailey on the couch. "She fell asleep."

"Doing too much too soon. Did you find the dog?"

"No."

"She'll be worried about that."

"I plan to keep looking."

"That'll make Bailey happy. Place a report with Animal Control so they're on the lookout, too. That'll impress her." The elderly woman walked into the room, her excitement visibly bubbling over. "I brought lunch. There's plenty for you, too."

So, what if he was supposed to meet Kent for lunch? Justin would rather stay here with a sleeping Bailey and her surprise visitor.

"By the way, I'm Lilah Cole, Bailey's grandmother."

"Nice to meet you, Mrs. Cole."

She shuddered. "Lilah, please. Mrs. Cole makes me think of my mother-in-law. Those aren't fond memories." She handed him one of the bags. "Come in the kitchen. I need help with lunch and while we work, you can tell me about yourself."

He stared at the bag in his hand. He could guess where Bailey got her strong personality. He had no idea what she would say to his hanging out with her grandmother, but he had a feeling Lilah would be nothing but smiles. That was good enough for Justin. Maybe helping Lilah prepare lunch would earn him some points with Bailey. He could use them. "What do you want to know?"

Chapter Six

Bailey blinked, allowing her eyes to adjust to the light. She wasn't ready to wake from her nap, but she'd heard something. Voices? Laughter? Except the TV was off. The radio, too. Maybe she'd dreamed the sounds.

She sat on the couch with her leg propped on the table. Light streamed through the front windows. The clock on the DVD player showed she'd slept over an hour. Felt like longer. She stretched her arms over her head.

An afghan, crocheted by Grandma, fell to Bailey's lap. She didn't remember covering herself. Had Justin done that? No, he would have left by now. At least she hoped he hadn't stuck around while she slept.

Bailey cringed.

She couldn't believe she'd confessed her personal worry to him. Shame poured through her, like the water rushing from the Columbia River to the Pacific Ocean. Tiredness and worry about the dog had lowered her defenses, allowed her to open up. That rarely happened, even with her family.

Laughter sounded from the kitchen. Female. Familiar. Grandma. She must have brought over lunch.

Bailey heard another voice. Male. Not one of her brothers.

Oh, no. Justin was still here. Her back straightened like a piece of rebar, no longer against the sofa. Seeing him would be too embarrassing after blurting out her feared ineptitude about having a family. Even if she'd appreciated his advice.

She glanced around the room, looking for an escape. The bathroom? Her bedroom? A closet?

And then she realized Grandma and Justin had spent time alone. Flutters filled Bailey's stomach like a bevy of blindfolded butterflies.

Her grandmother finding Justin here while Bailey slept could be the start of a Lilah-induced apocalypse. Instead of four horsemen, her brothers would ride in and wreak havoc. This was bad, so bad Bailey debated pretending to be asleep so she wouldn't have to deal with…

"You're awake." Her grandmother stood in the doorway to the kitchen.

Too late to play possum. Bailey forced a smile.

Lilah Cole was a short, wiry woman with white curls, wrinkles from a lifetime of laughter and a bright-as-the-sun smile. She would turn eighty-one next month, but she acted like a spry sixty-year-old, doing Jazzercise classes at the rec center twice a week.

"I must have needed that nap." Bailey fingered the edge of the blanket. "I didn't hear you come in."

"You were out cold. Big Foot could have stomped around, and you wouldn't have stirred. Justin kept me company. Such a nice man. So polite. And handsome, too."

Uh-oh. Bailey recognized the twinkle in her grandmother's eyes. That was how she looked when she talked about Emma Markwell, AJ's fiancée. If Grandma decided Justin was the man for Bailey…

Time for damage control. "Not nice. He wants to tear down the inn."

"To build a better one."

"A glass box to take advantage of the views, but a building with zero personality. I did an internet search, saw pictures of the remodeling job he did in Seaside. No, thanks." Bailey couldn't believe she was having this discussion with her grandmother. "Where is he?"

"In the kitchen doing dishes," Grandma said in a low voice. "We ate while you napped."

"Great." Not really. Bailey had no idea why Justin had stuck around unless he wanted to pump Grandma for info. "You always bring too much food."

"That's what grandmothers do. Feed our grandbabies."

"I'm way past the baby stage."

"Not in my eyes." A faraway expression filled Grandma's gaze. "Seems like only yesterday you were running around in a diaper and nothing else. Your grandfather would chase you down the hallway. You'd giggle. Two pigtails sticking out on each side of your head like Pippi Longstocking. Crayons in each hand. A giant grin on your face as you looked for something, usually a wall, to color."

Justin entered the room carrying a tray. "Braids and a grin, I can imagine. The crayons, too. The diaper, not so much."

This was going to be a problem. Bailey blew out a breath.

Grandma laughed. "Bailey wanted to be naked, but I had my hardwood floors and rugs to protect."

Heat spread up Bailey's neck. She bit the inside of her cheek. In less than ten seconds, her face would clash with her hair. "Grandma. You're as bad as Mom."

"What?" Grandma feigned innocence. "You've always been a free spirit. Nothing wrong with that."

Bailey's insides twisted while she kept a straight face.

Justin was looking at her, and she felt unusually self-conscious. "I prefer wearing clothes these days."

"You look wonderful in whatever you wear," Grandma said.

"Except for those paint-splattered coveralls." Justin handed Bailey the tray containing a plate full of lunch, utensils, napkin and glasses of lemonade. "If the fashion police had been patrolling the streets the other day, we'd still be trying to raise bail."

Bailey grimaced. "They aren't that bad."

"Yes, they are." Grandma's scrunched face matched her disapproving tone. "Please tell me you're joking about wearing them."

"I've only worn them once in public," Bailey admitted. "Satisfied?"

"Yes, but that was one time too many." Grandma motioned to the lunch—meat loaf with mashed potatoes, green beans and homemade biscuits. "You need to start chowing down. There are brownies for dessert."

"You made my favorites."

"Anything for you, dear. And Justin." Grandma picked up her purse. "I have to go."

Bailey's muscles tightened into a tapestry of knots. Her grandmother leaving them alone was a bad sign—a matchmaking sign. "We haven't visited."

"You see me almost every day." Grandma waved her off. "Risa is busy, so I need to pick up the kids from school."

"Amelia and Maddox don't get out of school for at least two hours. And they take the bus home whenever I babysit them."

"I'm a busy woman. Places to go. People to see." Grandma headed toward the door, then glanced over her shoulder. "Delighted to meet you, Justin. See you soon."

He nodded. "Thanks for lunch."

"I'll pick up the containers later. Have fun, you two."

With that, Grandma strode out the door, a small hurricane about to be set loose on Haley's Bay.

"The woman is a spitfire." He sat on the far side of couch. "She asked so many questions."

"I'm sorry. Grandma wants to know everything about everybody. She uses her newfound knowledge to meddle. Managing others' lives—well, trying— keeps her young."

"No apology needed. I got a great lunch and made a new friend."

"You don't mind that your name will be bandied about town? Might already be happening."

He moved to the cushion next to her, cutting the distance between them in half. His smile hinted of mischief and something else Bailey didn't want to name. "Your grandmother is a sweetheart, but I caught on fast that she was trying to pry me open with her charm."

"You should have woken me up. I would have run interference."

"You were tired."

"You didn't have to stay."

Justin shrugged. "Lilah asked for my help with lunch. I couldn't say no."

Bailey shook her head. "My grandma can whip up a meal for forty without blinking an eye."

"Yeah, she seemed to have everything under control."

"But you went along?"

"She's your grandmother. There's no other place I'd rather be right now."

The sincerity in his voice tugged at Bailey's heart. The last thing she needed from Justin. "What about Kent?"

"I texted him. He's at the courthouse." Justin pointed to her lunch. "Eat. The meat loaf won't taste as good cold."

She stabbed her fork into her lunch. Food would distract her from the man. She took a bite. Spices and flavors exploded in her mouth. "Mmm."

"Your grandmother's a good cook."

"The best." Bailey scooped up another forkful. "My mom conceded defeat in the kitchen, but one-upped Grandma by having seven children to her three. My mom, however, would never admit that was her reason for having a big family. She adores Grandma."

"Cole family gatherings must be interesting."

Bailey wiped her mouth with the napkin. "They are. Crowded and loud, but no fighting unless we're talking sports."

"Seahawks fans?"

"My brothers and sister are. Sundays at my grandma's house during football season are mandatory. Doesn't matter if you like sports or not, so I watch the commercials."

"Your way of fitting in."

Once again he'd said something that made Bailey think he could see right through her. Not about to admit anything, she focused on her lunch. Bailey ate. Maybe silence would convince him to leave. The seconds turned into a minute, then two.

"I reported the stray dog to Animal Control," he said.

She choked, coughed, grabbed her lemonade to wash down whatever had gone down the wrong way. She cleared her throat. "Did my grandmother tell you to do that?"

A beat passed. A sheepish grin appeared. "She didn't want you to worry."

Bailey's fork slipped from her fingers, clattered against the tray. "Crap. This is worse than I thought."

"Excuse me."

She took a breath. "My grandmother's picked you. For me."

Justin's eyebrows drew together. Lines crinkled his forehead. "She said that a minute or so after meeting me."

"Timing doesn't matter to Grandma. She's a romantic at heart. Love at first sight. Cupid's arrow." Bailey rubbed her aching temples. "My grandmother married my grandpa after knowing him three days. They eloped and were married for over half a century before he died. I bet she's over at the B and B where you're staying, telling my aunt Ida Mae that we're making out on the couch right now."

"We'd better get started, then."

Bailey ignored his joke. "Grandma's been wrong about her picks in the past, so I'll remind her about that when she brings you up."

He scooted closer, until his thigh pressed against hers. "Is that going to be before or after we make out?"

Bailey's pulse sprinted as if she were running a hundred-yard dash. "Very funny."

"You're smiling."

Was she?

He slid his arm around Bailey's shoulders.

His breath tickled her neck like a cat's whisker against her skin. *Speak up. Say something. Stand.*

But she couldn't. Because a part of her wanted to see what happened next.

Justin leaned forward.

She met him halfway, driven by a mix of curiosity and desire.

His lips touched hers. A spark flared, made her stiffen, but then the feel of his lips relaxed her, turning her into a mass of goo.

Heat, salt, wow. Justin's kiss tasted better than any she'd experienced or imagined. She arched against him.

His lips moved over hers.

Time stopped. Her brain short-circuited, not wanting to think but feel and enjoy. Her heart wanted more...wanted him.

He drew back. His gaze met hers. "Time for dessert."

Bailey's mind went straight to her bedroom. So. Not. Good.

She looked away from him, touched her lips. The kiss

was short, but hinted at…possibilities. "Why did you kiss me?"

"Because I wanted to. I've thought about kissing you since the first day we met."

"Even though I looked like a crazy clown?"

"You had your moments of normalcy. Though the clown look was a little endearing."

Her heart sighed. She needed to make it stop doing that.

"I'm glad I did." He smiled. "No regrets."

Her lips tingled from his kiss. She kept thinking how easy kissing him again would be. But she…couldn't.

The inn. The staff. Her family.

If she wasn't careful, this was going to erupt into a huge, tsunami-type mess. Cleanup could take years.

Bailey took a breath, then another. "Kiss me again and you'll have regrets. A lot of them."

He flinched, a surprised look on his face. "You didn't seem to mind when we were kissing. You seemed into it."

"Maybe I was. Now I'm not." Bailey swallowed around the lump in her throat. She had to get away from him. "Thanks for your help. But you need to leave. Now."

Before she changed her mind and kissed him and showed him what kind of dessert she'd prefer instead of brownies.

Seven days passed. Seven days Justin spent thinking about Bailey and her amazing kiss that made him want more. Seven days he looked for the stray mutt after finding out Animal Control had yet to catch the dog, so he'd have a reason to contact her. The damn dog must have worn an invisibility cloak because he hadn't seen a glimpse of dirty brown fur. Maybe Bailey had one, too. He hadn't seen or heard from her.

No texts, no calls, no meetings about the ownership of the inn or the dog.

His fault for kissing her, but he still had no regrets. Her

kiss had been both a surprise and electric. She'd met him halfway and her kissing him back had been a turn-on. Was that why she'd gotten so upset? Because she'd wanted the kiss as much as he had? Women had gotten mad over less. He guessed he would find out in a few minutes.

He parked his truck on the street in front of Lilah's stately, three-story Victorian that overlooked Haley's Bay. He glanced at the horizon to see the sun setting. The rhyme he'd learned from a fisherman in Depot Bay, Oregon about a red sky at night being a sailor's delight played through his mind. Tonight's red sky would please fishermen and boaters wanting to head out in the morning.

The invitation from Ida Mae to attend Bailey's Chardonnay and Canvas event at Lilah's house had come at the perfect time. Saying no had never crossed Justin's mind. He wanted a chance to see Bailey, to figure out why she'd gotten under his skin.

Colorful painted pots with blossoming flowers sat on the front steps. The bright color combination looked like Bailey's work.

This evening would be interesting. An artist, he wasn't. The only painting he'd done involved drywall. But to see Bailey, he'd happily pick up a brush and pretend to be Picasso for the next three hours.

A white swing hung on the left side of the porch, inviting visitors to sit and enjoy the view. He imagined Bailey out here, the breeze toying with the ends of her hair, her bare feet pushing the swing back and forth. He could almost smell her floral perfume.

A woman had never been on his mind the way Bailey was, not even his ex-wife. He and Taryn had met in college and become good friends. A romantic relationship had been the next step. After they married, they'd bought a bungalow in Lincoln City, but she soon tired of life in the small town on the Oregon coast with him away so much on job sites.

She wanted to move to Portland, where she'd grown up. He wanted to live near their company headquarters. Taryn decided to move without him. She hadn't cared about his job or anything except what she'd wanted. She'd filed for divorce shortly after that. Better off without her.

Justin stood on the welcome mat, stared at the word written in black script. Lilah and Ida Mae might want him here, but what about Bailey? A weird feeling settled in the pit of his stomach.

Sure, he was attracted to her, but he couldn't be distracted. He wanted life to return to normal, where his every thought didn't revolve around a pretty, copper-haired woman. He didn't want to be kept on his toes or have his emotions go from one extreme to another or be tempted to kiss her again. He liked being single and not having to explain himself to a woman.

He knocked.

The door opened. Lilah's white curls bounced. Her smile reached her twinkling blue eyes.

"You're here. Wonderful." She pulled him into the house. "I'm so happy Ida Mae invited you. We had a last-minute cancellation and she thought you'd be the perfect substitute. I hope you don't mind hanging with our garden club tonight painting flowers."

"Thanks for including me. I've been curious about Bailey's classes."

Lilah patted his arm. "You'll enjoy yourself."

Justin didn't need a PhD in human behavior to know grandmother-style matchmaking was afoot. Bailey had made him uncomfortable when she asked him to leave her home. His turn to do the same to her, but in a more fun way. "I'm ready to paint, though a mechanical pencil is more my tool of choice than a brush."

"You'll do fine. Bailey is an excellent teacher. She's

also a fantastic cook. Did you know she used to work in the kitchen at the inn?"

He thought Lilah might pull out Bailey's scrapbook next to show her winsome, braided, diaper-clad babyhood. He wouldn't mind. She was probably a cute, hard-nosed, in-your-face kid. "She told me, but mentioned something about being a better artist."

"Bailey's too modest. Have her cook you dinner. I promise you won't be disappointed with the meal she'll serve."

Subtlety wasn't the woman's strong point, just like her granddaughter. "I'm sure I would love it, but she shouldn't be standing in the kitchen while she heals."

"That's true. Tonight will be hard enough. But her brother Declan, one of the twins, dropped off a stool earlier for her to use."

Twins? Bailey had never mentioned she had twin siblings. But then again, he hadn't known her long. "She's lucky to have her family take such good care of her."

Lilah tsked. "Bailey is too independent to allow anyone to take care of her. Been that way since she was three and the twins, Camden and Declan, were born. But we help where Bailey allows. She's let us do a little more with her injury, which tells me how much her toe must hurt."

Justin wasn't surprised. Bailey's middle name could be self-reliance. He followed Lilah into a large room filled with long, rectangular tables holding easels, white plastic paint trays and brushes. A black apron hung over the back of each chair.

"A couple of my grandsons moved the furniture out earlier," Lilah said. "Good boys, though a tad on the wild side. They need to find good women to straighten them out."

Over toward the side of the room stood a group of white-haired women chatting, laughing and sipping wine. The average age appeared to be seventy-five, maybe eighty.

"Your garden club?" he asked.

Lilah beamed. "Friends since before you were born."

He didn't have many long-term friends. He'd grown up moving from town to town, as resorts were opened, never staying longer than two years in one place except when he went to college and then got married. Until he came to Haley's Bay and met the Cole family, his transient life these past few years hadn't seemed bad. After the divorce, he'd sold their house and rented a condo because he spent more of his time at job sites than at home. But now he wished he'd had…more.

"Chardonnay for the gentleman." Ida Mae handed him a wineglass. "So glad you could join us. Linda Ross had to cancel, and we didn't want her spot to go empty."

"Thanks for the invitation and the wine." Justin took a sip. He was a beer drinker—craft beer was his favorite— but this was tasty with a hint of oak and touch of vanilla. "I'm looking forward to tonight's class."

Especially seeing Bailey. He searched the crowd of women, but didn't see any copper ringlets. Maybe she was sitting…

"Justin?"

He turned toward the sound of Bailey's voice. His breath caught. She stood, as if a vision, in a maroon, ankle-length skirt, a slightly oversize T-shirt with colorful swirls and her hair pulled back in a loose braid. He hadn't conjured her in his imagination. She was real, standing in front of him within arm's reach.

"Hi." He forced a greeting from his dry throat.

Her gaze narrowed. "What are you doing here?"

Ida Mae raised her wineglass. "When I heard we had an open spot, I invited Justin. Much better than having him spend another night hunched over blueprints in his room. I want my guests to have fun while they stay at the B and B, not work all the time."

Justin fought a grimace. She made him sound like a

workaholic. "I'm new in town. Don't know a lot of people yet. And I have a lot of projects to finish."

Well, *start*, once they gained possession of the inn.

"Working is important, but you need to have fun, too. A good thing you have us to keep you company tonight." Lilah patted his arm. "Won't having Justin here be fun, Bailey?"

"Letting Linda's spot go empty would be a waste." Bailey sounded on edge. She dragged her teeth over her lower lip.

He remembered kissing those lips. "I've only painted on construction sites. I'll try not to be too much trouble."

"A man who looks like you has trouble written all over him," Ida Mae teased.

Lilah shooed her away, then looked at Bailey. "I'm going to check the appetizers and wine. Why don't you give Justin a quick intro about how tonight will work?"

Bailey watched her grandmother head to the food table. "I can't believe my great-aunt dragged you into my grandmother's scheme."

"Matchmaking?"

"Aunt Ida Mae is Grandma's partner-in-crime. Be glad my sister-in-law Risa isn't here or we'd be dealing with a trio instead of a duo."

He wanted to wipe the embarrassment from Bailey's eyes. Though he liked the cute blush on her cheeks. "Hey, no one dragged me. I'm curious about the painting class. Might be something to add to our guest offerings. And I'm honored your grandmother approves of me. Even if we both know nothing will happen between us with the inn's ownership at stake."

Relief filled Bailey's gaze. "You're really being nice about this."

Crap. Justin rocked back on his heels. Inn or not, he didn't want her to think of him as nice. Sexy, handsome, not nice. "How else would I be? I get a night where I'm the only man in a roomful of women."

"Into cougars?"

"These ladies might be considered lionesses."

"Word of warning." Bailey leaned toward him. Her warm breath against his neck made his pulse hiccup. "Don't let any of them hear you or they might attack."

He laughed, trying not to think about her lips so close to his ear. "I'll be careful. So, what's going to be happening during the class?"

She stepped back. "You want to do this?"

"I so want to do this, even if my painting will look like something a preschooler made. No laughing, okay?"

"Promise. Though am I allowed a giggle or two?"

The light in her eyes brightened her face. He wanted to snap a picture of her to capture the moment. She looked so happy.

"Three giggles," he said. "That's all."

"I can live with three."

He'd never understood people who danced without music, but he wanted to take her in his arms and swing her into a dip. He shook the crazy thought from his head, then noticed she wore an oversize sandal on her left foot. "You're wearing a shoe."

"Sort of. This one belongs to Grady. Never thought his big feet would come in handy, but they have this time. I can't wait to wear my own."

"You look great. Better than the last time."

"Thanks. My foot's healing." She glanced around the room, not meeting his gaze.

He wanted her to look at him. "Animal Control hasn't found that dog. They've had reports for a few weeks now."

Bailey's gaze met his. "Poor dog. I thought for sure he'd be in the shelter, maybe adopted by now."

"I've looked, but not seen him again." He took a quick

sip of his wine. "If I find him, I'll let you know. So to-night…"

"We socialize at the beginning. After that, everyone takes a seat. Each person has a canvas on an easel and supplies at a spot. Just follow the directions and at the end, you'll have a completed painting. We have dessert before heading home."

"Sounds easy."

"Painting is easy and fun." She glanced at the clock on the mantel. Her lips parted, making a perfect O. "I need to get the class started or we'll be here all night."

Spending all night with Bailey sounded good to Justin. He watched her cross the room, a sexy sway to her hips. If she was still limping, he didn't notice.

"Take your seats, everyone," she said. "Put on your aprons. It's time to begin."

Maybe after the class finished he could convince Bailey he needed private instruction. Not here, but back at her place, the two of them and a leftover bottle of Chardonnay and a few of the chocolate-dipped strawberries. Playful images filled his mind. He sipped the cool wine to keep his temperature from rising.

Would Bailey say yes? Or turn him down cold?

Wait a minute. He wasn't looking for romance. A relationship was the last thing he wanted.

Stop with all the r-*words.*

He downed the wine in his glass.

Focus.

He'd allowed himself to get worked up over Bailey because of not seeing her for a week. Now that he'd seen her…

No big deal, he told himself. All he had to do was concentrate on painting. Chat with the nice old ladies. Then he could return to his room at the B and B.

Alone.

Chapter Seven

"Ready to have fun tonight?" Bailey loved sharing her love of painting with people. These social art-and-wine events were a fun way to do that. She smiled at the eleven Garden Club members, women she'd known her entire life, sitting at the four rectangular tables her brothers had set up this afternoon.

Her gaze met Justin's. Held. His blue shirt brought out his eyes, deepened the color. Not quite cobalt…

Aunt Ida Mae coughed.

Oops. Bailey looked away. She hadn't expected to see him here. She'd been trying to forget about him, but the memory of his kiss lingered on her lips. She needed to focus.

"I've picked out a fun floral project." She lifted her sample from behind one of her supply bins and kept the painted side away from the guests. "I'll give you a clue what type of flower you'll be painting. Holland."

"Tulips," a woman named Sharon shouted.

"That's right." Bailey turned the canvas to show them her rendition of a Dutch-inspired landscape of a tulip field and optional wooden clogs in the front with a windmill. People would use her design to make their own. "This is what you'll be painting."

The Garden Club members oohed and aahed.

Justin peered around the canvas on his easel. "Wow. You did an amazing job."

Bailey ignored the urge to stand taller. His opinion didn't matter. But she wanted everyone, including him, to enjoy the project.

Mabel snickered. "Maybe you should think about becoming a painter instead of using your wrecking ball to destroy lives. My son worked the inn's front desk for thirty-three years. My granddaughter was a server there for five. Now they're on unemployment and trying to find new jobs."

Other women nodded or mumbled their agreement. Justin's smile no longer looked natural. Bailey wanted to say something, but she was supposed to be looking out for the inn, not comforting the man who wanted to destroy it. She clutched her canvas.

Aunt Ida Mae touched his shoulder. Her reassuring smile seemed to help Justin. The lines around his mouth relaxed.

Bailey needed to get these women painting ASAP. "Let's get started."

She instructed the class on sketching the design, then adding the first layer of paint. She discussed mixing colors, as well as techniques for loading brushes. She made her way to each table, watching first splashes of color appear on blank canvases. This was not a paint-by-numbers course. Here, creativity reigned.

"That's lovely, Faye." Bailey loved seeing how her friend, a sculptor, added texture with the paint. She moved on to the next person. "Great use of color, Mabel."

Getting around to each person wasn't easy with Bailey's injured foot, but she moved better today than this past weekend. Progress. She explained the next steps.

"Any questions on painting flower stems?" she asked.

Brushes in hand, the class set to work on their canvases, ignoring the full wineglasses sitting next to them. Plenty of time to socialize later.

Bailey returned to the three seated at the first table. She glimpsed the back of Justin's head, two rows in front of her.

Why was he here? Boredom? Maybe. Curiosity? She could see that. To annoy her? Most definitely. But a part of her—make that a small part—was happy to see him.

Bailey pointed to a flower on Darla Watson's canvas. "I like the shading you've done. If you use an even darker color along this edge, the flower will have more of a 3-D effect."

She continued on to the second table, then the third. Aunt Ida Mae sat next to Justin, no doubt trying to be her grandmother's ears and eyes during the painting class.

"Love the golden flowers, Aunt Ida Mae. Not maize, more like saffron. I also like the ochre shading with the pale yellow. The colors will match the breakfast room at your B and B."

"That's exactly where this one will go, dear." She worked on one of the stems. "Though I can't decide between a black and a white frame."

"I have some you can try and see which you like best." Bailey glanced at Justin's canvas, did a double take, gasped. She'd expected straight lines and a symmetrical design, given his architectural background. But this work of art brought a sense of wonder and awe. How could he have done this? Made her feel this way?

Her gaze traveled from the painting to Justin. "I thought you only painted walls."

He lowered his brush, stared up at her. The dazed look in his eyes spoke of being totally lost in his little world.

That was what she called being so into her work she forgot about everything else.

"Huh?" The surprise in his voice matched the confusion on his face. "I'm sorry. What did you say?"

Bailey recognized his clouded gaze and disorientation. She moved closer and gave him another minute. "You said you didn't paint."

"I don't. Unless you're talking construction." He used his brush to paint a pink tulip. "But I must admit, this is almost meditative. Stress-relieving."

"You know what you're doing," she said, trying to keep the emotion out of her voice. His painting affected her not only as a teacher, but an art lover. She didn't want to be impressed, but she couldn't help herself. Unlike other students, he'd used different colors for the flowers. No monochrome fields and rows. He painted the flowers with no pattern whatsoever.

He looked over his shoulder at her. "Thanks, but I'm using the trial-and-error method, one step above paint by numbers."

"Could have fooled me." She pointed to the top of his canvas. "I love how you used smoother strokes for the sky, then short, choppier ones that added texture to the tulip field. Your windmill is elaborate and realistic. Especially the perspective with the lattice-framework sails. They look like they'd spin off the canvas if I blew hard enough. You're a natural. I knew an architect could draw, but this…"

Okay, he'd talked about shabby chic that first day at her cottage. Justin knew who Anubis was, but he seemed more left-brain, a straight-lines-and-angles kind of guy.

"That's because I have a good teacher," he said.

"You have talent." Raw, sure, but that was part of the charm. His eye for color was first-rate. "The way you shadowed the flower stems is perfect. They look like they're blowing in the wind."

"Your directions were clear. I just added paint."

"There's nothing about art that involves just adding paint." Bailey peered over his shoulder, wanting a closer look. She touched his back, then realized what she was doing and stepped back. "I'd better see how everyone else is doing."

Walking away, she pretended not to notice Aunt Ida Mae staring at her with a can't-wait-to-see-what-happens smile. Grandma, too.

Bailey's stomach did a cartwheel. She'd given Justin attention for his painting, but the gray-haired matchmaking Mafia would exaggerate. Embellish. Embarrass.

This was part of being a Cole and living in Haley's Bay. For better or worse, her family cared. But how was she ever going to meet a guy, let alone date, with so many busybodies around? Not that she was interested in dating Justin. But if she were…

Grandma carried a bottle of Chardonnay and topped off people's glasses. "Want a refill on your wine, Bailey?"

She'd had a couple of sips to check the bottles when she'd opened them, but didn't drink while teaching. A good thing. She needed to be fully cognizant around Justin with her grandmother watching. Now that she saw his hidden talent, she was amazed and more attracted to him. "No, thanks. I'll stick to the sparkling cider."

"Sweet and bubbly." Aunt Ida Mae's lips spread into a curious smile. "You don't want to act silly or make googly eyes."

Her aunt spoke to Bailey as if she were fifteen and knew nothing about boys. Get a little wine in Aunt Ida Mae, and she was the one who got goofy. Bailey hoped Justin wasn't watching and couldn't hear.

She didn't dare glance his way. That would only play in to their shenanigans. She had never wanted a class to be finished early until tonight. "No worries about me doing either of those things."

"Too bad." Justin studied her as if she were a painting and he was analyzing the artist's usage of design and color. People looked at her all the time, and she'd been staring at him moments ago, but his appraisal bothered her. She shifted on the couch. Not wanting to care what he thought, but wishing she knew at the same time. "I was hoping to see some goofiness tonight."

Darn the man. He was playing along. She stuck her tongue out at him. "There you go."

Instead of waiting for a response, she headed toward the food table.

His laugh echoed behind her.

A ball of heat settled at the center of her chest and spread outward.

Don't say a word. Don't cause a scene.

She checked the desserts, plates and napkins. Sliced brownies, chocolate-covered strawberries and Snicker-doodle cookies filled a three-tiered serving dish. Leave it to Grandma to go overboard.

Bailey sensed Justin's presence behind her. Her nerve endings tingled with anticipation. Crazy, since the two were in a room with eleven other women.

She straightened the stack of napkins. No turning around or she might end up making googly eyes.

"I finished the painting." His voice rumbled over her, low and rich, delicious like the sweets on the table. "Earned my dessert."

"You did." She stepped to get out of his way, but he went in the same direction. She brushed against his chest. Fireworks exploded, surprising her with their intensity. She stumbled.

He placed his hands on her waist. "Be careful. Don't reinjure yourself."

Bailey nodded, not trusting her voice.

"I may have to try another," he said.

"Cookie?" she squeaked, aware of his hands touching her, even though she was standing fine now. Problem was, she didn't mind all that much. Everything she thought she knew about Justin McMillian was proving her wrong each time she saw him. His possessive touch ignited a flame deep in her belly. Her lips ached for another kiss. *Stop thinking about his kisses.* "There are plenty of cookies."

"I'm talking about another painting class."

"Oh." Being so close to him unsettled Bailey. At any moment, she might win the klutz-of-the-year award. Walking seemed hard around him. Sure, her foot made her clumsy, but her awareness of him made a simple task ten times harder. She didn't like that. "You should."

He let go of her waist, reached around her and snagged a Snickerdoodle. "Though I'm not going to turn down one of these."

His lips closed over the cookie. She watched him take a bite, wishing he was nibbling her.

What was wrong with her? Only a week had passed since he'd been at her cottage. Seeing him tonight was nothing, and no more kisses were on the horizon.

Talk to him about...his painting. Yeah, that would take her mind off his lips.

"Do you know where you're going to display your painting?" she asked.

"Probably my office. I'm there more than I'm home, unless I'm out in the field."

She took a cookie. Maybe the sugar would quench her craving for, well, him. "Must be hard being away from home so much."

"Part of the job."

"Your family..."

"We don't see much of each other because of work. Right

now Rainey is in Gold Beach on the southern Oregon coast redoing the interiors of a resort. My parents are at a property in Cannon Beach. Paige is holding down the fort in Lincoln City."

"Do you ever get together?"

"Not often. Everything in my family has always revolved around the business. Even when we were kids."

How sad. She couldn't imagine. "What about holidays and birthdays?"

"Sometimes, but holidays are big business when you're in the resort industry. Birthdays can be celebrated anytime."

She remembered having to work holidays at the inn, but she'd gotten off in time to attend her family's gathering here at Grandma's. "I forgot about that part."

"You'll remember quickly if you own an inn."

"I do own one. Well, half of one, for now."

"Funny, so do I. For now." His smoldering look sent her pulse into the stratosphere. "We have two choices. Remain serious or try silly."

Stay in control. "Silly is always more fun than serious. But the last time I made a fool of myself in front of a man, I was mistaken for a psychotic clown. That left horrible scars."

He brushed strands of hair from her face, and she almost swooned. "I don't see any."

"Internal scars, not external ones." She noticed women standing up. Her grandma said something to Aunt Ida Mae, pointed and smiled. That satisfied expression on her grandmother's face meant one thing—more matchmaking. "Dessert time."

"I'd better grab a brownie and get out of the ladies' way."

He did, then moved toward the tables with the easels. A part of Bailey wished he'd stayed, but then again, after Mabel's outburst, she didn't blame him for retreating.

Grandma came closer, leaned her head toward Bailey's and whispered, "Go talk to him."

"I just was talking to him."

"Not enough." Grandma placed a brownie in a napkin, then handed it to Bailey. "Give this to Justin. The way to a man's heart is through his stomach. Is he a good kisser?"

Bailey stared at her grandmother in disbelief. "That's not something I want to discuss."

"The night's still young, dear," Aunt Ida Maid said. "The two of you could have a lot of fun before the sun rises."

"Go for it," Faye encouraged. "If you can forget about the inn. If I were twenty years younger…make that forty."

The women laughed.

"Well, if you don't go over to him," Sharon said, "some of us will. He might like mature women."

"I'm game."

"Me, too."

Bailey wasn't going to say a word. She couldn't. Gossip would be raging in the morning, possibly by bedtime.

Brownie in hand, Bailey made a beeline for the other side of the room, wanting distance from everyone. She didn't need the Garden Club's advice about Justin. She didn't need to be pushed into talking to him. What she needed was chocolate.

She bit into the brownie.

This would have to do. For now.

Three hours later, Justin folded the legs of the last table. He and Bailey were the only ones still at Lilah's. No one had asked him to stay, but Bailey's pale face and the circles under her eyes bothered him. He wanted to make sure she didn't do any heavy lifting.

"Where do the tables go?" he asked.

"In the storage room, but Declan will be here in a few

minutes to help and then drive Bailey home." Lilah swept the hardwood floor. "It'll go faster with the two of you."

Declan, one of the brothers who would mess up Justin's face if he got too close to their sister.

"Should I be worried about meeting another one of your brothers?" he asked Bailey in a lighthearted tone, hoping he could squeeze a smile from her tired face.

She sat on the floor and packed away her supplies in two large plastic containers. She didn't look up at him. "Not if you behave yourself."

He had touched her at the dessert table. Having his hand around her waist felt natural. She hadn't seemed to mind. At least he hadn't kissed her, though he'd been tempted once. Maybe twice. Okay, a lot of times. But he knew better without an invitation.

"I always behave myself. But you might not agree with the behavior."

Bailey tilted her head toward Lilah, who seemed to be working extra hard sweeping imaginary crumbs. A not-now look followed.

The door opened, then closed. A twenty-something man wearing shorts, a ripped T-shirt and flip-flops entered the room. He looked like a modern-day pirate with a scruff of whiskers, shoulder-length dark hair and tattoos on his arms. He had green eyes like the other Cole siblings.

The guy gave Justin the once-over, didn't look impressed by what he saw. "You the resort guy who wants to tear down my sister's inn?"

That summed up the situation succinctly if you happened to be a Cole.

Bailey hung her head. "Declan…"

"I'm Justin McMillian, resort guy."

"Declan Cole, fishing guy and boxer." He didn't extend his arm. Must not be a shaking-hands type. "You an artist or do you just like hanging with older ladies…and my sister?"

"I'm not an artist. Architect." Justin kept his tone light. This guy didn't just talk tough. He was rough 'n' tumble and ready to fight, the kind of man you didn't mess with in a bar or anywhere. "Your aunt invited me. I'm staying at her B and B. But I must admit the Garden Club ladies are a fun bunch."

Declan cracked his knuckles. "And my sister?"

"An excellent artist and instructor."

Lilah stepped forward. "Justin's quite a painter, isn't he, Bailey?"

She looked up. "Yes, very talented. Surprised the hell out of me."

Lilah gasped.

Declan laughed.

Justin smiled. He could always count on Bailey being honest.

The front door opened. Grady or Ellis must be making an appearance. Justin looked at the doorway to see which brother had arrived. Tyler Cole entered. He wore dress slacks and a button-down shirt. No tie or jacket, but he looked as though he might have come straight from work in those clothes.

"Tyler." Lilah sounded surprised to see him. "What are you doing here?"

The lawyer rolled up his sleeves. "Thought I'd help move the furniture back in."

"Wonderful, wonderful." Lilah rubbed her hands together. She looked at her two grandsons. "Have you boys eaten?"

"No," Declan and Tyler said at the same time.

"I'll heat up dinner." With that, Lilah scurried from the room as if she were about to feed royalty.

Justin assumed that was how the woman saw her grandchildren. He loved seeing the family dynamic between the Coles. Ever since arriving in Haley's Bay, he hadn't felt like hired help, which was how his parents treated him and his sisters. Not only now, but when they'd been younger, too. What Justin wouldn't give for a family like Bailey's...

Tyler's gaze narrowed. He looked at Justin. "You decide to help out, too?"

The lawyer's less-than-curious tone suggested he knew Justin was going to be here. Those old ladies spread gossip faster than bees scattered pollen in the springtime. No wonder Bailey was so worried.

He wouldn't be deterred. "I attended the paint night, figured Lilah might need an extra hand moving tables. Didn't realize the Cole cavalry was riding in."

Bailey looked up from her storage. "The cavalry better be polite to the guests."

Her words didn't contain a warning, but a threat.

Hard-nosed and in your face, yes. But he liked that about Bailey.

Declan and Tyler exchanged a glance. Something was going on, but Justin didn't know what.

"Want to help me carry the tables to the storage room?" Declan asked him.

Justin picked up the one closest to him. "Lead the way."

Bailey stood. "I'll help."

"No," he and Declan said at the same time.

Justin motioned to Bailey. "Sit on the bar stool and relax. You've been on your feet too long."

Declan's chin jutted forward. He pointed to Justin. "Do what he says. Or you won't like the consequences."

Bailey's lips curved downward. She looked not only tired, but also fed up.

At least Justin might get out of here with his face intact. Spending an evening with Bailey and learning to paint was worth whatever happened to him. And his face.

He raised a table. "So, where do these go?"

* * *

Bailey put her paint tubes in the plastic supply box. Her foot hurt, so sitting on the floor was the best position for now. She'd caught a glimpse of Justin leaving the room from her peripheral vision. She hadn't wanted to look at him. Not when Declan seemed ready to pounce if Justin said the wrong word. And Tyler…

She glanced at him. "Why are you really here?"

Her cousin stood over her, casting a large shadow. "Mabel Sawyer called me. Told me McMillian was getting chummy with the other co-owner of the Broughton Inn. Thought I'd want to know."

"Did you?"

"Yes."

The one word spoke volumes. The kissing, the low-key flirting and her attraction to the man suddenly felt naughty and wrong.

"Why?" she asked.

"The inn."

"Tonight had nothing to do with the inn. Mabel is the one who mentioned it. And rather rudely, if you ask me."

"You shouldn't be around Justin without legal counsel present. That's me, in case you forgot."

"I know that."

Tyler kneeled. "You're an attractive woman, Bay. A guy like McMillian might try to take advantage of you. Put undue influence on you to gain possession of the inn."

Her cousin made her sound like an idiot. "I'm not some naive person, ready to be taken in by a scam artist from a developing country."

"I know that, but the last thing you want is an impropriety. You've got people counting on you. Any kind of conflict of interest is going to look bad."

"I didn't invite him tonight. That was Aunt Ida Mae and Grandma's doing."

"Matchmaking?"

Bailey nodded. "Single men between the ages of twenty-five and forty seem to be her target. Justin falls squarely in that range."

"I'll talk to Grandma, but you can't see Justin outside of any meetings I set up."

She rearranged the paint tubes in the box. "We haven't discussed the inn."

"Doesn't matter." Tyler's voice sharpened. "Got it?"

She nodded, even if her cousin's—make that her *lawyer*'s request—seemed harsh. She'd wanted distance from Justin. Looked as though she got her wish. So, why did she want another wish to come true instead?

Glong. Glong. D-ding-a-ting-glong.

The sound woke Bailey. She rubbed her eyes. The bells continued to chime. She needed to change her ring tone to something else.

Light filtered in around the window blinds. Bailey glanced at the clock—7:23 a.m. She yawned, stretching her arms over her head.

Better not be Tyler again telling her to stay away from Justin McMillian as if she were sixteen. Her cousin had loaded her art supplies and driven her home before anyone returned. She hadn't even said good-night to Grandma or to Justin.

Bailey's family needed to get out of her personal life, the conflict of interest about the inn aside.

She glanced at her cell phone on the nightstand. No name and an unfamiliar number. The 541 area code belonged to Oregon. "Hello."

"It's Justin."

Hearing his voice brought a smile to her face. Not a bad way to start her day. Except she shouldn't care if he called or be smiling when he did, at least according to Tyler. "How did you get my number?"

"An internet search on your Chardonnay and Canvas events. Sorry to call so early, but I might know where the stray dog has been hiding."

She sat. "Where?"

"The yard of an old deserted house on Bay Street."

"Mr. Potter's place. It's been deserted since he passed fifteen years ago. His son in Boise owns the house, but he hasn't been back to Haley's Bay since the funeral. The overgrowth could hide a family of five."

"Or a stray?" Justin asked.

"Definitely."

"When I was driving home from your grandmother's last night, I saw something—looked like the stray—dart into the yard. I stopped, but it was too dark to see anything."

"Last night is a long time from today when you're talking about a stray dog."

"I know." He hesitated. "I drove by this morning. I didn't see him, but it's worth taking a look."

She glanced at the clock again. "Have you called Animal Control?"

"They haven't had much luck, given all the sightings."

"So, are you going to give Animal Rescue a try?"

"Thinking about it."

She had to give him kudos, given his lack of dog experience. But she'd seen last night how much more there was to Justin McMillian. Still, she didn't want him to fail. For the dog's sake. "Need help?"

"That's why I'm calling. I've never had a pet. I know dogs bark and wag their tails and shouldn't be fed chocolate. I could use someone with dog knowledge."

Tyler's words about staying away from Justin echoed through Bailey's head. But an image of the dirty, skinny dog was there, too. Right next to one of Justin.

Focus on the dog. Who had probably taken off for some-where else by now. She bit her lip. "When?"

"Ten minutes."

Not the answer she expected. She glanced down at her nightshirt, touched her tangled hair. But if there was any chance they could help the dog… "Sure. I'll be ready."

Bailey disconnected from the call. She thought about texting Tyler, but he would tell her not to go. Better to keep quiet and apologize later if someone happened to see her. She hoped no one did.

Crawling out of bed, she remembered her plan for today—painting. Oh, well…how long could catching a dog and going to the shelter take?

Chapter Eight

Eleven minutes later, Justin pulled into Bailey's driveway. He hadn't expected her to be ready, given that she sounded as though he'd woken her up, let alone waiting for him on her front step. Yet there she was. The woman continued to surprise him.

Bailey wore a pair of faded jeans that hugged her hips. The bottom of a blue shirt hung out of her green fleece jacket. Cute. Typical Northwest attire and perfect for being outside this morning. There was no heavy coastal fog, but the temperature was cooler than yesterday when he'd gone for a run in shorts and tennis shoes.

He jumped out to open the passenger door for her. "Good morning. I swung by the Java Cup. There's a coffee in the cab for you."

"Thanks."

Her lopsided ponytail bounced. She climbed into the truck. "I hope the dog didn't wander off again."

Her voice held a note of worry, but something else…anxiety. She sounded…impatient. He wanted to make her feel better, but a hug or another kiss seemed wrong right now.

He'd asked for her help. He didn't want to take advantage of her.

"Me, too." He climbed into the cab, backed the truck out of the driveway, caught a glimpse of Bailey biting her lip.

The gesture gave her up. He'd learned to read tells and Bailey was an open book. "Your foot okay?"

"Almost good as new." No relief over her recovery showed on her face. Only worry.

He drove toward the bay. "You look…stressed."

"I'll feel better once we get the dog."

The dog was a means to an end for Justin, a way of spending time with Bailey. Seeing her this morning was a great way to start his day. Maybe they could grab breakfast after they took care of the dog.

"There is something you should know." She picked up her coffee from the truck's drink holder. "Tyler told me not to see you without legal counsel present. That means him."

Justin tightened his fingers around the steering wheel.

"He's concerned about a conflict of interest and jeopardizing the inn," she added.

"Seems strange he didn't say this before."

"Mabel contacted him after the paint night."

"I remember Mabel."

Bailey flicked her fingernail against the cup's sleeve. "I'm sure you do."

"Mabel has a reason to be upset. I get that."

She looked at him. "You do?"

"Yeah. Usually by the time I start working on a place, time has passed. Employees are long gone. But jobs are difficult to find these days. No one wants to see loved ones out of work."

He sure didn't. But the longer the question of the inn's ownership dragged on, being fired by his parents seemed more likely. His mom and dad were the dream destroyers. Or would be when the pink slips got handed out.

Once the company was sold, Justin had no doubt his sisters would move to bigger cities with more job opportunities. Portland, Seattle, maybe San Francisco. He'd never see them or his parents, who wanted to spend their retirement traveling the globe. All would leave Lincoln City without a glance back, the way Taryn had left.

Not Justin. He might not have a hometown where he grew up, but he considered the entire coast home. He wasn't leaving. He'd find a way to keep his family together and show them work wasn't everything. Maybe they could be more like the Coles, watching Sunday football games and eating dinner.

If only they could locate Floyd Jeffries… But the man seemed to have disappeared. No sign of him, his shady girlfriend or the money. Private investigators were searching, and half-jokingly said the pair was probably on some tropical island sipping cocktails.

"Mabel shouldn't have run to Tyler like a tattletale."

"So I shouldn't call Tyler and tell him you're with me?"

Bailey tightened her ponytail. "This is about the stray dog, not the inn."

Yes, but her hunched shoulders weren't normal. Everything from her facial expression to her posture looked off. "I know your family means a lot to you. I don't want to make this harder on you. Let's agree not to mention the *I-N-N*, okay?"

"Sounds good." She took a sip of the coffee. "This hits the spot."

"I'm on my second cup." He'd needed more caffeine. He hadn't slept well. Too much thinking about Bailey and painting.

He parked his truck in front of 717 Bay Street. Weeds

and twenty-five-foot-tall overgrowth hid whatever house might be on the property. "Ready to go dog-hunting?"

Bailey placed her coffee back in the cup holder. She pulled two plastic baggies from her jacket pocket and handed one to Justin. "I watch Declan's dog, Chinook, when he goes out of town. I brought some of her treats for the stray."

Justin tucked the bag into his pocket. "I knew I called the right person."

"I'm guessing I was your only choice."

"There was Animal Control, but you're cuter."

She smiled, unbuckled her seat belt. "Cuter or not, don't know that we'll have better luck than them."

"They look for lots of animals. We only need to find one."

A twisted gate hung on one hinge barely attached to a dilapidated, fence post with its paint peeling. Two-thirds of the fence was cracked or missing. What once was lawn gave way to a jungle of huge shrubbery, a mix of green and brown, up to his neck.

"Can't imagine anyone wanting to live here," he said.

"Some animals don't have a choice. They have nowhere to go. Every day is a fight to find food to eat and survive. Chinook was a rescue dog living in a hoarder situation, but you'd never know it looking at her now."

By the time Justin rounded the truck to help Bailey from the cab, she was already at the gate. She gave a push.

The hinge creaked.

She jerked her hand away, looked at him. "I can't believe the gate didn't fall off."

"Failure looks imminent."

"The gate, yes. Too soon to know about the dog." Bailey stepped through, her feet tromping on weeds providing a strange backdrop, but she looked beautiful in the morning light. "Here we are. Two enemies blazing a trail like Lewis and Clark."

"I'd say we're more like frenemies."

"I can go with that."

She tripped on a root but caught herself before he could act. His smile faded at the missed chance to touch her.

"Be careful," he warned.

"I'm trying, but this place is a jungle." She headed toward the left. "If I remember correctly, the backyard is this way."

He eyed the two-foot-wide passage through the plants. If Bailey was game, so was he.

Halfway in, a wayward branch scratched his jacket. No rip, but a mark remained. Walking through the tall walls of weeds reminded him of the corn mazes at pumpkin patches, only this wasn't planned. "I hope the dog is here. Somewhere."

The gap narrowed ahead. Bailey walked sideways. "I remember a staircase that leads to the back deck. We can stand up there and look for him."

Justin followed her up the steps, enjoying the view from behind. This was his first time seeing her in jeans. He wouldn't mind trading places with the denim cupping her butt. Sexy and a turn-on.

She stood at a wooden rail. "The backyard is worse than the front, but maybe we can see the dog walking around."

He stopped next to her. A view of the bay greeted him.

"Wow." If the Broughton Inn had a million-dollar view, this one was worth double. Given the waterfront location, this property was a find. "I wonder why Mr. Potter's son hasn't sold his dad's old house."

"Wanting to buy up the entire town now?" Her voice sounded stiff, almost suspicious.

"Curious, that's all."

Justin's father had taught him to keep his hand hidden

from both friend and foe. The distance to the water and elevation of the bluff where the house sat was far enough to stave off high tide or storm surges. He estimated the lot size to be a quarter of the Broughton Inn, but the bay frontage more than compensated and a smaller rolling lawn could be added.

"Any sign of the dog?" she asked.

He'd forgotten their reason for coming. He scanned the yard. "No, but I'll take a closer look."

That would give him a chance to get a better feel of the slope to the shoreline. He wondered if he could find the exact dimensions of the lot on one of the town websites.

"I don't see the dog." Bailey sounded disappointed. "Here, puppy."

No dog appeared.

The breeze tossed the ends of her ponytail about. She shook her bag of dog treats. Nothing. She gave the bag another shake. No movement below. She whistled.

Bailey's gaze met his. "I don't think he's here."

"Look at the brush down there. If he's skittish…"

"I just wish we could find him." Her lips parted slightly, pink and soft and smooth.

He needed another taste of her, a longer one. "I wish…"

"What do you wish?" she asked.

He lowered his mouth to hers. Slowly. To give her time to decide if she wanted a kiss or not.

She didn't say no or back away. Justin took that as a yes.

He covered her mouth with his, the urge to kiss her stronger than common sense.

Her kiss was as sweet and as warm as he remembered, a tasty confection he wanted to devour. His lips moved over hers, but he kept his hands at his side. He'd made the first move. Twice now. He was leaving the next one up to Bailey.

This time she didn't stiffen, but leaned into him. Her muscles remained loose. She pressed against his lips, kissing him back. Her eagerness surprised. Now, this was a real turn-on.

Heat roared through his veins.

Her hands didn't touch him. Lips locked together, but nothing else.

He wasn't complaining. Her kiss was as spectacular as she was. Unique. Perfect.

She wrapped her arms around him finally. Her breasts pressed against his chest.

He circled his arms around her, pulling her closer. This was what he wanted. All he needed.

A moan escaped her lips. She backed away from him, her eyes clouded, her lips swollen.

"Kissing isn't going to help us find the dog." Her tone was stunned, amused.

He'd take it. "No, but consider the kiss a warm-up for our search."

"You think we needed one?"

He shrugged. "When it comes to you, I have no idea what we need."

She'd crashed into his life like a runaway train. Okay, she'd been standing there, unmovable, but he hadn't been the same since that morning at the inn.

Justin knew one thing…he was happy he'd kissed her again. "I do know this kiss was better than the first one. I can't wait to see how the next one turns out."

Bailey's mouth gaped. She was speechless, a memorable occurrence.

He bit back a smile. "I'm going to check down below. Care to join me?"

Join him? The man had some nerve. That was the last thing Bailey wanted to do. Her ragged breathing matched her rapid pulse. Cheeks burning, she didn't want to acknowledge how much she'd wanted to keep kissing Justin.

Her lips didn't tingle. They throbbed. Her body ached for more.

She clutched the deck railing, thankful the weathered wood was smooth beneath her palms, not full of splinters. Her skin felt hypersensitive as it was.

What had she done? And what was she going to do now?

Justin McMillian had kissed her again, unexpectedly and thoroughly, as if she were his to command with a touch of his lips. Worse, she had been willing, eager, hungry. Responding to him like a woman starved for kisses. She'd wanted to gobble him up. A part of her still did.

Stupid. Stupid. Stupid.

For all she knew, her reaction was exactly the response he wanted. Tyler's warning seemed more ominous postkiss. Nothing good would come from spending time with Justin. Conflict of interest. Uh, yeah. Kissing was not exactly professional behavior. The inn's staff and their families were counting on her to win.

She needed to keep her distance from him and keep her guard up. He could be playing her. Why wouldn't he? A charming hotelier and construction hottie who oozed sex appeal must be good at that kind of game.

Thank goodness she'd remembered the dog or she might still be kissing him. And happily enjoying the kisses.

She tightened her grip on the railing. Her gaze narrowed on Justin heading down the stairs. He looked like a fashion model, handsome in his worn jeans, Henley shirt and flannel jacket. His boots were durable enough to withstand the weeds and rocks below. Handsome, check. Capable, check. Under control, check.

The opposite of her.

The urge to bolt was strong. So what if doing so would be rude? But she doubted she could walk home without doing some serious damage to her foot, and she had the dog to consider.

Justin waved from the bottom of the staircase. "I want to see if the dog is by the shoreline. Come on down if your foot's up to it."

Her foot was fine. Her heart, she wasn't sure.

Bailey gave him a half wave but didn't answer. Her nerve endings jangled as if they were dancing and wanted a new song.

He disappeared into the weeds.

She breathed a sigh of relief. A second kiss changed nothing. This was a spur-of-the-moment action brought on by worry over the dog. Once they found the stray or confirmed he wasn't here, she wouldn't see Justin until another meeting at Tyler's office or in a courtroom. That made the most logical—

"Bailey," Justin shouted. The way he said her name made her stomach drop. "I need your help."

His words rushed out.

Concern shot through her. She hurried down the staircase and followed his path, mindful of her foot. The mix of weeds and rocks and uneven ground made walking difficult, but she didn't slow down. "Justin?"

"Over here."

A moan.

The deep guttural noise prickled the hair on the back of her neck. "Are you okay?"

"I found the dog. He's stuck in some rocks. Hurt."

Oh, no. Picking up her pace, she followed the sound of Justin's voice talking to the dog until she found him, one knee on the ground. He steadied the dog's head with his hands. The scruffy dog lay next to him, barely moving, covered in mud and dirt and burrs. So thin. Her heart broke.

"I freed a leg that was caught between two rocks, but there's a bad gash on his back leg. He doesn't have much strength."

She kneeled and let the dog sniff her hand. "Hey, pup."

A lick was her reward.

"What a sweetie." She removed her jacket and covered the animal, careful to avoid the injured leg. "You're a nice doggy."

The dog's tail wagged.

"That's a good sign," she said. "How did you end up here?"

"No collar."

"A vet can check for a microchip. That's the easiest way to see if he has, or had, an owner."

Justin scratched behind the dog's ear. "You're going to be fine, buddy."

Bailey hoped so. She rubbed the dog's dirty face. "Some doggies don't like to go to the vet, but you look brave."

Justin looked over at her, an odd expression on his face. "You're good at this."

"I watch Chinook and babysit my niece and nephew." Bailey eyed the wound on the dog's injured leg. "We need to get to the vet now. You carry the dog. I'll call to let them know we're coming."

"Come here, buddy." He picked up the dog.

The stray yelped, a pathetic sound that physically hurt Bailey to hear; then a soft whine emerged, constant, but fading.

Justin cradled the dog as if he were a fragile, premature baby, only bigger and covered with fur.

His tenderness and concern melted her heart. Nothing solid remained, only a warm puddle. He might not have had a pet before, but he was kind and gentle and caring with the dog. She had a feeling he would be the same way with children.

With their children. Her pulse quickened. Everything she'd dreamed of having suddenly felt in reach. All because of this poor stray dog.

He continued to talk to the dog.

Cell phone in hand, she followed Justin to the stairs. "I'm calling Declan's vet. It's nearby."

The dog rested its head on Justin's arm. The whining had become quieter, not more than a whimper.

"Let's hurry." He speeded up. "The pup's not looking so good."

Bailey opened the door to the animal clinic. Justin carried in the dog. A gurney was waiting.

"What happened?" a scrub-clad vet tech asked.

"He's a stray. His paw was caught between rocks. There's a bad gash."

"We'll take a look." She pushed the gurney through a door that closed automatically behind her.

"I need some information about the dog," the receptionist behind the window said. "Name."

"Buddy," Justin said without any hesitation.

"You said the dog's a stray."

He whipped out his wallet and handed the woman a credit card. "As far as we know. Do what needs to be done with him. I'll cover all expenses."

Bailey whispered, "Vet bills can be expensive."

He smiled at her. "I can afford it."

Not only kind and nice, but also generous. Justin's actions warmed her heart. "That's very thoughtful of you."

The receptionist nodded. "Would you mind filling out this treatment authorization form?"

Justin did. Bailey went to sit. The smell of freshly brewed coffee filled the air in the waiting room, slightly masking a lemony-bleach scent. A television hung on the wall, a home-and-garden channel playing with the sound muted. Phones rang and doors opened and closed in the distance.

Bailey sat on an upholstered chair. The thin layer of

padding didn't offer much comfort, but she was in a better place than the dog.

And Justin.

For the next hour and a half, he paced the length of the waiting room, staring at the screen of his smartphone. He'd been checking missing pet websites trying to find info about "Buddy," the name he'd given the dog when they checked in. He'd also contacted Animal Control again, too, who had little information on the dog other than multiple sightings since spring.

The bell on the door sounded. A man entered the clinic with a black Lab on a leash.

Too bad Tyler wasn't here. If her cousin saw Justin in action today, he might change his mind about the guy trying to take advantage of her or exert "undue influence" to get the inn. Okay, she still had concerns. His being worried about a dog wasn't enough to make her dismiss all misgivings, but she liked this side of Justin. Liked it a lot.

He sat next to her. "No one has reported a lost or missing dog that looks like him."

"The vet should know soon if he's got a microchip."

An elderly couple with a meowing cat in a pink carrier checked out at the receptionist counter.

"They're taking a long time. I hope he's okay." Justin stared at the door to the exam area. Lines on his forehead deepened. "I thought we'd hear something by now."

The worry in his voice tugged on Bailey's heart. She reached toward him, then pulled her arm back, resting her hand on her lap.

Yes, she wanted to comfort him, but she was unsure if that was okay or crossing a line or giving him the wrong idea. Boy, that second kiss was messing up her thought process. "We should hear something soon."

Justin rubbed his lips together. "I've never been to a vet office before."

"Tests and X-rays take time. Just like with people," she said. "I'm sure they want to be thorough with the exam and not jump to any conclusions. He looks like he's been on his own for a while."

"Makes sense." He stared at the closed door leading to the exam rooms. "But I wish I could do more."

"You found him. You're paying for his medical treatment. You're doing plenty." Her words didn't change the serious expression on Justin's face. Bailey wished she could bring back his smile. "And this is an excellent vet clinic."

"I knew you'd pick the right place."

She straightened. His words meant more than they should. "Want another cup of coffee?"

"No, thanks."

"The Burger Boat is across the street. I can get sodas or milk shakes."

"Appreciate the offer, but I'm not thirsty." His gaze returned to the closed door. "Buddy's paw didn't look that bad. All he needs is a bath and a few good meals to put some meat on his bones. He'll be fine."

She recognized something in Justin's tone. Years ago, she'd sounded the same way after finding a baby bunny in the field by their house. She'd waited for hours for the mother rabbit to return, but that never happened. She'd begged her parents to let her bring the young bunny home. Instead her father took the bunny to a nearby farm, saying their house was already too much of a zoo. He'd never told her where. She'd cried for days. "You seemed to hit it off with Buddy."

"Yeah, it's weird." The edges of his mouth curved slightly. "I hadn't considered getting a dog. But Buddy's all I can think about. Crazy?"

"Yes, but I'm all for crazy."

His mouth swooped down for a quick kiss. "Figured you would understand."

She was the one smiling now. "I do, but if you're serious, you need to take some time and think about it. Adopting a dog isn't something you do lightly or temporarily. Dogs get attached. They can be expensive and need attention. You'll need to figure out what to do with him when you're at a job site. Or here in Haley's Bay. My aunt doesn't allow pets at her B and B. So there are logistics you'll need to work out. If you're not committed—"

"I am." A surprised expression flashed across his face. "I can't believe I said that."

"Why not?"

"I haven't committed to anything in a long time. But that mangy mutt…"

"Stole your heart."

His gaze met hers. "Yes."

Her heart melted. "Everything happens for a reason. That's what my grandma always says."

Bailey expected him to look away. He didn't.

"This feels…right," Justin continued.

Being with him felt that way. She kissed him. He tasted the same as he had before—delicious, one minute some fresh-from-the-oven baked goods, then a gourmet entrée the next. His warmth seeped into her as if she was home, comfortable and warm, wrapped in a bed of handmade quilts.

His lips took hers, awakening something deep within, a longing for…more. He brought his arm around her back. A fire ignited low in her belly. A wanting heat. She leaned into him to get closer.

A ding sounded. The clinic's door.

Bailey jerked away, nearly falling off her chair, but Justin caught her. A blue carrier was being brought inside. A cat meowed. Next came…

Risa. Her sister-in-law.

No. No. No. Bailey slid down in her chair, wishing the

door to the restroom wasn't next to the receptionist's desk where Risa stood.

"What's wrong?" Justin asked.

Bailey placed her finger at her mouth. "Shh."

By dinnertime, every single Cole, including Tyler and AJ, would know…whatever Risa had seen when she entered the clinic. Bailey didn't want to make this worse.

Risa turned. Her gaze met Bailey's. "What are you doing here?"

"Found an injured dog over on Bay Street." She didn't like the way Risa studied Justin, as if he were on display in a department-store window. "How about you?"

"Annual exam for Skippy." Risa gave Justin another once-over. "Who's your friend?"

He stood and approached her. "I'm Justin McMillian."

Risa looked impressed. "McMillian Resorts?"

Justin nodded, shook her hand.

"I'm Risa Cole. Bailey's sister-in-law."

"She's married to Ellis," Bailey said in case he didn't remember.

"I met your husband last week," Justin said. "He's a lucky guy."

Risa grinned as if she'd won a year's worth of mani-pedis at the nail salon. "Why, thank you. Grandmother Cole was right when she said you were sweet as her graham-cracker pie."

Great. Bailey leaned back. Her head hit the wall. The result—a dull ache.

He was at her side in an instant and touched her shoulder. "You okay?"

"That's Bailey for you. Always acting without thinking." Risa's attention hadn't left Justin, nor had she missed him touching Bailey. "So you're here for the Broughton Inn?"

"I am." He tilted his head toward Bailey. "Except your sister-in-law is trying to get in the way."

Bailey raised her chin. "And I have succeeded."

"For now." His wink caught her off guard.

"Bailey, like all of the Coles, tends to see things from only one side. They'll fight you to the end whether they're right or wrong."

"When have I been wrong?" Bailey asked.

Risa and Justin shared a glance and a smile.

A vet tech called Skippy's name. Risa headed toward the door. She glanced back. "I'll be wanting to talk to you later. Don't do anything I wouldn't do."

The door shut. A call from her mom should be coming in, oh, five or six minutes, followed by one from Grandma.

Laughter gleamed in Justin's eyes. "So that's your grandmother's matchmaking apprentice? Guess I should expect a call for dinner soon?"

His words brought a much-needed smile to Bailey's face.

"Risa is as subtle as your grandmother and great-aunt," he continued. "I was waiting for her to ask my height, weight, IQ and yearly income."

Bailey grimaced. "My family is insane. The women set me up, and the men scare the guys away."

"Does your sister fix people up?"

"No way. Camden's not interested in having a relationship at all. All she cares about is fishing."

"So then it's not the Coles who like setting people up, but the ones who marry into the family."

"I hope that means I'll never become one of them. But related by blood or not, they are family, and I'm stuck with them."

"They care about you."

"In a nosy-I-know-what's-best-for-you way." She thought about kissing him. A flush of heat went up her neck. "Do you think Risa saw us…?"

"No. Only the cat. So unless Skippy can talk or was wearing a GoPro camera to film a cat's view of a vet visit and be the next YouTube sensation, we're safe. Unless you want to kiss me again."

"No way. Not with Risa here. I already know she's going to tell my family I was here with you."

"Could be some major fallout."

"Grandma and Aunt Ida Mae will be happy."

"Don't forget Tyler."

Bailey had. "Oh, no. He's going to flip."

This was not going to be good. For her. She looked at Justin. Or for him.

Chapter Nine

Justin had paced the animal clinic's waiting room so many times he knew the length and width and had a pretty good guestimate of the height. Bailey sat on one of the uncomfortable chairs, a worried expression on her face.

Buddy? Her family? A combination?

All Justin knew was his relief at having Bailey here with him to wait, to hold his hand, to kiss him. If not for Bailey and her family, he doubted he would want to adopt a dog.

Hell, he wasn't even sure what he was going to do with Buddy. But if no owner claimed him and he recovered from whatever they'd spent hours working on him in the back, Justin wanted him.

A forever home. That was what Bailey had called it.

He could do that.

Maybe Buddy would give new meaning to the word "home," too.

A blonde who looked to be in her early thirties and wore

green surgical scrubs entered the waiting room through one of the doors. She carried a clipboard.

"I'm Dr. Nora Hayworth." She had bright green eyes. "You brought in Buddy?"

"Yes." Justin stood and helped Bailey up, not that she needed his assistance, then introduced them. "How is he doing?"

"For what he's likely gone through, he's holding his own. We didn't find a microchip, and Buddy's unaltered."

"Unaltered?" Justin asked.

"Buddy hasn't been neutered. Most owners spay or neuter their animals, which means he's likely abandoned or always been a stray." The vet ran down her notes. "We've cleaned him, run blood tests and taken X-rays. His leg isn't broken, but his wound is infected. He's also underweight and dehydrated. We've given him subcutaneous fluids. Once he's more stable and closer to a proper weight, we can discuss vaccines, heartworm medicine and flea treatment, since we don't have any medical history on him."

Justin's tension lessened. "Whatever he needs."

"So Buddy needs to stay overnight?" Bailey asked.

"Yes, he's been on his own for a long time. Possibly since birth. We can make sure he's hydrated and eating. Small meals are best for now. He's also going to need to wear a cone so his wound can heal properly."

All in all, that didn't sound too bad to Justin. "So, what do I need to do?"

The vet looked at her paperwork. "We can call Animal Control—"

"No," he said quickly. "If the dog doesn't have an owner, I want him."

"Justin's interested in adopting Buddy," Bailey said. "Is there anything about Buddy's personality that he should be aware of?"

"Not that I've seen so far," Dr. Hayworth said. "Buddy's

quite friendly and wants to play. He isn't that old. Based on his teeth, approximately nine months old. Still a puppy. Likes other dogs and cats and gets along well with the vet techs. His behavior indicates a good disposition."

Justin felt as if Buddy had brought home a report card full of A's. "That's what I wanted to hear, Doc."

Bailey nodded. "I wish we knew how he ended up alone and injured."

"Sometimes people don't understand the responsibilities that go with pet ownership. Puppies are cute, but more work than some realize. Or a person picks the wrong breed for their lifestyle. That leads to dogs being given away, dumped or surrendered at shelters. Other times a dog will escape or get lost. Often a stray will have a litter of puppies." Dr. Hayworth looked at her notes again. "Any other questions?"

"None from me." Justin looked at Bailey. "Do you have any?"

"Nope."

He laced his fingers with Bailey's and squeezed. "We're good for now. Thank you."

"Always a pleasure to see a happy ending. You're more than welcome to visit him each day he's here. If there's a change in his condition, we'll contact you. Make sure reception has your number." Dr. Hayworth left the waiting room.

Justin released a loud breath and Bailey's hand. "Sounds like Buddy's going to be okay."

"Great news." Her grin made him feel warm, as if he were still touching her. "Looks like you're a doggy daddy. Congrats."

"I'm going to have to go shopping."

"You have a couple of days."

"Right, but I need to find a place to stay that allows dogs."

"Buddy can stay at my place while you're in town."

Justin straightened. "What about Tyler?"

"This isn't about the inn. Though I'm sure he won't be happy." She tilted his head. "I'll go out when you visit him. That should solve any conflict-of-interest problems."

"I'll want to spend a lot of time with him." Justin would like to spend more time with her, too. "I don't want Tyler to be upset at you."

"I love dog-sitting. This will be fun for me. And that's what I'll tell my cousin."

"Thanks so much." Justin's smile spread across his face. "That'll be better for Buddy than boarding him until I go back to Lincoln City. Especially given his condition. You're the best."

"You are, for giving Buddy a home."

"I need a book on being a dog owner."

"Lots are out there."

He put his arm around her. "Plus, I have you."

Each day, Buddy got stronger, put on weight, healed. Thanks to help from Bonnie, the clinic's receptionist, Bailey timed her visits to avoid Justin. That was the only way to keep Tyler's wrath, Grandma's innuendos and her family's curiosity at bay. Even her mother was asking questions.

After Risa told the entire family at Sunday dinner about seeing Bailey with Justin at the animal clinic, Tyler had given her two more lectures. Not nice ones.

But Bailey had no regrets.

Buddy would be coming to her house soon. No one in her family would know that, a secret she wanted to keep. She crossed her fingers.

Bailey entered the waiting room from the back of the clinic and waved goodbye to Bonnie. "Thanks for the text about when to come in."

"I'll do the same tomorrow." The woman smiled warmly. "Though I don't know how much longer he'll be here."

"I'm getting my house ready." That meant dog-proofing

her cottage and trying to get all paintings done ASAP. She needed to put away her art supplies with a dog—make that a puppy—running around the house. No way would she chance Buddy getting into something toxic. "I can't wait."

"Or maybe you can't wait for Buddy's owner to pay a visit to your house."

Her cheeks felt warm. She recognized the flush of heat and hoped her face wasn't too red. "I'm sure Justin will want to see his boy."

"No doubt. He's here three times a day."

"I had no idea." But Bailey wasn't surprised. Even though she hadn't seen him in a couple of days, she'd picked up bits and pieces of what he'd been doing from people around town. Though she wondered why they thought she cared.

Okay, she did. A little.

The clinic door jingled. "Bailey."

A chill ran through her. Justin had arrived.

She faced him. "Hey. I was just visiting Buddy."

Justin's brow furrowed. "How is he today?"

"His leg is healing." She jiggled the zipper on her purse. "He's putting on weight, too. Handsome guy."

"Takes after his dad."

"Yes, he does." The words popped from her mouth like a champagne cork. *Oh, no.* Had she said that aloud?

His smug smile was proof she had. Great.

He moved toward Bailey, causing her to take two steps back until she bumped into a counter.

He placed a hand on either side of her. "You're…interesting."

She leaned back, afraid if she moved forward, he would kiss her. Or maybe she would kiss him. Not good with Bonnie watching them. "That's like saying I have a good personality."

"You do."

"Funny."

"Come on, I'm kidding." He leaned close enough that she could feel his warmth and smell the scent of his after-shave. "What I mean is you're passionate about what you do, yet have a practical streak at the same time."

She raised her chin, a satisfied feeling settling in the center of her chest. "Not many folks around here call me practical."

"It's true." He lowered his voice. "Got plans tonight?"

"What do you have in mind?" Oops. Her answer should have been yes, she had plans. She wasn't looking for a date.

"Takeout, then head over to the south point to eat."

"Hiding from the crowds."

"I'm not suggesting that for me."

Okay, more proof he was a good guy. He was aware of her family and others who might see them together. She should still say no. That was what Tyler would want her to do. Except she wanted to say yes. "Sure. Sounds good."

An act of rebellion or one of attraction? She had no idea, but Bailey wanted to spend more time with Justin.

"Burger Boat or Ying's Chinese?" he asked.

Dinner sounded like a real date, and that appealed to her. "Ying's. I feel like some orange chicken."

And she was curious to see what her fortune cookie said. Her life sure hadn't been the same since Justin came to town.

The sun dipped toward the horizon, and an evening breeze traveled over the water. Justin sat on the south end of Haley's Bay. Summer meant extended daylight. He wanted to make the most of this time with Bailey.

She sat on a rock, finishing up her dinner. "Did you get enough to eat?"

"Plenty. Egg rolls are one of my favorites. Good choice."

"I like Chinese food."

Another thing they had in common. "Me, too."

He only wished the Broughton Inn wasn't the biggest thing they shared. He stared at the buildings along the waterfront.

The quaint town of Haley's Bay was growing on him. He glimpsed the facade of the Candy Cove, lit up with white bulb lights. He couldn't decide if the peanut-butter fudge or the saltwater taffy was his favorite.

"You're quiet," she said.

"Long day. One full of surprises."

"That seems to be most of my days." Her gaze focused on the marina, making him wonder what artistic image her creative brain was conjuring.

"Come here often?" he asked.

She nodded. "Can't beat the views. It's a fun place to hike, too."

The wind teased her hair, but she didn't try to smooth or fix the blowing strands. Her casual, careless beauty appealed to him, but he also appreciated her sharp mind and caring heart. Three things that made him want more kisses. "You're a hiker?"

She wiped her mouth with a napkin. "Hiking is the closest thing I do to a sport, much to the chagrin of my athletic family. Though I enjoy watching the Olympics."

He laughed. "That'll keep you in shape."

"I stand for the National Anthem and jog to the kitchen for snacks during commercials," she joked. "Seriously if I don't keep myself busy, I morph into a couch potato. I'm trying to cut back on sugar, eat healthier. If not for good genes and a fast metabolism, I'd be in trouble. Unlike you. Let me guess. Runner?"

He nodded. "Triathlons."

"My brother Flynn does those."

"He's the one in the navy."

She nodded. "Swimming, biking and running on the

same day seems like torture to me, but he enjoys the challenge. You must, too."

"Nothing like it. Challenging and rewarding."

"I'll take your word on that." One corner of her mouth rose in a sideward smile. "My idea of a triathlon is parking my car in a compact spot, walking into the ice cream parlor and eating a Scoop-a-licious Super Sundae with two cherries on top. Of course, I'd need to be rolled back to my car afterward, so maybe I should call that a quadrathlon."

She really was something. He took a step toward her. "I've done those, too, with an added kayak, but I like your kind better. More fun and tastier. You're a unique woman, Bailey Cole. You start artist co-op galleries. Save old buildings. Babysit your niece and nephew. Take in other people's animals. What else do you do for yourself besides hiking and quadrathlons?"

"I paint," she said without any hesitation.

"That's your job."

"It's what I love to do." She glowed with an enviable look of contentment. "I'm fortunate to earn my living doing what I enjoy. Or will again, once my foot isn't holding me back."

"Wouldn't a couch potato sit when she paints?"

"You'd think so, right?" Bailey joked. "I sit when I'm working on smaller projects, but my current piece is too large, so I was standing before I got hurt. Declan brought over a stool. I tried sitting, but that affected my process. I need to keep moving and circling to bring the piece alive and see the various angles and lighting." Her cheek turned pink. "Sorry, I get talking about painting…"

"Don't apologize. I like hearing about your work."

The creative process—especially hearing about hers—fascinated Justin, reminding him of the times he'd designed outside-the-box prototypes. Those were his favorite projects, but they were rare. Some of his best work had never been approved by his parents or built.

Maybe he could do something on his own. It seemed a waste to not do anything with those designs.

Her smile spread to her eyes. "That's because you're thinking about your own process."

"Didn't know I had one."

"Maybe not consciously, but the interest has been sparked."

"Maybe."

"Definitely," she countered. "How does your painting look in your room at the B and B?"

"Very nice. Still can't believe I painted it."

"That's what's so fun about the Canvas and Chardonnay classes. People discover a hidden talent once a paintbrush is in their hand." She stared across the water. "The sun's starting to set. This was a good idea. No one around to bother us."

He'd also gotten a good view of the backside of the Potter property. But Justin didn't want to tell Bailey that. He didn't want business to be part of their…whatever this was. He might have considered trying to charm her out of the inn, but that was before. Before getting to know her better. Before kissing her. Before having her offer to take in his dog. Now he wanted only to spend time with her.

"We needed to celebrate," he said.

"What are we celebrating?"

"Buddy put on more weight. He should be released in a day or two."

"That's awesome."

"You sound happy."

"I am." Her grin lit up her face. "I can't wait for my surrogate doggy to come home."

"Won't be long until he's there. Though you'll have to put up with my visits."

She met his gaze, then looked down at the rock. Her face flushed.

Adorable.

"So, what do you think of this view?" she asked, changing the subject. He'd let her. It was either that or kissing her. On second thought…

He focused on the overgrowth and junkyard disorder of the Potter property.

"I—" Ideas exploded in his head. The structure, the landscape, a dock, everything. His fingers itched for a pencil and paper so he could sketch the designs running through his mind like a slide show. A smaller inn or B and B. Not one to match the Broughton Inn, but to stand alone and complement those plans.

Oh, hell. He looked from the lot to Bailey.

"What?" she asked.

Guilt coated Justin's mouth, the taste bitter compared to Bailey's sweet kisses. His design for the new Broughton Inn was one of his favorites, and if he added the Potter place to the mix, he had both a first and a second place for his best designs.

Forget kissing her again. That wouldn't be a good idea if he wanted to go after both properties.

She smiled at him. "You had an idea. For a painting?"

The hope in her voice stabbed Justin like a dagger.

Damn. She had no clue what he was thinking about doing. He didn't dare tell her. She might not understand. For all he knew, Potter's son would say no to him. "I was thinking about the inn."

She pursed her lips. "It's never far from my mind. The people who count on the inn for their livelihoods need jobs."

Justin picked up a stone and tossed it into the Columbia River. "You think about everyone but yourself."

"That's not true. I want the Broughton Inn for a consignment gallery. There's also the historical piece, the preservation and the beauty aspects."

He didn't agree with using the word *beauty* to describe

the inn, but he knew she didn't see the place as he did. "You've mentioned that, but those things can be preserved with pictures, special displays and placards."

Her nose scrunched. "You mean like a museum?"

"The Hotel del Coronado near San Diego, California, has a section that documents its history."

She thought for a moment. A wistful expression formed. "The inn has meaning beyond history books and architectural value for my family. My grandparents were married at the Broughton Inn. My parents went to their senior prom together there."

"Those memories will always remain."

Bailey started to say something, then stopped herself. "What about making new memories? Ones to add to the old?"

"Does the actual building matter? If not, people can still remember their experiences there and enjoy a new inn."

He waited for her to respond.

Finally she shrugged.

"It's clear the inn has special meaning for you and your family, but let me ask you this," he said. "Will owning the inn hold the same kind of passion you have for painting, or will it turn into an obligation you must uphold?"

Justin knew the question might not be easy to answer. He'd felt that way himself on occasion, wondering if there was more to life than building resorts and hotels so other people could relax. He didn't want Bailey to experience the same frustration when creating works of art made her happy.

"I don't know, but I'm willing to try." A faraway look filled her eyes. "Owning the inn is good for those around me."

"That's noble. I mean that in the most sincere way, but consider what you're taking on."

She raised her chin, giving him that stubborn look he'd

grown to know and not mind so much now. "I worked there for years. I know what's involved."

"As an employee, yes, but not as the boss signing paychecks. Details like payroll, insurance, benefits, profits and losses weigh on you, become a burden," he explained. "You care about people. Leaving their problems when you walk out the door will be difficult. If you can leave them at all. There's not much time to take a day off or go on vacation. Family gatherings and celebrations might have to wait."

"That does sound boring."

Taryn had said the same thing over and over again, but he thought she'd grow to understand what his job entailed and how the resorts were part of his family. But she could never understand why he needed to work so many hours and be away so much. She got angry when he brought work home. Would Bailey be the same?

Stop. He was getting off track. What Bailey thought about his company's business wasn't relevant to the discussion.

But an idea popped into his head, one that might solve both their problems. "What if McMillian Resorts offered to hire back the laid-off employees and maintain contracts with vendors?"

She pressed her lips together. "I didn't think we were going to discuss the inn after what Tyler said."

They shouldn't. Justin understood what the lawyers meant about conflict of interest. "Hypothetically."

"Hypothetically, I might be open to that if you preserved the original building. I've had time to think about the various additions. Much of those are dated and uninspiring, lacking historical significance or architectural detail. But the original portion is worth saving. You were wrong to include that in your teardown."

Another surprise. Maybe she wasn't as stubborn as everyone thought, if she could admit he was right about something and compromise. That kind of renovation didn't fit McMillian's business model. But he hadn't planned on adopting a dog or kissing Bailey, either. "Anything is possible. Hypothetically."

His thoughts flip-flopped between Bailey and the Potter place. She was a jewel with faceted edges and a brilliance that drew his eye time and time again. The lot across the bay was a rough stone with potential. He imagined everything—weeds, plants, house—bulldozed from the lot, leaving a clean slate, a blank canvas, to create something stunning that would take advantage of the location and views.

Would she object to that teardown, as well? The place was old and in disarray. Would she see reason? Would she ever see that new was not only easier and more comfortable, but *more* beautiful? Or would she be disappointed in his lack of vision and slam the door on them being friends or something more?

Justin wasn't ready to find out the answer.

He needed to get her home and stop talking about the inn before he did or said something he would regret.

Chapter Ten

The next morning, a knock sounded at Bailey's front door. She glanced at the clock on the microwave—nine o'clock—and wiped her wet hands with a dish towel. She wasn't expecting visitors, but that never stopped her family from dropping by. Calling wasn't in the Cole DNA. At least she'd changed out of her pajamas. Not that her ratty green sweatpants and ripped gray hoodie were much of an improvement.

She trudged from the kitchen. The traction on the bottom of her fuzzy socks kept her from slipping. She yawned, tired from dog-proofing the house and a sleepless night thinking about Justin. He hadn't kissed her when he dropped her off after dinner. He'd simply walked her to the door and said he'd see her tomorrow.

No biggie, she'd told herself. Just like the kisses. The only things she and Justin would have to discuss in the future would be Buddy and the inn. But she couldn't help from feeling a tad…disappointed.

Another knock.

"I'm on my way." She opened the door.

Justin greeted her with a smile. "You should keep your door locked."

"I, um…" Seeing him left her tongue-tied. She hadn't expected him to stop by this early. "What's the word on Buddy?"

"I might be able to pick him up tomorrow. Want to go dog supply shopping? I'm not sure what he needs."

The request was what a friend would ask, except they weren't friends. She wasn't sure what they were. Part of her wanted to spend more time with Justin. The other part kept thinking about what Tyler had said. She could write him a list of supplies, but that didn't feel right, either.

Bailey touched her hair, realizing she'd twisted the strands into a messy bun held in place by a paintbrush. She remembered what she was wearing. "I'm not dressed to go out."

"You look fine."

So said the man in the khaki pants and cornflower-blue polo shirt that did amazing things to his eyes and funny things to her insides. The guy looked good no matter what he wore. Unlike her.

But she supposed clean sweats were a step up from smelly, dirty coveralls. This was how she dressed when cleaning or doing yard work, and that was what she planned to do today, so why was she worrying about her clothes? Shopping at a pet store wasn't a date. "Okay. Let me grab my purse and a pair of shoes."

"Fuzzy ones?"

"Excuse me?"

"You like to wear fuzzy things on your feet. Socks, slippers, shoes."

"I hadn't noticed." Bailey was surprised he had. She thought about her choice of footwear. Interesting. He was correct. "But why wear boring socks and shoes when you can wear fun on your feet?"

His grin gave her chills, the good kind. "Until coming to Haley's Bay I've had a fun deficit. I've been sketching some landscapes. Being here is good for me."

"Buddy will give you the perfect reason to have more fun." She opened the door wider. "Come in. I won't be long."

She retreated to her bedroom, rubbing her hands over her arms. Chills were not a good response to having fun with Justin. Maybe she should start a list for herself—no throbbing lips, no chills, no kisses.

Even though kisses weren't on the agenda, she brushed her teeth—for general hygiene's sake—put on shoes, the nonfuzzy kind, and grabbed her purse. "I'm ready."

He stood in the empty dining room. "What happened to the drop cloths and your painting?"

The guy was more observant than she realized. "I put them away."

"Your foot is healing. You'll be able to stand and paint in no time."

"True, but I didn't want to take any chances with Buddy here."

Brow furrowed, he studied the empty dining room. His lips parted. "You put away the painting and supplies because of my dog."

She nodded, noticing a cloudy area that had been covered by the tarp. Something must have soaked through to the floor. She would have to see if denatured alcohol would repair the damage.

After Buddy left with Justin. Whenever that might be.

"Why?" he asked.

"Paints and brush cleaners are toxic. Didn't want to take a chance of Buddy getting into something he shouldn't," she explained. "I have so many other projects I can do while he's here, things that won't hurt him if he's the curious type."

"Thank you."

The sincerity in the two words made breathing difficult. The connection she'd felt when he held her hand at the vet clinic returned. Her every nerve ending went on high alert. Her lips tingled in anticipation. She forced the words "you're welcome" from her tight throat.

He reached for her.

Bailey wanted him to touch her, to kiss her, more than anything, but she knew that wasn't smart. She backed away, adjusted the strap on her purse. "There are two pet stores in the area. One in Astoria, the other in Long Beach."

"No rush." He held up his hand. "We have time."

"I know, but remember what Tyler said."

A sheepish expression flashed across Justin's face. "We're seeing each other because of Buddy."

"That doesn't mean we have to..."

He gave her a look.

Was he going to make her say the word? She waited. He kept staring at her. Fine. She would say it if he wouldn't. "Kiss."

Justin grinned. "I like kissing you."

At least she wasn't the only one, but she didn't feel better. "I like kissing you, but more kisses might complicate us resolving the ownership of the Broughton Inn."

Justin raised an eyebrow and grinned wryly. "So I'm a complication, huh?"

Yes, and a big distraction. But there was no need to answer. He knew that.

"Probably a good idea, then. No kissing," he added.

"Thank you." Except Bailey wished he hadn't agreed with her so easily. Wait. She should be relieved he had. When Justin McMillian was involved, she had no idea what was going on inside her head. "Astoria is the safest choice for dog shopping. Less chance of being seen."

"All set, but don't get your heart set on doggy designer wear. I will not be dressing Buddy in clothing."

"Come on," she teased. "No rain slicker for those wet days?"

"I'm a true Oregonian. I don't carry an umbrella. Buddy and I will both get wet."

She opened the door. "What about bunny ears come Easter time, or reindeer antlers for Christmas?"

"No way." Justin stepped outside. "A bandanna might be okay. Depends on the pattern."

"Picky."

"I must protect Buddy's dignity."

"At least until you decide to use a picture of him for your Christmas card and wrap him in garlands with a Santa hat on his head."

"Never."

"It's only July. Time will tell." But she would never know. Her heart panged with regret. She shook off the feeling, stepped out of the house and locked the door. "So, how do you feel about doggy booties?"

After having fun shopping with Bailey and spending more money then he'd ever imagined spending on a dog, Justin climbed the steps of the Astoria Column, a 125-foot-tall tower built in the 1920s and one of the most popular tourist attractions in the area. Of the 164 steps, they were about halfway to the top.

He glanced back at Bailey. "How's your foot holding up?"

"I'll let you know if it hurts."

She continued upward, a smile on her face and her breasts jiggling with each step. Too bad he couldn't walk backward.

"The view is worth the climb," she added.

The stop at the tower had been her idea when she found out he'd never seen the view from the top.

"I can't believe I'm the Oregonian, but someone from Washington brought me here."

"Then we're even because I've never been to the top of the Space Needle in Seattle."

"Spend time on the Oregon coast?"

"Some. Mainly Cannon Beach. It has such a strong artistic community, more so than on my side of the Columbia, which has been underserved by coastal galleries."

"Until you."

"That's right." Pride filled her voice. "The co-op gallery will be back one of these days."

"Do some tourists enjoy local art?"

"More than some," she said. "From my experience with the inn's gallery, people want to take home more than a souvenir magnet to stick on their fridge. A piece of art that captures their vacation destination is a memento to treasure."

"You're not like other artists I've met," he said.

"Should I take that as a compliment?"

"Yes, you should. You've done your research."

"Art is as much a business as a passion. After the Broughton Inn co-op gallery opened, art sales tripled. There's also been an increased interest in classes and art-centered events from both tourists and locals. That's huge, given the current economy."

He moved to the side to let a couple pass by on their way down.

"You're almost there," the man in a Mariners cap said.

"Hear that, Bailey? We're almost at the top." Two minutes later, Justin reached the final step and walked out onto the viewing platform. He looked past rooftops toward the bridge that connected Oregon to Washington. The water of the Columbia River shimmered, a contrast to the green shrubs and trees both nearby and in the distance. He saw the coastal ranch. "Incredible view."

"See Young's Bay?" She wore her sunglasses on her head. "Then there's the Pacific Ocean. It's quite a sight to see all the boats and ships sailing under the bridge."

He could imagine. The part of the bridge closest to Oregon was elevated. The Washington side seemed to float on the water.

"Breathtaking." Like the view of Bailey, her eyes bright and her smile wide. Beautiful. He couldn't stop staring at her. "Do you ever come up here to work?"

"Not enough room." She closed her eyes and tilted her face upward. The sun kissed her cheeks, making him wish he could have a turn. "Too many tourists, too."

"That's what we are today." Though she didn't look touristy at all. Someone looking at her would guess she was an artist or a cook, or maybe a writer.

She opened her eyes, then gave him a look. "You know what I mean."

Did he? Justin liked how she treated him like an artist, assuming he understood, when all he'd done was complete one painting. Still, he appreciated the way she included him. "I'm figuring it out."

"Have you done any more painting?"

"I knew you would ask that."

"So, what's your answer?" The dog-won't-let-go-of-the-bone tone had returned.

The wind blew off the water, stronger up there than on the ground. A large ship sailed under the bridge.

"I've sketched a few things," he said finally. She didn't need to know that he loved every minute, lost himself in the work and found himself refreshed when he returned to working on blueprints and resort designs. "I don't have the supplies to paint."

"Borrow some of mine. I'm not using any right now."

"Because of my dog."

"I want to see more of what you can do."

"That sounds like a challenge."

"Maybe." The wind tousled the ends of her hair. She moved out of the way so a young family could pass. "I'm excited whenever I find someone with natural talent."

He raised an eyebrow. "So you're only interested in my painting ability?"

She grinned wryly. "Your kisses aren't too bad."

Justin thought that might be an invitation, but she moved to the other side of the viewing plaza. He followed her. "You can't leave me hanging."

"Was just making a comment about your talents. Remember what we said."

"No kisses."

"How about a peck?" he asked.

She shook her head. "Semantics."

He wrapped an arm around her back. "So you'll let this amazing view go to waste."

"If we're kissing, we can't see the view." She scooted away. "You don't give up."

"Neither do you."

A thoughtful expression formed on her face. She stared at the horizon with a faraway look in her eyes. "Guess we have more in common than I realized."

"We'll have even more after Buddy gets released."

She half laughed. "Better enjoy your final day of freedom, Dad."

"You, too, surrogate Mom."

"We're almost a family." Her eyes widened, as if she hadn't meant to say the words aloud. "Well, a little like one."

"Yes. We will be." For as long as he was here. The idea appealed to him on a gut level. "Until I came to Haley's

Bay and met you, I had no idea what family was all about. I'm glad I met you, Bailey, and a few of the other Coles."

"Let's hope you feel the same way when you leave town."

He rubbed his face. "Still worried your brothers might mess up my face?"

"No." A wicked gleam lit her eyes. "That I will."

"Guess I'll take a rain check on those kisses."

"Smart thinking."

"I try." But he had to try harder when he was around her.

Buddy, Bailey and him. A family. Justin had to admit, the idea appealed to him. Too bad the Broughton Inn had to get in the way. And her family.

Two days later, Justin sat on Bailey's couch with Buddy at his feet. They'd come straight from the vet clinic that morning.

Best. Dog. Ever.

All dog owners probably thought that about their pet, but in Justin's case the words were true. Buddy was amazing. Still recovering, but now clean and fresh-smelling, as well as flea-free.

And most important, happy.

Buddy seemed thrilled to be inside, have toys to play with, his own doggy bed, food and a kick-ass colorful collar that Bailey had picked out at the pet store in Astoria. A part of Justin wished he were staying here instead of the B and B. But that had as much to do with Bailey as Buddy.

"You are such a good dog," Justin said. "A lucky one, too."

Buddy stared at Justin with big brown eyes and a look of total adoration. The dog panted, wagged his tail. Not even the cone bothered him.

"Sorry, boy. No more treats." Justin had learned within five minutes of arriving at Bailey's that Buddy could sit and lie down and shake. Food was the best motivator for the tricks, but the dog didn't seem to have an off switch when it came to eating. "You'll get a tummy ache."

The dog made a noise that resembled a whine.

Smart dog, but spoiled already. "Cry all you want. I'm not changing my mind."

Buddy looked at him, then lay down on the throw rug, not quite defeated. It was more like that he wanted to rest up for his next round of treats and rubs.

Yeah, one smart dog.

Bailey stepped through the kitchen doorway, a cup of strawberry lemonade in her hand. "Thought you might be thirsty.

She knew him well. Justin smiled. "I am."

"How's Buddy doing?"

"Great. Explored the living and dining room. Did a few tricks. Ate too many treats."

Bailey shot an accusing glance Justin's way. "Whose fault is that?"

He took the glass from her. "Just making sure he's comfortable."

"Looks right at home."

"Yeah, he does." Justin wanted to spend lots of time with Buddy so the dog was used to him before they went to Lincoln City. "Figured out in the first two minutes that he's addicted to petting. Thought I should warn you, one or two rubs aren't enough for my pup."

"If Buddy didn't know that before, he knows it now."

Justin sipped the lemonade. Tasty. Was there anything Bailey couldn't do well?

Buddy's ears perked up. He sat, looked at the front door, barked once.

"What is it?" Justin asked the dog.

The doorbell rang.

Bailey gave him a pat, then walked toward the door. "Good, Buddy."

"Knew he was a great dog." Justin was finding something new to love about Buddy every five minutes. "Expecting company?"

"No, but that doesn't mean someone won't drop by." She opened the door.

"Surprise," a group of people shouted.

Buddy barked.

Justin looked over his shoulder. A crowed gathered on the front porch. He recognized a few—Grady, Ellis, Risa, Lilah and Ida Mae. The others, including a couple of cute kids, resembled the people he knew. It looked as though the Cole family had come calling. They'd brought food and gifts.

"What's going on?" Bailey asked.

Risa beamed. "When I had to take Skippy back to the vet the other day, one of the techs mentioned Justin was adopting the dog you'd found and the receptionist said the dog would be staying with you so I thought a doggy shower was in order. So here we are with gifts and food."

Bailey's face paled. She clutched the doorknob. None of her family seemed to pay attention to her as they walked in, making themselves right at home.

As usual.

Justin held on to Buddy's collar. The dog sniffed the air but seemed content to stay near him. No growling or barks, just watchful eyes.

Two children, a boy and a girl, ran up. "Can we pet your dog?"

He remembered what Bailey had done yesterday when they found Buddy. "Put your hand out and let him sniff you."

They did.

Buddy licked each of their hands.

The girl giggled.

The boy pulled his hand back. "That tickles."

Buddy raised his paw so the little boy would shake.

"Wow." The boy's eyes widened to the size of silver dollars. "That's one smart dog."

"Can we play with him?" the little girl asked.

Even Buddy seemed to be waiting for an answer.

"Sure," Justin said. "But no running. He's got an injured paw."

The kids scrambled toward the kitchen with Buddy at their heels.

Justin joined Bailey as her family continued to stream in with food and presents and beverages. Even cousins, including identical twins, a frowning Tyler and his smiling brother, J.T., a firefighter, were there.

"I'm sorry," Bailey mouthed to Justin.

He helped her carry the presents to the fireplace hearth. "Wow. It's like Christmas."

She nodded. "You're going to have more dog supplies than you could ever imagine."

A tall, tanned fifty-something-year-old man entered the house. One look at Bailey in her yoga pants, old T-shirt and bare feet, and he grimaced. "Holy crap, Bailey. You've already got the whole artsy-fartsy thing against you. Please tell me you didn't go out in public looking dressed like a hobo. Do you know what people are going to say?"

She took a deep breath and another. "Love you, too, Dad."

So this was the patriarch of the Cole family. He looked like a fisherman, and someone you wouldn't want to upset or bump into in a dark alley. Not that Haley's Bay had any.

Justin extended his arm. "I'm Justin McMillian. Nice to meet you, Mr. Cole."

"Jack Cole." He shook Justin's hand. "Word of warning. That dog of yours better be the only thing sniffing around here."

"Understood. Feel the same way about my two sisters."

Justin wouldn't be surprised if the fisherman father had driven away more than one potential boyfriend.

Bailey sighed with twenty-seven years' worth of exasperation. "On that note, I'm going to crawl into a hole and die."

"Don't be overdramatic," her father said.

She winked at Justin, as if she weren't too upset, but playing along. "Fine. I'll go change into something too artsy-fartsy so you'll have at least one more thing to complain about, Dad." She kissed his cheek. "Remember the number one rule in my house...no fighting."

She walked to her bedroom.

Her father's frown deepened. Her brother Declan looked disappointed. Apparently battles were part of the family fun.

Justin bit back a smile. He'd wanted to know what a Cole family gathering would be like. Looked as though he was getting his chance. For better or worse.

Though this wasn't what he expected.

Tyler looked unhappy, and Declan looked ready to punch a wall. Justin hoped the Cole males remembered the no-fighting rule. For Bailey's sake. And his.

Bailey stood at the back door, staring out at her yard. Food covered the picnic table. Her family members and Justin occupied folding chairs setup on the lawn. They ate, drank and laughed. Buddy, the guest of honor, went from person to person getting pets.

Warmth balled in the center of her chest. She had to give her family credit. When the Coles threw a party, including an impromptu dog shower, aka an excuse to check out Justin, they went all out. Buddy had enough toys, supplies, treats and clothing to make him the most stylish pup on the West Coast.

She carried another pitcher of strawberry lemonade to

the drinks table, a folding card table with various sizes of plastic cups and a permanent marker to write someone's name on their drink. Three ice chests full of soda, juice boxes and beer were underneath.

Tyler grabbed a bottle of amber ale from one of the coolers. The serious expression he wore when he'd walked into her house remained. He was dressed like a surfer, but he still looked like a lawyer. "Buddy's staying here. Is McMillian?"

"No." She lowered her voice. "He's over at Aunt Ida Mae's."

"I texted AJ."

"About?"

"Justin trying to charm the inn away from you."

"He's not."

Tyler sipped his beer. "Looks that way to me. Ask anyone else here, and they'll agree."

Her cousin's words hurt. "You're wrong, and so are they. I'm not stupid or naive, Ty. I've been around the block a couple of times. I'm not going to give away the inn to some handsome sweet talker."

"It's been a while since you've dated."

"Not that long. Remember Oliver." Just saying his name left a bad taste in Bailey's mouth. "And just so you know, I'm not dating Justin."

Kissing and dating were two entirely different things. She looked over to see him surrounded by the Cole women—her grandmother, great aunt, mother, sister, sister-in-law and niece. They'd have a précis on him within the hour.

"We found Buddy at the Potter place," Bailey said. "Keeping Justin's dog has nothing to do with the inn. You know I like animals. I'm just trying to help."

"Knowing the McMillian reputation, chances are he'll want to buy the Potter property, too."

"What reputation?"

"The company is cutthroat when buying real estate."

"Justin isn't like that."

Tyler raised a brow. "You know him that well?"

"No." Nothing she'd seen so far gave her such an impression, though what she'd heard about his sister Paige made her wonder if she was the source of rumors.

"It's a moot point anyway." Tyler wiped off the condensation dripping from his beer. "Phil Potter has shown no interest in selling in the past. He won't now."

"Maybe they'll make Phil an offer he can't refuse," she countered. "He hasn't been back to Haley's Bay in forever. The place is a hazard. There's no reason for him to hold on to the property."

"What about sentimental reasons?" Ty's gaze narrowed. "That was something you understood before spending time with Justin McMillian."

"I still understand that. Why do you think I want the inn? But if McMillian Resorts buys another property, they might not want the inn. Then it's mine."

He lifted his bottle. "Still dreaming of saying 'I do' there, cuz?"

Justin joined them. He refilled his cup with strawberry lemonade. "What's this about 'I do'?"

Oh, no. Please no. Her gaze implored Tyler not to say anything, but the devilish smile on her cousin's face made one thing clear—he was going to spill.

Her stomach churned with a potent mixture of dread and embarrassment. "Ty—"

"For as long as I can remember, Bailey has wanted to get married at the Broughton Inn," Ty said.

"Like your grandmother?" Justin asked.

Bailey nodded, heat rushing up her neck. Declan approached, eating a brownie. Oh, no, she didn't want him to get in on this conversation, too.

If a big earthquake were going to strike the Pacific Northwest, this would be the perfect time for the fault lines to shift. Everyone was outside. Nothing to fall on them. No one would remember the topic of discussion.

Except Justin was waiting for an answer.

She took a breath. "Most girls dream about weddings."

Declan grabbed a beer from a red ice chest. "Not all eight-year-olds put on a wedding and make their brothers and cousins attend."

"That was a dress rehearsal, not a wedding," she clarified, praying the ground would start rocking and rolling any second now.

"She made us wear paper bow ties," Tyler said.

Declan laughed. "And black hats. I'd forgotten about those."

Ty grinned. "We must have looked like idiots standing on the gazebo in funny hats with a boom box playing the 'Wedding March.'"

So much for an earthquake. Might as well go all in. She squared her shoulders. "You were wearing top hats. And the music was Bach's 'Jesu, Joy of Man's Desiring' and Pachelbel's 'Canon' in D."

Justin's eyes twinkled. "A formal affair."

"Oh, yeah," Tyler said, seeming to enjoy her discomfort. He and J.T. had no other siblings, but both treated her and Camden like sisters. "Bailey wore a white nightgown and borrowed a friend's First Communion veil."

"She had on white gloves and shoes, too," Declan added. "Mom was so pissed she scuffed up those shoes before Camden could grow into them."

Bailey remembered that. "I was grounded for a week and was assigned extra chores when they found out I cut Aunt Ida Mae's white roses for my bouquet."

"I thought Camden did that."

"She did, but she was my maid of honor and younger. I

couldn't let her be punished when this was my idea." Bailey smiled at the memories, both good and bad. "I don't think I wore white shoes for the longest time after that. But I got to play bride, so the punishment was worth the crime."

"Sounds like an elaborate rehearsal," Justin said.

She nodded. "Important stuff when you're little."

Declan looked from Justin to her, an odd expression in her brother's green eyes. "All Bailey needed was a groom to make the wedding complete."

That hadn't changed. There was still no groom.

She forced herself not to glance Justin's way. "I asked one of you to stand in, but had zero takers."

"I was too short," Declan said.

"You were lucky we showed up at all." Tyler walked away. Declan followed him.

Justin stared over the lip of his cup. "Do you still want to get married at the Broughton Inn?"

Buddy nudged her leg. She bent over and rubbed his back, trying to avoid the cone secured around his neck as well as Justin's questioning gaze. "He's doing great with all these people around. Did you see him playing with the kids?"

"Answer the question."

The firmness in his voice made her look up. He stared intently at her. She swallowed around the lump in her throat. "Yes. That's what I meant about making new memories."

"I see."

He did? Maybe he would consider sharing what he saw. "Any other questions?"

"No, but the gazebo could stay."

"Huh?"

"The gazebo wouldn't have to be torn down. The structure could be repaired and strengthened. Painted, too."

Bailey thought about what Tyler had said about the inn being charmed out from under her. "Hypothetically?"

"I'm trying to make sure you get what you want."

Her pulse skittered, matching her erratic heartbeat. No one had ever done that for her. Oh, AJ tried. His way to make up for staying away for ten years, perhaps? She'd been the middle child with three older brothers and three younger siblings. The forgotten one. Her older brothers were always giving her—not to mention their parents—a hard time. The twins and Grady had needed constant supervision. No one had time to think about Bailey's desires, just her basic needs.

She struggled to find the right words. "Thanks, but I can take care of that myself."

He glanced around the backyard at her family until his gaze reached hers. That connection she'd felt was stronger now.

"I know you can," he said. "But you shouldn't have to. Not all the time."

Tingles poured down her spine and she knew then what she'd been denying all along. Justin McMillian might be the wrong man, but she was falling for him anyway. Falling hard.

And if the Broughton Inn was coming between them, she might have to choose. The question was…which one would she pick?

The first answer that came to mind surprised her. Justin couldn't be the right one…or could he?

Chapter Eleven

For the first two days after Buddy arrived, Bailey left her house when Justin visited. She knew that was what Tyler, her family and everyone else in town wanted. Saying hello followed by goodbye a minute later got old fast, but she was trying to do the right thing.

Except leaving home each time wasn't the right thing for her.

Or Justin, who wanted her to stay.

Or Buddy, who tried to block the door when she was leaving.

On day three, when Justin came over, she gave in and stayed home. Tyler didn't call. None of her family showed up. No one seemed to notice, let alone care. So she did the same thing the next time. And the time after that.

One week passed, then another, each day sweeter than the last. Bailey was getting attached to Buddy. She looked forward to Justin's visits. Their no-kissing mandate fell by the wayside.

When he was at her house, she could almost believe the three of them were a family. A part of her—a big part—longed for this arrangement to become permanent.

Crazy? Yes, but she didn't care.

Bailey was happy in a way she hadn't been before. Not with any former boyfriend or date. Nothing came close to this. She didn't want the feeling to end. If only she didn't have to worry about the inn...

But she wouldn't think about that now. She had chocolate chip cookies to make. By the time Justin finished playing with Buddy in the backyard, she would be finished baking and they could spend time together.

The ingredients sat on the counter. Parchment paper lined the cookie sheets. The oven was preheating. She reached into her kitchen cupboard and pulled out a large mixing bowl.

"Whoa. That's commercial-size."

She glanced over her shoulder toward the sound of Justin's voice. He stood in the doorway and looked way too good in his khaki shorts and green polo. A good thing she'd decided to wear a skirt and a tank top, rather than her work-around-the-house clothes. She knew he didn't care, but she did.

Buddy peered around Justin's legs. The pup sniffed the air.

"I haven't started yet," she said to the dog.

"How many cookies do we need to make?" Justin asked.

We. The word made Bailey's heart sigh. She hadn't asked him to help. She'd assumed he wouldn't want to bake when he could be playing with Buddy. "Ten dozen."

"I had no idea the Coles were related to Cookie Monster."

Grinning, she stuck out her tongue. He made a silly face in return.

She placed the bowl on the counter. "Sorry to disappoint you, but there are no fuzzy blue relatives in the Cole family tree."

"Only fuzzy blue shoes."

"Purple fuzzy slippers."

He exhaled, louder than a sigh, as if he were exaggerating the sound on purpose. "I have fond memories of seeing those slippers for the first time."

"Revising history?"

"Embracing it."

Bailey wished he'd embrace her. She felt as if she'd known Justin longer than a few weeks. He fit so perfectly into her world. Or would, once the problem with the inn's ownership was resolved.

She pulled out her measuring cups and spoons.

"So why ten dozen?" he asked.

"That's how many Grady asked me to make for his department's barbecue tomorrow night."

Justin shook his head. "I can just imagine what Paige would say if I asked her to bake cookies for me."

"What about Rainey?"

"She would go to the nearest bakery and buy them. None of us learned to cook growing up. It wasn't something my mom had time to teach us." Justin put on the apron hanging from a hook. "What do you need me to do?"

He really was a good guy. Too bad Tyler couldn't see this side of Justin. "Thanks, but you don't have to help. Go play with Buddy."

"I want to help. Buddy, too. He'll be happy to clean up anything that drops to the floor." Justin walked toward her. "You're going to need help making twelve dozen cookies."

"Ten."

"Twelve." He rubbed his stomach. "The other two dozen are for us. Well, me."

Smiling, Bailey faced the counter and scooped flour

into a measuring cup. "I might be able to stretch the dough into more cookies."

"Might?" Justin stood behind her, his chest pressed against her back. "What's it going to take to get you to say you will?"

A thrill ran through her. She was ready to bake twenty dozen cookies, if that was what he wanted. She'd do anything to make him as happy as she felt. "I…"

"Need more convincing?" He showered kisses along her neck. "How's this?"

A moan escaped her mouth. Talk about talented lips. She leaned back against him to give him better access. "I could make an extra half dozen."

"Only six more?" Justin nibbled on her ears. Sensation shot from her earlobe down to her toes. "That won't do."

"No?" Her voice sounded husky.

"Nope." He turned her so she faced him. "Two dozen."

She held the measuring cup full of flour between them. "How about a dozen? I can't stretch the recipe any more without having to pull out a calculator and refigure the ingredients. Math was never my best subject."

"A good thing it was mine." He ran his fingertip along the side of her face. "I'll help you calculate measurements. And whatever else you need."

He brushed his lips across hers, the kiss feather soft.

A list with several more kisses on it formed in her mind. "I might need a lot."

"That's okay." The desire in his eyes matched the way Bailey felt. She arched toward him.

Justin pulled her closer.

Something pressed against her stomach. Huh? The measuring cup slipped from her hand and crashed to the floor. The sound echoed in the small kitchen. Flour flew up, a cloud of white dust.

Justin jumped back.

Bailey reached for a dish towel. "Sorry. I forgot I was holding the cup."

"If our kissing made you forget, then it's worth the cleanup."

"Good point." She stared at his legs. His feet were completely covered in white. "You've got flour on you."

"So do you. All over."

Bailey glanced down. She was covered in white from her waist down. She laughed. "At least it can't get any worse."

Buddy bounded in between them. Flour went flying again, all over them and the dog.

Justin laughed. "It's worse."

The dog ran in circles, spreading more flour around the kitchen and on them.

"He thinks this is a game," Justin said.

"Well, he won, if that's the case." She laughed. "So much for wowing you with my cookie-making skills."

"You've wowed me with all your other skills. And you've cooked for me already. I know your cookies will be killer."

His words sounded genuine. Her cheeks warmed, a regular occurrence around Justin. "Thanks."

"Thank you." He gave her another kiss. "You taste like flour."

"I must have touched my face."

He grabbed a roll of paper towels. "I'm going to put Buddy in the backyard so we can get this mess cleaned up. He'll need a bath, but we have cookies to make."

"Yes, twelve dozen is a lot." She grabbed a dish towel. "If you're good, I'll let you taste the dough."

"Oh, I'm always good."

Smiling was so easy to do around Justin. "I had a feeling you'd say that."

"Cookie dough is one of my favorites." His grin spread. "What's yours?"

She liked the cookie dough, but she liked tasting something better. "You."

On a Saturday morning under an overcast sky, Justin sat at the picnic table in Bailey's backyard. He tossed a neon-green ball toward the fence. Buddy ran after it.

She was inside on a phone call to one of her brothers. Justin had no idea which one. Keeping track of all the Coles in Haley's Bay could be a full-time job.

Buddy barked. Now that the uncomfortable cone was off and his leg healed, running and chasing had become his favorite playtime activities.

"Bring the ball here."

The dog picked it up in his mouth, but decided to take a roundabout way back.

Justin preferred going the direct route, point-to-point. He didn't make a habit of sniffing every blade of grass like Buddy. But his dog seemed to be having fun and enjoying the journey, not speeding by to arrive at the destination. Maybe the dog could teach him some new tricks. Bailey, too. "Come on, boy."

Buddy ran and dropped the ball.

Justin threw the drool-covered ball once more. He'd yet to reach the point where the dog gave up first. Maybe that wasn't in Buddy's nature. "Wait until you see your new house. It's on the beach. You can chase balls into the water."

The dog was more interested in running after the ball than listening to him. Justin didn't blame Buddy. Playing was more fun.

Staying in Haley's Bay had been fun. The quaint coastal village had a different vibe than his hometown, Lincoln City. He wouldn't miss the everybody-knows-your-business factor here, but he would miss the everybody-knows-your name part. And Bailey.

He might be ready to go home, sleep in his own bed and introduce Buddy to his new home, but he would miss the pretty, kind artist who'd opened her home to his dog and, by default, him.

Buddy ran toward him with the ball once more.

Justin's growing attraction and affection were too deep to think of Bailey as only a friend. Romantic was the only way to describe his feelings.

But they were stuck in some kind of limbo, which he hated. Buddy drew them together. The Broughton Inn kept them from becoming closer. The thought of leaving Bailey and going back to Lincoln City depressed him. She'd mentioned visiting, but that didn't make him feel any better.

The dog dropped the ball. Justin threw it again, this time aiming for the opposite side of the yard.

He tried to think of reasons he needed to stay in Haley's Bay longer, but things were winding down.

The property inspections, done by two different inspectors, each hired by one of the "owners," showed typical problems with a building that age, but nothing on the reports required demolition.

Of course not. A teardown recommendation would have made this too easy. But now that he knew what the inn meant to Bailey, a part of him was glad her dreams for the place hadn't died. And maybe there could be a solution where they both got what they wanted.

While Justin fine-tuned the renovation applications for the various historical committees, he'd tasked Paige with finding Mr. Potter's son in Boise, Idaho, and buying his land. So far, the man had turned down two offers, but Paige had gone back with a third. The guy would be a fool if he said no.

Justin had blueprints he'd drafted in his free time, but

he'd wait to show them off until the deal closed. No reason to jinx the project to stroke his ego. Or, if he was being honest, open himself up to criticism.

Bailey's opinion of his plans meant more than he understood. Sure, she had a style he admired, but the need for her to appreciate his work borderlined on pathetic. Yet he kept the stupid tube in his truck, in case she asked what he'd been up to in the time they were apart.

She hadn't asked.

He hadn't told her about trying to purchase the Potter lot or the blueprints.

A bird swooped down over the grass. Buddy dropped the ball and went for the bird that wisely flew into the neighbor's yard.

Justin shook his head. "You'll have better luck with the ball."

His cell phone beeped, signaling a text message.

He glanced at the message from Paige displayed on the screen: Phil Potter said no to third offer. Told me not to call again. It's dead. Get the Bro. Inn deal closed. NOW!

Not the news Justin wanted to hear.

He and Bailey had avoided any discussion of the inn since the dog shower. But the sooner this was resolved, the sooner he could figure out where he and Bailey stood, now and in the future.

"Hey." Bailey sat next to him. "That was AJ. His private investigator might have a lead on Floyd in South America. Someone matching his description was in Cartagena."

"Let's hope they find him.

She stared at the dog. "Buddy looks like he's having fun."

"That makes one of us."

"You bought the bag of balls."

"Who knew a triathlete's arm could tire from fetch?" She wasn't smiling. "Something wrong?"

"Not wrong." She moistened her lips. "It's just… I've been thinking. That's why I wanted to talk to AJ today. He told me to go through Tyler and formally present my offer, but it's Sunday and you're here, so I'll just tell you what I told my brother. If McMillian Resorts agrees to put in an art gallery that I could lease, hire the former employees, maintain vendor contracts and keep at least a portion of the main building in the new remodeled design, I'll give up my ownership claim."

Wow. And like that, it was done.

Still, her words shocked Justin. He searched her face to see if she was uncertain about her decision, but she looked almost serene. "You're positive?"

"Yes." She didn't hesitate. "I've been thinking about a compromise for a couple of weeks now. I think this would work."

"You're full of surprises. I never would have guessed."

"I do my best pondering when I'm alone. Or with Buddy." She rubbed the dog's head and he gave her an I'm-in-love pant and lick combo. Buddy being able to touch her made Justin almost jealous.

Definitely jealous.

"I'm an artist. I've never wanted to be an employer or manage people." A gleam entered her green eyes. "And I want to do this without feeling like I'm doing something wrong and letting people down."

She leaned toward him and kissed him on the mouth. Hard.

Oh, man. Him, too. Her warmth, her sweet taste. He wrapped his arms around her, pulling her close. Her hands splayed across his back. She kissed him with a hunger that matched his own. He wove his fingers through her hair, relishing the feel of her mouth.

Buddy barked, jumped on top of Justin so he fell back away from Bailey.

She laughed. "Someone is jealous."

Better you than me. Buddy panted. He looked happy, not upset, and gave each of them a lick.

"Guess he wants kisses, too." Justin petted the dog's head. "We'll have to do some training."

"He's too cute."

The dog wasn't the only one. Justin's gaze locked on Bailey's. Funny, but a shared glance was as much of a turn-on as one of her kisses.

"About the inn…"

"I'll have Paige draw up a contract."

"Sounds good." Bailey gave Buddy another rub. "AJ's hoping they can track down Floyd and get some restitution. But I can't let this drag on any longer. The employees need to know what's happening, and so do the artists. The inn is the best place for the co-op gallery. And the truth is, I'm ready to move on."

So was Justin. But he wasn't sure what he wanted to move on toward. Renovating the inn wouldn't take as long as new construction, but he would have to draw up new plans. His part wouldn't last as long. After that…

No complaints. He had the Broughton Inn and Bailey. What more could a guy want?

Three days later, Justin sat in the company's conference room in Lincoln City. He skimmed through the contract Paige, Kent and the two other attorneys had drafted for Bailey—an inch-thick worth of mumbo jumbo legalese.

The growing tension behind Justin's eyes spread down his neck. He dropped the contract onto the mahogany table. The papers hit with a thud. "I'm not giving this contract to Bailey. This piece of crap has enough loopholes to confuse the Supreme Court. She made us an offer with conditions, but those are nebulous at best with the contract wording you used."

"You received a verbal offer." Paige lifted her chin. "This contract ensures that the Broughton Inn will be ours. You can't expect us to hire just anyone without knowing whether they meet the McMillian Resorts standard of customer service or locking ourselves in to unknown vendors who could cut into our profit margin by raising prices. We also both know a gallery is not what the inn needs."

"I'll concede the first two points, but you're wrong about the third." He rolled his shoulders, but the movement bunched his muscles more. "A gallery would give the inn a local look, invest in the community and lead to more event business."

"Don't let an infatuation cloud your judgment," Paige said. "Bailey Cole is an artist. She's too flaky to run a gallery."

"She did a great job running the gallery until we purchased the inn."

"There's no business plan. She brings nothing to the table except her limited experience with Floyd Jeffries. Look how well that turned out."

He leveled his gaze at Paige. "The same could be said about your experience with Floyd."

"What's going on?" Her eyes narrowed. "All you used to care about was getting a project completed on time and under budget. Not even Taryn got in the way of that. Now your priority is some artist and a gallery. You need to keep our business interests the priority. Not hers."

Until today, Justin had never paid attention to what his sister and the other lawyers did to close a deal. He took over once they'd obtained the property. Negotiating wasn't his area of responsibility. This wasn't his concern. But Bailey's warm, enthusiastic smile appeared in his mind. He couldn't let this go. For her sake and his.

His gaze traveled from Paige to the two attorneys. "There has to be a way to make this deal fairer."

"The contract was written for McMillian Resorts' benefit." Kent leaned forward over the edge of the table. "The company has the sole option of deciding if any of Miss Cole's conditions will be met, and if opening a gallery is in the best interest of the inn or not."

"Not," said one of the newer attorneys, a man Justin had only met once and whose name he couldn't remember.

His sister and the rest of the attorneys laughed.

The hard knot in Justin's stomach grew into a large rock capable of damaging a keel and causing a boat to capsize. He felt unbalanced, uptight, out of place. All he could see was a beautiful woman with copper ringlets, expressive green eyes and a go-to-hell attitude. "These terms aren't what Bailey had in mind when she made her offer."

"So?" Paige gave him a look, the kind she hadn't given him since they were teenagers and he was about to get caught by his parents for sneaking out of the house past curfew. "This is the contract we're offering. The 'we' includes you."

That was the problem. Justin eyed the contract. He was a part of this because he'd brought Bailey's offer to Paige, and each page was an affront, a selfish grab on the part of his company—really, his family. He'd wanted Bailey's appreciation and gratitude over the formation of a partnership with the art gallery, one that could exist beyond business. But the terms would only make her see McMillian Resorts as an adversary. Not only the company, but him, too. "That still doesn't make the terms right."

Kent twirled a pen between his fingers. "Bailey will have Tyler look over the deal. He can counsel her on whether to sign or make a counteroffer. Negotiations rarely are settled the first go-round."

"That wastes time and money," Justin said.

The pen froze on Kent's fingertips. "Her brother's

money. AJ Cole could use hundred-dollar bills for kindling and not miss them."

"That's beside the point." Justin didn't like any of this.

Paige rolled her eyes. "Don't let a pretty woman mess with your head. This is what we've always done in the past and what we'll continue to do to make McMillian Resorts successful."

Maybe he hadn't cared how deals were carried out or turned a blind eye in the past. But the underhanded tactics now made him sick to his stomach. How many other people had been confused or even...swindled? He wasn't sure he wanted to know the answer. "Success at what price?"

"Any price." Her voice hardened. So like their father. "That's how it's been. And will be. You should know that."

"I do now." The words tasted like sand.

Relief filled Paige's eyes. "The only person standing in our way right now is Bailey Cole. Once she signs this contract, the inn is ours. Thanks to you."

Victory. That was what he wanted, what he'd been working toward these past weeks, so why did winning feel hollow? He felt off his game, as if he'd been playing by different rules. But Paige was correct about one thing. McMillian Resorts needed to salvage and close this deal. Should he change how he normally operated because he'd fallen for a passionate artist, one he'd only known a few weeks? If a gallery at the Broughton Inn didn't work out, couldn't AJ help Bailey out? She would understand, right?

"Do you want to take the contract to Bailey or do you want us to courier it to her?" an attorney asked.

Logically Justin knew the contract was necessary to ensure the inn's success and protect McMillian Resorts. This was business, nothing personal, but he wanted to make sure Bailey knew that. "I'll deliver the contract."

He could explain what was going on, make her see... What? That McMillian Resorts cared only about the inn?

No, that might be the truth, but he wanted Bailey to know that he cared about the art gallery and her.

Especially her.

The next day, Bailey sat on her living room couch with Justin and a sleeping Buddy. The ride up the coast to Haley's Bay, followed by chasing birds in her backyard, had worn out the dog.

She flipped through the thick contract, scanning the pages. "Seems a bit much for a few conditions."

Justin dragged his hand through his hair. His heavy eyelids matched his tired eyes.

His quick trip home to Lincoln City hadn't seemed to agree with him. He was more relaxed when he was here with her in Haley's Bay.

"You know lawyers. They are the definition of anal." He leaned back against the sofa. "Have Tyler review the contract so you understand what you're signing."

"Trying to pull a fast one to get the inn," she joked.

"Not me, Bailey. I—" He covered her hand with his. "I want this to work out."

"Me, too." She glanced from the contract to him, a weird feeling in her stomach. "So, why do I feel there's a 'but' coming?"

"There isn't, but promise me you'll review the contract with Tyler before putting pen to paper. Understand what you're signing. I can't stay much longer. I need to drive back to Lincoln City today."

She stiffened. "You drove all the way up here to deliver the contract?"

"I wanted to see you, too."

But an hour wasn't a long enough visit. She'd hoped they'd have the whole day together. Should she tell him that?

"Hey," he said. "Don't be sad."

"Okay. I know something that will make me feel better."

She brushed her lips over his. Forget chocolate. He was her favorite flavor. One she could easily become addicted to if she wasn't already. "I wish you could stay."

"I'll be back in two days. We'll go out."

She waved the contract. "And celebrate."

He held her hand. "I'm going to miss you until then."

"Same here."

"I want you to know that when I'm with you, I can't imagine being anywhere else. When I'm not with you, I can't wait until we're together again."

Tingles shot through her. *So sweet.* "I can't wait, either, but sounds like you have it bad."

He nodded slowly.

"Good," she said.

Justin drew back. "Good?"

"I feel the same way."

"What are we going to do about this?"

"No time to do anything today, though you could kiss me."

"Happy to oblige."

He pulled her into his arms and lowered his mouth toward hers. His kiss was gentle, not as raw and on-edge as before. She recognized the familiar urgency and desire, but this time a new tenderness to his kiss made her think of picket fences and forever, not sweaty sheets and one night.

This kiss. This man. This feeling of completeness was what she'd been waiting for. Oh, she had a good life, a career, a home and a family who loved her. But Justin brought something different, something new, something totally unexpected and welcome. Buddy, too.

Justin pulled her closer. She went willingly, wrapping her arms around him.

His kiss made her feel as if she could conquer the world, whether creating a new work or taking on a project for the historical committee. Sure, she'd felt that way before, but this was better. She wasn't alone. Oh, she had her family, but she'd wanted someone not related to her to care. Not just humor her. She had never known the boost this kind of unconditional support could give her.

She gave into the sensations pulsing through her, ran her fingertips through his clipped hair. He wasn't the kind of man she thought she would end up with, but he was exactly the kind of man she wanted, needed, loved.

Love.

She loved him.

Bailey had known she was falling for him, but somehow in this mess Floyd had made for them, she'd completely fallen in love with Justin McMillian. Only time would tell what would happen, but so far so good.

Especially if he kept kissing her this way.

Slowly he dragged his lips from hers. "I wish I could stay, but I need to head back to Lincoln City for another meeting."

"Business or family?"

"One and the same when you're a McMillian."

"Your family is so different from mine. My mom gets upset if we talk too much business."

"Your mother is a smart woman. I see where you get your beauty and brains from." He brushed his lips across Bailey's hair, then woke Buddy. "Be back soon."

Everything was coming together. Finally. Bailey never thought she'd want to thank Floyd Jeffries for his criminal behavior, but if not for his breaking the law by selling the inn to both AJ and McMillian Resorts, she would never have met Justin.

She wiggled her toes, her excitement growing. Instead of the Broughton Inn pushing her and Justin apart, the old hotel was bringing them together. This was the start of something new, something big.

Her, Justin and Buddy.

Cole and McMillian.

A family.

The next day, Bailey sat on the opposite side of Tyler's desk. Tapping her toes, she opened her mouth, then pressed her lips together. She'd arrived at her cousin's office confused. After listening to him, her understanding hadn't increased.

"I must be missing something. The contract reads like there's no guarantee of anything I asked for, including an art gallery."

"That's correct." Tyler rested his elbows on the desk. His serious eyes and expression made him look every bit a lawyer and not the cousin who used to have who-can-burp-the-loudest competitions with her older brothers. "The contract is written strictly for the benefit of McMillian Resorts with more escape routes than the latest tsunami evacuation plan. Based on the convoluted verbiage, I'd say the inn will not hire past employees, honor current vendor contracts or have an art gallery when it reopens."

Bailey's heart cracked wide open, the newly found love she felt for Justin bleeding out. Her world tilted. She gripped the sides of her chair to make sure she didn't fall off.

She hadn't wanted her first impression of him to be right. She wanted to be wrong. Dead wrong.

"I don't understand." Her voice shook. "Those were my conditions if I gave up my ownership claim."

Each breath hurt. She blinked to keep the tears at bay. No way was she going to cry over Justin McMillian. Not in front of Tyler.

"I'm sorry, Bay."

She nodded, not trusting her voice when her insides felt as if they'd been mixed up in a food processor. Her fingers dug into the chair. It was a good thing she wore her nails short or she'd cut through the leather upholstery.

"What were your exact words to Justin?" Tyler asked.

His harsh tone startled her. She leaned back. "I... I don't remember."

"You should have come to me. We could have officially presented an offer with your conditions."

"That's what AJ said to do, but I didn't want to bother you over the weekend."

"Doing legal stuff like this is my job, Bailey. And given their contract, the offer you made to Justin may have put your claim on the inn at risk, whether you agree to their terms or not."

Her muscles seized. "What?"

"No one with half a brain would sign this contract. They know that. So that means they expect us to make a counteroffer or..."

She slumped in her chair. "Why do I have a feeling I don't want to hear the *or* part?"

"Or," Tyler said, "depending on how you worded your offer to Justin, the McMillian legal team may claim you've verbally forfeited your claim on the inn."

She jumped out of the chair. "What?"

"No worries yet." Tyler motioned for her to sit, but she didn't...couldn't. "That's only one possibility, given the scenario."

"Let's hope it's not the one they go with."

"You care about Justin."

"I don't believe he planned to screw me over. I really don't. He'd been too shocked and happy about my offer. But his family..."

"He's part of that family."

"I know." Justin had chosen not to fight his family over her and what she wanted, even though he had seemed to say he would. But family came first, a lesson she'd known but pushed aside because of her feelings for him.

"I'm sorry." She tried to control her breathing. "I should have listened to you and AJ. I did so many things wrong."

She might love Justin, but he wasn't her Mr. Right. As long as he retreated into what was safe for him, work and the family business, he was Mr. Wrong. Words about needing her were easy to hear, but his actions told the truth. He didn't care as much for her as she did for him.

"All we can do is start over. I can't promise anything, but I'll do my best," Tyler said. "This contract tells me McMillian Resorts plans on playing hardball. You should resign yourself to a protracted legal battle. Likely a messy one. Your relationship with Justin McMillian may come up."

"My fault. I'll deal with it."

The contract changed nothing with the inn. Not yet anyway. But something had changed with Justin. She couldn't keep seeing him. Not knowing what she knew now. He wasn't the man she thought he was. Her heart panged at the loss.

Bailey should have known better than to put her heart and the inn on the line. "I accept full responsibility. The complete blame."

She felt like an idiot for stupidly risking the inn for a man. She blinked away the tears. Crying was not going to happen. "Let them know I'm not interested in their contract."

"Do you want to make a counteroffer?"

Bailey raised her chin. "No. I'm all in. I'll fight until the end."

Tyler looked proud of her. That had to count for something, right?

"Go buy yourself a cup of coffee and a donut while I make the call," he said. "Bring me back a maple bar."

"Yes, counselor." She tried to joke, but her voice sounded flat. That was the same way she felt inside, pummeled by a semitruck. "One maple donut coming up."

She forced her feet to move, to keep a smile plastered on her face, to pretend that her world hadn't spun off its axis and rolled into a different dimension. She went to the donut shop first, then headed to the coffee shop. She wasn't ready to face Tyler yet.

Fifteen minutes later, she still wasn't ready, but slowly made her way back to the office. Somehow she managed to carry her coffee without spilling—okay, the cup had a lid—and the bag of donuts without sneaking a bite. Not that she had an appetite.

The emptiness inside threatened to swallow her whole. Bailey's splintered heart cut like shards of glass. But she wasn't giving up hope. She couldn't. Perhaps this was a mistake. Tyler would have good news, and she could laugh off the way she'd believed Justin would betray her.

She entered the law office. Tyler sat on one of the upholstered chairs in the waiting room. He stood when she entered.

Bailey raised the bag. "That hungry for a donut?"

Her cousin took the food and drinks from her hand.

She didn't need a PhD in rocket science to decipher the look on Tyler's face. "It's bad."

"As soon as I told them you weren't signing, Paige McMillian said they were petitioning the court that the verbal agreement between you and Justin nullified your ownership rights to the inn."

Bailey's stomach roiled. She staggered back until she fell into a chair. "That's… I didn't. There were conditions."

"We'll fight them."

She trembled. "Is this Paige's doing? Or Justin's?"

"I don't know," Tyler said. "But this is only the beginning."

The fight over the inn might be in the early stages, but things between her and Justin were over. "I—I should have—"

"Don't think about what you should have done. You can't change the past."

No, the past was set, but she could change. A part of her had been trying to change by making that compromise to Justin, but her stubbornness and drive to be independent put the inn at risk.

"Hang in there." Tyler touched her shoulder. "The Mc-Millians don't know what they've taken on. We Coles are fighters."

She nodded. "I'm not giving up without a fight."

The inn was one thing, but Justin...

Her dreams about the two of them and Buddy went *poof*, disappearing like a child's bubble blown into the air. Her eyes had been opened to the man she'd fallen in love with. He wasn't who she'd believed him to be. She forced herself to breathe.

Her heart felt trampled upon, battered and bruised, but only time would let her know the full effect. The inn, however, would be lost forever. Replaced by a modern monstrosity and a staff not from here, and that was her fault. All the employees and Haley's Bay residents had been counting on her. She'd let them down. She was the one responsible for following her heart and not her head. For thinking she knew better when she didn't. She'd been warned. And now she felt like a complete fool. She had only one person to blame—herself. But she never wanted to see Justin McMillian again.

Chapter Twelve

"Hey, it's Justin." He left a voice message on Bailey's cell phone. "Wanted to confirm dinner plans for tomorrow. Call me back."

He disconnected from the call, then checked his text messages. No reply from Bailey. Where was she? His calls today had gone straight to her voice mail. Weird. She usually called right back. Maybe she was teaching a class he'd forgotten about, but he missed hearing her voice.

Paige bounced into his office, reminding him of when she was eight and had pulled out a tooth. "We won!"

"Won?"

"The inn."

His pulse accelerated. He stood. "Bailey didn't tell me she signed the contract."

"She didn't."

"Then how…?"

Paige shook her head. "Tyler Cole called. The guy acted

so put out. Turned down the contract we offered. Said no counteroffer would be made."

"Wait a minute." Justin rubbed his chin. "Without the contract, how do we win?"

She didn't say a word, but her I've-got-a-secret-gleam gave him a funny feeling in his stomach.

"Tell me what's going on," he said.

"This morning we filed a claim for sole ownership."

"On what basis?"

"The verbal agreement made between you and Bailey where she relinquished her claim to the inn."

"There wasn't a verbal agreement. She made us an offer, one that came with conditions that you and your legal crew ignored."

"Not true. We took her words very seriously. Giving her that contract gave us time to get everything finished on our end."

"What you're doing isn't ethical. It's wrong."

Paige shrugged. "We'll let the court decide. Bailey may decide to give up her fight."

"Give up?" Frustration threatened to overwhelm Justin. "The Coles of Haley's Bay do not give up. Tyler will go after you like this is a personal attack, which it is, since you're twisting Bailey's offer. AJ has enough money to fund a war. They aren't going to let this drop. Why did you do this?"

Paige looked perplexed. "Why wouldn't I? Our dream, our jobs are at stake. Whatever it takes."

"Not like this."

"This is what I always do. What Dad taught me to do. I get whatever property you want. Just because you don't see the fallout or backroom dealings doesn't mean there aren't any."

He stood speechless.

"The Broughton Inn is going to be ours, so you'd better get busy with the approval process," she said. "A complete teardown is what we're after, but if not, do your best to make the old look brand-new."

He couldn't shake Paige's words about how his family did business or stop wondering if Bailey knew what had happened, and that was why she hadn't called or texted. She must know if Tyler knew.

Paige touched his shoulder. "Hey. What's wrong? I thought you'd be excited. You look like you've lost your best friend."

Justin hoped he hadn't. "I'm wondering how Bailey's going to feel about this."

"Come on," Paige said. "Did you not learn your lesson with your divorce about dating women who are the opposite from you?"

"Bailey's not opposite. We're quite similar."

"You're kidding yourself. Can you imagine what Mom and Dad would think of her?"

"I hope they'd like her because I do." But if that was the case, why hadn't he driven down with Bailey and introduced them? Because of the inn? Or was there more? "I'm heading up to Haley's Bay with Buddy."

"Better bring a hazardous waste suit. There may be fallout."

That was what Justin was afraid of. He only hoped the inn wouldn't be what kept he and Bailey apart, because he wanted them both in his life. He didn't want to have to settle for only one. And wouldn't if he had the choice.

The knock at Bailey's front door made every muscle tighten, including ones she hadn't known existed. She rolled her neck, but the action did nothing to relax the tension gripping her like a straitjacket.

She didn't have to peek out the window to know Justin was standing on her welcome mat and rapping his knuckles against her door. Buddy had barked, and four people had texted they saw Justin driving on Bay Street. That was life in a small town, where everyone knew not only her business, but also her secrets and, in this case, her pain, broken heart and shame.

She walked to the door, keeping her head high, each step moving her closer to a confrontation that wouldn't be pleasant but must be done. She wasn't prepared.

How did a person prepare herself for saying goodbye to someone she'd come to care about…come to love? And Buddy. She didn't want to say goodbye to the sweet dog.

Focus. She'd been played for a fool. Forget about the good times and magical kisses they'd shared.

Not magical. Stupid. They no longer mattered.

She squared her shoulders. His excuses would not sway her. If he even made any. Time to get this over with.

With her hand on the doorknob, Bailey took a deep breath. She opened the door. Buddy ran inside.

"Hey." Justin's smiled loosened the lines around his mouth. "I wasn't sure you'd be here."

The relief in his voice poked at her heart. She tightened her grip on the doorknob. "I'm here."

He stepped inside. "You never called back or replied to my texts."

She closed the door. Better to do this in private than in front of the watchful eyes of her neighbors, who were likely timing the length of the visit so they could report in to her grandmother and Tyler.

"I thought you lost your phone," Justin continued. "Or might not want to talk to me."

"I…"

Bailey knew what she wanted to say, but words failed her. All her practice had been for naught with him standing so close to her and looking far too handsome for her own good. The urge to fling herself into Justin's arms and forget the mess she'd made was strong. She had to be stronger.

Bailey swallowed. Twice. "I didn't want to talk to you."

He flinched. "The inn."

She nodded once.

"You spoke to Tyler."

"At length." She moved into the living room, wanting to put distance between them. "How could you lie about my offer to you?"

"I didn't lie. Paige and the legal team decided to do this on their own. I had no input."

"So you're not guilty, just complacent."

"You don't understand." He brushed his hand through his hair. "You're a free-spirited artist who doesn't care what anyone thinks of you. My parents expect me to live up to certain expectations."

Bailey wasn't buying his words. "You still could've stopped them."

"No, I couldn't. My family is at stake here."

She struggled to remain in control and not lose it. "Your company. Not family."

"It's the same thing when you're a McMillian. Paige didn't tell me about filing until after the fact. You have every right to be upset, but it's just business."

Baily's mouth gaped. She couldn't believe him. "If this goes to court, you'll be forced to testify under oath."

"We'll settle before this ends up in court. That's what we always do."

She wasn't sure if he sounded confident or cocky, but she didn't like his tone. Or any of this. She stared down her nose at him. "That doesn't make your tactics right. And I'm not settling."

He didn't flinch. His facial expression didn't change. "I told Paige you would fight."

That surprised Bailey. "Not just fight. I'm going to win,

so you'd better start practicing for your deposition, since it'll be your word against mine. And I'm not the one who'll be lying on the witness stand."

He reached for her. "Bailey."

She leaned away so his hand only found air. This...*he* wasn't what she wanted. Not any longer. "Don't touch me. I don't want you to touch me again. Or contact me."

"Is that what Tyler said to say?"

"Oh, he told me that weeks ago. I foolishly didn't listen. But I won't make that mistake again."

Justin's forehead creased. "You're willing to let the inn come between us?"

"Us?" She half laughed. That was better than crying. "There's never been an *us*. You've wanted the inn from the beginning for your family. I happened to be the way for you to get what you wanted."

"That's not what—"

"Nothing you say or do will convince me otherwise."

"These past weeks, we've shared something special."

Her eyes stung. She blinked. "Special? Not from my perspective. I understand you putting your family first. I should have listened to mine, but you're no better than Floyd. And like him, you have no idea what you're losing by doing this. I deserve so much better. So does the inn."

"That's not how this is."

"It is. I trusted you. That's why I made the offer." Her voice cracked. Darn, she needed to stay in control. "I thought..."

"What?"

That they had a future together. But she'd die before she admitted those words to him. She raised her chin. "It's too late, but I wish I'd never gotten involved with you."

He flinched.

Good. Except it wasn't. Not really.

He straightened. "Let's talk about this over dinner."

"Your family is trying to steal the inn using lies about my offer. I have nothing left to say to you." She motioned to the door, hoping her fingers wouldn't tremble the way her insides were. "Please go, and don't come back."

His eyes darkened. "So that's how you want things to be."

She hesitated, crossed her arms over her chest. "Yes."

Justin called for Buddy. She hugged the dog and kissed his head. Oh, how she would miss this adorable furball.

Without a word, Justin grabbed Buddy and walked out of the cottage. Out of her life.

An engine started. She waited until she couldn't hear the car's sound anymore. She slid to the floor, buried her head in her hands and let the tears fall.

The sun rose each morning, but Justin found getting out of bed and heading to the office harder and harder to do. Nothing satisfied him. Today had been the most difficult. All he could think about was Bailey. Her pretty, warm smile and gorgeous, caring eyes were imprinted on his brain. Whether his eyes were open or closed didn't make a difference. He still saw her.

Wyatt—Justin's foreman and closest friend—spit out a sunflower seed shell. "That artist girl got under your skin."

Justin nodded, but Bailey had done more than that, She'd found her way into his heart, too. He'd kept telling himself he liked her when the truth was, he'd fallen in love. Fallen headfirst. Fallen hard. Every cliché rang true where she was concerned.

Damn. He hadn't been this messed up by his divorce. He hadn't felt this emptiness inside, as if someone had ripped out his heart and not put anything back in its place. "I don't know what to do about it."

"You got over Taryn. You'll get over this one."

"Her name is Bailey." Justin didn't like the way the people closest to him ignored her existence. She was more than an artist or the obstacle standing between McMillian Resorts and the Broughton Inn. She was a daughter, sister, aunt, friend. A kind, beautiful, intelligent woman. Damn, she was right. He had it bad. "And I'm not sure I will."

Wyatt eyed him warily. "Never seen you like this."

"Never been like this. Not even with Taryn. I—" Justin shook his head, trying to dislodge Bailey from his brain. "The only place I want to be is Haley's Bay."

"Not at the inn."

"I wish I'd never heard of the Broughton Inn. No, that's not true. I wouldn't have met Bailey. Too bad my family is hell-bent on seeing this project through to the end."

"You were spearheading that mentality."

"At the beginning, but now..."

"Because of her."

He started to say yes, then stopped himself, because she wasn't the only reason. "Bailey is the biggest reason, but my family's tactics to close this deal..."

"Dude, that's how it's always been. You never cared. Or maybe you didn't pay attention."

Justin hadn't. He'd focused on the result. The means hadn't mattered. A part of him had known or guessed how the legal team operated, but he hadn't let that stop him. Not until he'd seen the repercussions. Years of not paying attention, of focusing on his role and no one else's, had caught up to him. Their method of business and the resulting damage was too much. "I don't like it."

"So tell them."

He should, except...nothing would change. No matter what he said, the course was set. He knew that in his heart.

Because he'd been the same way with Taryn.

She'd wanted him to work less and spend more time with her. Move to Portland, away from his family and their company. He'd said no. That they could figure out another way.

But what he'd offered to save their marriage hadn't been enough. No wonder Taryn had left. He'd wanted his wife to do all the work and make all the compromises. Exactly what his family was asking of him now.

Taryn hadn't been the one to blame for their divorcing. He was responsible, but he hadn't realized it until now. Crap.

Justin didn't want to make the same mistake this time. The way he'd felt about his ex didn't come close to his feelings for Bailey.

He didn't want the inn. He wanted her. "I screwed up."

"What's new?" Wyatt joked.

"Nothing. That's the problem. I'm finished." Justin rose from behind his desk. "I can't keep doing this."

Wyatt's brow furrowed. "Do what?"

"Let McMillian Resorts ruin my chance at love and happiness again. I didn't see it the first time with Taryn. I do now. Time to make a change." He walked out of his office toward the conference room where he knew his family would be assembled. His heart pounded with purpose; every fiber in his being agreed.

"Took you long enough," his dad grumbled as he entered.

"Now, now." His mother patted his father's hand. "Justin's here. We can get started."

Rainey, his younger sister, the baby of the family, fingered the pendant on the chain around her neck. Dark circles under her eyes and her pale complexion made him wonder when she'd last had a full night's sleep. She needed a vacation.

Paige tapped her fingers against the table as if she'd rather be somewhere else. He knew how she felt. He was impatient, too. He wanted this over with now.

His father motioned to an empty leather chair. "Sit. Now that the three of you have shown us what you're capable of doing, we're ready to sign over ownership of the company to you and retire."

Justin stood in the doorway. His and his sisters' dream handed to them on a platter of lies. Unbelievable.

The only thing he knew was this company. He'd never worked anywhere else. This was his family, but until going to Haley's Bay he hadn't realized how much business defined them, as individuals and a collective group. Living like this was no longer enough. Family should mean more. And being without Bailey was not an option.

He sucked in a breath. Exhaled. "I quit."

His father laughed. The gut-busting sound echoed through the conference room. "Stop being an idiot and wasting our time. Take a seat."

"I have at least two months' vacation and personal time off. Wyatt knows where all the projects stand. He's overqualified but can step into my position without any problems."

His family stared at him, mouths gaping.

His mother pursed her lips. "You can't be serious. We're giving you the company."

"I am serious. I don't want a company that's run this way. I'm in love with a woman named Bailey. She's the other owner of the Broughton Inn."

His father's nostrils flared. "If this woman's got half a brain, she won't want an unemployed bum for a boyfriend."

"She's very smart, and I won't be unemployed for long once I tell my side of Bailey's so-called verbal offer to the judge."

Paige's face dropped. "You wouldn't."

"Don't be so sure about that."

A weight lifted off Justin's shoulders. He had no doubt he was doing the right thing.

He tossed his office keys onto the table. They clattered against the wood. "I'm sure this will take time getting used to, but I hope we'll be over this by the time the holidays roll around."

His mother stood. "Justin—"

"I've got to go."

"Where?" Rainey asked.

"Haley's Bay."

His father frowned. "This artist is more important than your own family."

"You're important, too," Justin admitted. "But I've lost one woman to McMillian Resorts. I won't lose another, especially one who means as much as Bailey does to me. I need more in my life than work. I need her."

The words *I'm sorry* were on the tip of his tongue, but he wasn't going to apologize for wanting more, wanting to be loved, wanting more from a family than sharing a common work interest.

"I love all of you, but I love Bailey, too. I need to tell her and hope that's enough for her to give me a second chance."

"And if it's not?" Paige asked.

Justin hadn't thought that far out. He shrugged. "I'll keep trying until I convince her or she has me arrested."

Rainey beamed. "A good thing we have an attorney in the family. Though sounds like a bail bondsman might come in handy."

"Likely. Bailey's youngest brother is a police officer."

Paige shook her head. "This isn't going to end well."

"I've gotta try." And Justin would. Because he didn't want to live with the *what-if.*

The phone vibrated against the living room end table. Bailey rolled her eyes. What part of "no" didn't Justin McMillian understand? He'd been texting and calling all morning. She should have turned off her phone instead of only muting the sound.

A stupid mistake. One she would remember not to make again.

As she stood on a plastic tarp in her dining room, her vision blurred, the colors on the canvas blending together in an odd-shaped rainbow. Distractions always made her lose sight of a project. One reason she liked being alone.

She just needed to keep reminding herself that.

And forget about how much she missed having Buddy around, and…

She blinked until the canvas came into focus, the landscape of her grandmother's house as clear as the robin sitting on the bird feeder outside the window.

More vibrating. That one sounded like a text.

A week ago Bailey might have been flattered. Okay, she would have been. But now Justin's attempts at contacting her left her aching heart hurting more.

She hated that, hated…

No, she didn't hate Justin.

But she was angry with him. A part of her felt sorry for him. But she didn't hate him. She kept trying for indifference, but so far that hadn't happened.

Stop thinking about him.

She needed to finish this commissioned piece if she wanted to pay her mortgage without having to dip into her savings.

Bailey used her forearm to push stray hairs off her face with her forearm. Paint splatters covered her hands. She didn't need paint on her face.

Another text from Justin arrived. She would turn off her phone once she washed her hands.

She wasn't interested in anything he had to say. She didn't need him. Or anyone.

Bailey had what she needed to be happy—a loving family, her own home, a career that might not make her rich, but one she loved. So why did she feel so miserable?

She knew the answer, a six-letter word that started with a capital *J* and ended with a small *n*.

Not fair.

But her brothers, all five of them, would tell her life wasn't fair. As they'd always done.

She got back to work. If she concentrated on finishing the painting, then she wouldn't have to think about anything else. She could put everything into her work, including her heart.

Time seemed to stop. Minutes…hours…she had no idea how long she'd been working.

The front door opened. Three of her brothers—Ellis, Declan and Grady—walked in.

"See?" Grady said. "I told you she would be working and her door wouldn't be locked."

Declan double-checked the lock. "Not broken, which means you didn't lock the door again."

A headache threatened to erupt. "I'm working. Go away."

Ellis looked at her painting. "Pretty good, but you haven't answered your phone for two days."

Declan picked up the cell. "Sounds off. Battery's almost dead."

"Go away." She focused on her painting. "I need to finish this."

"Mom sent us over," Grady said. "Worried you were upset over breaking up with Justin. She wanted to make sure you were eating."

"Sleeping," Ellis added.

"Not crying nonstop." Declan studied her. "Your eyes look a little red, but I thought they'd be swollen."

"Oh, man," Ellis said. "Remember the time Bobby Steele dumped you for that hot blonde?"

"Cecilia Remming." Declan whistled. "As much as I love you, sis, can't say I blame the guy."

Bailey sighed. "Just because a girl has a D-cup in high school doesn't make her the be-all, end-all. You do realize Cecilia ended up having breast reduction surgery last year because of back trouble."

Declan checked her empty water bottle, then tossed it to Grady. "Don't ruin the fantasies."

"Fine. I take it back." Bailey wasn't a dream crusher. That title belonged to Justin. She waved her paintbrush, sending splatters of coral pink onto the tarp beneath their feet and causing her brothers to step back. "As you can see, I'm fine."

"You don't look so good." Grady raised the water bottle. "I'm going to refill this."

Ellis dug through the candy wrappers on the floor. "When did you eat last something that wasn't all sugar?"

"Showered?" Declan sniffed. "I'd say at least two, maybe three days, based on the smell."

Her shoulders sagged. Bailey straightened. She wasn't about to answer them. If she did, they would know that she wasn't exactly fine, but she was doing okay. Surviving. Hoping the emptiness inside would go away sooner rather than later.

"I'm working." She motioned to the almost finished canvas. "I'll do those things as soon as I complete my painting."

Ellis studied her. "So the way you look, how messy your place is, has nothing to do with Justin?"

Bailey fought the urge to say something sarcastic or biting. No fighting with them, either. She counted backward from five. "This is how I work."

And it was, except work usually left her feeling refreshed, able to stay up late and wake early. This painting hadn't done that. If anything, work was draining what energy she had left.

"It's okay if you're upset." Declan stacked empty cups lying on the floor. "We know you liked Justin."

Ellis nodded. "You were different with him."

"Yeah, not such a hardnose all the time," Grady teased.

Declan glared at their youngest brother. "Shut up, Grady."

"We're not trying to butt in." Ellis folded the throw she'd used for a nap. "We're your brothers. It's our job to take care of you."

"No, that's my job." Bailey placed her brush on the easel. "I appreciate the concern, but I'm not a kid anymore. My heart's been battered, but this isn't the first time I've lost in love. This won't be the last."

At least she hoped not.

"You've been hiding out," Ellis said.

Her shoulders sagged. "What part of working don't you understand? I'm not doing a spin-art project. Creating a painting takes time. I lose track of things, including staying in contact and time. Go tell Mom all is well and as soon as this painting is finished, I'll be over there."

Her brothers exchanged glances.

"Really," Bailey added for emphasis, then motioned them to the front door. "Go. Risa is expecting you home, Ellis. I'm sure you two single guys have hot dates tonight."

Declan winked. "A lukewarm date, but no complaints if the night ends the way I expect."

"I'm giving a talk at a Boy Scout meeting, then calling it an early night," Grady said. "I'm on duty in the morning."

Their little brother sure had grown up. All of them had. Bailey gave each one a hug. "I'll charge my cell phone. But I'm not answering until the work is finished."

"Fair enough," Ellis said.

"And, sis—" Declan reached out to her "—we give you a hard time, and you can be a pain in the ass sometimes, but McMillian's an idiot for letting you get away."

The tension wrapped around her chest loosened. "Thanks. I appreciate that."

Her brothers filed out of the house, one by one. She closed the door.

"Lock it," the three said in unison.

Bailey bolted the lock, then leaned against the door. She loved her family, and how her brothers wanted to take care of her was sweet. But she wished someone other than her siblings wanted to watch out for her. She wished she had someone to kiss good-night and wake up to each morning. She wished she had finally found her Mr. Right.

Being disappointed by Mr. Wrong, time and time again, was getting old.

Chapter Thirteen

"I don't know what I should do next." Justin sat in his parked truck with the windows rolled down. The temperature in Haley's Bay had cooled to the sixties as soon as the sun had set. "Probably shouldn't go back to Bailey's house again."

He'd been twice. No answer when he called her. No replies to his text.

"She's shut me out of her life completely. I miss her."

He stared at his cell phone charging. Not many options remained except giving up. He wasn't ready to admit defeat. Not yet.

Buddy sat in the passenger seat. The dog had been the definition of loyal.

Justin rubbed his dog. "So glad I've got you."

Buddy placed his head on Justin's leg.

He rubbed the dog. "I screwed up. Took me too long to stand up to my family. But I'm the reason I lost her. Can't blame anyone else."

His throat was dry. He'd finished his last bottle of water an hour ago. No wonder he was thirsty. He checked Buddy's portable water bowl—full. "I'm going to grab a drink. I'll be right back. Stay."

Buddy sat for a moment, then lay down.

The side and back windows were open. Buddy would be cool enough.

Justin saw the sign for a place called the Crow's Nest, what looked to be a dive bar, halfway down the block. One beer; then he'd find a place to stay for the night that allowed dogs. Or he and Buddy could sleep in the back of the truck.

A night's sleep would help him regroup. He'd try something else in the morning.

Inside the place, the smell of beer and grease filled the air. The place was crowded, but a few open spots at the bar remained. The jukebox's sad country-western song about lost love matched his mood and situation.

He took a seat at the bar and ordered a beer on tap from a local microbrewery. The bartender set the pint in front of him. "Here you go. Compliments of Declan Cole."

Justin looked over his shoulder. Declan sat at a table for two, but only one glass was at the table. Justin picked up his beer and walked over. "Mind if I join you?"

"Seat's empty."

"No date tonight?" Justin asked.

"She canceled."

"There's always tomorrow night."

"Gonna cut this one loose. She's got commitment on the brain. All I want to do is have fun."

Justin took a sip. The beer felt cool going down his throat. Might as well get the one question he had off his mind. "How's Bailey?"

"Working hard on her newest painting and trying to convince everyone she's fine."

"Is she okay?"

Declan's jaw tensed. He raised his glass. "Do you care?"

"More than you know." Justin stared into his beer. "I want her back."

"Tell her."

"I've tried. She won't answer my texts or calls. She wouldn't answer the door tonight. I tried the knob. Locked."

Declan laughed.

Justin took a long drink. He might need two beers. "Go ahead and laugh at some other guy's pain."

"No, it's Bailey. She finally listened to us about locking her door."

"Wish she would listen to me."

Declan raised his pint. "What would you say to her?"

"I messed up. I was wrong to let my family try to take advantage of her offer. That I quit."

Declan pinned him with his gaze. "You quit your job?"

"I don't approve of the way my family does business."

"How'd they take your resignation?"

"No idea. I didn't stick around. I drove up here. No one's called or texted, so I'm guessing they're still getting used to the idea."

Declan stared at two women who'd entered the bar, then looked at Justin. "What are you going to do now?"

"Figure out how to get Bailey to talk to me. She won today, but I'll go back for more rejection tomorrow. Maybe try a new tactic."

A blonde waved at Declan. He shook his head. "Like what?"

"No idea. I'm hoping inspiration strikes tonight." He stared at the white foam in his beer. No answers there. "Got any ideas?"

"You think I'm going to help you get my sister back after you broke her heart?" Declan sounded incredulous.

"I didn't ask for your help, only ideas."

"She would never admit it, but she likes fairy tales. And

romance. Big into that. But if you say that I told you, I'll deny it, then beat you up."

"Fair enough." Justin took another sip. "I'm sure Bailey would see past any suit of armor or white horse. She prefers wildflowers to cut ones. And she's been trying to cut back on eating sugar."

Declan stared over his beer. "Bailey doesn't diet."

"No, but giving her chocolates would tell her I wasn't listening. I've got enough cons against me. Not going to add any more."

Declan studied him.

"What?" Justin asked.

"You like my sister."

"Yeah, I like her." Justin downed the rest of his beer. "I'm pretty sure I'm in love with her. Not that I can tell her."

"Want another?"

"Nope. One's enough. I need to find a motel, then put together my plan for tomorrow."

"Your plan?"

"To get Bailey to listen to me for five minutes so I can tell her how much I love her. I'm assuming that's as long as she'll give me. So I need to be prepared." He removed a diamond engagement ring from his pocket. "I hope this will be enough. Thanks for the beer."

"Hey. Skip the motel. I have a spare bedroom."

"I've got Buddy with me."

"He can play with Chinook," Declan said. "I'll call my brothers and cousins. Maybe we can give you some ideas."

Justin's heart pounded. "You'd do that?"

"Hell, yeah. Any guy stupid enough to spend money on a ring for my sister when she won't text him gets bonus points in my book. But I swear if you hurt her, you'll—"

Justin raised his hands. "If I hurt her, you're free to do whatever you want to me."

Declan pulled out his cell phone. "I'll text the boys to meet at my place. Camden, too."

Amazing. Justin had Bailey's family on his side. Well, at least one of them. All he had to do was get her on his side, too. He wasn't superstitious, but he crossed his fingers. He was going to need not only help from the Coles, but lots of luck, too.

This had better be good.

6:00 a.m. was too early to be up on a Saturday. The rising sun provided enough light for Bailey to see the paved walkway at the Broughton Inn. She'd much rather be in bed after another restless night. She doubted she'd slept more than two hours each night this week. But Grady had said meeting him this morning was vital to the future of the inn, so here she was.

Her steps barely sounded against the stones. Dew clung to the grass and dripped from the lights that normally lit the way. They were off today. Electricity must have been turned off until ownership of the inn and someone's name went on the account.

The past few days had crystalized her thoughts about her future. Yes, she wanted to find love, but she also wanted to do something more to help artists in Haley's Bay. She wanted to open an art center, one that housed a gallery, classrooms, even a retreat. Ideas had been exploding in her mind like fireworks. She would figure out a plan once she knew if this was all a pipe dream. But thinking of something other than Justin helped her broken heart.

Better not think about him or she might cry. She'd wasted too many tears already.

Bailey headed toward the gazebo. She loved this place, even if the structure needed repairs and a new coat of...

She looked up. Froze.

The gazebo had been painted white and the flower boxes

hanging off the sides filled with colorful blossoms. Tule and miniature white lights had been draped around the top and along the rails. Her heart beat in triple time. Exactly the way she imagined her wedding day.

She blinked. Closed her eyes. Opened them.

Nothing had changed. The gazebo still looked like a dream come true. "Grady?"

Justin stepped from behind the gazebo. He wore a tuxedo. Buddy, wearing a black bow tie, was at his side.

Her heart slammed against her rib cage. She opened her mouth to speak, but words wouldn't come.

He looked handsome, mouthwateringly good, even though she shouldn't care what he wore or looked like. But she did, and didn't like that.

A million questions ran through her head. She went with the most obvious one. "Where's my brother?"

"Grady, along with Declan, Ellis, J.T. and Tyler, is standing watch. I don't want to get arrested for trespassing on private property, even though we both own this place. For now, at least."

She glanced around at the decorations gracing the gazebo. "Did you boys decide to play decorator?"

"Risa was happy to help. She had the supplies in her craft room, and tying bows is beyond these hands of mine. Camden joined in, too. Your sister is amazing with a paint sprayer in the dark."

Bailey wanted to believe she was dreaming. That she wasn't standing in a place set for a wedding with the man she'd dreamed of marrying. This was too…much.

Tears stung her eyes. She turned away. "I have to go."

He touched her shoulder. "Five minutes. That's all I need."

She didn't have five minutes. Five seconds were going to be difficult enough. She rubbed her eyes, trying not to lose it completely.

Justin lowered his hand. "Please."

She nodded, not trusting her voice. Breathing was automatic, but right now she felt as if she had to remind herself not only to breathe, but to also think and stand. Nothing seemed to be functioning except her tear ducts.

"I'm sorry." His voice cracked. "The more times I go over what's happened, the sorrier I am."

The regret in his eyes pushed her back a step until she bumped into the gazebo's railing.

"I've been focused on work for so long, I couldn't see what was in front of me." His gaze met hers. "You."

Her breath caught in her throat. "Justin—"

"Until I met you, I put McMillian Resorts first. That was a mistake. I couldn't let my family and the inn come between us. I quit."

Bailey gasped. "You quit your family's company?"

"I couldn't continue to work there, knowing what they'd done to you. You're not the first. I turned a blind eye, but not any longer. I'm not going to lose you."

"What about the inn?"

"They won't ask me to testify for them now. That means they have no case. If you still want the inn, I'll do everything in my power to make sure it's yours. I'd suggest you have Tyler call Paige ASAP. My family members are most likely ready to make a deal themselves."

Bailey was having trouble thinking straight. "What will you do now?"

"Find a new job. Start my own business. I haven't thought that far ahead. All I've been thinking about is you. We have something special. I'd like another chance."

"That's what this is all about? Trying to charm your way into my heart?"

"I was hoping I was already there, but I figured this couldn't hurt."

She wanted to scream yes, jump into his arms and kiss

him hard on the lips. Fear held her back. Justin had messed up her nice, not-so-neat world. She didn't want him to do that again with even worse results. Together, they were good, but he also pushed her buttons, made her want things, want him. "I…"

The twinkling lights covered by the white tulle caught her attention. Common sense told her to say no. No good would come of trying again. She'd followed her heart once and ended up possibly losing the inn. What would she risk this time?

But, her heart countered, what could she gain? Was she willing to walk away from the possibility of something wonderful and awe-inspiring? She had done so in the past, but now she wasn't sure she wanted to do that again.

"I'm scared," she admitted.

He held her hand. "I am, too. But life is scary. It'll be less scary with the two of us together."

"You sound confident."

"I am." He squeezed her hand. "I love you, Bailey."

Heat pulsed through her, and joy overflowed. Had he really said that he loved her? She wanted to hear the words again. To be sure. "What did you say?"

"Your expression tells me you heard me the first time, but I'll say the words again. I love you. I love your passion and your creativity. The way you care so deeply about the people, animals and the things in your life, including your family. You're unique, and I can't imagine being without you."

She'd longed to hear those words. She just hadn't thought they'd come from him. But let this man go? No way.

"I love you, too. Even when we disagree. I love how you gave Buddy a forever home. I appreciate how you hear my side, and don't try to change who I am."

"I would never want to change you."

"Just every building you see."

"Not every single one. I have a feeling you're going to like some of my new ideas."

"For the inn?"

"For the Potter place," he said to her surprise. "Phil Potter turned down three of Paige's offers, but I'm not going to give up. The spot is perfect for a gallery and small inn."

"An artist retreat center."

"That works."

Of course it would. Because she and Justin were meant to be. Grandma had always said everything happens for a reason. She was right once again.

He held out his arms. "Come here."

Bailey did with Buddy at her heels. She kissed Justin hard until she couldn't think straight and clung to his shoulders to keep her knees from giving out.

He drew back. "I've missed everything about you, especially holding you in my arms and kissing you. We'll have to do more of that."

"Most definitely." But something kept her from being totally ecstatic over reconciling. "What about your family? Aren't you sad?"

"This is the right decision for me. They'll see that, too. I doubt my leaving will make them change the way they've done business, but maybe they'll rethink how they close deals in the future. Everything in our family life has always revolved around the business. Whether I'm involved or not, won't matter."

"I love you."

"You don't know how long I've waited to hear those words."

"As long as I was waiting."

He laughed. "I have one more thing to ask you."

"About the inn?"

"This has to do with you and me. I want you to know I'm serious and want to make a commitment." He kneeled and showed her a black velvet ring box. "Will you marry me, Bailey Cole?"

Her heart skipped four beats. She covered her mouth with her hands. "I... I..."

He opened the box to show a gorgeous diamond engagement ring; its setting was not traditional, but an asymmetrical, artistic one. So...her.

"I love it."

"Is that a yes?"

"Yes." She extended her hand. He slid the ring on her finger. Satisfaction pooled in her chest. "I know we'll create a wonderful life together here in Haley's Bay."

Buddy barked.

She gave the dog a rub. "All three of us will."

* * * * *

MILLS & BOON®
By Request

RELIVE THE ROMANCE WITH THE BEST OF THE BEST

A sneak peek at next month's titles...

In stores from 11th January 2018:

- **A Diamond in the Rough** – Catherine Mann

- **Call Me Cupid** – Fiona Harper, Nina Harrington *and* Heidi Rice

In stores from 25th January 2018:

- **One Passionate Night** – Susan Meier, Jessica Gilmore *and* Caroline Anderson

- **Save the Date!** – Michelle Douglas, Lucy Gordon *and* Kate Hardy

Just can't wait?
Buy our books online before they hit the shops!
www.millsandboon.co.uk

Also available as eBooks.